D1356554

the
distant dead

Lesley Thomson grew up in London.
Her first novel, *A Kind of Vanishing*, won the
People's Book Prize in 2010. Her second novel,
The Detective's Daughter, was a #1 bestseller
and the series has sold over 750,000 copies.
Lesley divides her time between Sussex and
Gloucestershire. She lives with her
partner and her dog.

Stella Darnell runs a successful cleaning
company in west London. Her father was a
senior detective in the Metropolitan police.
Like him, Stella roots into shadowy
places and restores order.

Jack Harmon works the night shifts as a
London Underground train driver. Where
Stella is rational and practical, Jack is
governed by intuition. Their different skills
make them a successful detective
partnership.

By Lesley Thomson

Seven Miles from Sydney

A Kind of Vanishing

Death of a Mermaid

The Detective's Daughter Series

The Detective's Daughter

Ghost Girl

The Detective's Secret

The House With No Rooms

The Dog Walker

The Death Chamber

The Playground Murders

The Runaway (A Detective's Daughter Short Story)

Lesley
THOMSON

the
distant dead

Map reprinted from The Project Gutenberg EBook of *Bell's Cathedrals: The
Abbey Church of Tewkesbury*, by H. J. L. J. Massé (EBook #22260)

9 7 5 3 1 2 4 6 8

A catalogue record for this book is available from
the British Library.

ISBN (HB): 9781788549752
ISBN (XTPB): 9781788549769
ISBN (E): 9781788549745

Typeset by Divaddict Publishing Solutions Ltd

Printed and bound in Great Britain by
CPI Group (UK) Ltd, Croydon CR0 4YY

Head of Zeus Ltd
First Floor East
5–8 Hardwick Street
London EC1R 4RG

WWW.HEADOFZEUS.COM

For Melanie, always

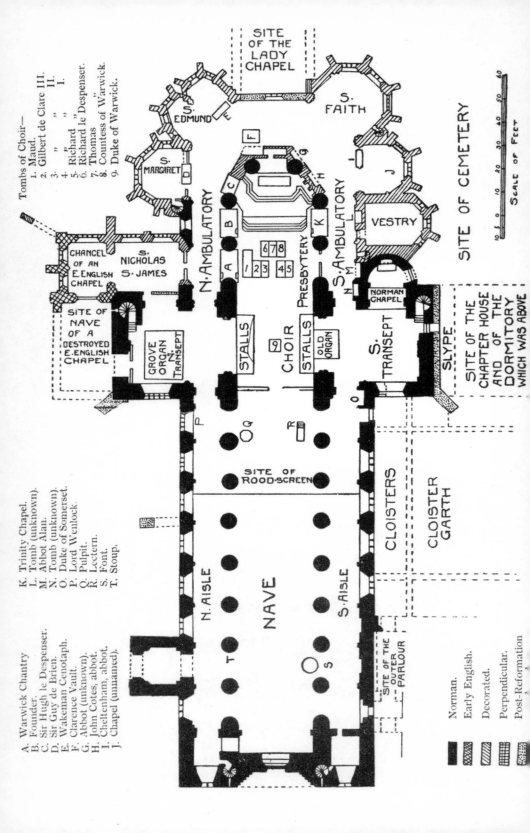

Tombs of Choir—

1. Maud.
2. Gilbert de Clare III.
3. „ „ II.
4. „ „ I.
5. Richard „
6. Richard le Despenser.
7. Thomas „
8. Countess of Warwick.
9. Duke of Warwick.

SITE OF THE LADY CHAPEL

S. EDMUND

S. FAITH

S. MARGARET

F

G

H

J

VESTRY

D

CHANCEL OF AN E. ENGLISH CHAPEL

S. NICHOLAS

S. JAMES

N. AMBULATORY

C

B

A

6 7 8

1 2 3   4 5

K

S. AMBULATORY

NORMAN CHAPEL

SITE OF CEMETERY

Scale of Feet

10 5 0   10   20   30   40   50   60

SITE OF NAVE OF A DESTROYED E. ENGLISH CHAPEL

GROVE ORGAN N. TRANSEPT

STALLS

CHOIR

PRESBYTERY

STALLS

9

OLD ORGAN

N   M

L

S. TRANSEPT

SLYPE

SITE OF THE CHAPTER HOUSE AND OF THE DORMITORY WHICH WAS ABOVE

O

P

Q

R

SITE OF ROOD-SCREEN

CLOISTERS

CLOISTER GARTH

N. AISLE

NAVE

S. AISLE

T

S

SITE OF THE OUTER PARLOUR

A. Warwick Chantry.
B. Founder.
C. Sir Hugh le Despenser.
D. Sir Guy de Brien.
E. Wakeman Cenotaph.
F. Clarence Vault.
G. Abbot (unknown).
H. John Cotes, abbot.
I. Cheltenham, abbot.
J. Chapel (unnamed).

K. Trinity Chapel.
L. Tomb (unknown).
M. Abbot Alan.
N. Tomb (unknown).
O. Duke of Somerset.
P. Lord Wenlock.
Q. Pulpit.
R. Lectern.
S. Font.
T. Stoup.

Norman.

Early English.

Decorated.

Perpendicular.

Post-Reformation.

PART ONE

Prologue

Thursday, 12 December 1940

It used to be that a clear night with stars and a full moon spelled romance and love. Now, with the end of the longest period of all-clears since intensified raids began, the cloudless sky spelled death.

In the small hours, the sky billowed with smoke from fires caused by incendiaries that pulverized pavements, destroyed homes, eviscerated lives.

Etched against the smog, in a street near the River Thames, blacked-out windows offered blank countenances, their occupants crouched in shelters, cellars and under kitchen tables. The tide had turned and the river welled over the camber near the eyot. In the moonlight the flotsam of bottles and lengths of scorched timber resembled severed limbs.

A man and a woman, clinging close, wove along Eyot Gardens. The woman flinched at a crash which sounded nearby but was miles to the east. In trilby and mac, the man was her hero as he hustled her into a house on the corner by the Thames. Inside, he kicked shut the front door and when he flicked an electric light switch, a glass chandelier, at variance with a suburban villa, flooded the herringbone-tiled hall in remorseless light. Clasping his lover's chin with an elegant hand, his whisper might have been 'I love you'. Or it might not.

Hours passed. Fog rolled in, slick and poisonous, shrouding the river. Yet, obscuring London from the Luftwaffe, it was the city's friend. The roar of engines and the thunder of explosions ceased as planes returned to Germany. Destruction done, they dropped the last of their payload over Sussex before they crossed the English Channel.

A scream, elemental, animalistic. Silence. No doors were opened, no sashes were flung up. If walls had ears, they did not hear.

Chapter One

December 2019

Jackie

'Clean Slate for a fresh start, Beverly speaking, how may I help you?' Beverly Jameson, blonde hair streaked with silver and a diamanté-beaded scrunchie snatching it high up in a palm-tree effect, a short skirt over leggings and cherry blossom Dr Martens, rocked back in her chair, pen aloft.

Jackie felt satisfaction at Bev's opener. It was a good while – eight years? – since she'd weaned Bev off her dreadful sing-song rap to answer in lovely warm tones. Not that it was genuine, with Stella no longer there; neither of them felt as cheerful as Bev was sounding. In the mornings, it was all Jackie could do to get out of bed.

'Hello? Clean Slate, Bev here… Hello? Look, is someone there?' The tone was cooling. 'Please speak?' Bev put down the receiver. 'That's got to be the sixth time this week. I should have kept a record. Thursday morning, ten past nine. Right,' she flung down her pens and addressed the phone, 'whoever you are, *bring it on*.'

'Could be a wrong number,' Jackie said.

'I swear someone's there. He listens and doesn't speak.'

'You think it's a man?' Jackie was completing a contract on a bi-weekly clean of a church hall. Usually by the start of December her in-tray was groaning with new business, people wanting super-clean homes for Christmas, but at this rate they'd be letting go of those cleaners who hadn't already migrated to a more successful company. Jackie dreaded the possibility she might have to give the loyal old-timers, Wendy and Donnette who'd been at school with Stella, their cards. Once, good operatives were hens' teeth, now Clean Slate had teams to spare, but no work for them.

'Has to be a man. What woman would do…' Beverly jerked her shoulders in an exaggerated shudder. 'Creeps me out.'

'Could be a mystery shopper.' Jackie couldn't bear this idea. The vultures were circling. It was, however, a distraction from her constant fretting about Stella. If Clean Slate didn't need cleaners, they wouldn't need office staff. Suzy, Stella's mum, was in Sydney visiting her son, but she could update the customer database from there and anyway she'd stopped drawing a salary. Of all of them Suzy was the least worried. *Just like her father leaving the baby for others to hold, Stella will sort herself out and be back.* Jackie could manage, she and Graham had savings and were mortgage free. Bev and her wife had just bought a flat in Richmond, so if Jackie had to let her go…

'If it was mystery shopping, he'd probe us about our services and waste time so we couldn't bring in real new business.' Bev was grim-faced. 'I've got a nasty feeling it's some weirdo after Stella. But why now? She hasn't done any interviews.'

'I'm sure it's not.' Jackie felt queasy. More than once she'd encouraged Stella to do an interview with reporter Lucie May for the local paper. The detective's daughter who cleaned for a living had, after her father's death, solved several murders. In the past, publicity had drummed up new customers for Clean Slate. But a recent article had also drummed up admirers who, seeing Stella's photograph in the paper, wanted her to do more for them than clean. Jackie sought to reassure Bev – and herself – about the anonymous caller.

'At least he won't find Stella in Tewkesbury.'

Chapter Two

December 2019

Stella

Stella Darnell loved cleaning, to make surfaces shine and retore order from chaos. Deep cleaning was her passion, but it wasn't allowed in the abbey. The handout from the Churches Conservation Trust said to ignore your usual standards, a church will never be free of dust or cobwebs. No aggressive cleaning products like furniture cream or silicone polish, the favoured weapons in Stella's usual armoury. The handout said to clean 'gently and sympathetically'. After several shifts in Tewkesbury Abbey, Stella found this worked for her too. She loved her mornings being sympathetic with the tombs.

'That's a warning to the living.' A man was leaning against the portico to the south ambulatory. 'To remember the grisly gruesome aspect of death. It's not all angels and lambs.'

Taken by surprise, Stella dropped the dusting brush.

'What is?' She scrabbled for the brush on the stone floor of the side chapel.

'What you're cleaning, it's a cadaver tomb.' Arms folded, the man smiled. 'Christ, have you got to clean the whole abbey with a small brush?'

'Only the carvings, otherwise I've got a larger one.' Stella flicked the sable into the crevice between the upturned feet of the figure lying on the tomb.

'They were a macabre thing in medieval times. You're cleaning vermin which feast on the rotting corpse. See, there's a mouse, that's a toad.' He took a step closer. 'Fascinating. Those indentations were scored by early visitors to the abbey leaving their mark. These days they have historic value.'

He was too close. Security patrolled regularly; ten minutes earlier one had pointed out Stanley lifting his leg against a pillar by the nave. Stella had mopped it up.

'There are about fifty cadaver tombs in churches in Britain. I mean, they had a right to be obsessed with death, there were many visitations of pestilence in the last part of the fourteenth century.' He came over and rested his arms on the recumbent figure. 'This one is the starved monk, aka the Wakeman Cenotaph. Not that Wakeman himself is interred here.'

Stella shot a glance at Stanley. Dogs were for protection, but her miscreant poodle had twisted round and was preening his tail.

'Seriously, though, you do this every morning?' The man was grinning. 'One hell of a gig!'

'No, this week I'm cleaning here in the Wakeman Cenotaph at the end of the North Ambulatory, we have a rota—' Stella stopped. There had been several recent muggings: a handbag snatch in the presbytery, a verger attacked by a gang in balaclavas, his arm broken and his watch stolen. If this man was checking out Tewkesbury Abbey, he'd start by buttering up one of the cleaners. 'The abbey is closed. How come you're here?'

'In my job it's my business to flout rules, that's how you learn stuff.' He moved towards Stanley, presumably thinking fussing her dog was the way in. Stanley whipped around, panting from his preening, and bared his teeth.

'That's a warning to the living,' Stella said. The Ralph Lauren combat jacket, hair escaping from under a black beanie and glasses stamped with Armani didn't fit a mugger, unless he was wearing what he'd nicked. He was late forties, surely too old for mugging. Except Stella's inner policeman's daughter voice proclaimed that rubbish. *Anyone could mug anyone.*

'Never approach a dog unawares.' The man was holding out a hand for her to shake. 'Roddy March. Of course.'

Of course? Stella laid her brush on the ribcage of the starved monk and made a quick decision: 'I'm Beverly.'

'Beverly? I thought—' March appeared wrong-footed.

'I have to get on.' Stella withdrew her hand and swished the brush over the monk's protruding bones. March was likely a harmless geek who toured churches collecting weird facts, but her three mornings cleaning the abbey had become precious and Stella wanted to clean alone.

'I'm a podcaster,' March said.

'Oh, right.' Stella felt that in this conversation – which she didn't want – she had nothing to say; she never listened to podcasts and what she knew about history could be cobbled into a handout.

'Deep reporting is the way forward.'

'On cadaver tombs?' *Deep cleaning certainly was.* Stella gave the monk a final brush.

'You could say that.' He laughed. 'Hey, I'm building tons of followers, you should join the conversation.' He was rummaging in one of the pockets of his jacket.

'I have to work.' An inane response, but Stella had no inclination to join in a conversation now, or any time. She'd come to Tewkesbury, she had told Jack, because she needed space. So far, she had found it, but not this morning.

'Here, you need my card. Check out my podcast. Radio Public's a cool platform, but I'm everywhere. I've podded out one ep, so you don't have to play catch-up.' March tossed his fringe. 'Actually, if you fancy it, we could—'

Stella was reprieved by March's phone, the ringtone a haunting electronic tune which he allowed to play out as, spinning on his heel, he answered the call out in the ambulatory.

'Wotcha...'

Stella stuffed the card in her fleece pocket. She was interested in the concept of a cadaver tomb. She looked closely at the starved monk. She no longer saw a collection of surfaces with crevices into which she must flick her brush. The emaciated body lying on the plinth was indeed teeming with creatures: lizards, snails, the mouse – Jack wouldn't think them vermin – and, although the stone had weathered over six centuries, it had originally been carved to represent decay. Stella caught March's conversation.

'...when do you start?... Yeah, so what did you expect, planting cabbages isn't rocket science... Wait, what do you mean you're *here*? Go outside. *Now*. Christ, I'm *not* flirting, she's just a cleaner and no, actually she's not. Her name's *Beverly*... I'm on my...'

March's voice faded. Stella heard the boom of the north porch door shutting. Twice.

Just a cleaner. Over the decades, she'd grown used to those whose carpets she vacuumed and toilets she sluiced discounting her; it was almost worse when they treated her as a friend and told her their problems.

Whoever March was talking to had been in the abbey. Perhaps one of the other cleaners, there were three on today. But he'd ordered whoever it was to leave and the team's shift wouldn't be finished for an hour. Likely it was a jealous partner. Stella felt for whoever it was, Jackie reckoned people were jealous when the other person was distant and ungiving, it made the jealous person think others got what they didn't. Since Stella had been in Tewkesbury, this had made sense. Jack got jealous. Was Stella ungiving? Whatever, Stella did know that jealousy was a scary emotion, it could lead to murder.

Once a woman of action and super-efficiency, Stella Darnell, fifty-three last birthday, would have been impatient at having to consider the 'age and fragility' of an object when cleaning. Her job was to make things look as good as new. She would have been horrified to abandon usual standards. But nowadays Stella understood fragility; she didn't require a cadaver tomb to warn her about the reality of death.

Stella retracted the handle of the spider-web brush and packed it in her trolley. Never mind if the likes of Roddy March dubbed her just a cleaner. She hoped that if she looked after the abbey, it would look after her.

Stella wandered the streets in the village of Winchcombe, steeped in nostalgia for past times laced with grief for all she had lost. In the grounds of Sudeley Castle she unclipped Stanley's lead and threw him a tennis ball. He quickly tired of the game, leaving her to fetch it herself.

Stella was recovering from what she thought of as an emotional melt-down. After years of working at full tilt to keep her grief at the sudden death of her father seven years before at bay, she had been engulfed by it. She had upped sticks from her London life – running her cleaning company, the man she loved – and had retreated to Gloucestershire.

Winchcombe was forty minutes from Tewkesbury. The last time she'd been there was with Jack. A different life. Stella had to admit – idiot – that she had hoped to find him there. Stanley had too, perhaps, because when they passed what had been a mean tumble-down cottage squeezed between larger buildings in a back lane – the scene of a murder that she and Jack had solved – he'd strained towards the door. Now adorned with hanging baskets and a slate name plate, it had become a Cotswold dream home.

On Abbey Terrace, the other 'murder house' caused Stella's heart to take a dive. She and Jack had fantasized about living there. His kids would join them, Jack had said. 'We're not put off by a body in the hall.' As they passed now, Stanley showed no interest, as if, like Stella, he'd never believed in the dream.

Stella was unfazed by murder; it was life and all it threw at her from which she shrank. The business of a live-in relationship, all the day-to-day stuff. Then one day you die.

Dusk was gathering as Stella trundled the van along the Old Brockhampton Road. She wasn't expected anywhere, but as she disliked driving in the countryside at night she knew she should soon set off for Tewkesbury. But she had one more visit.

Angling her van onto a verge by a five-bar gate, Stella released Stanley from his jump seat and, checking for vehicles, let him out. Stanley, who all day had been as sluggish as she felt, shot out, wriggled under the gate and galloped off across a ploughed field. In the dwindling light, his champagne-coloured coat was a smudge against the ploughed soil. Stella climbed the gate and stumbled along a claggy furrow. No panic, she knew exactly where he'd gone.

Crow's Nest stood in the middle of the next field at the end of a track. When she and Jack had stayed there, initially Stella – rarely afraid – was spooked by the darkness and silence. A townie, every field looked identical and, for the boss of a cleaning company, too muddy. Regardless, with Jack there, Crow's Nest had soon felt like home. She had come to see the specificity in wild flowers, the hedgerows and clusters of grasses. She could appreciate blackthorn, beech, teazels and sedum.

That was then. No longer the boss of a cleaning company, now she was in the countryside alone and again she saw only fields and mud.

When Stella reached the track, she found Stanley rigidly staring into the gloom. She saw why. He did not recognize where he was.

In place of the ramshackle mock-Tudor house with a sagging roof and rotting timbers was a glass and steel cube with wrap-around balconies.

Stella's ghosts had fled. She could not evoke Jack. The quiet was profound and all encompassing. A thing in itself.

She stumbled back to the van, Stanley at her heels. *Never go back, you can't cheat the passing of time.* No more memory lane.

As she accelerated out of Winchcombe along dark winding roads bordered by impregnable hedges, Stella lamented the lack of light. Shadows leapt and shrivelled in the headlamps as, grim-faced, she hugged the wheel and fervently hoped that nothing would come towards her. The twisty byways with hidden ditches and protruding dry-stone walls offered few passing places.

Spears of light pierced the darkness ahead. As she rounded a bend, Stella saw that they were rear lights. A van was travelling in the same direction as her. But where most locals averaged sixty, hounding her bumper before overtaking, the van – white like her own – was crawling at fifteen miles per hour. Stella hung back. In daylight she wouldn't have minded tootling along, but now she wanted to get back.

The van stopped. Stella slammed on the brakes. The interior of her own van was washed with lurid red light from the rear lamps. She waited. It must have stalled. She rapped a tattoo on the wheel then caught herself on the edge of another simmering rage. Grief could make you angry, she'd read. The driver could have been taken ill. She should get out and check. Her own lights were on full beam, she dimmed them. She'd dazzled the driver and he or she had stopped to let her know. *Sorry.* She toggled the lights.

The brake lights went out. All the lights were off. Although Stella was also driving a white Peugeot Partner, she assumed the driver was male. She shivered. Not from cold, the heater was on full. Stanley growled.

The man might have been taken ill or unconscious. Or his battery had died. She had jump leads. Thinking to help, Stella reached for the door handle. Stanley's whimpers recalibrated to a dreadful cry that was eerily human. The thing about dogs was they could be reassuring company or crank up your nerves to sheer terror. Stella was paralysed.

The van was stationary, the lights were off. A spattering rain began to fall; automatically Stella flicked on the wipers. The creak of the blades dragging across the windscreen nearly stopped her heart.

Stella had no way out. In the narrow lane, she couldn't turn or reverse. The rear mirror reflected black like a void. Stella grabbed her phone from the console. No signal. Exactly why she preferred towns.

The van's driver's door was opening. Stella stiffened, her mind racing. Her own doors were locked, but a wrench like the one in her van, therefore likely in his too, could smash through glass. She smacked clammy hands on her trousers and dry swallowed.

Stella knew, even as she got out, she was making a mistake. Stanley gave a shrill bark. She was watching herself in slow motion, *one foot on the tarmac, the other…*

Light speared through the back window of Stella's van. Another vehicle was coming down the narrow road behind her. Stella slammed her palm on the hazard light button. The 'phantom' van in front trickled forward, still with no lights. It gathered speed and slipped away into the teeming dark.

Fired by adrenalin, her breathing ragged, Stella's foot shuddered on the accelerator and she bunny-hopped the van a few metres. It was then she noticed the time on the dash. Ten to six.

On the Tewkesbury Road, wipers swiping away streaming rain, Stella reached forty. It wasn't true that she didn't have to be anywhere. The Death Café began at six.

Chapter Three

Wednesday, 11 December 1940

7 p.m., Wednesday. Thirteen shopping days until Christmas. In the sulphurous dark, pedestrians, shopworkers, as if in a giant game of Blind Man's Bluff, fumbled across Hammersmith Broadway. Blackout had been in force since 5.24 p.m. Late commuters, emerging from the Underground station, jostled with shelterers descending into the Hades of makeshift camps, patrolled by looters and chancers, that every night lined the Piccadilly line platforms.

Epitaph For A Spy read the headline of a copy of the *Daily Express* lying in a gutter and captioned beneath a photograph... *judgement of death was duly executed...* of *one of the two notices outside Pentonville Prison yesterday...*

Maple Greenhill set her jaw. Her dad had said that, little older than Maple at twenty-four, Jose Wahlberg, one of the spies, was too young to die. Old enough to be a traitor, Vernon had said. Crisply elegant in a reefer coat, blonde hair rolled, sabots crunching on fragments of glass littering even those streets that had escaped bombing. Maple felt the draught of a trolley bus – the 'silent peril' – and veered away from the kerb. When anyone could be killed at any moment, two men who planned to kill them all deserved to hang. You couldn't feel sorry for spies. What if it was Vernon?

Aleck had promised Maple that, when it was conscription, he'd put in a word for Vern. Aleck knew people.

Maple was haunted by the memory of William, her boy (at three in no danger of dying as a soldier), sobbing in his nana's arms on their doorstep. She'd promised she was only going up the shop for cigarettes. She'd heard his cries all the way up Corney Road. Her mum stayed there to make her feel bad. *Don't tell him lies, he'll never forgive you.*

The arrest of the spies was meant to reassure the British public that the Germans were losing, but if two men could land in Dungeness with recording equipment in posh suitcases, Maple reckoned William's nightmares of Nazis coming down the Thames or out of the sky was likely.

Her mum had shouted, 'It's your baby you should be with, not some fancy man.'

'I'm seeing Ida,' she had shouted, almost believing it. 'I don't have a fancy man.' Not a lie. Aleck was her fiancé, not some fly-by-night like William's dad.

'I'm thinking of Will,' Maple had said to herself as, on the tram, she'd wiped William's teary snot off her gorgeous plum-red coat and rearranged the mink which made her mother's lips pucker in mute disapproval. That was after Maple had offered to do the blackout curtains, which nearly killed her.

St Paul's church bells chimed seven. The thickened air rendered the peals directionless – they came from everywhere as if rung by God himself.

As it trundled away, the trolley bus missed a taxi which, hearse-like in the swirling dark, turned into Brook Green Road and halted outside the Palais de Danse. A crowd was milling around the blacked-out doors. Tonight, it was rumoured, Glenn Miller and his band would do a spot before flying out of RAF Northolt.

'I say,' Aleck paid off the taxi and, trim in belted coat and trilby, stepped up to Maple and took her by the shoulders, 'it's Tallulah Bankhead.' He kissed her forehead.

'Get on with you.' Maple reached up and brushed his cheek, noting his smooth skin. She adjusted her stole. No bloke ever compared her to a film star. Fancy her, typist at the dairy, being engaged to a man with a proper job. She'd whispered to William as she pinned up the living room blackout that very soon they would be living *happily ever after*. Now, Maple said, 'Dad says, seeing as we're engaged, he wants to meet you.' She gave a light laugh to smother the little fib. 'You've to come to tea Sunday.'

At that moment, in Corney Road, Chiswick, crouched in the Anderson shelter with his wife, son and little grandson, Keith Greenhill knew nothing of this. He did indeed want to meet Aleck – the nameless scoundrel who was playing about with his daughter. The mink told Keith, as it had told his wife, that Maple's fancy man was at best a trickster who'd signed up to the forces to escape responsibility, like the shiftless fellow who'd left Maple in the lurch. As he gazed at Maple's distraught lad, cried-out in his wife's arms, Keith Greenhill vowed to get him by the scruff of the neck and tell him... Neither of them would sleep until Maple got back, which, from recent experience, they knew would be the small hours.

'Whoever he is, the scoundrel lacks the decency to walk her home.' Greenhill leaned close to his wife to be heard above the cacophony of the guns. 'We'll have to have it out with her.'

'Give her time, she'll tell us.'

'She's had time.'

'See how the land lies in the morning.' Audrey stroked a cow-lick from William's forehead. 'She really could be seeing Ida.'

'Pigs might fly.' Vernon, the Greenhills' twenty-one-year-old son who was slumped by the shelter's entrance, roused himself.

'Do you know something?' Keith demanded.

'Course not.' Vernon pulled the horse-hair blanket up over his chin and rolled over to sleep. His parents exchanged a look; they didn't believe him.

The ground shook with a bomb that they knew wasn't as near as it sounded. Huddled in the cold damp of their newly constructed shelter, which Keith complained was cheap and nasty and not up to the job, the Greenhills retreated into private terror. Everyone knew the Nazis were not the only enemy. There was talk of women being raped in public shelters, old people attacked in their homes for savings and gold watches. Danger lurked around every corner.

Maple should hurry up and come home.

The Palais doors shifted briefly ajar and, gripping Maple's elbow, Aleck piloted her into a world of glitter and magic where Hammersmith Broadway was Hollywood and, even as sirens wailed, one might believe the Blitz could be kept at bay.

Lamps, wreathed in a bluish canopy of cigarette smoke, cast ghostly light over a boiling mass. Ecstatic faces were caught in a match's flare, red lipstick, sleek oiled hair. The floor was marked with scuffed chalk marks from where the BBC had snaked cables for the Force's Sunday broadcast of *Services Spotlight*, the dance hall slot in *The Sunday Nighters*.

Tonight's swing band's sound, not Glenn Miller, bounced off walls plastered with posters that urged women to take up factory work. Tonight's Gas Mask Ball was thrown to encourage Londoners to carry masks. Not really Hollywood.

For Maple, as she danced her life away, a gas mask and doing war work were the last things on her mind.

Last week, when she'd told Aleck about William, he'd just kissed her quiet and undone her blouse. 'We all make mistakes.' The next time they met he'd given her the mink and, from deep inside her, his hands around her hips, asked her to marry him.

William wasn't a mistake. Maple hadn't told Aleck the toddler with pudgy legs and such a cheeky smile was the best thing in her life. Every man liked to come first.

Aleck always got the barman's attention. As he handed Maple the first of several daiquiris, he told her, 'Chin-chin, baby.'

They swooped and swirled to 'I'll Never Smile Again' and 'Easy to Love'. Aleck's hand, on the small of Maple's back, slipped lower. He pressed her to him and she felt his love. For her. If she was Tallulah Bankhead, he was James Stewart from *Mr Smith Goes to Washington*. She'd tell him later. Maybe when he came to tea.

Watching the couple from the bar, a woman whose husband had been killed in a U-boat attack, who expected never to smile again, felt gin-infused hope. It was for such love Britain was fighting. A better world in which everyone cared. Then the man and his girl were lost amidst the throng. And the woman felt desolate as if, with their departure, had gone all chance of happiness. Later, spotting a polite notice for customers at the Palais on the night of the eleventh to come forward with any information about a murdered girl, Una Hughes recognized her. She was able to give the divisional detective an excellent description of the couple.

On the corner nearest the river, an incendiary had ripped away the front of a house to reveal a tableau of shattered domesticity. In dancing flames, as if in a magic lantern show, was a carpeted staircase cut off before the landing, the bathroom mirror above a pallid sink still intact. The stern portrait of a Victorian grandee hanging askew above the drawing room mantelpiece frowned upon the front area infilled with smashed brick and timber, crockery and broken furniture displaced by the blast.

Maple couldn't believe it would happen to her mum and dad's home, their pride and joy. Since Aleck, she felt she and all those she loved would be safe.

The road was blocked by an AFS team attacking flames from a burst gas pipe in the kitchen. In intervals between guns and distant bombing was the grind of the pump engine. Urgent shouts – *Ruddy low tide, Where's the fire-boat?, Shift the turntable* – helmeted fire-fighters, two of them women, like cut-out figures in the orange light which suffused the cobbled road as if it were paved with gold.

Guiding Maple past the criss-cross of vehicles, between pooling water and rubble, Aleck whispered in her ear, 'Wardens dug the family from the cellar two nights ago, crushed to a pulp, all of them. Mind you, the wife was on short commons, and riddled with cancer when I opened her up – handy really, she got a painless death.' He nuzzled into Maple's neck.

Maple imagined telling her mum and dad how there was little Aleck *doesn't know about London's dead*. His phrase. Now, she said, 'It's not fair getting ill in a war. Everything like that should stop. At least we got those spies.' She liked to show Aleck she was up on things.

'Nothing's fair, Maple. Blighters got their just desserts.'

Smoky clouds were thinning to the west. Light from a fitful moon flickered on the Thames. A mud-slicked cobbled causeway, accessible when the tide receded, led to the eyot, an outcrop of land overgrown with reeds and stubby trees. The stench of charred timber and damp mortar was stronger on the shoreline.

'It's the smell of death,' Maple said to sound clever.

'Death doesn't smell like that,' Aleck said. 'Here we are.'

Skirting poles on trestles that protected a large house on Chiswick Mall, he flicked his torch over a board propped against the gate – *Danger. Structure Unsafe* – and led Maple up the path of a house on three floors with rooms either side of the door. Despite the danger sign, it looked undamaged.

Maple would tell her dad that Aleck saw past danger, she felt safe with him. Her dad was always worrying, he'd cried during Chamberlain's speech.

Aleck said the war had been good to him. It was good to her too. If not for Hitler, she wouldn't have met Aleck and he'd never have proposed.

'This is yours?' Maple gasped when Aleck fitted a key into the front door. Aleck usually found an alley at the end of gardens, behind shops, hidden by bins. The first time Maple had worried they should wait until it was decent. Aleck told her, 'There's a war on, rules have changed.'

'Of course not.' He pocketed the key and opened the door.

'Are we allowed?'

'I'm allowed.'

'Who does live here?' Maple blinked in the encompassing light of a vast chandelier. A small voice suggested, *We will.*

'A friend.' Aleck shucked off his coat, folded it and placed it across the post at the bottom of the staircase.

'Is he here?' Maple darted a look up the stairs.

'So many questions.' Aleck gave a braying laugh.

'We've never done it in a bed, will your friend mind?' Shouting above the endless clatter of guns, Maple felt appalled. It had to be Aleck's idea to *do it*, and she must act surprised. 'What if he comes home?'

'He won't.' Aleck lifted off Maple's mink stole and pulled off her coat, his gift. Tugging her, he went into a room off the hall. A table lamp gave a soft circle of light. Aleck tossed Maple's things onto a wing-back chair. The coat slipped off onto a Turkey carpet, but he didn't notice. Without it, Maple shivered. The ashes in the grate looked cold and she imagined asking Aleck to make up a fire, but, in another man's house, that would be cheeky. 'He's never coming back. Oliver Hurrell, aged fifty-three, solicitor of this parish, unmarried with no living relatives, was killed by shrapnel fire-watching at the Commodore yesterday. Our acquaintance began and ended at Hammersmith Mortuary.'

Aleck often said the dead were his friends. Sometimes, despite her pride in him, Maple wished he wouldn't.

Afterwards, flicking on his lighter, Aleck lit them each a cigarette. He shuffled to sitting, his back against the sofa.

'Tallulah Bankhead wouldn't sit in her birthday suit in a dead man's house without a ring on her finger. James Stewart wouldn't let her.' Not used to smoking, Maple took kissing puffs of her cigarette. A settee was a far cry from an alley but it was not a bridal chamber.

'What are you talking about now?' Aleck blew smoke-ribbons at the rose ceiling moulding.

'I think we should not meet like this, not until we're married.' Ida said you had to put your foot down or things got out of hand.

'It's not me you lost your virginity with, dearie.' Aleck narrowed his eyes. 'And let's face it, you never take persuading.'

'What about Sunday? Dad's expecting you. Mum's making a cake with eggs.' Coughing as she inhaled, Maple began gathering her clothes from the carpet where Aleck had strewn them. Her toe snagged a stocking and tears pricked. Real silk, they had cost more than a day's wages.

When she'd fallen pregnant, her younger brother Vernon called her a tart. He'd gone with her dad to Bertie Spence's lodgings in Fulham to find that the hod-carrier had signed up the day before. Keith Greenhill had made Vernon say sorry, *treat your older sister with respect*, yet Vernon was only saying what her parents felt.

'A bed would have been nice,' Maple mumbled. Watching Aleck tap his cigarette into an ashtray on an occasional table, she noted that, apart from tie and jacket, he hadn't so much as dropped his trousers. She'd never seen him in the altogether.

'Have sense, Maple.' Aleck flipped up his braces. 'I couldn't raise the flag in a dead man's bed.'

'I bet you could.' Pressing a dampened finger to the silk, Maple made a fruitless attempt to close the nick. 'Mum's gone to town with baking.' She made it up as she went along, then, seeing her coat in a heap, felt annoyed that Aleck had treated it badly; not caring meant his present to her was worth nothing to him.

Aleck didn't help her into it as he had in the Palais. Watching him tighten his tie, her fingers rummaged restlessly in her coat pockets as, tottering on one high heel she trod into the other shoe. To fend off the feeling of being dirty and wrong, she persisted. 'What time on Sunday? Will three do?'

'Let's not rush it, Maple.' He smoothed back his hair.

'It's been three months. By rights you should have asked Dad about marrying me.' Maple probed at something – not in the pocket, it was caught in the pocket lining.

'I didn't mean it, silly girl. We men promise anything in the heat of the moment.'

Maple knew that. The hod-carrier had promised her a diamond ring. Aleck was meant to be quite different. She worried at a tiny tear in the lining and hooked out a bit of paper. Smoothing it, she showed it to the lamplight.

'Who's Julia?'

In the street the all-clear sounded.

'What?' Aleck mashed his cigarette in the ashtray.

'This is a mending ticket, for Julia Northcote, I think it says?'

'My sister.'

'You said you were an only child.' Maple might be an optimist, but she was no fool. When not blinded by dreams, she could tell when a man was lying.

'My wife.' Aleck looked angry. 'Good God, who else would it be?'

'You're married.' Cold as ice, Maple rivalled Tallulah Bankhead. 'You're a liar. My dad will have your guts. All the time you, *you*—' Maple shoved the paper back in her pocket and strode to the door. She turned, incandescent. 'You think you can palm me off with her cast-offs. We'll see about that.'

Maple never reached the herring-bone tiled hall. Aleck caught up with her and whipping off his tie, slipped it over her head. He yanked her close.

Several Londoners, creeping back to their homes after the raid, heard the scream. One woman told the detective she assumed the lady had seen a mouse; the caretaker at nearby flats said it wasn't his business what went on behind closed doors.

Chapter Four

December 2019

Stella

Stella hesitated at the door to the Abbey Gardens teashop. Through the steamed-up window, a group clustered at the servery: a man, and two women. Another woman, tall with a mass of curly black hair, was handing out teas and coffees from behind the counter. She looked faintly familiar, but Stella knew no one in Tewkesbury. The smaller tea tables had been pushed to the wall, leaving the large circular table in the centre of the parquet floor which, as cleaner for the teashop, Stella would be mopping at 6 a.m. tomorrow.

Not too late to change her mind and leave. But after the scary incident on the lane, Stella was in no hurry to return to the empty flat and spend the evening alone. Choice was taken from her when the door opened and a man greeted her.

'I'm a bit late.' Stella saw it was three minutes past six.

'Dust is the enemy of time, it clogs the cogs. Come inside, my dear, punctuality is a concept. 'Fraid there's no booze.' His bass tone was surprising for such a tall reedy frame. Stella caught the aroma of coffee and could see a fire burning in the grate.

'I didn't expect alcohol.' Stella planned to keep a clear head. 'Are you in charge?'

'Good *God* no. Mademoiselle Felicitations is running the show. The Amazon lady doling out weak tea and no sympathy over there. Come, come, you're letting in the cold air.' Doffing an imaginary cap he scooted Stella inside. 'Clive Burgess at your service, ma'am.'

'Stella.' The man smelled of something which, after a moment, Stella identified as Horolene, the cleaning fluid for clocks she knew from a museum she'd cleaned in London.

'And I bet you are.' Clive Burgess shook her hand and perhaps seeing her quizzical expression said, 'Stella. Star.'

'Oh, right.' Stella looked around for a means of escape. The tearoom had been transformed. The table, draped with a dark mauve tablecloth shaded by a lamp, put her in mind of a séance. An impression not lessened by the sugar-dusted Victoria sponge perched on one of the teashop's pottery cake-stands. Stella kept Stanley on a short lead; it would be disastrous if he snatched the cake.

'Tread carefully, it's her first bash at this Death Café malarkey, she's a bit windy about it. Upset her and death might come to all of us quicker than we'd like.' Hands resting on the back of the chair the man laughed wheezily. Looking at him properly, Stella saw he was even older than his jaunty energy suggested, perhaps eighty. Seeing Stanley, he said, 'I say, are dogs are allowed?'

'I didn't ask. I'll leave.' Stella grasped the legitimate escape route.

'Don't you dare.' The man stretched his arms across the door, barring Stella's exit. 'We'll sink in this ship together.'

'I'm sure it will be fine.' Stella hadn't anticipated small talk. The notice in the tearoom described the Death Café as an opportunity to explore the meaning of death. Stella had promised to come so would not bail out. She slung her anorak over a chair at the séance table and approached the servery.

'Are dogs allowed?' Nervous, Stella repeated Clive's question and forgot to say hello.

'I don't see why not, as long as he behaves himself.' Up close Stella realized she did know the woman, who had signed her email Felicity Branscombe. Or not so much know her as had seen her before. She had conducted the choir in the abbey when Stella had been there for evensong. She, too, had to be over seventy. In her early fifties, Stella wondered if she should come back later. Twenty years later.

'I'm Stella,' she told Felicity.

'We'll do introductions in a mo. There's builders' tea, sachets of a ghastly herbal concoction that promises to send you to sleep and coffee. No milk, it got spilt. Serving beverages is harder than performing an autopsy.' Felicity banged a bowl of sugar onto the counter. 'I hope you weren't expecting wine. As I told Clive, the purpose of this evening is honest discussion, not getting plastered. The Death Café lot say you have to provide refreshments or, frankly, I'd get on with it.'

'Black coffee please.' Stella was startled at the reference to an autopsy – presumably Felicity had to keep on a death theme.

Once everyone was seated, Felicity distributed perfectly cut slices of the cake on paper plates. Opposite Stella and Stanley – held tightly on Stella's lap – was an overweight woman, the fringe of her iron-grey bob clamped with a slide shaped like an elephant's tusk. Stella reckoned the woman was late sixties. Her demeanour was grim, a weird contrast to her brightly coloured Elizabethan-style tunic embroidered with deer and rabbits who were being chased by men firing arrows.

'Does he moult?' The woman was looking at Stanley. 'I'm allergic.'

'No.' Stella clutched Stanley tighter which made him struggle to jump down. 'He's made of wool.'

'I do hope so,' the woman said.

'Don't panic, Joy.' An elderly woman shut the door to the toilets next to the servery. 'You're more likely to get asthma from my angora jumper.' Sitting down next to Stella, the woman winked at her. Stella took in the auburn-coloured bob and turquoise polo-neck. The woman arranged a silver quilted jacket around her shoulders.

'Evening, Gladys,' the Tudor woman said.

Seeing how smartly dressed all three women were, Stella felt embarrassed by her fleece, worn since cleaning the abbey that morning. She'd left time no go home and change.

Sticking to the rules of a Death Café, Felicity informed them she was their facilitator and asked everyone to 'go gently into the night with me, it's my first time in the hot seat'. She listed ground rules, 'mobile phones off' and said not to:

'...promote your business particularly if you are an undertaker or sell wreaths. A Death Café is not a bereavement support group, if your loved one is recently deceased and your grief raw, this ain't for you.' She rested her gaze on Clive who was on a second slice of Victoria sponge and looked to Stella the picture of chirpiness. For herself, she welcomed the no tears rule. Were she to start crying, Stella feared she'd never stop.

'Tell us why you have come tonight. Offer us a point for discussion. What do you hope to take away?' Glancing up from what looked like a crib sheet, Felicity's smile revealed a row of expensive-looking teeth. All Stella could think she must take away was her rucksack which last week she'd left in the abbey after evensong.

'We'll start with Mrs Gladys Wren.' Felicity pointed her fountain pen at the woman in the silver jacket. 'Please tell the group your name and what you do for a living.'

'You've given it *away*.' Gladys Wren raised eyebrows dyed to match her hair. 'Landlady, for my sins. Now, what do I say?'

'Why you're here.' Tudor tunic rolled her eyes.

'Call me Gladys.' Gladys toyed with her cake. 'It was recommended by a friend. Death is never far away, is it? My hubby Derek always said, when it was my turn, they'd have found a vaccine. He said I got younger by the day. God rest him.'

'That's nonsense,' the Tudor woman said. 'How terrible would it be if everyone around this table never died.'

'Lovely contribution, Gladys,' Felicity said. 'What will you take with you?'

'A bit of this lovely cake if Mr Burgess hasn't scoffed the lot.' Gladys angled her fork at Clive, the elderly man who had greeted Stella. 'It's so light and buttery, did you make it, Felicity?'

'Shop-bought.' Felicity made an irrelevant gesture with her hand.

'I came here...' Poking about in a plastic crocodile-skin bag, Gladys dug out a well-thumbed Donald Duck notebook and flicked through the pages. 'For shopping lists, ah, here it is. "To face death in the face." That sounds silly when you say it out loud.'

'Death is all around, everywhere you look,' the Tudor woman said.

'Now *there's* a song.' Gladys waggled a finger. '"Love is All Around".

'It was fifteen weeks in 1994 for Wet Wet Wet.' Stella liked statistics.

'After Derek's time or he'd have swept me off my feet.' Humming the tune, Gladys swayed in her seat and, unprompted by her Donald Duck book, 'Grief never leaves you, no day goes by when Derek isn't with me. Ten years is ten minutes.' And to Felicity, 'Don't you worry, lovey, I shan't cry.'

'Do any of you have a subject we can air as a group?' Felicity tapped her paper.

'While we're on the subject of death...' Gladys flicked to the back of the notebook and, flattening the pages, read out in halting tones a sentence written across two pages. Stella was no handwriting expert, yet she didn't associate the bold scrawl in green ink with Gladys. 'What. I want to. Know. Is.' Gladys turned the book diagonal to better read, '"Who here wishes someone was dead? I know one who shall remain nameless."'

Stella was impressed that Gladys had come prepared. She herself had not.

'I'm sure we all do, but it's not our purpose tonight. Is there anything apart from cake you hope to take away?'

Stella felt for Felicity, chairing the group was like herding cats.

'Happiness.' Gladys heaved her shoulders. 'Since Derek. *Oops*, there I go again, he *will* pop up.' She hunched into her silver jacket and fell silent.

'*Lovely*, Gladys.' Felicity crossed out what looked to Stella like Gladys's name. She imagined Felicity thinking *one down, three to go*. Stella hoped time would run out before Felicity got to her.

'Joy, you're next,' Felicity said. 'Name, occupation, why you're here, et cetera.'

'Joy by name. Joy by nature,' said the woman called Joy in the hunting tunic.

'You hide that well, lovey.' Gladys grinned at Joy.

'Welcome, Joy, lovely that you could come with all you have on your busy plate,' Felicity cut in.

With a tendency to think literally, Stella noted that Joy hadn't touched the cake on her plate. Stella had nibbled at hers; the scary incident on the dark lane had killed her appetite. She hugged Stanley closer, not forgetting that, however sleepy he appeared to be, the cake would be the only thing on his mind.

'I expect to take away what I came with. Common sense. We will all die and for some of us the end will be sooner than for others.' Joy jutted a determined chin. 'No point in beating about the bush.'

Stella came out in a sweat. Going clockwise around the table, after Joy was Clive who was consulting a silver fob watch attached to his waistcoat. Then it would be her turn.

'...organist at the abbey, I'm the first woman. My male predecessor died.' Joy nodded. 'I'm not a feminist, but it was time. My dear father taught me: leave your mark, don't let sleeping dogs lie. The marvellous Grove organ on the north side of the Choir is my path to immortality, I shall not be forgotten.' She traced one of the embroidered rabbits with a stubby finger.

'I want to discuss the last image we want to see as life ebbs from the corporeal form. Mine is da Vinci's *The Last Supper*. His Jesus is my father to a T.'

Joy seemed to be one of those people like Lucie who, the more confidential what they had to say was, the louder they said it.

'My old man was more of a Tommy Trinder,' Gladys said. 'The person I want to see as I die is Derek, he was my saviour.'

Joy made a short scornful sound that made Stella want to rescue Gladys.

'No one man can be a saviour. We have to save ourselves.' Joy looked disapproving. Stella felt blind panic: she had no idea what she wanted to see. It haunted her that her father's last view – he died outside the Co-op – was a grubby pavement in a small seaside town. It had been a huge mistake to come.

'Who would like to speak next?' A flush was creeping up Felicity's neck. Stella supposed that her first Death Café wasn't going to plan and considered stepping in. Jack said Stella had to stop wanting to rescuing people, they must find their own way. *She hadn't rescued Jack.*

Stella was considering holding her nose and getting it over with when the door flew open and a blast of wind and rain blew in a tall woman, beanie pulled over her ears, mud-streaked parka coat dripping on the parquet. She flung herself onto a chair between Clive and Gladys and, shrugging out of her parka, bashed at the knees of equally muddy denim overalls as if to clean them. Her face was almost hidden by a khaki snood yet it was easy to tell she was scowling ferociously. All Stella cared about was that now the newcomer would speak before her.

'You're late. What is your name and why have you come?' Felicity said, which, to Stella's mind, sounded really quite rude.

'I only remembered once I got home, I had to cycle back,' came the muffled reply. 'Andrea.'

'We've only just started.' Stella came to the rescue.

'I know.' Andrea did a 'duh' expression as if this was a no-brainer.

'Yes, ducky, you settle down. I'd take those wet things off or you'll get a chill in your kidneys.' Gladys Wren's concern nearly had Stella crying after all. Her own mother loved her, but expressions of concern came out as terse strictures. Gladys was explaining to Andrea, '...we have to say what we hope to get from here.'

'Get warm and then not get soaked on the way home.'

'We've all made sacrifices to be here.' Felicity beamed at the group. 'This is Andrea, everyone. *Welcome*, Andrea.'

'Hardly,' Andrea said.

'Hi there.' Stella nodded to her, but Andrea was scowling at Stanley.

'Didn't know we could bring dogs.'

'Have you got a dog?' Clive leaned unnecessarily close to Andrea.

'No,' Andrea said.

It amazed Stella, brought up to be polite by warring parents, how perfect strangers could think nothing of being rude to each other. Although, aside from Andrea and herself, it seemed that everyone else knew each other. Only to be expected in a small town. Stella knew it was contrary but, horrified at making light conversation with the group, she also felt obscure resentment at being an outsider. No question of pairing with Andrea, she appeared to have taken an instant dislike to Stella.

'I'll throw in my hat.' The elderly man cleared his throat loudly. 'Clive's me name, footloose and fancy free is me nature.' He snatched off his wire-framed glasses and puffing on the lenses buffed them vigorously with his stained tie. 'Joy, if by feminist you mean one who loves women, *c'est moi.*'

'That's not being a feminist, that's a lesbian, which I doubt you are, Clive. Some women are frightened they'll be mistaken for gay if they admit to preferring women-only spaces.' Joy spoke to the fob-watch man as if he were a child. 'I, for example, am *not* a lesbian, however I won't hide bitter disappointment that my expectation that this discussion would exclude men has proved to be false.'

'I'll be whatever you like, *Joyous*.' Clive waggled his glasses like Eric Morecambe.

'Is that about death?' Andrea glared at Joy and Clive. 'Men die as much as women, why wouldn't they be here?'

Paying attention to the group's dynamics – Jack would if he was there – Stella decided Andrea's animosity was indiscriminate and not aimed at her. But how odd to come since she clearly didn't want to be there.

So, I'm an—' Clive was drowned out by Rod Stewart. Stella recognized 'The First Cut is the Deepest'.

'That's mine. I have to go.' Felicity was frowning at her phone.

'Ooh, hoisted by your own – mobile phones off – petard, my dear.' Clive's glasses were steamed up, Stella couldn't see his eyes.

'We'll tell you what we all took away with us.' Joy appeared marginally more cheerful.

'...sorry, but it means you all have to leave too. I'm responsible for locking up the tearoom. We shall continue tomorrow night.'

'What if we're busy tomorrow?' Andrea ran the zip up and down her parka, reminding Stella of Jack's four-year-old daughter Milly when she was cross.

Heading across the tearoom with the remains of the cake, Felicity flung up the counter flap and shouldered the door to the servery.

Stella and Gladys were gathering up mugs when they heard her call, 'Don't help, I'm far better on my own.'

No one noticed Stanley hoovering up crumbs under the table.

Chapter Five

Thursday, 12 December 1940

'Good to see you, doc. 'Struth, you got here quick.' George Cotton strode into a room crammed with several dark-wood cabinets, a high-backed sofa, armchairs and plant stands. A technician was arranging arc lamps delivered by one of the police vans.

'I was close by.' Dr Northcote smiled.

The two men shook hands. One, a divisional detective, pulled away from retirement on his allotment to replace conscripted police officers, the other, at thirty-nine already a celebrated Home Office pathologist, were divided by class and did not meet socially, but mutual regard ensured each was relieved to find the other at the scene of a murder.

'Not quick enough to save French Annie.' Northcote indicated the body of a young woman lying twisted at the foot of the sofa. 'Killer can't be far, she's still warm.'

'*Chrissakes.*' Cotton spun on his heel and rushed out of the house. His voice rang in the street as he bellowed at the three constables clustered by the gate.

'Check every house, alleyway, the dustbins, shelters in gardens, there's a public one near the Black Lion. Boats, skiffs. If he's on the eyot, he'll be stranded, comb every ruddy inch. And,' Cotton waved a hand at a houseboat moored nearby, 'take that apart.' He heaved a breath. 'There's a monster out there. *Find him.*'

Cotton was still panting when he returned to the murder room. He noted the upturned chair and rucked Turkey carpet. 'She must have struggled. Surprising not more neighbours didn't hear.'

'There was a raid on, don't forget.' Dr Northcote was crouched, the skirts of his coat between his haunches. 'Anyway, people keep themselves to themselves these days, you know that.'

'Unless they're nicking stuff from dead people's destroyed homes. I could swing for the schoolteacher we nabbed last night; he'd stolen a wireless set off a woman killed by a strike, because his own had stopped working. How such minds work, beats me.' Cotton raked through dark hair, which took years off his actual age of forty-six.

'No morals,' Dr Northcote agreed.

Standing next to the pathologist, George Cotton considered the corpse. He didn't need Northcote to put her at between nineteen and twenty-five, and she'd been pretty, with looks that needed no make-up. Her fake blonde hair was washed and curled. If she'd been anything like June, that would have kept her busy – she'd probably worn curlers to bed last night. This picture pierced his heart. Thinking of June, Cotton said, 'I'm thinking that black velvet dress and her silk stockings cost a bob or two.'

'The coat and this mink must have been given by a satisfied customer.' Northcote was reading his thermometer.

One stocking was torn at the calf. The tear too slight, Cotton reckoned, to have occurred in her attempt to escape. One shoe was half off, the leg twisted beneath her at a dreadful angle.

'Definitely murder?' Not a question.

'Strangulation, George.' The doctor pointed with a six-inch rule. 'See those abrasions? My guess is a ligature. A length of material, a tie most probably. Wound on the back of her head is with a blunt instrument of some kind.'

'The poker, perhaps?' Cotton went to the large marble fireplace and examined a silver companion set beside the grate. 'It's here, at the back. I doubt he had the presence of mind to return it.'

'I think an ashtray. The wound is less specific than the head of a poker. There isn't an ashtray here, bet he pocketed it.' Northcote got to his feet.

'Spur of the moment thing,' Cotton mused. 'Still warm, you said?'

'I hate to give you a time, but on this occasion, I can safely state French Annie here's only been dead about half an hour.'

Cotton didn't like Northcote's habit of referring to all dead women as Annie, whether French or Old.

'No sign of anyone in the vicinity, sir.' A young man with acne-scarred cheeks in a suit of what Cotton fretted was black-market tweed – crime was no longer the proclivity of seasoned criminals – hovered by the door.

'Check if this address is where this lady lived, Shepherd.' Cotton fiddled with the rim of his hat.

'There, I can help you, George.' Northcote picked up his bag. 'The house owner is one Oliver Hurrell, aged fifty-three—'

'You know him?' Cotton dreaded being called to the fatality of a friend.

'Only by death. Hurrell, solicitor of this parish, was killed by shrapnel fire-watching at the Commodore yesterday. Germans got there first, but the chap would have dropped dead of apoplexy soon enough – arteries furred like London Underground cables and riddled with disease.' He gave a tight smile. 'No relations. I'll show you the file on him.'

'In that case what was this woman doing here?' Cotton rubbed his chin. 'All dressed for a night out.'

'Not my job, but I'd say this lady was one of the blooms of the night.' Northcote clipped shut his bag.

'She doesn't have the look of a prostitute. Her skin is too good, she looks well.' Cotton wasn't arguing, this was how they worked. One posing a theory, the other expanding on it or countering with another. 'If she is, that outfit is too dear for picking up customers from the street – her clients would be too high a class to meet her in deserted premises. Any evidence of sexual activity?'

'More than once, I'm afraid.' Northcote leaned down and, almost tenderly Cotton noticed, took up one of the dead woman's hands. 'Like you say this girl fought like a cat, look at her nails. I did find skin underneath them so somewhere on his person, our man has scratches.'

'Any hair?'

'Not one strand, so either he was as bald as a coot or, more likely given the wound at the back of her head, she was caught by surprise.'

'Some men see women's lives as cheap.' At times like this, Cotton hated his job. Only an hour ago, this woman had her life before her.

'Another case of girl lures gentleman into vacant house for sex then expects to fleece him.' Northcote sighed.

Cotton knew he and Northcote differed on this subject because, in his experience, men did the luring.

'How did she know it was empty? Hurrell was living here only days ago.' Cotton thought aloud.

'I'm always saying, George, we should recruit tarts to spy for Britain – they know exactly what's going on. They'd take on those German kids we hanged today.' Northcote adjusted his scarf against the chill in the unheated house and added, laughing, 'Perhaps we do employ them, what?'

'Perhaps.' Cotton knew Northcote meant the two spies who, stumbling ashore at Dungeness last month, had got themselves caught immediately and hanged at Pentonville on the morning of the 10th. One, at twenty-four, was Shepherd's age. Cotton was alone amongst his colleagues in thinking capital punishment brutal. It never put felons off from killing people or surely, in a war, committing treason.

'That was a decent score.' Northcote's satisfaction reminded Cotton the pathologist had performed the post-execution autopsies. While Cotton could sometimes tire of policing, he never envied Northcote his job.

. While Northcote was packing up, Cotton did his own check of the house and ascertained it unlikely the woman and her killer strayed beyond the living room. When he returned, he said, 'If her killer knew this place was empty, maybe he planned to kill her here.'

'How would he know?' Northcote said.

'There's a danger sign outside, for a start.'

'It rather suggests our man has killed other girls. Were that so, I might have expected to have them come through to me,' Northcote said.

'One thing: no handbag. Women always carry one. Mark you, he's deposited it in a nearby bin.'

'Spot on, George, our killer won't want to be seen prancing along with some fancy handbag on his arm.' Northcote was as much a detective as Cotton.

Cotton was gazing at the twisted corpse. The set of her features, the determined chin, suggested Maple Greenhill had known her own mind. How had she ended up dead in an empty house?

'Sir.' Shepherd was back. 'Fingerprint man from the Yard's here.'

'Get him in toot sweet.' Unlike some officers, Cotton welcomed anyone from the Yard. You couldn't have too many cooks in the kitchen and these days fingerprinting was more often than not a clincher.

'I'll start on her first thing, George.' Pausing, Northcote bowed his head to the dead woman and, donning his trilby, went out into the night.

★ ★ ★

Two hours later PC Shepherd was driving George Cotton past the brewery on their way to Corney Road, the address on the young lady's ID card. As Northcote had predicted, police found her handbag in a bin near Eyot Gardens.

Maple's purse contained no cash, but along with the ID was a wage slip for the Express Dairies. On her modest weekly income, it would have taken Maple months to pay off her Jaeger coat. Otherwise, one lipstick, a powder puff in a squashed cardboard box and, somewhat of a surprise, a copy of *The Woman in White* by Wilkie Collins which Maple had borrowed from Boots. Her bookmark, an oblong of felt embroidered with the letters MVG, was tucked near the end. That Maple liked reading didn't fit Cotton's – and surely not Northcote's – portrait of a prostitute.

'Two sets of prints in the house. Not much to go on, sir.' Shepherd crawled the Wolseley past Chiswick House on their right. 'Inspector Cherrill said one set will be Hurrell, the man who lived there. He reckoned the other is a right thumbprint which he said was Dr Northcote. Fancy him just knowing that and why would Scotland Yard have the doc's fingerprints?'

'Cherrill's got the dabs of all manner of distinguished personages. I, too, am honoured to be filed in his system. Come on, chin up, lad. In the past, I'll have you know, we've got a result with less than that. In the end it's about wearing out shoe leather, and nous.' Cotton discouraged pessimism in his reluctant recruit. The lad had been in the police only two years when war was declared; Cotton himself stopped him joining up because he needed him in CID. He'd told Shepherd: *'There's a job to be done here on the home front. If we all go off to fight, we're leaving London to the criminal fraternity.'*

'One stroke of luck is they've still got Mr Hurrell at the Co-op undertakers.' Untypically, Shepherd was quick to rally. 'What with his funeral being tomorrow. The inspector is sure he's not on file, otherwise we'd have been faced with exhumation.'

'I'm sure he could have obtained plenty from all over the house. Just convenient having the original to hand, so to speak.

One thing we know is Hurrell's not a suspect.' The brightest of CID having been called up, Cotton had to exercise patience.

He'd explained the ID card wasn't sufficient evidence to name their dead woman. You could get yourself in hot water relying on paperwork. Rifling through her bag and along the lining, tucked in a secret compartment with a folded ten-shilling note, Cotton had discovered a photograph. Edges crinkle-cut, it showed a boy aged about two perched on the lap of a young woman against a painted backdrop draped in velvet.

It was Shepherd who confidently pronounced, 'That's her, sir.'

It should be good news that the woman in the photo matched the body currently being transported to the Hammersmith morgue, but what Cotton would give for the bag to have been a false lead. For the picture to portray a mother still alive and able to cuddle her baby.

Five past five. The raid had ended but blackout wouldn't come off until 8.40 a.m. As the car crawled at ten miles an hour, Cotton, the bearer of bad news, did not want to go where they were going.

Under the cover of his coat, he shone his electric torch on the photograph. Maple Greenhill's smile was broad, he could almost see that she must have burst into laughter as soon as the shutter clicked. *Maple had enjoyed life.*

In last night's raid, many had lost their lives, but dwelling on one, Cotton vowed to catch the man who had ended that life.

Except, as the car tracked tramlines, a trick that in the dark lessened the chance of straying to the other side of the road, Cotton privately agreed with Shepherd: so far, they had sweet Fanny Adams.

Chapter Six

December 2019

Jack

Midnight. St Nicholas's churchyard. By the faint light of a lamp-post on the pavement beyond the railing, Jack Harmon bent to make out the name.

GEORGE COTTON
1894–1979

Simple facts, nothing to get his teeth into. No dates with which to nourish his need to flesh out the dead. For example, if a person died on their birthday you could imagine they'd been fighting a life-limiting illness and had exerted the last of their will to round off their life. Those whose death was in early January had wanted a final Christmas.

Shifting his gaze to an adjacent grave, Jack read that John and Victoria Cotton had died on the same day in 1935. *Innocent victims of the Welwyn Garden City railway accident.* Odd phrasing. Was the driver considered guilty? A train driver himself, Jack blanched at the idea.

After dark the cemetery gates were locked, but Jack knew a way in. He liked the prospect of the Cotton family meeting again. Did you haunt where you had been buried or where you died? Ghosts were not limited by geography. Their graves were their resting places.

These days it was all about confectionery and dressing up. Jack never abandoned hope that one night, wandering in a cemetery between the serried ranks of dead, one person would join him. His mother.

Her grave was miles away in Sussex but she was murdered beside the River Thames, ten minutes from the cemetery, two years after George Cotton's death. Yesterday, Jack's son had asked if the dead did walk, did they take it in turns? The little boy had worked out that the dead outnumbered the living, there would be a crowd of ghosts. Bella, Jack's ex, had been cross with Jack: *You tell them such crap.*

Without – literally – meeting a soul, Jack climbed back through a gap in the cemetery wall, crept alongside the ancient walls of the darkened church and out through the lychgate onto Chiswick Mall. Like the cemetery, the street was timeless. Victorian wrought-iron lamps, now casting bleak LED light onto cobbles, had once hissed with gas. In the threaded dark, cars became hansom cabs.

He told Stella she had rescued him from his half-life. Well, now she had put him back there. Saying that had been a mistake. Stella shunned even a whiff of dependency. A woman of action, she had no truck with ghosts, or signs Jack believed defined fate. Stupid him, his signs, ghosts, amulets had led him here. Alone.

Jack felt Stella's absence like a death. He was the walking dead.

Jack felt a weight in his pocket and took out the pebble. A driver on the London Underground, he'd come off the dead-late shift on the District line at Ealing Broadway. He'd walked through the terminated train checking for passengers, asleep or drunk or both. He'd found the pebble on the floor of the last car and, picking it up, saw a face had been scratched into the flint, eyes and mouth wide as if in horror. He intended to hand it to Lost Property, knowing they'd laugh at him for bothering, but now, the aghast face was company.

The tide was receding. The causeway was littered with flotsam, broken glass and bits of wood which, lit by the waxing moon, looked like limbs. The mud gleamed as if phosphorous. Careful not to slip in his rubber-soled shoes Jack went down slime-ridden river stairs onto the beach. He walked a rotted plank to the causeway and from there to the eyot, a scrap of land only accessible by foot at low tide.

Jack Harmon walked the streets of London. It was his habit to follow home late commuters, night-shift workers, couples keeping their distance, love long over. He'd linger in shadows to keep watch on his chosen house until the grey light of dawn. Jack knew most of us trust that bad things only happen to other people. Set in our routines – dog-walking, jogging, journeying to and from work or the supermarket – we don't see what else is happening.

We move house and, excited to collect the key, never consider who else has a copy. We tell the chemist our address without heed to who is queuing behind. We banter with the window cleaner, meter reader, we give the plumber the alarm code. We leave doors unlatched to nip out for chocolate we shouldn't have and we express horror at a murder in the local paper, never thinking that we ourselves may die that way.

Standing amongst tall reeds on the eyot, Jack whispered on the breeze.

'Have you seen the cold-hearted shadow who waits so patiently for a chance to know you better?'

Jack knew, it takes one to know one.

Chapter Seven

December 2019

Stella

Since she'd moved to Tewkesbury, Stella was appreciating that she worked for someone else. She could do the job, and leave. Today had begun by cleaning the Abbey tea shop, an auctioneer's office on the High Street, then a couple of domestic visits, before ending with deep-cleaning a probate house for sale that was opposite the secondary school.

This last, a favourite activity, raised Stella's spirits and, having resolved not to return to the Death Café – last night had been worse than her worst fears – Stella changed her mind. The session had hardly started so she hadn't yet kept her promise to try out a Death Café. Remembering Joy was allergic to dogs, and in case there was cake, Stella went without Stanley.

The clock struck five fifty-five. She sheltered from the rain beneath the vast flying buttress on the abbey's south wall. Pale light from the tearoom tinged the grass. Through steamed up windows Stella could see several figures and felt mild relief; not just her then.

It was like a repeat of the night before. Again, Stella hesitated outside the door and was startled as it was flung open. Although the man who ushered her in was not Clive.

'Twice in two days, we can't go on meeting like this, *Beverly.*' Collar of his combat jacket up, Roddy March flicked back tumbling locks of ebullient blond and, raising an Abbey Gardens mug to Stella, tossed the rest of a piece of cake into his mouth. 'Thank God you're here, these others are dodo dead.'

It was the man from the tomb of the starved monk. *The man in the beanie to whom she had said that her name was Beverly.*

'Have you come about cadaver tombs?' In confusion, Stella said the first thing that came into her head.

'You remembered.' March looked pleased as he shut the tearoom door. 'That's what I told that Felicity, she was already antsy that I've started on the nosh.' He gestured to the table where Stella saw a coffee and walnut cake, a large chunk missing, had been placed on the stand. Irrelevantly, she wondered what had happened to the rest of the sponge from the previous night. 'And for God's sake don't ask for biscuits, Clive said he was in the dog house last night.'

'I'm not hungry,' Stella snapped. Although, seeing the cake, she realized that she was.

'Is March your friend?' Felicity asked when Stella went to fetch her coffee.

'No. I don't know him.' While this was strictly true, Stella felt she had lied.

'He's a gatecrasher, come for the free cake.' Felicity looked furious. 'I had to say he could stay.'

'That was nice of you,' Stella said for something to say. She wondered why anyone would gatecrash a Death Café for any reason. Roddy March had sat next to what last night was her chair. She would move.

But when she brought her coffee to the table, Stella found that Gladys had saved the seat for her. Irritated to have March beside her, Stella was nevertheless touched that Gladys had done so. Everyone had placed themselves in the same chairs as the night before. Joy was opposite Stella with Clive to her left, on his left was Andrea then Gladys, Stella, Roddy and finally Felicity.

'I never said what I hate yesterday.' Joy had swapped her tunic for a thick knitted cardigan which, Stella saw, depicted more deer and rabbits.

'I never actually asked you to—' said Felicity.

'What do I hate? Well,' Joy held up a fragment of walnut, 'I utterly loathe that ghastly euphemism for death, "*passed on*". As if life is a conveyor belt. We do not "pass on", we die.' A hunter swooping on its prey, Joy snatched up a morsel of cake and popped it in her mouth.

'Joy, who encouraged you to feel this hate?' Roddy was smoothing out a new page in a notebook.

'We are avoiding the personal, please stick to death,' Felicity cautioned him. 'Joy, your point about euphemisms for mortality is cogent. We're here tonight to stare death in the face.'

'Are we?' Gladys gave a nervous laugh. 'I'm not dressed for that.'

'Waves roll in and level the sand until there's nothing to show you were ever there.' Clive tapped his fob watch pocket. Stella saw he was wearing the same tie as last night. The same shirt too. 'We kill time, we waste time and we fill in time. Beware, we cannot *defy* time.'

'Nice.' Roddy March wrote it down. Felicity's expression darkened. Stella supposed taking notes was discouraged.

'It was my turn when our host received a text from an admirer who couldn't wait.' Clive sucked in his cheeks. Stella felt for Felicity – yet again the evening was slipping from her grasp.

'It wasn't a... Oh never mind, go ahead. Introduce yourself.' Felicity pulled out her Death Café crib sheet from a leather doctor's bag.

'I am an horologist.' Clive rolled the r. 'Should you suppose I can read your stars, don't. I can't tell me Virgo from me Piss-cees. My vocation is to serve Old Father Time. I construct clocks, watches, automatons, those that *tell* the time and those with no face, the pendulum swings, but we are none the wiser. The secret keepers of time.' He was flicking a brown plastic thing along his fingers, back and forth. 'For me, as the big hand approaches eighty-two, time ain't on me side. However, time is a construct, hours and minutes are the petty invention of man.' He produced his fob watch from its pocket in his waistcoat and, tapping the face as if, like a barometer, this would tell him, said, 'I will live for ever.'

Everyone laughed except Stella who suspected Clive wasn't joking, and Joy who hadn't yet smiled.

'Secret keeper of time, *love* it.' Roddy March was writing.

'Children are our legacy, new life to replace old.' Felicity was back on script.

'Not if you don't have kids,' Andrea said.

'"Flesh perishes, I live on, projecting trait and trace through time to times anon",' Clive intoned, then, in his ordinary voice, 'Never married. My family face dies with me.'

From where she sat, Stella noticed his fob watch was an hour slow. It was a month since the clocks had gone back; in his business Clive couldn't have forgotten. The plastic thing he was playing with was a spoon from the lid of an ice-cream pot like those sold at the tearoom during the day.

'...dead parents, dead brother, dead neighbours. It's a chain, one leads to the next. Dead. Dead. *Dead*.'

'Yes, Clive, we get it,' Joy said. 'We will all die.'

The Death Café was in free fall. Stella wanted to chair it, set an agenda, objectives, allocate actions, but she'd left Clean Slate and didn't chair anything. Her own free fall was when Roddy March found out that Felicity and the rest of the group called her Stella when he thought her name was Beverly. *It never paid to lie.*

The abbey clock chimed six fifteen. The meeting finished at seven thirty. Stella couldn't hope for Felicity to get another text and send them away two evenings running.

'Thomas Hardy said our face lives beyond us. Family is legacy.' Felicity flicked a look at Andrea whose own face was behind the snood. Stella wondered why Andrea had come again, she looked as if she was on detention.

'I have three kiddies, but seeing as they all take after Derek my face will perish when I die.' Gladys Wren flicked droplets of rainwater off the sleeves of her silver jacket. Stella noticed Gladys had redone her nail varnish cerise. Stella, in the black suit she used to wear for client meetings, felt better turned out than the night before.

Cheered by this, she said, 'I started a cleaning company called Clean Slate, I guess that's a legacy.' Stella saw Felicity's rictus expression and realized it could be construed as promotion. Hastily, 'I have nothing to do with it now, so that's that, I suppose. I do have stepchildren... *had*...' Jack had wanted her to consider Justin and Milly hers, but his twins already had a better mother than Stella could ever be.

'Death is part of life.' Felicity was reading from her crib sheet.

'That implies a nice natural end.' Roddy March turned his head this way and that, easing his neck as if it was stiff. 'What about having the life strangled out of you in an empty house or, say, your skull stove in and gouts of blood leaving a trail as you crawl to the phone only to die inches from the receiver? There is no euphemism for murder.'

'Bumped off. Rubbed out. Offed.' Andrea pulled down her snood. 'It's sick how some people are obsessed with it.'

'Murder is part of life.' While not acknowledging that Andrea had effectively contradicted him, Roddy March wrote down what she had said. 'Anyone can be murdered.'

Stella was propelled back to the lonely dark lane, the lights of the white van extinguished. The stillness. If another car hadn't drawn up behind her would the van driver have attacked her. Or worse? Taking a large swallow of coffee, she saw the fire was dying, the café had grown cold.

'Let's hope not, my boy.' Clive was winding his watch. Perhaps he'd seen it told the wrong time.

'Children kill.' Andrea disappeared back behind her snood. 'What about that kid who shot his father? Children can be evil.'

'He'll be branded a killer for life, poor lad,' Clive said. 'Murder is one disease time cannot heal.'

'It was an accident.' Stella joined in unintentionally. *Boy Kills Dad* – the Gloucestershire *Echo* had reported how a local gamekeeper's son, mistaking his father for a poacher, had shot him, *clean through the heart*. Nothing clean about it. The story had saddened her. If time could heal grief, it could never heal guilt.

'He was eight, quite old enough to know better.' Joy pursed her lips. 'Children of that age know right from wrong. They get up to all sorts, blackmail, robbery, murder.'

'Eight-year-olds know exactly what they're doing.' Andrea's voice was blurred by the snood.

'We were all young once.' Felicity offered round more cake. Roddy March was her only taker. 'Andrea, as a gardener, you're used to being around dying organisms, tell us your impressions of death?'

'Who says I'm a gardener?' Andrea looked hostile.

'Probably your get-up.' Roddy smirked. 'That fabulous outdoor look.'

Stella took in Andrea's soil-encrusted nails – the opposite of Gladys's manicured hands – ruddy cheeks, hair tousled from the wind and rain. Glancing at March's pad, she was disturbed to read: *Andrea, loose cannon, Worzel Gummidge, needs a wash.* A cruel summary.

'It's the signature on your email. Gardener at Tewkesbury Abbey.' Twitching inverted comma forefingers, Felicity looked impatient. 'OK, folks, let's sum up what we have so far. We've agreed to dispose of euphemisms. Certainly, in my past life, we told death as we found it.'

'You've had another life?' Joy looked thunderous as if this was cheating.

'We could have a séance,' Gladys said.

'She means before she retired.' Andrea sighed.

'I was a pathologist, a renowned one, actually. Death really was all around me. My name, Dr Felicity Branscombe, aka Cat

Woman, and the villain's enemy, will trip off the tongue to those of you who follow great murder trials.' Felicity flushed pink.

'Yes.' Stella sat up. She'd never heard of Felicity – although as a child she'd liked Cat Woman – but felt bound to rescue her from the table of blank faces. Felicity's autopsy analogy when she was serving drinks yesterday now made sense. As did her Rod Stewart ringtone which showed Felicity had a sense of humour... *The first cut is the deepest...*

'Cool. You and I need a chat.' Roddy nodded at Felicity who didn't nod back.

'Andrea, my dear, this must be familiar territory for you, the abbey gardens is jam-packed with the dead.' Clive patted Andrea on the shoulder which made her recoil.

'I don't see dead people when I'm gardening – flowers and plants are alive,' Andrea said. 'My discussion point is what's best: burial or cremation?'

'Cremation is warmer.' Clive said.

Unable to bear the cold any longer, crossing to the fireplace, Stella rattled the handle under the grate and urged dying embers into flames. She laid another log on the fire.

'...want burial, you'd better book pronto,' Clive was saying. 'My great-grandfather invested in a mausoleum in the abbey, and one day they'll prise off the marble slab and shove me in. With your talents, my girl, you can dig your own grave.' To Stella's surprise Andrea smiled.

'I'd like a woodland burial.' Andrea shot a look at March. 'Better than being in a tomb.'

'Lovely.' Stella hoped to goodness Andrea hadn't seen his notes about her. Andrea mentioning tombs, it occurred to Stella that perhaps she'd heard March's podcast on cadaver tombs. She had earbuds around her neck, she might listen to podcasts as she gardened. When cleaning Stella preferred to feel present with no distractions. Now she regretted that, after meeting March in the abbey yesterday morning, assuming she'd never see him again, and what with the van on the lane and the Death Café experience, she'd forgotten about his podcast. The trouble with small towns was people could come back to haunt you. Brushing the starved monk gently twice a week, Stella felt a responsibility to him, so March's cadaver tombs podcast interested her. Keeping to the subject of disposal she felt bound to add, 'In our family we're cremated. With the Co-op.'

'Cremation is horrible.' Joy stroked one of the rabbits on her cardigan. 'By the end you're nothing but hip joints and fillings and don't be thinking you can take your teddy or some cuddly toy with you into your coffin.' Her stern expression took in Stella whose own teddy had come with her to Tewkesbury. 'That's illegal. Stuffed animals pollute the atmosphere and kill off the rest of us.'

'Burial uses up space, but it is so much nicer than incineration.' Felicity clamped a hand over her mouth. '*Damnation*, I'm not allowed to voice an opinion.'

'Why not, Feli-ci-*tee*?' Roddy March's eyes twinkled. 'There's so much you could tell us, all those murderers you've chopped up, bottled, sliced and placed between glass slides. We'd love to hear your thoughts.'

'That's not why we're here,' Joy said. 'We could all talk about our lives. It's death that matters.'

'*Mea culpa*, Joy, was it?' Roddy clasped his hands in prayer. 'Me, I don't want to slide through the curtains into the flames as if into Hell. Although, with my past, maybe I'm headed there anyway.' He guffawed.

'That's a myth,' Joy said. 'Your coffin comes off the turntable through a hatch into a room where it's received onto a gurney. When it is your turn you are wheeled to a cremator that is affixed with your name tag. The door is flung wide and your coffin shoved into the oven with a huge metal poker. It takes an hour or so to be consumed by the intense heat. Your ashes are raked onto a tray and left to cool. Even in death we queue. That's right, isn't it, Felicity?'

'Why should I know?' Felicity was consulting her notes.

'I expect Joy means because you're a pathologist.' Andrea's lip curled.

'What happened to the deceased's remains after I was done was not my business. Unless a re-examination was required. One good reason why I'm not in favour of the fire,' Felicity said. 'Introduce yourself, Stella. In your email you claimed to be a cleaner.'

'Stella Darnell, aged fifty-three, and I *am* a cleaner.' With the discussion in full swing, Stella had dared be confident she'd get away without saying her piece. The Death Café website had stated it wasn't mandatory to speak. 'Offices, people's homes, institutions.'

'How interesting.' Felicity was encouraging. Everyone else looked blank.

'Not forgetting the abbey.' Roddy March had written, *Joy by name, horrible by nature!!!* next to Joy's name.

'You know each other?' Andrea asked.

'No.' Stella was worried that Felicity would think she had lied earlier. 'I was cleaning. Roddy, Mr March, passed by.'

'*Passed*, did he?' Clive wheezed at his joke.

'Dad died on Monday the eleventh of January 2011. Heart attack. Outside the Co-op. He was a detective in the Met CID—' Thinking of Roddy March's excoriating jottings on Andrea and Joy, Stella shifted to avoid seeing what he'd written about her.

'Is this relevant?' Andrea suddenly said. 'I thought we couldn't mention personal stuff. That's what you said.' She jabbed a finger towards Felicity.

'Stella is setting the scene,' Felicity said.

'Did you want to tell us about your father, Andrea?' Roddy March waited with apparent fascination. Andrea ignored him.

'Yes, I am setting the scene.' Stella's own patience had worn thin. Since leaving London, she was easily overtaken by a volcanic rage that surged up from nowhere. Right now, she pictured pushing Andrea's face into the remains of the cake. What right had the woman to be so rude and unpleasant? 'This café is about death. My dad's death is why I'm here. It was eight years ago so, like Gladys with Derek, I won't cry.' She wished Jack was there to hear her, he was always encouraging her to express emotions. 'I inherited Dad's house but even now, it's like he's just left the room.' Stella didn't say how when she and Jack solved one of Terry Darnell's cases, a newspaper headline had read, *Cleaner Follows Detective Dad's Footsteps*.

Or that two months ago her world turned upside down when her mum remarked that Terry was *dead and gone*. Stella had, on some level, been storing up her achievements to tell her dad when he came back and, in that moment, had understood deep in her heart that she had no footsteps to follow. He was never coming back.

'Dad said when you're gone, you're gone...' Stella lost her thread and ground to a stop.

'Thank you, Stella,' Felicity said after a pause. 'We hold different views on death, there's no right or wrong way to view it.'

'Except murder,' Roddy muttered, and Stella caught herself nodding.

'...we die at our allotted time. It's written on our graves, if not in the stars,' Clive intoned.

She will never be stirred
In her loamy cell
By the waves long heard
And loved so well...

'Not more Thomas Hardy.' Joy groaned as if she was inundated with Hardy's poetry.

'My grave will be on a hillside overlooking the sea where I can bask in the sun and be refreshed by gentle rain.' Felicity must have forgotten she wasn't meant to express an opinion.

'Only the headstone will have that,' Joy said. 'You'll be six feet under in a loamy cell.'

'Mr March, why you have come today?' Felicity sounded more accusatory than curious.

'Why have I come? *Ooh*, tough one.' Roddy March sucked his pen. 'Long story short. Most of you will have heard the first episode of *The Distant Dead*, my podcast about murder victims whose real killers never paid for their crimes because the cases were firmly closed.'

'Not had the pleasure, old son,' Clive said.

'Yes.' Andrea sounded grudging.

Joy murmured something which might have been 'certainly not'.

'I thought you were...' Stella realized she'd misunderstood – March had never actually said his podcast was about cadaver tombs. She was rather disappointed.

'Ooh yes, lovey. Very good, kept me guessing, you should listen, Joy.' Gladys looked at Joy. Stella thought if Jack was there, he'd say there was little love lost between Joy and Gladys.

Felicity said nothing, and Stella assumed that, as a pathologist, Felicity wouldn't care for a podcast which sought to prove that the police – and by extension her own profession – had made a mistake.

'I'm clawing back justice for those who, as Clive says, did *not* defy time. If you go to your grave with an innocent person charged with your murder, your story has the wrong ending. You are robbed of your legacy.' Inexplicably, he nodded at Joy, then Stella remembered Joy had talked about legacy the evening before. '*The Distant Dead* will name the true killers of murders committed in the last hundred years. Murders by the likes of James Hanratty and Timothy Evans.'

'DNA proved that Hanratty *did* kill that scientist,' Andrea said.

'Don't split hairs, love,' Gladys Wren said. 'For years he was supposed innocent, that's what Roddy means.'

'I'll be starting with a murder familiar to many of you. The Tewkesbury Murder Mystery. Although, since 1963 when it occurred, many have been *bumped off* in this town, it is the brutal killing in Cloisters House by the abbey wall that remains etched in the public's memory.' March took the last piece of cake.

'Not that many murders.' Andrea sounded defensive. 'Fewer than in Cheltenham.'

'And it's no mystery,' Joy said. 'Another instance of son kills father.'

'Trust you to rain on his parade, Madame Joy.' Clive raised an eyebrow.

'It was an open and shut case.' Joy shut her mouth, lips pursed.

'Joy, Clive, *go, you guys*. I intend to provoke just this conversation. The hive mind will shine a light on the true killer.' Roddy March splayed out his palms. 'Of course, the twenty-second of November 1963 was etched on memories because—'

'You said etched already,' Andrea said.

'—many of you can recall what you were doing when President John F. Kennedy was assassinated, but Kennedy wasn't the only famous man to meet his maker that day. On that same Friday, renowned Home Office pathologist Professor Aleck Northcote was having a nightcap when there was a loud knock on the door.'

'You can't know it was loud,' Felicity said.

'Did you know him?' Gladys Wren asked Felicity. 'With you both being in that business? Small world, I'd suppose.'

'No,' Felicity said. 'Obviously I've heard of him, his textbook is the bible. Northcote would be 118 if he was alive today. I'm younger.'

'You don't look anything like it, dearie,' Gladys said, although Felicity hadn't given her age and everyone in the room looked younger than 118.

'And what if the intruder had a key?' Andrea said.

'Professor Northcote signed my copy of his autobiography when I was a student.' Felicity appeared to be off down memory lane.

'The son was guilty, they proved it beyond doubt.' Joy abruptly scraped back her chair and crossed to the servery. 'I was eight at the time.'

'Like you said, kids of that age know right from wrong,' Gladys said, apparently without point. 'We all have occasion to know about that night.'

'Stella doesn't know what the hell you're all talking about, do you?' Andrea rounded on Stella.

'Well, I—' Stella felt the atmosphere had taken an unpleasant turn.

'That evening, while the world was reeling from Kennedy's death, Giles Northcote takes the mid-morning train from Paddington bound for Tewkesbury to tap his old pater for another loan.' March talked as if no one had interrupted. 'Giles has run up yet another gambling debt, he risks being blackballed from his club. Yes, there's a sweet Victorian feel to this narrative. He is expected. Aleck tells his trusty housekeeper that Giles is coming and that he knows it's not a social call. The young buck is seen drinking in the Black Bear at lunchtime and later pacing the Victoria Pleasure Gardens, presumably getting up courage to face his dad.'

'You don't know that,' Andrea said again.

'Then around eight that evening, Giles Northcote weaves his way along the high street to Cloisters House. The story is one played out all over the land for generations: Papa refuses to cough up and by now pissed and desperate, Giles batters him over the head with a handy poker. He steals cash from Northcote's wallet, swipes a silver cup Aleck won for running round the world or some such in his gilded youth. Miss Fleming, aforesaid housekeeper, comes back from the pictures to find her master dead in the hall, his groping fingers centimetres from an original 1930s Bakelite telephone.'

'The kind of phone doesn't matter,' Andrea said.

'He's setting the scene.' Gladys seemed to have taken to Roddy March.

'I lead my listeners on a journey, they see what I see,' March told Andrea. Although Stella rather thought Andrea had earned it, she felt a bit sorry for her. March was hijacking the Death Café and Andrea was the only person who appeared to mind. Stella saw it as a get-out from having to say any more about herself.

'Northcote was my customer.' Clive rubbed his chin. 'His skeleton clock was the first timepiece I handled, as a wet-behind-the-ears seventeen-year-old,' he said in a dreamy voice as if they were at a séance. 'The chap was terribly conceited, but he took me under his wing. I suspect I was the son Giles was not. My father couldn't get on with him so he was happy to let me loose on the man's clock. Think he wanted me to botch it, one in the eye for me and Northcote. I was the fourth Burgess at Burgess and Son, and, like his father before him, my old man was jealous of my skills. You never forget your first piece, an elegant Charles MacDowell clock, simple design with oblique toothed gearing. Exquisite.'

'What has this to do with death?' Andrea asked.

'It did end badly because when Northcote's boy did for him, Northcote hadn't paid. He'd promised to give me double. I'd forgotten to get him to sign a receipt, we had no proof of the work. Got it in the neck for that, I can tell you. When I heard the news, I wanted to motor to Wormwood Scrubs for *How to Kill Your Father* tips from Giles.' Clive scratched at a blob of food on his tie. 'You'd be on the right track. Many in Tewkesbury had reason to bash Professor Northcote's head in. The blighter supposed that, being knight of the realm, he needn't pay for *The Times*, his pipe tobacco or bar tabs run up when he was ingratiating himself with the masses so they'd make him mayor.' Clive was revving up. Northcote's murder might have been days ago. Clive had said time was a construct; maybe, for him, the murder *was* yesterday.

'I'm afraid that there was no doubt the son did it,' Felicity said. 'They found Aleck's cup – for the four-minute mile, two seconds slower than Roger Bannister – in Giles's flat. He was going to sell it.'

'I thought you didn't know him?' Andrea said.

'No more I did, but we path. students venerated Professor Northcote. He was Aleck the Great.' She looked nostalgic.

'Here's what really happened.' Roddy March held up his pen. 'After Giles left that night, Aleck received another visitor.'

'Who?' Perhaps Felicity had forgotten it was meant to be a Death Café.

'He's not going to tell us.' Joy was at the servery counter. Roddy March jumped up and took one of the mugs she'd left there. The scented steam coiling into the cooling air, Stella knew was chamomile. She hadn't heard March ask for the tea, but befuddled by the occasion, could easily have missed it. 'He's here to plug his pod-thingy, aren't you, Mr March.' The teabag dripped over the plate. Watching it slowly revolve, Stella pictured a body dangling from gallows. 'I've heard of these podcasts; mostly you never find out who did what, they merely sensationalize the crime.'

'The murderer still lives amongst us.' Roddy March's tone would have gone well in a séance. Although the fire was still burning in the grate, the atmosphere was distinctly chill. Stella regretted that she had come.

'For the guilty, time knows no statute of limitation, the clock of crime is always ticking,' Clive said.

'True-crime podcasts are done to whip up drama. You should consider the families of the victims.' Stella cast about for how to get the discussion back to cremation and burial. Except Jack would say that was her rescuing.

Joy did it for her. Complaining it wasn't Agatha Christie, she rapped the table with her cake fork. 'I came here to talk about death, not murder.'

'Murder *is* death,' Clive said.

'Mr March isn't dead *yet*,' Joy said. 'None of us is.'

'The mystery *will* be solved,' Roddy cried. 'In the last episode I do the big reveal. You learn the identity of Northcote's true killer. You'll hear the why, the when and how the true murderer escaped justice for decades. This is a case of cause and effect. Northcote's murder is an echo from a long-forgotten murder that took place in London during the war. As you'll discover, time ain't always a healer.'

'Time is *never* a healer. It simply passes.' Clive winked at Joy. 'I do not mean it *dies*.'

'You will be hooked.' Roddy dropped his voice. Stella was startled to see he was talking to her.

'Mr March.' Felicity jumped up. '*Enough*. You weren't here yesterday when I outlined Death Café ground rules. You are promoting your business. If you have nothing about death to share with us, you must leave.'

'Roddy's not an undertaker or a coffin-maker.' Gladys seemed to have taken a shine to March. 'Although, I wouldn't make a song and dance about doing either of those.'

'You'll need both one day,' Joy said.

'I do have something to share,' Roddy told Felicity.

'Seriously, can we move on?' Andrea said. 'We're wasting time.'

'There's always time,' Clive said.

'Someone wants to kill me,' Roddy said.

Chapter Eight

Thursday, 12 December 1940

Divisional Detective Inspector George Cotton had the stomach for an autopsy. Thirty years in the Metropolitan police had hardened him to the reek of bodies and disinfectant. With the morgue attendants banging in and out of the swing doors to the yard, he covered his nose and mouth with his scarf, not for the smell but to ward off the arctic cold.

How he longed for a different reality. Him in his office, chair up to the radiator, and Maple typing away at Express Dairies on King Street. At five, she would begin her journey home to Corney Road, back to her family.

Instead, Maple lay on Northcote's porcelain slab, her head cushioned on a block. Hammersmith's cheery mortuary attendant Ed White – Weissman until the war – stripped her, calling out each item for PC Shepherd to record in his notebook and dropping it in a brown paper bag. *Camisole. Boned brassiere, silk stockings, right leg torn at calf...*

Cotton's thoughts were halted by the crack of the ribcage as Dr Northcote made the first incision. Cotton clenched his jaw as he observed the stony-faced pathologist working with nimble craftsman's fingers.

Months of the Blitz had exposed Cotton to twisted, mangled corpses, burnt in the fires of incendiary bombs, crushed by masonry, shredded by shrapnel. Nothing had inured him against the pain of seeing someone's loved person, whole and as if asleep, be butchered, however skilfully, by a pathologist. It was that very finesse which upset Cotton. Stamping on the tiled floor as the chill seeped through his soles, he felt as if Maple Greenhill was to be murdered all over again.

As Northcote worked, he murmured a commentary which Alberta Porter, his pretty and very capable secretary, perched on a camping stool, took down in shorthand. Porter's sensible brogues were yet not sensible enough for the wading into rivers and ditches she did to assist her boss examine a corpse in situ. Northcote called Porter his right-hand girl.

While Northcote talked about listening to the corpse, Cotton heard only silence. Maple Greenhill would never speak again.

Today, Cotton felt that, aside from assisting the pathologist, Alberta Porter was also there to represent her own sex. Porter's cool and steady manner equalled Northcote's, but now, Cotton knew, the rising pink in cheeks that never saw rouge was for the blunt-faced blokes, himself included, who were gawping at Maple Greenhill in the altogether.

The doctor believed all his deceased – including hanged murderers and the 'ladies of the night' of whom he so disapproved – deserved his best. He delved into the truth of their deaths however they had lived.

Cotton knew Northcote suffered with his back but he never spoke of the pain. Lifting out Maple's organs – kidneys, liver, her heart: 'healthy as the day she was born, no appendix' – he passed them to White, ready to receive them into enamel dishes.

Somewhat soothed by the background splashing and gurgling as White chased runnels of blood into the gutters with water from a rubber hose, and by the scratching of Alberta Porter's HB2 pencil, Cotton made himself concentrate on Northcote's findings.

'...as I said at the scene, Greenhill was strangled. The hyoid bone is broken. There's evidence of damage to the larynx, see this bruising to the skin around the neck?' He indicated Maple's skin, now lifeless as tallow, with the tip of a blade of what Cotton knew was a cartilage knife. 'It's livid where the blood settled after he flung her down. Gravity's pull. That's skin in her nails, one hair from the pubic region, I suspect from their consensual love-making. She didn't argue. Blunt force trauma at the back of the skull. As I said early this morning she was probably hit by an ash tray, a square one judging by the indentation.'

'That nail's broken.' Cotton tried to avoid pre-empting Northcote. Like his mother always said, don't go telling the doctor what's wrong with you. Now he pointed at the middle finger of Maple's right hand.

'Unrelated. Down to cheap varnish, these girls don't look after themselves, with their sordid existence, they're used up by thirty. She had a way to go, look at this lovely elastic skin.' Northcote's brow furrowed. A highly respected expert witness, he carried the jury with him the moment he stepped into the box. Defence counsels buckled before his opinion, uttered with granite authority. True to science, Northcote wasn't swayed by prejudice. However, a practising Christian, he loathed prostitutes.

'It is a hard life.' Cotton was one of the few prepared to part company with Northcote. 'It would help if men didn't go after them.'

'Most lives are hard, George, but can you see your daughter resorting to this?' Handing Porter his white coat for laundering, Northcote indicated Maple, her ravaged body shrouded now under a sheet. He began scrubbing his hands over the sink, working up a carbolic lather, sluicing to his elbows.

'No, but—'

'Blimey, what cat was that?' White was looking at livid score marks which ran the length of Northcote's forearm.

'Bloody wife's rose-bush.' Northcote rolled down his sleeves and, businesslike, clipped gold links into his cuffs.

'You want to watch for sepsis, sir,' White warned.

'Julia slathered me in iodine, unnecessary fuss.' His back to Porter holding out his overcoat, Northcote shrugged it on.

Outside in the yard, Alberta Porter climbed in the passenger seat of Northcote's Daimler. The two men sheltered from a vicious wind by the entrance to Hammersmith Crematorium, next door to the morgue. Failing to find his lighter, Northcote accepted Cotton's match. Like a conclave's signal, the detective and the pathologist sent wreaths of blue smoke up to the dull grey sky. Job done.

'I'm thinking Maple knew her assailant. She had dressed up for last night.' Cotton looked through the car window at Porter leafing through her notes. Few pathologists took personal secretaries with them to the morgue or the places of execution. Northcote treated Porter as one of the boys. Cotton liked that about him.

'That's your department, Cotton, you know my view. These French Annies have to dress to command the cash. Empty houses are a tart's Mecca.'

'It's the wrong sort of looking good. She was dressing for a man she loved, not for some drunk soldier on leave.' Cotton was always disappointed by Northcote's crude language; although it was how blokes at the station talked, Northcote was an educated church-goer. Cotton crushed his cigarette on the asphalt. 'We found two cigarette butts in the grate. If there was an ashtray, her killer removed it. They stopped for a smoke. Most of the girls I meet don't hang about, time is money.'

'They ring the last blood from the stone, stupid risk.' Northcote looked pained. 'Oliver Hurrell was a smoker, the chap whose home she decorated. Those butts were probably his.'

They both hated it when the victim was a young woman, whatever her occupation. Northcote performed hundreds of autopsies every week, he was one of the fastest which was why the police liked him on the job. Fearless, he dodged bombs, crossing and recrossing London, cutting open the dead killed by raids, blackout accidents, natural causes and murder.

'Perhaps.' Cotton knew Northcote and his wife had problems. The doctor had once said that, with their son at boarding school, Julia Northcote got lonely and gin was her preferred medicine. Cotton's wife Agnes had said it wasn't good for patients to know that a doctor's wife got ill. Not even if his patients were dead to start with? Cotton had joked.

'How else did she afford that mink? It's worth at least ten guineas. I bought one for Julia. To cheer her up,' Northcote said.

'Perhaps her sweetheart promised riches then backed out. She's upset and he kills her.' Cotton was thinking aloud; he would never convince Northcote to change his mind about women who sold their bodies for sex.

'Porter will post over my report. My guess is fabric, a tie perhaps, pulled tight from behind. Stockings would work, but she was still wearing them. Man catches her unawares, she twists and claws like a cat, and protecting himself, he quietens her. For good.' Eyes narrowed at the sky, Dr Northcote took a drag of his cigarette. 'Odd he didn't try to hide her body. There's a burnt-out house a couple of doors down. That's why the house we found her in was declared unsafe. Christ, the Blitz is open house for murderers and looters.'

'I'm betting he was disturbed.'

'Didn't you say the all-clear was sounding when neighbours heard the scream? He would have got the hell out.' Northcote crushed his cigarette on the ground. Alberta Porter was out of the Daimler and ready with the door open.

'I'll check with the PC who got there first,' Cotton said. 'You said Maple was still warm when you arrived. Last night's temperature was below zero. Like you said, she'd been dead minutes.'

'Don't get too exercised, George. We both know that as long as girls like these take advantage of the blackout these murders will increase.' Northcote climbed into the car and nodded to Porter to do the same. One foot on the running board he gave a wry smile. 'Maple's man will be an inebriated soldier called back to base without a care in the world. We both know that.'

'You got there damned smartish.' Cotton could always rely on Northcote. 'I thought we had a chance with you on the scene so quickly.'

'It was damn near on my doorstep.' Northcote sounded offended by this. He shut the door and, winding down the window, started the car. 'Just as well I did or she could have lain there for weeks. If I remember, poor old Hurrell had no relatives. A bit of a recluse.'

'That would have made your job harder,' Cotton agreed.

'You forget the hyoid bone.' Northcote was smooth in his correction.

'Of course.' Cotton touched the knot on his tie. Northcote had given them a sketch of the murderer. Blood group AB negative, greying hair, the downward pressure on Maple's throat suggested he was tall. If the cigarettes Cotton had found in the grate were chucked there by the killer, he smoked Chesterfields. It seemed Hurrell, the house owner, had not kept cigarettes at home. There had been a full packet of Player's in Maple's handbag so he'd given her one of his. The likelihood that he'd strangled her with his tie might say the killing was unplanned.

Northcote reached up out of the car window and shook Cotton's hand. They enjoyed batting about ideas. Cotton was always grateful to have Northcote doing the PM rather than his younger colleague, Dr Bradman, a spiv who had an inflated belief in his talent coupled with a tendency to underestimate Northcote's.

Settling into the police-issue Wolseley, Cotton asked PC Shepherd to drive back to the house by the river where Maple Greenhill's strangled body was found.

Chapter Nine

December 2019

Stella

Within the ancient walls of the grounds, insipid lamplight projected hazy shadows across the headstones, the writing worn to impenetrable hieroglyphics by centuries. The tower rose up and beyond, curdling clouds threatened more rain. Every now and then, as indeterminate as a passing thought, a bat flicked across the mauve-black between the yew trees.

The suspended silence was shattered by a scream. Across the dappled cemetery came crude skeletons, red-toothed werewolves and ghouls, luminous faces grinning. Teenagers were enacting a party-shop horror show. They ran close to Stella, standing by the south wall, without seeing her in the gloom. Then, as quickly as they'd appeared, they were gone.

As Stella skirted the abbey, she saw a light in an upper window of Cloisters House. She had passed by the large detached house many times without noticing it. Now she knew it was where Professor Northcote had been murdered in 1963. Stella did in fact know about the murder. As part of what she called due diligence, she had read up on Tewkesbury. One website called Northcote's death a classic murder story; Wikipedia said the news got little press attention because of Kennedy's assassination on the same day. Spotting a reference to a biography of the pathologist, Stella realized it was in her dad's collection of true-crime books that she'd found in his attic. On impulse, she had dropped it into her suitcase. She hadn't unpacked it. She decided to begin it when she got back to the flat.

Outside the abbey, Stella peered through the bars of a tall iron gate to the back garden of Cloisters House. She made out wigwam frames and a line of raised beds made from railway sleepers. The gate was secured with a padlock and chain. Unlike Jack, she would not dream of trespassing.

When March said he'd received anonymous texts and a dead bird had been left on the bonnet of his jeep, losing patience, Felicity had made him leave. Had Stella, instead of Felicity, gone outside with March and given directions to Cheltenham police station, she could have escaped. Although having to hear more on his take on the Northcote Murder Mystery might have been no escape at all. Recalling March's phone call in the abbey yesterday, it was better his jealous partner accompanied him to the police station

Stella wandered across the abbey grounds unconsciously, and, as Jack avoided cracks in paving for bad luck, she stepped only on lozenges of light cutting through the splaying branches of a vast oak tree. Disappointed though she was that March's podcast wasn't about cadaver tombs, she might give it a listen.

Andrea had told them that no way would March go near the police, men like him handled the world alone. Felicity had made a feeble attempt to get them back on track, but no one seemed keen to discuss modes of body disposal or coffin choices so she wound the Café to a close and everyone left. Stella had stayed to clear up, but as she had the previous evening, Felicity, doubtless dejected at the failed Death Café, said she'd prefer to do it alone.

Stella had gone to the Death Café to face the subject of death and put grief for her dad finally to rest. Instead she was back in familiar territory. Murder.

A strip of light slanted over the flagstones. The south door to the abbey was ajar and from within came the deep strains of the organ. Joy must have gone straight to the abbey after the Death Café. Stella didn't blame her; it must be Joy's version of deep cleaning. Drawn by the grand tones, she crept inside.

On Stella's first day in Tewksbury two months ago, she had discovered that the abbey allowed dogs. It had been raining so, Stanley in her arms, she'd dashed inside. She'd hoped that Stanley, who barked his head off at the drop of a hat, would stay quiet. Evensong had been beginning – Stella now knew Joy was on the organ – and seeing Stanley lulled to sleep by the prayers – like baby Jesus, an elderly woman had whispered – Stella had stayed.

After that Stella was a regular at evensong. Reliant on facts and evidence, she was sceptical about God, but she liked the music.

Now, keen to avoid Joy and guessing it would be mutual, Stella chose a chair behind one of the giant pillars nearest the north ambulatory. She let her gaze rest on the screen with, she'd read somewhere, its *delicate foliated tracery*. Not a classical music fan – that was Jack – yet Stella had no trouble recognizing Chopin's Funeral March. Was Joy practising for a service or had she been influenced by the Death Café?

The triforium walk high up near the ceiling was not lit but, craning up, Stella could still distinguish the bosses carved above the piers, ill-tempered faces leering down at her. It was said they had been carved by a monk, who took out the teasing and insults he received from fellow craftsmen on his work. Was he the starved monk? Generally, the grotesque creatures amused her; tonight their expressions appeared terrible. She felt afraid.

Stella liked being alone and over the weeks the abbey had become another home, but now she knew Joy, Stella had forfeited anonymity, she felt hunted, like a rabbit on one of Joy's colourful garments.

Stella caught a movement. In the gleam of a lamp a shadow was etched on the wall. *Someone was on the other side of the column.*

The music from the north transept ceased. Whoever it was would shortly leave. Joy must appear at any moment. Stella was about to inch along the row of chairs and cross the nave, away from the Grove organ, when she stopped.

Three figures lurked in the gloom of the south ambulatory. Stella shrank back into her seat, pointlessly – they must have been watching her for some minutes. Clustered outside the door to the vestry, they waited patiently. Although he would have been no help, Stella wished she had Stanley. Heart thudding against her chest, she told herself she was not afraid.

As she stared, the trio resolved into life-size effigies of the Three Kings. It was beyond paranoid to suspect the kings had been placed there to frighten her. It hadn't worked, *she would not be afraid.*

The shadow of the person beyond the column had gone.

He or she had left silently, as if they didn't want to be seen. *So what?* Stella would have done the same herself. She got up and, stepping into the north ambulatory, walked around the column. No one was there. All the chairs were unoccupied. Had there ever been anyone there? She looked at the wall. The low-angled lamps highlighted indentations in the stone, but nothing resembled the profile of a human face. Her mind was playing tricks. She had imagined the shadow.

A shoe scraped. *Joy.* In trying to avoid an imaginary person, Stella had forgotten Joy whose nature, if she found Stella there, would be far from joyful.

The organ struck up again and Stella let herself relax. Not music this time, but a series of jarring chords that did nothing for Stella's jangled state. She moved to the north aisle; she wanted to regain a semblance of calm before she left. The abbey always improved her mood. There was something on one of the chairs, a prayer book or a Bible. It wasn't a book. A peaked cap lay on the chair where she had imagined the shadow. *She had not imagined it.*

Stepping out into the darkness, talking in a low voice to Felicity who was obviously trying to stop him going on and on. Stella's last sight of Roddy March had been of him cramming this peaked cap on his head.

Andrea had got March right: he hadn't gone to the police, he had come to the abbey. That he had been listening to Joy on the organ faintly warmed Stella to him. She hadn't associated his brash, thrusting personality with enjoying church music. After he'd gone, Joy maintained March was exploiting the fiction that Giles Northcote was innocent of killing his father in order to drum up interest in his podcast. Thinking this, Stella felt obscurely cheated. She'd have a word with him for ruining Felicity's Death Café. He'd ruined it for her too.

Discordant notes reverberated around the abbey as Stella made her way past silent kings, towards the choir. Passing the vestry, she trod carefully past the presbytery on her left. In the apse she was closer to the north ambulatory and the Grove organ. *Closer to Joy.* Passing sepulchral monuments of various abbots, the lattice fretwork as fine lace, she stepped around the grating covering the Clarence Vault. Stella entered the Wakeman Cenotaph and she took refuge by the tomb of the starved monk.

Stella sniffed musty air, centuries-old dirt that no cleaner could attack. Aside from the Vulpex liquid soap she'd used to wash the floor of the chapel there was another smell. *Citrus.* Gifted with hyper-olfactory powers, Stella recognized cologne. She'd cleaned enough people's bathrooms to have encountered Versace's Dylan Blue. The scent was cut with another. A coppery odour, like old pennies.

The monk looked unchanged. Vaguely, Stella expected more of his emaciated body to have rotted and the creatures crawling over his ribcage to have nibbled away more of his flesh.

The body lay face up, blood pooled through the combat jacket to the stone floor, where a saturated lock of hair glistened. His arm was outstretched, his forefinger pointed at Stella. His face was twisted in a terrible grimace not unlike the carved bosses in the nave.

The podcaster's assertion that someone wanted to murder him had not been a publicity stunt. Someone *had* murdered him.

Roddy March's finger twitched. *He was alive.*

'Roddy, oh, Roddy, talk to me. What happened?' Stella knelt down, oblivious to the blood soaking into her trousers and put her face close to his. She touched the bloodied patch on his chest. Hardly a nick, how was he bleeding so profusely? *It was an exit wound.* She dare not turn him over – even if she could, Roddy was heavily built. Stella dabbed clumsily at her phone, fingers, slick with blood, sliding on the screen – 989... 96... 999.

'Ambulance, police. Please be quick. Please.' Stella described the situation. Good in a crisis she answered the operator's questions decisively. He was breathing faintly, his airwaves were open. She dare not try to get him on his side. 'I think he's been stabbed in the back.

'His lips are moving.' Stella stopped being calm. 'What? Roddy, tell me. Who did this?' Dimly, she noted she might ask Roddy for a message to his loved ones instead of who had stabbed him in the back. Stella pulled off her jacket and shirt and feeling it pointless, pressed the bundle on the exit wound in Roddy's chest.

'...Cah... ca... wo... my...' His eyes were fixed on Stella, wild, his pupils enlarged. He looked terrified.

'Car? Wo my.' Stella felt stupid, it couldn't be that hard.

'C-c-chh...'

'Cawomy.' Stella imitated Roddy's first attempt. *Jack would say don't overthink.* 'Chamomile'. The tea Joy had given Roddy at the Death Café. 'Was your drink poisoned?' Crazy, no poison would cause Roddy to bleed out.

'Chhh.'

Stella pressed on the wound; blood was coming through the jacket.

'Is this a message for... for...?' Stella remembered the person who had followed him into the abbey yesterday morning. 'Someone who loves you?'

Stella leaned down to make out the expression in his eyes, but a gossamer film had turned them milky, opaque. Roddy was dead.

Chapter Ten

December 1940

The river had filled and submerged the causeway to the eyot beneath grey-greenish water. A cry pierced the silence and a V-shaped squadron of geese passed over the eyot where, the osier trade long gone, reeds grew dense and tall. The formation broke up as each bird vanished into the smoky mist.

George Cotton leant on a rail opposite the eyot. Last night the east of London had got a basinful; even from Chiswick a pall of smoke was visible. He transferred his gaze to the immediate below, but the Thames offered no comfort. The tide delivered the debris of smashed buildings and – a doll's head drifted by – of smashed lives. Detective to the core, Cotton kept an eye out for a corpse. In winter the Thames tended to keep hold of her dead, but this was no usual December; since the Blitz nothing was the same. No season could be relied upon. He followed the eddying progress of a length of window sash, the cord trailing, and imagined that someone had once flung up the sash on a summer morning to greet a better day. Agnes called him fanciful.

Cotton had paused to take stock before returning to the house where Maple's body had been found.

The plash of oars. From a pontoon off a garden that belonged to one of the grand houses behind emerged the bowed figure of a man seated in a rowing boat. Cotton watched as the man rowed skilfully through the channel between the eyot and the river bank. As he cleared it, he glanced across at Cotton. His BBC Home Service voice cut the chill air.

'Lovely morning, ain't it.'

Cotton tipped his hat in reply.

'Nothing ruddy lovely about it.' Shepherd was at Cotton's elbow. 'Not when you haven't slept a wink.'

'He's alive. That's what matters, lad.' Cotton pushed off the rail. 'With a young woman waiting for us to catch her murderer, our beds are a way off yet.'

Jalalpur Villa was on the corner of a terrace of three Edwardian houses, each named after towns in British India. Cotton reckoned the villa called Amritsar, where, twenty years ago, the British Army committed a massacre, could have done with a new name. Looking at Jalalpur Villa, black door shabby with the dirt that coated everything these days, Cotton felt a moment of despair.

'This will always be a house where a young woman was murdered,' he said.

'I expect in, say, fifty years, no one will care,' Shepherd said. 'What if we don't find him, sir?'

'What have I said? Sunny side up, Constable.' Cotton wasn't confident. Since September 1939, there had been eight murders in his division. Only three solved. Two of those were women. One pushed off Hammersmith Bridge by a drunken serviceman of the ilk Aleck believed murdered Maple. He was let off and shipped out to France where he'd been hit by friendly fire – justice of a sort. The eighteen-year-old burglar who beat a pensioner to death for a pathetic amount of savings was judged insane and went to Broadmoor. Bert Whitaker, a fifty-year-old coal lorry driver and fire-watcher got manslaughter for strangling his wife for 'carping on and on'. Cotton had got scant satisfaction seeing Whitaker on Aleck's table when, perhaps unable to live without being carped at, he'd hanged himself with his belt. The killer of a middle-aged secretary working late at an employment agency off the Broadway who was beaten to death with her typewriter carriage was never caught. What chance, when CID was two men and a dog? Forget the dog.

Inside Jalalpur Villa, although the body had gone hours earlier, the air smelled fetid. Taking another tour of the house, Cotton was amazed at the sheer number of antiques, the china figurines superior to Agnes's factory-made collection of ladies with parasols that paraded on their radiogram. Vases, bowls, glasses in display cabinets in every room. A devil to clean, Agnes would say.

He confirmed that the silk coverlets on the sumptuous four-poster in the main bedroom were undisturbed: Maple's killer had not taken her upstairs. He'd been in a hurry from the start.

In the living room – Aleck had called it the drawing room – Shepherd was bending over a pianola set next to a towering oak tallboy.

'Mum and Dad saved for ever for one of these and he's got one and more things besides. How do you get that much money? Mum's always saying having something means doing without something else.'

'Some people can have their cake and eat it. Oliver Hurrell hasn't got anything now, poor chap.' Cotton pulled back the brocade curtains. In daylight, the room lost the look of a museum and became the dreary setting for a brutal slaying. Cotton scrutinized the settee and saw again the faint dents in the settee cushions where the man had had his way. *Had Maple been willing or was she raped?*

'What's this?' Shepherd was looking at the Turkey rug. Stepping back, he knocked a hexagonal occasional table inlaid with ivory. He righted it and, crouching, lifted the edge of the rug. He held up a silver cigarette lighter. 'No cigarettes in the house.'

'I'll make a detective of you yet.' Cotton flapped out a fresh cotton hankie and took the lighter. He caught a whiff of fuel. 'You're right. None of the rooms smell of tobacco. Dr Northcote said that Hurrell didn't smoke. 'This can only mean—'

'—that it has to be his, sir. Stupid bastard didn't do a sweep of the room after he'd killed her. It belongs to our murderer.' Shepherd, the reluctant detective, came alive.

'Well done, lad, this could be the clue we need. Even the cleverest murderers make careless mistakes.' Cotton held up the cigarette lighter. 'Crikey, it's a Dunhill, our killer had some cash.'

'A-X-E.' Looking over his shoulder, Shepherd read out the three letters engraved on the side. 'Could be a secret society, fifth columnist, my dad says they're everywhere.'

'That's an N, not an E. I'd guess they're initials.'

'What kind of name starts with X?'

'Xavier,' Cotton said without thinking. Then he let out a groan. He thought back a couple of hours to the chill mortuary yard. He'd used his Swan Vestas to light Northcote's cigarette. 'Aleck Xavier Northcote. False alarm. Dr Northcote must have left this here last night.'

'Careless, if you ask me,' Shepherd said.

'Luckily I'm not asking you, Constable, though I grant you it's out of character,' Cotton snapped. Aleck Northcote forbade smoking when examining a body in situ or at the mortuary. He said the dead told their story through his senses as much as by their flesh and insisted nothing must mar the truth. Not like Dr Bradman, who, Cotton knew from colleagues, could be influenced by police to find the right result.

It was inconceivable that Northcote, the pathologist who never made mistakes had made a mistake.

'Come on, Shepherd, best boots to the fore. Time to tell Mr and Mrs Greenhill their daughter died last night.'

As they drove past Chiswick House grounds, Shepherd remarked that an incendiary had dropped there recently. 'They do open-air concerts, my nan goes sometimes – suppose she'd been there?' One of Shepherd's habits was to suppose what if someone he knew happened to be in the wrong place at the wrong time. Cotton never said how it was likely, for them both, that one of his 'supposes' would come to pass.

'Turn left here,' he said instead.

Corney Road, built in the last decade as a suburban escape from London, comprised one line of semi-detached houses, the brickwork yet to be stained by smog. The kerb line of pollarded willows did not quite obscure the cemetery opposite. Many of the front gardens were turned over to vegetable patches, fences were freshly whitewashed; residents in Corney Road cared about their homes.

'It looks respectable.' Shepherd also believed Maple Greenhill was a part-time prostitute.

'So was our victim. And, even if she was a prostitute, you treat her the same as if she was your nan.' Cotton was now sure Maple had been meeting a sweetheart. 'First law of detection, lad,' he told the young constable. 'Rules have exceptions and exceptions are the rule.'

Although Corney Road was outside D Division, Cotton could give Shepherd directions because five years ago he'd buried his parents in the cemetery. That rainy Thursday, watching the two coffins lowered into the ground, a gale inverted his brolly, snapping the spokes. Lashed by rain, his funeral black hung heavy as he'd thrown what was mud onto the caskets. Walking away with Joe, his thirty-five-year-old baby brother, they slipped and their shoes squelched on the sodden grass. Joe never got over them dying in the Hertfordshire rail crash. Signalman error. An irony, if you thought about it, with their signalman dad just retired from the Southern Railway. Cotton did not think about it. He hadn't been back to the cemetery. It had been Joe who kept the grave tidy. Agnes did it now.

Nerving himself for Maple Greenhill's parents, Cotton felt a crumb of comfort that his mum and dad never knew the war. They didn't know Joe had been killed a few weeks ago when HMS *Royal Oak* was torpedoed off Scapa Flow.

As he and Shepherd crossed to the Greenhills' house, Cotton reckoned, on balance, his family's deaths were trumped by a child raped and murdered. If that happened to June, it would slay him.

'What's Maple done now?' Vernon Greenhill's forearms were streaked with grease and this reminded Cotton that Maple's twenty-one-year-old brother worked as a mechanic. Seeing biceps bulging beneath his shirtsleeves, Cotton knew that, on hearing bad news, family could go for the messenger.

'Mother and father indoors, son?' Cotton clasped his hat.

'If she's got herself arrested, tell me. Mum's got a weak heart.' Vernon Greenhill barred the way.

'She will have to hear this, Vernon.'

Perhaps cowed by the use of his name, Vernon Greenhill retreated into a hallway, gleaming parquet giving off a scent of beeswax. Pausing to drop his hat onto an antler stand beside an aspidistra on a tall spindly table, Cotton stepped into what Agnes called her parlour. A fire crackled in a grate. On the mantelpiece Maple and Vernon's framed faces beamed, kids' shiny complexions flannelled clean.

'It's the police about Maple.' Staying by the door, Vernon wasn't beaming now.

Keith and Evelyn Greenhill, in their early forties, but, dressed in what for Cotton would be his Sunday best, seemed older. Seated on a green velvet sofa they stared out of the window to the graves. Cotton had the uneasy impression they had got ready for the news he was about to give them.

'What's she done now?' Keith Greenhill was a masculine version of his daughter, the same wide mouth, hazel eyes, but with a short back and sides, combed and oiled. On Maple the looks were pleasant, augmented, Cotton guessed, by a lively character. On Greenhill they were handsome. Cotton caught himself wondering if Greenhill was faithful. These days too many crimes involved adultery.

'Who says she's in trouble, Keith?' From her expression,

Cotton saw that Evelyn Greenhill was frightened of what her husband might let slip. Perhaps they hadn't reported that their daughter had failed to come home last night because they had not expected her. Her lips were pale, her eyes glassy. Tipping his head, Cotton told Shepherd to get Mrs Greenhill a glass of water.

During his long career, Cotton had told many a relative that their son, daughter, loved ones were dead. Seeking to reassure the Greenhills that Maple had done nothing wrong, he had to say what had been done to her.

'How?' Vernon was the first to speak.

'She was strangled.' Cotton didn't believe in mincing words.

'Who on earth would...?' Evelyn Cotton took the glass from Shepherd, but didn't drink from it. 'Everyone loved her.'

'That's what we will find out.' Burning up, Cotton stepped away from the fire and nearly trod on a boy sprawled on his front on a rug near the window. The face considering him was what Cotton's mum would have called a proper little cherub. Rosy-cheeked, sandy curls. Cotton knew instantly he was the boy in the photograph that Maple had carried in her handbag. Her son.

Awkwardly, the boy clambered up onto sturdy legs, reaching up to Cotton, a lead soldier in his fist. Cotton stared down. Then, God love him, Shepherd stepped in and, taking the soldier, aimed the tiny musket at Cotton and said, 'Bang bang.' This set off peals of laughter.

'More,' the boy squealed.

Cotton expected someone in the room to get the boy to be quiet, but no one moved. Instead, kneeling down to the toddler's height, Shepherd told him, 'I've got a soldier just like this in my toy box.'

'Have you caught him?' Vernon Greenhill asked.

'No. Not yet.' Cotton felt perspiration trickle down his brow and he dashed at it with a sleeve. He said, 'Someone will hang for this.' *And there was him not holding with capital punishment.*

'You'd better mean that,' Vernon said.

'Don't be rude, Vernon,' his mother scolded. 'The police will do their best.'

'I'm afraid we do need to ask you some questions about Maple. Anything you can tell us to identify this man. Like was she seeing someone regular or—'

'Or what?' Vernon Greenhill squared up to Cotton. 'You saying Maple was a, was a... *prostitute*?' He reddened.

'Take it easy, sir.' Shepherd touted the lead soldier.

'She didn't go with men,' Vernon Greenhill spluttered.

The boy, making choo-choo noises, pushed a tin engine over Shepherd's boot. Incontrovertible proof that, some four years ago, Maple had gone with at least one man.

'I have to ask... could Maple have been working in the evenings?'

'You wash your mouth out.' Vernon stepped up to Cotton. Although much shorter, his biceps would carry the day. Cotton was out of shape. Maybe Shepherd reckoned the same: he was on his feet in a jiffy.

'Steady, son.' Cotton braced himself. 'It's a capital offence to threaten a police officer.'

'Vernon, *enough*.' Evelyn Greenhill reminded Cotton of his own mother. A small, slight woman who demonstrated that size is no indicator of strength. Maisie Cotton had kept her two boys in order with just such a look. Evelyn looked at William tootling his engine over the braid rug. 'Maple put everything into her baby.'

'She wasn't a prostitute,' Vernon said.

'Was there a regular chap? Someone she had a shine for?' Cotton was kindly.

'Not that we knew.' Evelyn was on the edge of the settee, hugging herself close to the fire. It needed more coal, but no one had seen. She told him that they'd said goodbye to Maple on the doorstep, she was seeing her friend Ida.

'Mummy didn't bring Plaay-yer's,' the boy piped up. Agnes

used to warn him about children's big ears, and not to mention any horrible things from work with them there.

'Maple told William she was just getting fags.' Keith shook his head. 'He's got the memory of an elephant.'

'You knew that was... not the case.' Cotton guessed young William understood the word 'lie'. 'Did Maple tell you where she was actually going?'

'Down the Palais,' Vernon mumbled. 'I should have gone but Mary, she's my fiancée, had a shift the next day so...' He stopped and Cotton saw that, like his nephew, Vernon Greenhill knew about lying. He had never been accompanying Maple to the dance hall. And nor, Cotton would confirm, had the friend called Ida.

'Mary's a clippie on the 27.' Evelyn's note of pride sounded by rote, for her son's benefit. She was probably prouder of her secretary daughter.

'I'd like to see Maple's room, to get a picture of her, things she liked, any hobbies and such, anything that could help find who did this.' Cotton sidestepped Vernon at the door.

'Stay with your dad.' Evelyn Greenhill got up and took Shepherd and Cotton upstairs. The landing window was still blacked out with fabric pinned to the frame. Switching on a light, she sighed, 'Maple does the blackout, we don't ask much, not even keep for the baby, but she makes a song and dance every time.'

'My girl's the same.' Cotton winced at his tactlessness – Mrs Greenhill had snared him by speaking of Maple as if she was alive. 'It is a palaver.'

'Just spent nearly fourteen shillings on her linen sheets, what a—' Mrs Greenhill's face contorted. She wasn't complaining, Cotton realized, but mourning that her daughter wouldn't benefit. 'Make yourselves at home,' Mrs Greenhill told them as she returned down the stairs.

'We're hardly going to do that,' Shepherd whispered once they were alone.

'You say all sorts when you've had bad news.' When he was told about his parents' deaths Cotton had asked which bit of the train they'd been in. Not an idle question. On holidays, knowing what could go wrong, his dad always insisted they sat on suitcases in the guard's wagon. That day, his mum's birthday treat, they'd gone in the first-class carriage behind the engine. Cotton flicked a hand as if at the memory and said, 'Master Vernon knows something he's not telling.'

'How do you make that out, sir?' Shepherd said.

'He's too convinced Maple wasn't a prostitute.'

'My sister sends me spare, but I'd be browned off if a copper hinted she was a prostitute, not that she is,' Shepherd said.

'Good lad, that's what brothers are for,' Cotton said. 'I think he's upset because he knows there was a man and he didn't protect her.'

'If he knows and isn't saying then we should arrest him.' Shepherd saw arresting people as a perk of the job.

'Vernon doesn't know, or mark my words, he'd have high-tailed it, fists ready, when we told them. He will be kicking himself for not finding out who his sister was courting. My guess is this man is married or Maple would have been over the moon to tell her family.'

Maple's bedroom was a poignant illustration of her switch from child to mother. A teddy bear and a feeding bottle, children's books – *Out With Romany*, *The Family From One End Street*, Lamb's *Tales From Shakespeare* – too old for the boy were in a bookcase also stacked with wooden building bricks and a Peek Freans crackers tin filled with more lead soldiers. Errol Flynn, cut from the *Sunday Pictorial*, was on the wall. A scratched and mended cot was hard up to a bed that Maple must have slept in since she was a girl little older than her son.

A double-doored utility wardrobe left scant floorspace, bought, Cotton decided, to accommodate Maple and William's things. He opened it and recoiled. The delicate flowery scent evoked the dead girl far more than viewing her body on Northcote's slab.

Inside hung some frocks and blouses and a couple of work skirts. Unlike the silk dress Maple had been wearing when she was murdered, all looked hand-made. Another coat, of cheaper material than the fancy one Maple was found in. He said, 'Maple appears to have led two lives: secretary at the dairy, and for nights out she dolled herself up in garments that were so dear a girl on her modest wage would have to save up half her life to afford.'

'If Maple was selling herself, she was going for the highest bidder.' Shepherd whistled.

'Wash your mouth out, PC Shepherd.' Cotton whipped around. 'Damn well show respect to this young woman who, if she was alive, would have been ashamed to have you and me turning over her bedroom.'

Shepherd at least had the grace to look ashamed. To spare his blushes, Cotton got Shepherd checking under the bed, delving beneath the lumpy palliasse, pillows, shaking out sheets and blankets while Cotton sifted through Maple's undergarments. They were searching, Cotton told him, for a billet-doux, or something Maple's man had given her as a gift.

Wrapped in a flannel vest, which Cotton suspected had been rarely worn, he discovered her 1927 diary when Maple was ten. The flyleaf was inscribed, 'For Maple, every girl must keep her secrets, love Mum.' Had Evelyn hoped this would inspire Maple to share confidences with her? When did Maple's secrets become too dark to tell? The diary was pure innocence, scattered with declarations, Maple's favourite dinner – bubble and squeak – she loved the colour sky-blue and wanted to marry Cary Grant. Entries petered out after February. The back pages were crammed with bus tickets – the 11, the 15, routes into London – there was an entry ticket for the Victoria and Albert Museum and a photograph of a girl; he saw a younger Maple in the sun-bleached features, squinting in sunlight on a chair in a school playground. On the back she'd written: '1929, I'm the only one going to the grammer. I'll end up head girl at Burlington!'

Cotton's daughter June had gone to Burlington School for Girls six years before Maple. Cotton noted Maple's misspelling of *grammar*. June was always top in spelling. She too was a secretary, but worked for a solicitor who now she was going to marry. Cotton shut the diary. Maple was dead, for God's sake, it wasn't right to compare.

'Found something, sir.' Shepherd strained into the gap between the wall and the bed. Heaving himself up, he passed Cotton a small box.

'I was expecting diamonds.' Cotton whistled at what looked like a curtain ring nestling on a cushion of deep blue silk. 'Humboldt and Baxter's Jewellers have expanded to hardware. OK, it's time for a confab with brother Vernon.'

He closed Maple's bedroom door after Shepherd and went downstairs. Vernon Greenhill was sitting on a chair by the window, William asleep on his lap. Cotton felt warmer towards Vernon.

'We think there was a man,' Cotton told them.

'I said that. Those times she said she was round with Ida.' Keith rounded on his wife. 'Ida never saw her. I asked her.'

'I said leave it to me.' Evelyn rounded on her husband.

'You never did anything. If we'd had it out with her...' Keith Greenhill knew when to stop, Cotton was pleased to see.

'It's no one's fault,' Cotton said.

'We nearly lost her when she was carrying him, I couldn't let her go again or she would have been on the street.' Evelyn went and took William from Vernon.

'You were too soft on her.' Vernon pulled at the collar of his shirt. 'If you'd come clean when he was born, we'd know where we were. I'm sick of telling porkies every time I leave the house.'

'What porkies?' Cotton asked.

'William's passed off as theirs. Maple was his big sister. Only Maple let him call her Mummy on the quiet. You never stopped her.'

Cotton knew Maple having a child out of wedlock would have been a blow to what was a respectable family living in a respectable street. They had taken the boy into the family – it took courage. Cotton had recently attended two failed abortion deaths, one in a smart flat on the river, the other a backstreet affair not far from his home. Since the war, like murder and stealing from the dead, abortions had become more common. It was harder for wives to work the timings to fit when their men had been home on leave. Women like Maple who didn't want to lose freedom or be shamed out of town.

'If you'd had it out with her, mother to daughter…' Keith said.

'I did ask how she got that coat, it looked fearfully dear,' Evelyn said. 'She palmed me off saying she'd got a rise. I had a word with that pecky-mouthed manager of hers and he said he'd give her a raise when she bucked up her ways.'

'You never should have gone to him,' Vernon blazed. 'That's her business.'

'Buck her ways up how?' Cotton asked.

'He claimed she got in late in the mornings and took long dinner breaks. He did say she'd kept her job because when she did the work it was of the highest standard.' Evelyn said again, 'Maple put everything into her baby.'

'She wasn't a prostitute,' Vernon said, as if someone had just said Maple was.

'Can any of you can shed light on how Maple came by this?' Cotton opened the little box.

'She was engaged,' Vernon blurted then looked horrified.

'You knew that and never said?' his mother shrieked at him. William woke up and started crying. Evelyn rocked him violently. 'There, there, lamb, *there, there.*'

'Maple made me promise.' Vernon looked miserable.

'Who was he?' It was grey outside, but for Cotton it was as if the sun shone. If he could find Maple's killer, one day he'd retire happy. *Was he close?* Then he recalled what he'd told Shepherd:

if Vernon knew the man's name the boy would have been gone by now and someone wouldn't have been safe.

'I don't know.' Vernon looked away.

'You sister's dead, Vernon, she has no secrets to keep.' Seeing the boy hang his head between his knees, Cotton softened. 'You can help her now by telling us what you do know.'

'If I knew, think I would be answering your stupid questions? I'd have it out with him.' Vernon scrubbed at the back of his head and sat up.

Quite so.

'Leave that to the police,' Constable Shepherd sniffed importantly.

'Did Maple talk about him? Say why she liked him? Anything she said could give us a clue to who he is.'

'She said I'd like him, that's all. That we liked the same things.'

'What things?' Evelyn had got William off to sleep again. 'What things did she say you both liked?'

'I can't remember.' Blank-faced, Vernon stared at the grate, the fire long burnt out.

'What do you like doing?' Cotton asked.

'The usual.' Vernon spun the wheels on William's engine. 'Me and Mary go dancing, follow the dogs at White City.'

'You and Mary are saving for a house, what are you doing frittering away cash?' Keith scowled. Cotton knew that in the face of tragedy, people stuck to the everyday.

'What am I meant to say? He asked me,' Vernon said. 'When I won fourteen and three on Highland Rum last year, I didn't hear you complain.'

'Did Maple say this man liked greyhound racing?' Hopeless. Cotton knew there were ninety thousand at the White City stadium for the Derby. Needle and haystack was the story of his life.

'Maple's murdered and you're on about dog-racing?' Evelyn kissed the sleeping boy on the forehead. William looked so peaceful, but Cotton knew that soon enough he'd miss his mum. Or his 'big sister'.

'It's fake,' Keith Greenhill said. 'That ring. Two a penny in Shepherd's Bush market.'

'Keith's dad was a pawnbroker.' Evelyn caught her husband's look. 'Well, he was.'

'Anyone can see that's cheap tat. It certainly wasn't purchased at this jeweller.' Keith handed the box back to Cotton. 'He was having my daughter on.' He clenched a fist.

'Maple knew that, you think she's stupid? She didn't *care*,' Vernon spat out. 'It was temporary, until he could take her to choose her own, she said.'

'What was stopping him?' Evelyn's head snapped up. 'You knew?'

'He was married, of course.' Keith shook his head. 'That posh box will have had his wife's wedding ring in it. I know the sort.'

'He had a big house in the country,' Vernon said.

Cotton flipped open his notebook. 'Where?'

'Out west somewhere, she never said.' Vernon looked wrung out. He said, 'Automobiles.'

'Auto... Sorry, lad, what do you mean?' Cotton looked up.

'He means cars. Vernon likes to talk American. He mends Cadillacs, Daimlers, you name it.' It was as if, forgetting why the police were there, Keith felt momentary pride in his son.

'Daimler is British.' Impatient, his son missed the moment. 'Maple said his car would pay for this house.'

'This house is nearly paid for,' Keith said and glaring at Cotton who perhaps hadn't hidden his surprise, 'I'm an actuary. Maple comes from a respectable home.'

'Did Maple say what sort of car this man drove?' Cotton chased the smallest hare.

'No, I'd remember that.' Vernon frowned. Cotton knew the poor kid was on the foothills of the guilt he would feel, for the rest of his life, about his dead sister.

'My daddy isn't in the ar-my, Mummy says he's saving so-wells for England.' William had gone from fast asleep to wide awake. Cotton could envy him that.

'Tell us about your daddy, William?' Cotton stooped down to the boy.

'He can't make them bet-ter, he gives them to God.' Overcome with shyness, William buried his face in his grandmother's tummy.

'He makes things up. Hears about the other kiddies' dads being in the army and invents one for himself,' Evelyn said stiffly.

'His dad *is* in the army. The blighter signed up to shirk duty to his son and my sister. He deserves everything the Nazis give him.' No one disagreed with Vernon.

'What if William isn't making it up, sir? What if that stuff about his daddy is what Maple told him about this secret man?' Shepherd said when they were in the car.

'You might have something, Constable.' Cotton slapped the dashboard with his notebook. 'Maple tells William bedtime stories about her so-called fiancé. He's not a soldier, he saves *souls*. Oh,' he groaned, 'please God tell me that our killer isn't a vicar.'

Chapter Eleven

2019

The bells tolled midnight. Footsteps clipped on stone. All the lamps had been put on, animating censing angels, fierce-faced tabor players and exposing the triforium walk high up in the vaulted ceiling. Yellow numbered markers dotted the tombstoned floor. Tewkesbury Abbey was a crime scene. The plastic barriers left by workmen had been stacked against a pillar.

The rattle of wheels made Stella look up. Roddy's body was being wheeled to the north door on a gurney. Her teeth began to chatter. Stella had insisted she didn't need to go to hospital, but huddled by the rood screen, she was grateful for the beaker of sweet tea conjured up by a policewoman. Her fingers and toes had gone numb. Her mind was numb. Jaw clenched, Stella accidentally bit her tongue. She tasted copper. She smelled copper. Her trousers stiffened as Roddy's blood dried.

The rattling faded then Stella heard the boom of the north doors. Looking at Jesus on the Cross through the rood screen, she saw instead Roddy March, his teeth bared in agony, gasping for breath in her arms.

Cawomy. Had Roddy really been trying to say 'Chamomile'?

It could be the name of his girlfriend, the jealous caller. Caroline, Karen, Charmian?

Where the north ambulatory had been blocked off with plastic barriers because workmen were repairing was police tape and arc lamps.

Only when Roddy's body was extracted from her embrace had Stella understood help had arrived. Legs buckling, she was helped to her feet by two police officers. They leaned her against the starved monk to get her breath.

Someone wants to kill me.

Roddy had said that when Felicity told him he had to leave the Death Café. She had escorted him out and then he had been killed. Stella had so nearly followed him, but aware that Felicity's Death Café was already a disaster, had felt she should stay.

'Sorry to keep you, Stella.' A woman came out of the north ambulatory and wove between the chairs towards her. Dark-suited, high heels, short hair, foundation, mascara, red lipstick in the middle of the night, when the woman – the SIO, Stella guessed – had probably been called from her bed. Wait, surely not. *It was.*

Janet Piper belonged to Stella's old life in London – what was she doing here?

'Janet.' Stella was appalled to feel on the verge of tears. The Death Café, Roddy's murder and now surrounded by strangers, it was Janet Piper, once WPC Piper, one of her dad's favourite colleagues. Had Terry Darnell been a different kind of man they might have had an affair. Even as a girl, Stella had divined that Janet loved him. She'd organized Terry's leaving do and, later, the force funeral, the Union Flag draped on his coffin. Stella's mother had been certain Terry was unfaithful with Janet, but Suzy Darnell's facts required no evidence.

Janet, like Martin Cashman, her dad's best friend, had always had Terry's back. Stella had last seen Janet in Hammersmith police station when she'd given her a witness statement on the case Lucie May called The Playground Murders. Why was Janet in Tewkesbury?

Stella's expression must have betrayed this because, sitting down, Janet said, 'I moved to Gloucestershire two months ago. More trees, less murders, or so I expected.' Janet signalled in the direction of the cadaver tomb where Roddy had been murdered.

'Never mind me, you're the last person I expected to meet and, forgive me saying, in a church. Otherwise, business as per, you finding a body.' Despite her levity, Janet sounded concerned.

'It's a long story.' A very short story, but not one Stella wanted to tell.

'Catch me over a drink.' Janet touched her shoulder. 'It's great to clap eyes on a familiar face, especially yours. Don't get me wrong, I love my new job, I've got a top floor flat overlooking the Severn, above the floods, and the walks around here are to die— *ahem*, fantastic. Yet I'm homesick for the Shepherd's Bush Road and, get this, I miss Hammersmith Broadway in the rain.' Janet rapped her notebook. 'And no one's a patch on Terry, he was a one-off.'

'Did you find his notebook?' Unwilling to even think about her dad, Stella recalled Roddy scribbling in the Death Café.

'Terry's?'

'Roddy's. He was writing in one.'

'*Whoa*. Winding back,' Janet said. 'You saying you *knew* the victim?'

'I only met him twice.' As Stella described her encounter with March the previous morning by the cadaver tomb, and how he'd appeared at the Death Café, she felt herself flush with shame again for not going after Roddy. 'The facilitator will know more.' Then she remembered Roddy hadn't booked. 'She won't have his address.'

'No probs, we found a card for some boarding house in his trouser pocket, it's where he was staying.' Janet patted Stella's shoulder. 'Got to say, I'm made up my chief witness is equipped with the observational skills of a raptor and that you *knew* him is gold.'

'We only said a few words.'

'Let's hear them.'

'Roddy March was at the Death Café when I arrived. On the second night.'

'How many Death Cafés have you gone to, Stella?' Janet's tact sounded effortful.

'One, really – it was split into two.' Stella explained that Felicity had been called away. 'Roddy sat next to me, maybe because we'd met here the day before and he didn't know anyone. Like I say, he was writing notes.' Stella's so-called observation skills felt blunted.

'You met him here yesterday?' Janet stopped writing, in shorthand, Stella noticed. 'Where exactly?'

'By the cadaver tomb. This one's called the...' Stella swallowed. 'Exactly where he was attacked. By the starved monk.'

'You didn't plan to meet there?'

'No,' Stella exclaimed. 'I was cleaning and he appeared.'

'So that wasn't the first time Roddy March had been to the... what did you call it?'

Stella told Janet what Roddy had told her about the tombs and that he'd received a phone call and gone off. She hadn't seen him again until the second evening at the Death Café.

'Did you get the impression he was expecting to meet someone there?'

'No, the opposite. He told whoever rang him that he'd see them outside the abbey. It didn't sound as if he expected to meet them by the tomb. I felt he expected me to know him, due to his podcast.'

'Podcast?' Frowning, Janet was writing rapidly.

'He's doing one – *was* doing – on men hanged for crimes he believed they never committed. No, not quite that; it was about matching the true killer to their victim, which gave the victim justice. Roddy said he'd released the first episode.'

'Have you heard it?'

'No.'

'This is great stuff, Stella. Just a mo. Hey, Tony.' Janet waved to a middle-aged man, his rumpled look suggesting he'd had to dress in the dark, talking to a woman in forensics overalls. He looked like Terry. *Get a grip.* In London Stella had seen Terry everywhere, but – so far – not in Tewkesbury.

'Our victim did a true-crime podcast – check it out, has he upset someone? Who has he interviewed? What did he unearth? What's so interesting about that chapel? Our witness saw him there yesterday,' Janet fired at the man when he came over. She looked at Stella. 'What's it called, this chapel, and for that matter the podcast? No worries, that's what Google's for.'

'The tomb of the starved monk. He called it a cadaver tomb.' Up close, Tony didn't look at all like her dad. 'On my cleaning rota it's called the Wakeman Cenotaph.'

'Seriously?' Watching Tony hurry away already on his phone, Janet turned to Stella. 'What was March's mood in this Dead Café? Nervous, wired?'

'Death Café. I didn't notice, but he wrote a lot of stuff down in his notebook.' Stella told Janet what Roddy had written about Andrea.

'Did she see it?'

'I doubt it, she was on the other side of the table.'

'Not really a motive to stab him to death.' Unconsciously perhaps, Janet wore the same grumpy expression as the angel she was staring at. 'Sounds like March was interested in you? First, he meets you in the abbey, then fronts up at the Death Club – could he have followed you?'

'He wouldn't have known I'd return the second night.' Stella had not intended to return.

The white Peugeot van slows down, no lights. Silence. The darkness is tangible like thick cloth.

Her teeth began to chatter again. Janet reached over and pulled the foil blanket tighter around her.

'I'm sure not,' Stella decided. 'Roddy only wanted to talk about his podcast. About a murder in Tewkesbury years ago.

I suspect he was there to fact-find. The group was local and one man, called Clive, had known the victim.' Suddenly Stella felt Roddy *had* been interested in her. A feeling she couldn't substantiate, but couldn't dismiss. *Was he the van driver on the lane?*

'I see.' Janet was expressionless so Stella had no clue what it was that she saw. 'Did you think March knew who you are?'

'I'm not anyone.'

'Last I knew, you were running a detective agency and cleaning for half of London on the side.' Janet raised an eyebrow. 'Thanks to that Lucie May, you've been in the media. I don't miss *her*. No surprise if some true-crime podcaster had you on his radar.'

'Clean Slate is only cleaning now.' Horrified to be on anyone's radar, Stella didn't say she'd given up everything to start again in Tewkesbury.

'You sure March knew no one? Someone who might bear him a grudge? Did you notice if anyone was unfriendly towards him? You know the drill, Stella. However apparently irrelevant or everyday, give it to me raw.'

Stella said everyone in the group apart from Clive Burgess, who made clocks, had been sulky. 'Including me, I'm afraid.' Gladys Wren, the lodging house owner, had defended March, but Stella imagined Roddy had been charming to older women. Felicity was cross with him for gatecrashing and transgressing the rules, and on the first night she'd also been annoyed that Andrea the gardener was late. Stella presumed now that Felicity, a retired pathologist, preferred dead people.

'Who's Felicity?'

'The facilitator, she ran the group, it was her first time.'

'Felicity the facilitator. That's actually quite funny.' Janet did a shorthand squiggle which, to Stella, had no resemblance to anything she'd said.

'I think it was then Roddy told us someone wanted to murder him,' Stella said.

'Say again.' Bolt upright, Janet stared at Stella.

'Roddy claimed someone wanted to murder him. He'd had death threats, a dead bird on his car.'

'What sort of bird?'

'He didn't say.' Stella was surprised, it was the sort of off-the-wall question Jack would ask. 'That's about when Felicity suggested he go to the police in Cheltenham. The station here is shut.'

'I'm aware of that.' Janet pulled a face. 'Did you believe him? Great way to whip up followers for this podcast.' Janet was writing. Stella knew that, years before, having passed her sergeant exams, Janet had come top in Pitman's typing and shorthand. Terry made her keep it quiet to avoid becoming, as he'd said, CID's Girl Friday.

'I think Roddy wanted to stay talking to the group, but Felicity was firm. I saw her point, the session wasn't going according to plan. Afterwards, the man called Clive said more about the murder Roddy was investigating. It was in Cloisters House, that big house on the other side of the abbey wall.' Stella tilted a hand towards the altar. 'Andrea, she's the abbey gardener, complained Roddy was a time-waster who leeched off the attention of others. She seemed to have taken a dislike to him.' Stella rubbed her face. If only she'd gone after Roddy when he left.

'This Andrea, could she have disliked March enough to stab him?' Janet tapped her upper lip with her pen. 'Are you sure she didn't see his potted description of her?'

'I got the impression Andrea was like that generally. That, or she didn't like me either. I wouldn't expect her to attack me.'

'Sounds like, piss her off and you're in her sights,' Janet said. 'I'll look forward to my chat with her.'

'Roddy can't have got in her way, he hardly noticed her.'

'That March described Andrea as a loose cannon suggests she's a disrupter – but how did March know that?'

'Her attitude was combative, impatient. She pushed against the spirit of the Death Café. When Felicity asked what Andrea wanted from the session she said she hoped to get home without getting caught in the rain again.' Stella flapped the foil blanket. 'Thinking about it, that was the first night, when Roddy wasn't there.'

'What murder was March investigating?' Janet seemed satisfied with this.

'Friday the twenty-second of November 1963.' Stella was glad to have observed one specific fact; it felt that her supposed raptor skills had deserted her. She told Janet about the murder of the pathologist and how his son was executed for it. Janet was animated – she'd heard of Professor Northcote.

'Your dad heard Northcote got too big for his boots, the man's word was gospel. Terry said, in the early sixties, when he was stationed in east London, one old geezer at the Hackney mortuary could remember Northcote working through the Blitz. Terry mistrusted heroes, the best professionals work in teams. I never let myself forget that.' She gave a hollow laugh. 'The Northcote case was cut and dried. Sounds like March was creating fake news. There's many a failed reporter going for reinvention as a top-list podcaster. The lovely Lucie May comes swiftly to mind.'

'Roddy said he had proof Giles Northcote didn't kill his father.' At the mention of Lucie, Stella felt uncomfortable. No love was lost between Janet and Lucie May with whom, after Stella's mum left Terry, he actually did have an affair.

'Did anyone seem uncomfortable about this? Supposing for a second that March was on to something, him saying that could have put the wind up someone in the group. Perhaps that was his intention?'

'Hard to say. No one seemed bothered that he'd gone.'

'To your knowledge did anyone follow him? Apart from you, of course.'

'Joy was in the abbey when I arrived, she plays the organ. But I think he was alive during the music.' Cold and exhausted, Stella tried to think how it had gone. When did the music stop?

She couldn't get past the terrible vision of Roddy's stricken face. The blood.

'I just talked to her. Playing that thing, she claims not to have heard anything. As you know, March was stabbed in the back. The killer didn't require strength, just the element of surprise.' Janet returned to her earlier point. 'I'm tending to think March went to this starved monk tomb hoping you'd meet him. Are you sure he didn't suggest a rendezvous there?'

'No.' Stella's stomach plunged. Up until now Janet had been chatty, almost as if they were mates, now she was homing in. As Stella knew in a murder case, everyone's a suspect and especially the witness who found the body. 'This is probably nothing.' She told Janet about the van slowing to a stop on the road from Winchcombe.

'We'll check if March drove a white van. That could be kids, there's been a spate of muggings. One MO is fake car trouble. Driver behind offers help, kids wave a knife and demand cash. You had a lucky escape. We had a mugging in the abbey.' Janet dropped her pen and retrieving it said, 'Not all woolly lambs and rolling combine harvesters in the country.'

'I should have gone after Roddy,' Stella said.

'Don't beat yourself up. If you had we might be shunting you off to the morgue too.' Janet swished to a fresh page in her notebook and looking at Stella asked, 'While I think of it, why did you come to the abbey after you left the Death Café?'

Right at that moment, Stella was asking herself the same question.

Chapter Twelve

1940

'...Only that the Palais de Danse was the last place where the victim was believed to have gone. My constable will be there within the hour.' *Suffering Jesus.* Cotton replaced the receiver onto the cradle before he said anything that might land him in trouble. The manager at the Palais swore it was unlikely any of his staff recalled Maple, '...*and since she wasn't killed at the dance hall, what's it to do with us?'* The war had made people callous.

Chief Superintendent Hackett hadn't been best pleased that Cotton was canvassing alibis for vicars in the parishes of Hammersmith and Chiswick. 'No man of God would do that to a woman, let alone touch a prostitute.' Nor had it helped to hear it was the only lead they'd got.

Cotton took a gulp from the cup of tea Ethel had brought and, sitting back in his chair, arms behind his head, his eye fell on Aleck Northcote's Dunhill lighter beside Cotton's own tobacco tin. Grimacing, he got back on the telephone and dialled the pathologist's office in Whitehall. A snooty-sounding assistant informed him, 'Dr Northcote is unavailable, he is at the Hackney mortuary, then he will be motoring to Hampshire regarding a deceased male body found in a cow field.' The man's implication being that Northcote was more important than Cotton. He *was* more important, but Northcote was the last chap to rub that in.

'Please tell *Aleck* I came upon his lighter at the murder scene and have it safe at the station.' Cotton slammed down the receiver. He instantly regretted calling. Northcote had been careless leaving his lighter where Maple Greenhill was strangled. Northcote might be annoyed with himself, but he'd be properly browned off with Cotton for highlighting this to one of his assistants. Cotton could have saved Aleck's face by discreetly returning the lighter. Even slipping it in Aleck's overcoat pocket when he was working. Finishing his tea, Cotton had to admit he resented how the pathologist's error had momentarily given him false hope that they had a strong lead to Maple's murderer.

It was a relief to know that the giant of his profession got things wrong; Northcote was human like the rest of them.

Cotton got up and leaned on the back of his chair, gazing through the criss-crossed tape on the window at the traffic on Brook Green Road. The police station was a few doors from the Palais where Vernon said his sister had gone dancing with her friend Ida. If Maple had gone there, it hadn't been with Ida. Mulling over the facts, Cotton set about pinning up the blackout cloth, a job he refused to leave to Ethel.

After leaving the Greenhills, he and Shepherd visited the Lyons' on Kensington High Street where Ida worked as a Nippy. Clutching a tray of crockery, the girl, her hair rolled like Maple's in the photograph with William, had sat on a kitchen stool and wept as she told them she hadn't wanted to be Maple's excuse. 'I never expected she'd get in such trouble, she said she was marrying a real gentleman.' Again, Cotton had felt the rush, they were close on Maple's killer, but it had fizzled to nothing. Ida had never met the man, Maple wouldn't even tell her his name. She had told Ida that he was rich and had a lovely car.

'Did she say they had sexual relations?'

Convulsed, Ida had admitted how, sometimes, she and Maple had both seen their chaps in an alley. 'I won't ever again. I promise. I asked her why, seeing as he had cash, he didn't take her to a hotel. We had a bit of a tiff over that.'

'I'd never have thought it of her, she looks like a good girl, and what's more a Nippy,' Shepherd said after.

'Buck up, Constable, your cheeks are meeting in the middle like you've swallowed a horsefly. Good girls do it too.' Not that Cotton cared to think of June in a backstreet – anywhere – with her solicitor fellow. 'There's a war on, everyone's grabbing at life while they have it.'

Now, forehead resting against the pane, Cotton watched the street outside the police station. Maple would have walked on that pavement. Going by where she lived, she'd have got the bus to the Broadway. Did she meet the man at the dance hall or had he escorted her? Cotton doubted it, although he'd certainly escorted her out. The empty house was a step up from an alleyway, but he hadn't even had her in a bed. Cotton caught his fists clenching and recalled how Keith Greenhill, convinced his daughter had a man, said how the blighter never walked her home. *Not even to the end of the street, I keep an eye out.*

Three in the afternoon and it was nearly dark. Since the raids, London was under a permanent cloud of smoke from the fires. He turned from the window.

Yellow electric light washed over the room. The building was less than a decade old, but to Cotton it felt tawdry. His office with four desks, grey cabinets, buff folders awaiting Ethel's filing looked bleak as death. Two of the desks, wire baskets empty, ink on the blotters dry, were reminders of Evans and Franklin who had gone to fight. Evans had died when a prize fool lost control of a jeep training in the Phoney War. Cotton prayed in church on Sundays for Franklin to see the war out.

Next to a sepia-stained photograph of Agnes and June was another of Cotton's passing-out in May 1912. Cotton was on the end of the first row, wet behind the ears, all set to end crime.

Since then some had left the force, and a few enlisted and were killed in the Great War. Bob Hackett sat next to Cotton, like him a constable, now his boss. These days Hackett preferred golf to catching criminals. You could say that every man in the photo – each determined and keen – had died so to speak. Himself included.

A few years off fifty, Cotton had seen too much. There he was, trying to instil Shepherd with a detective's eye and a love of the job when more than ready to hang up his dancing shoes, Cotton himself had scant faith they'd find Maple's murderer.

Shepherd was at the mortuary fetching Maple's clothes. He'd pack him off to the Palais when he came back.

Sitting down again, Cotton was distracted by Ethel's blurry outline through the chicken-wire glass partition. He heard muffled clacks as she typed up his interim report on the murder. Cotton took refuge in a small dose of normal life. This jolted his memory that he hadn't booked tickets for *Aladdin* up in town. Ethel had offered but, unlike the chief super, Cotton would not have his secretary manage his family as well as his office.

'Temple Bar 3161 please,' he told the operator.

Cotton bagged three seats in the stalls, two rows from the stage. Since the Blitz, theatre performances ended before 9.30 p.m. If there was a raid, Agnes would make them find the nearest shelter. Were it up to him and June they'd stay in their seats.

Afterwards they'd have a bite to eat at that fancy Lyons' on Oxford Street. Cotton smiled; he liked splashing out on his family.

Chapter Thirteen

2019

Stella

'...why did you come to the abbey after you left the Death Café?'

So, there it was. Stella was a suspect. Every detective keeps in their mind that the witness who finds the body is the murderer.

'I heard the organ.' Not the reason. If Stella had said that since living in Tewkesbury, the abbey was home, Janet's suspicions would sky-rocket. She well knew neither Terry nor Stella believed in God. Stella couldn't admit she felt soothed by stained glass images of the Passion, the trefoil arcade, the spandrels depicting intricate foliage, the glow of the votive candles and the hum of the two gigantic stoves which kept the abbey warm. Best not to admit she liked to think murmuring voices in the vaulted space echoed from across centuries.

Stella had not followed Roddy to the abbey, but she couldn't prove it.

'My colleague said you saw someone in here.' Janet wouldn't seriously suspect Terry's daughter of murder. *Would she?*

If Stella were Janet, she'd suspect Stella.

'I didn't actually see a person, just a shadow. Over there, on that wall.' Stella pointed across the nave to the north ambulatory. 'I assumed it was Roddy when I saw his beanie on the chair.'

'Show me which chair.' Janet was up and striding away. Her foil blanket flapping, Stella went after her.

'I was here.' Too weak to stand, Stella sat down on the chair. 'The shadow was there.'

'You didn't speak to March?'

'I didn't know it was him.'

'You're sure the beanie was his?' Janet was merely doing her job, but it was making Stella nervous, as if she had something to hide.

'I'm not sure, it's just that Roddy wore one.' Detectives took a witness's nerves into account. Her dad had said the police could make the angels feel guilty. 'It was like the one Roddy wore at the Death Café and yesterday in the abbey. The shadow looked like a head and shoulders.' *The more you say, the more you incriminate yourself.* Stella crossed the flagstones and swept her hand over the sandstone to show where the shadow had been.

'You weren't afraid of being here on your own?' Janet cast about. 'This place is giving me the heebie-jeebies and that's with half of Gloucestershire police here. But what am I saying? Stella Darnell has faced down cold-blooded killers. This is a walk in the park.'

'I like it here alone.' Stella couldn't tell if Janet was being sarcastic. She stopped herself mentioning the Three Kings. Then Janet would think she'd lost it.

'You weren't tempted to see who it was?'

'No.'

'Since that door to the right of the nave is the only exit, anyone leaving would have had to pass you.' Janet nodded towards the north door off the ambulatory.

'I assumed they'd gone towards the organ, perhaps to speak to Joy.'

'If you go that way,' Janet was looking at a folded tourist map, 'and keep going, you reach the chapel where March was murdered. Keep going, you'll pass round the back of the altar and then find yourself over there. Since you were on the same route, did it occur to you that you might meet March, or whoever, coming towards you clockwise?'

'No.' *It had.*

While Janet had Forensics fingerprint the chair, the hymn book and the Bible tucked in the slot of the chair in front, Stella cast about for a raptor-like observation to toss at Janet, like meat to a lion, but the cupboard was bare.

'If March went this side to the monk's tomb, he'd have seen the organist. Name of Joy.' Janet shifted a stack of plastic barriers leaning against the pillar. 'Yet Joy says no one passed her.'

'The music stopped before I got up. It was why I got up – I was going to leave.' Stella had changed her story, earlier she'd said she didn't know when she got up.

'What made you go that way? Sorry to go on but I need to get spatials straight.' Janet began annotating her map of the abbey. 'You bypassed Joy.'

'I wasn't keen to chat.'

'That figures, she's a sharp body. No tears for March, just cross I was keeping her. I suppose it's feasible: deep in her organ, she missed March, if he did go that way.' Holding the map, Janet marked an X by the organ. 'You were leaving yet you went the opposite way to the exit.'

'I went to give Roddy the beanie.' Stella felt dizzy.

'You didn't take it with you.' Janet smiled pleasantly, as if the question was of no consequence.

'I wasn't a hundred per cent sure it was his.'

'Unless he had left his hat earlier and it wasn't him listening to the music. You don't sound a hundred per cent certain about the shadow.'

'Not all the lights were on so no, I'm not.' Stella caught the lifeline.

'No matter, we can return to that tomorrow. You'll be in shock. You did good tonight.' Janet touched Stella's elbow. 'Listen, Stella, you did your best to save March, but you had no chance. Even if the paramedics had arrived, he'd have died. The knife went through his ribcage at the back and into his heart.'

'Right.' Dwelling on this fact, Stella was not prepared for the trick question.

'What was the interval between you finding March and when you called it in?'

'Three minutes?' Stella reeled and caught the pillar for balance. 'I'm sorry, it's all a blur.'

'Don't be. This is great stuff. We'll get you home. Tony, my sergeant, will give you a lift.'

'I'd prefer to walk. Clear my head,' Stella said.

'I don't like you wandering around on your own.' Janet slipped the leaflet into her notebook.

'I'll be fine.'

'OK.' Janet didn't look convinced.

'What he said before he died was something like "Car Wo My".' Stella leaned against the pillar. 'It wasn't that, obviously.'

'*...Cah... ca... wo... my...' His eyes were fixed on Stella, wild, his pupils enlarged. He looked terrified.*

'*Car? Wo my.' Stella felt stupid, it couldn't be that hard.*

'*C-c-chh...'*

Joy brought him a mug of chamomile at the Death Café; Felicity told me beforehand that she hated the smell,' Stella added because she'd observed it.

'Did he want you to get him some perhaps? A last craving. Not heard that one before.' Janet folded her map. 'Car Wo My, chamomile – it could work I suppose?'

'No, when I asked him if he meant that his eyes said no.'

'If it becomes clearer, or you remember anything, call.' Janet passed Stella a card with the Gloucestershire Constabulary badge at the top. Stella noted with surprise that Janet was still an inspector; she hadn't moved west for promotion.

'I will.' Setting off down the nave, Stella was grateful she felt so weak or she might not have resisted the temptation to run, which would look guilty. She had reached the porch door when Janet called to her.

'One more thing, Stella.'

One more thing. Terry had taught Janet well.

'You refer to March as Roddy, not Roddy March. Odd when you didn't know him?' Janet tipped her head.

'He bled to death on my lap. I was the last person he heard before he died. So yes, I call him *Roddy*.' Stella stormed out.

She was on the main street when she got the call. '*Where's my rogan josh?*' said the corncrake voice.

Chapter Fourteen

December 1940

Sunlight washed the soot-darkened brick of Hammersmith's Coroner's Court. The sky was blue as an August day, but the bitter cold penetrating George Cotton's overcoat left no doubt it was winter.

Would spring ever come? Would there be primroses in his garden? He longed for the forsythia to bloom.

Last night Wailing Wally, as Agnes called the siren, had gone off at 6.32, with no all-clear until 5.18 a.m. The noise was terrifying, an assault on the nerves, but as he'd told June, it's our guns that make most of the racket, let's pray they bring down lots of Nazis. Agnes had been at the substation – she'd ignored his pleas and joined the Auxiliary Fire Service – another reason to fret. But never one to sit still, Agnes had great faith in Churchill, he was a decisive leader with the courage to put himself in the same danger he asked of his people. Cotton had his doubts about the man – you only had to go back to Gallipoli. Cotton was more for Clement Attlee.

Cotton had given up on vicars; as he'd told Hackett, the lead was dead. Hackett was pleased, it wouldn't help the war effort to put a man of the cloth behind bars.

The investigation had hit the buffers. Shepherd had interviewed Maple's colleagues at the dairy and tramped around Hammersmith and Shepherd's Bush showing Maple's picture in local pubs. No one at the Palais de Danse had remembered her. They had her photo flashing up in cinemas before the main picture. Vernon had remembered Maple said her fiancé was always comparing her to film stars. Vernon reckoned that was what had turned her head. A painful irony that it was not as a film star Maple had made it to the big screen. So far, nothing. Now Cotton had to find a way to get Aleck Northcote's lighter back to him without embarrassment.

'Doc's still in there.' Frank Tither, one of the coroner's officers, jerked a thumb at the mortuary when he saw Cotton. 'Go on in, George, he won't mind, seeing as it's you.'

'I'll wait.' Cotton could leave the lighter in the officers' room, but both officers kept their desks shipshape; Tither in particular had the eyes of a hawk. Cotton swore inwardly – who would credit this charade when he had a murder to solve?

Although the mortuary dealt with the dead, it was never quiet. Tiles reverberated with the bang of doors as police, undertakers and mortuary staff crashed in and out, and the rattle and clang of trolleys and trays.

'Come in, George, have a cuppa.' PC Cameron, the other coroner's officer, beckoned him.

Cotton couldn't resist the retreat into the cubbyhole where the two men worked. A coal fire in the grate overcame the razor-sharp draught from a bomb-shattered pane that, covered with hardboard, made the room more cave-like. Cotton accepted the tea which Tither 'squeezed out of the pot', and was 'honoured' with an arrowroot biscuit: '…we don't offer them to all-comers.'

Cotton got on with the two men which was good because they were Wolsey Banks's mastiffs. If they took against you then you waited your turn and that could be a while.

Tommy Cameron was a Gloucestershire man and, like Cotton, in his late forties and retained on the force for the duration of the war. Typically, he was mid-way through a story from the good old days. Son of a farm labourer, Cameron spent his boyhood snoozing in hayricks or against the side of a cow he was milking. He picked damsels from the hedgerows, his joke. He was regaling Tither with his runaway bull story. Tither rolled his eyes at Cotton, but the tale – taller with the telling – evoking a time before gas-mask training, fire-watching and the crushing blackout, meant they were only too happy to hear it again. Although Cotton was higher in rank, he envied them. Particularly this morning – what he'd give to be a pen pusher, expediting files for a boss he respected.

Wolsey Banks was the best coroner in the country. He'd fought in the Dardanelles in 1915, which made him an Eden man: *Churchill is a jackass.* Like Northcote, Banks was scrupulously fair to his deceased. Banks treated police officers with respect, unusual for his profession. Yes, right enough, Cotton reflected as he munched on the biscuit, he'd give a lot to see out his days working for Banks.

'You don't look in the pink, George.' Cameron had stopped talking and was scrutinizing him. 'You still on that prostitute's murder?'

'We have no fingerprints, no witnesses, no suspects.' Cotton didn't mention Northcote's lighter that led them nowhere except up the creek. 'She wasn't a prostitute.'

Cotton had to keep scotching the rumour; no wonder that Maple's brother Vernon Greenhill lost his rag.

'I beg to differ, George.' Aleck Northcote stood in the doorway. 'Why else was she there?' He waved away Tither's signalled offer of tea. 'Thank you, Constable, but I have to be in Hackney within the hour.'

'Could we have a quick word, Aleck?' Cotton went out to the yard with Northcote. Alberta Porter was waiting by the open driver's door. Cotton felt for her, standing in the cold, and, fleetingly, entertained the notion she and Aleck were lovers. He dismissed it – if Northcote was unfaithful, it was only to his work.

'What can I do for you, Cotton?' Gathering up the skirts of his coat, Northcote climbed into the Daimler and when Porter closed the door, he wound down the window a few inches.

Cotton felt almost worse than when he told the Greenhills Maple had been murdered, at least that was his job. Never had he had to draw attention to a senior colleague's mistake, especially Northcote, famed for never making one. Cotton braced himself to be ticked off for giving the game away about the lighter to Northcote's assistant when he telephoned his office.

He skirted the issue. 'In your report you said Maple Greenhill's vaginal passage showed evidence of frequent sexual intercourse typical of the average prostitute. Yet the Greenhill family swear blind Maple never went with men like that. Her brother was ready to clout me for hinting it. I just wanted to check if you were correct about that.'

'A man has to defend his sister's honour.' Northcote unknowingly echoed Shepherd. 'In that girl's case, I'm afraid the bird had long flown. As I say, the corpse is my bible, it renders unto me facts and facts alone. I have to dash, George, another Annie awaits. Shrapnel casualty while up to tricks in a shelter by the Homerton Hospital.'

'Maple's mother says not—' Cotton felt angry that Northcote had to call every dead woman 'Annie'.

'Horrible though it is to hear that the fair sex transgresses, I can assure you it is no *mistake*. Your victim indulged in sexual activity up until the last minutes of her life.' Northcote was also famed for disliking his opinions challenged, it was a brave man who took him on. 'Mothers believe their most delinquent child is a saint. Julia would forgive Giles the most heinous crime. However, I admire your faith in human nature.'

'All the same—'

'I cannot alter my findings to suit your theory, I expect you to understand that, *Inspector* Cotton.' A warning that the conversation was over.

'Could the striations you describe have come from the same partner?' As Maple's defender, Cotton ignored the warning and said, leaning on the Daimler's roof, 'Vernon Greenhill says his sister was engaged, we found a ring. A cheap trinket, but the jewellery box will give us a lead.'

'That's more your area, sir.' Northcote gave a wintry smile.

As the car began to roll forward, Cotton kept pace. At the turn out of the gate he thrust his hand through the gap in the window.

'You left this.' He passed Northcote the lighter.

'What the *devil...* Where did...?' Northcote braked. Cotton saw truth dawn. '*Damnation*, I must have left—'

'Call for you, George.' PC Cameron was waving from across the yard. Tipping his hat at the car, Cotton hastened away into the mortuary.

'Sir. You'll never guess.' Shepherd always shouted into the telephone.

'I'm expecting not to try.' Cotton tapped on Cameron's desk with the brim of his hat. After his hash of telling Northcote, whatever Shepherd had to say it had better be good.

'A ticket.'

'A ticket?' Cotton stood in front of the fire.

'A mending ticket for Maple's coat.' Shepherd's excitement recalled Cotton's own, now long gone. 'It has the tailor's address on the back.'

'It's a tailor's mending ticket.' Shepherd was panting, he'd run up the stairs. The lad should do physical jerks, he wasn't fit. 'It was in Maple's coat.'

'Bright's Tailoring, Chiswick High Road.' Taking the card from Shepherd, Cotton flipped it over. 'What's this say?'

'I can't tell. It's not Greenhill. Could that be a J? The letter looks like an M.' Shepherd was fired up with success.

'We searched her coat, how did we miss it?' Cotton didn't dare hope they were on to something.

'It had been stuffed into a pocket lining, had almost reached the hem. I know where this tailor is, near Turnham Green Station where my nan had a flower stall next to the *Standard* seller. That's until the war stopped her.' The cat with the cream, Shepherd was gabbling.

'Shepherd, this is excellent police work, we'll make a Robert Fabian of you yet.' Cotton put Northcote and his ruddy lighter behind him. The case was looking up.

Chapter Fifteen

2019

Jackie

'Eleven fifteen and no stalker calls today so far.' Jackie handed Bev her coffee.

'The thing about stalkers is they don't stop.' Bev was grim.

'Is she here?' The door flew open and crashed against a filing cabinet. A man, tall, gaunt, overcoat buttoned to his chin, slammed it shut behind him and stalked past the photocopier, barging into Stella's room.

'No, she isn't.' Jackie came around her desk.

'That's her coat.'

'She didn't take it with her.' Beverly was on her feet.

A distant siren grew louder. Whoop-whooping as it stopped and then started again. Light strobed across the ceiling; engines revved as vehicles made way for whatever emergency vehicle it was. When the siren sounded again it was distant once more.

'Sit there.' Jackie motioned towards Suzy's empty desk. Trying not to sound too placatory, 'We've just made a pot of tea, we've got biscuits.'

Jack Harmon. Forty-two. Underground driver on the District line's dead-late shift. Single parent of four-year old twins and, on high days and holidays, cleaning operative for Clean Slate.

Not actually a sole parent, Justin and Milly lived with Jack's ex. He'd been coming to Clean Slate every day, except yesterday which had raised Jackie's hopes that he was mending. As if Jack was her third son, she hated to see him suffer. Stella was the love of Jack's life and when she left, he'd lost his soulmate. They all had.

Jack ignored her invitation to sit. He flew about the office, touching the filing cabinets, flicking at the curling corners of cleaning product posters, pausing at the framed ISO 9001 accreditation certificate and new jobs whiteboard which was blank.

'Jack, sit down.' Beverly was sharp. To Jackie's surprise, without a word Jack did as she told him.

Whereas Jackie and Beverly had been shocked by Stella's move to Tewkesbury with Lucie May, Jack had become a ghost of his former self. He *became* his former self. Jackie was sure that after he'd stabled his train, Jack had returned to his old ways of stalking through London streets. Walking until morning. When Stella met Jack, he'd been hunting the man who, three decades earlier, had murdered his mother. Against great odds, he and Stella had caught her killer, and the hunting – *haunting* – seemed to have stopped. Now, without Stella, even Jack's truly delightful children could not chase dark clouds from his sun. Stella had made it possible for Jack to love. Her leaving had frozen his heart.

'She's stopped answering texts,' Jack wailed. 'I was wondering if I should go there.'

'Go where?' Beverly looked fierce.

'To see... to Tewkesbury. Check on Lucie. After that injury, we should monitor her.' Jack bent and retied his shoelace. 'I'll give her an update on Endora.'

'Endora's fine,' Jackie said. Endora, a budgie, had been given to Lucie by her nephew. The pair, irascible, constantly tossing nuts and figs about, were suited. 'Gary said Endora's enjoying her holiday back with him.'

'*Bad* idea.' Beverly was blunt. 'If Stella wanted to see you, she'd have said. Instead she's stopped answering your texts. Lucie keeping you up to date is doing you no good, although it does tell you that Lucie herself is just fine.'

'Lucie thinks Stella might want to come back,' Jack said.

'Since when is Lucie May a judge of character?' Jackie couldn't help herself. 'She judges everyone by their story-value.' She gave Jack his tea. Stella was the younger sister Jackie hadn't had and she loved her as she loved Jack. Yet she was clear-eyed about Stella's flaws. Like her tendency to retreat when relationships got serious, and to bandy clichés from a bad drama. Stella had told Jack she needed space. At least, as Stella once had with another lovelorn man, Jack hadn't been dumped by text.

'She sent Justin and Milly Beatrix Potter books. That's a sign,' Jack said.

'It's a sign she's thinking of *them*,' Beverly barked.

'I'm glad she's keeping in touch.' Jackie tried to catch Bev's eye to go easy, Jack was a gentle soul. 'It's hard for four-year-olds to understand.' No need to remind Jack how a small child handled loss. He'd been one when he lost his mother. Jackie reassured herself that Jack's own children had a mother. Jackie knew Bella was cross with Stella. *I said she'd leave them in the lurch.*

Justin and Milly adored Stella and, to Jackie's surprise as Stella had never wanted to be a parent, she adored them. Jackie knew about the Beatrix Potter books – out of the blue, Lucie had texted, *Don't let Jackanory get his hopes up.* Lucie was Janus by another name.

'Did Lucie tell you it was a sign?'

'No. But surely Stella would cut all ties with them if she didn't want me,' Jack said.

'That doesn't follow.' Beverly was glaring at the jobs board. Not stupid, she'd know her job was on the line, Jackie would have a word later. Stella couldn't help having what amounted to a breakdown, yet Jackie wished she had taken refuge with Graham and her so they could administer love, care and fresh food with no ready-meals or takeaways. That said, Graham took Suzie Darnell's view: never mind what Clean Slate offered customers, Stella deserved her own fresh start. What did he know? Sixty-one and in love with his new motorbike, Graham was in the midst of his own life crisis.

The phone rang and Beverly snatched it up. 'Clean Slate for a fresh start... Sorry? Oh, I'm not sure... Oh, would you know, we've *just* had a cancellation. I can get a cleaner to you tomorrow.'

A real call. Jackie could have kissed Bev for not sounding desperate.

'This woman's letting her flat, she wants deep cleaning, including carpets.' Beverly paused. 'That was Stella's favourite kind of job.'

'Yes, Stella loved deep cleaning.' Anxious, Jackie glanced at Jack who must see the deep-cleaning request as a portent, but his expression was granite.

He said, '*Loves*, not loved. Stella isn't dead.'

A piercing police siren, this time from inside the room, made them all jump.

'Lucie's texted.' Jack waved his phone. Lucie had installed her ringtone on Jack and Stella's phones. At her most generous, Jackie had to admit the seventy-plus-year-old was a bit of a card. 'This is crazy – Stella's on the news. She found a body.' Tea splashed on the carpet tiles as Jack leapt up. 'Lucie says, "We have a new case! Jackeroo, this is your moment, get here now!"'

'Maybe wait until Stella—' Jackie was talking to a closing door as Jack's footsteps clattered down the stairs to the street.

Chapter Sixteen

2019

Stella

Watery sunlight drifting between drab curtains glanced off foil cartons, two glasses and a bottle of Merlot, empty now, on a coffee table. One glass, tipped on its side, was blocked from rolling onto the threadbare carpet by the splayed arm of a corkscrew.

Curled up on a leather sofa, a diminutive champagne-coloured poodle snoozed, chin resting on a stuffed rat whose greyed fabric indicated he was the dog's favoured companion. The scene – tossed cushions, the contents of an upended waste-paper basket, screws of paper, several scrunched-up packets that had contained dried figs scattered on the carpet – suggested the aftermath of an alcohol-fuelled fight.

The dog's ears pricked. A woman, tall and perhaps too thin, in workaday jeans, a fraying Christmas jumper (reindeer whose antlers reached her shoulders), black police issue boots, stomped into the room. Pushing back her hair, Stella Darnell viewed the mess with a critical eye then, taking the bin bag snagged in the back pocket of her jeans, set about clearing up.

The poodle, ecstatic to have company, danced around Stella on his hind legs as she moved about. Stopping to scruffle

Stanley's ears, she had soon restored order. Plumped cushions were arranged on the sofa. Stella stacked the takeaway dishes and tipped them into the bag. As everyone in the Clean Slate office was saying at that very moment, Stella Darnell was never happier than when tackling a mess.

In the kitchen Stella cut a wedge of dog food from a plastic container, mashed it and placed the bowl on a mat patterned with paws.

'Stanley, breakfast.' 'Breakfast' was a key word in Stanley's relatively extensive vocabulary and the dance became dervish-like. As Stella lowered the bowl, he abruptly sat down by the mat. Pummelling her aching temple, Stella commanded 'Release'. Leaving Stanley to his food, she wandered back to the living room.

Lucie had drunk most of the bottle. Stella's headache was due to tossing and turning for what remained of the night. She had kept seeing Roddy March beside the cadaver tomb. The coppery smell, his expression, soft locks of hair when she stroked it from his face. Stella had shouted at Janet because for Janet, Roddy's murder was simply a case to be solved. For Stella it was more profound. All she could think was, Roddy March had been alive – and annoying – and now he was dead.

Roddy's murder had kept Stella awake, but so had her conscience. She had told Lucie about the murder. Ultimately Lucie would have found out, a BBC Breaking News alert had come in at two thirty – *Man found dead in Tewkesbury Abbey* – but that wouldn't have been down to Stella spilling the beans.

After she'd accepted Auntie Lucie's prescription of a hot shower, capitulated to wearing one of Lucie's panda-bear leisure suits and drunk a glass of Merlot, Stella had basically run off at the mouth. She gave the veteran tabloid reporter the full story.

'Of course, off the record, Sherlock,' Lucie had cooed. Hours later – the last chimes of the abbey Stella remembered were 3 a.m. – Lucie started a new notebook.

Coshed by drowsiness, Stella had begun clearing up until Lucy shooed her to bed. 'I've got this, honey-bunch.'

Now, hunched on the sofa, Stanley on her lap licking his toes, Stella fretted about exactly what Lucie had 'got'. Not the clearing up, but that suited Stella.

Stella hadn't told Lucie the SIO was Janet, that would have definitely put flames to petrol. In Hammersmith, where Lucie was chief crime reporter on the *Chronicle*, Lucie had claimed Janet was jealous of her being with Terry. Lucie was as convinced as Stella's mother that Terry and Janet had been an item. She took it personally when Janet embargoed her stories or didn't pick her to ask a question at press briefings.

Some forty years ago, in the heat of separation from Stella's mother, propelled by a broken heart Terry had had an affair with Lucie. For him it was an affair on the rebound; for Lucie – self-styled truth warrior – it had been love.

It wouldn't be personal, Stella knew. It riled all police detectives when journalists subjugated reality for hypotheticals. When facts failed to fit her stories, Lucie defaulted to fiction. Yet Janet wouldn't allow her personal feelings to get in the way of her work. Lucie, on the other hand, gave resentments and animosities free rein.

Stella had no qualms about keeping back from Lucie that Janet was in Tewkesbury, but she should have told Janet that, convalescing from a head injury, Lucie May was Stella's flatmate.

Two months ago, Stella's friends – and Jack – had deemed it ludicrous that Stella would share a flat with Lucie. Jackie and Beverly warned Stella that money and domestics were always the stumbling blocks. Stella's mum, despite having left Terry, had been jealous that he'd taken up with Lucie and now told Stella that 'Lucie May will skin you alive'.

However, Stella and Lucie had surprised everyone by getting on famously. Stella accepted that Lucie's fulsome offers to shop, cook and clean never translated into deed. Stella preferred to do these tasks herself. Stella's own idea of cooking was an array of ready meals – shepherd, cottage and fish pies with frozen peas as a concession to Jackie's frequent suggestions that Stella eat more greens. Every week, Lucie treated them to a takeaway. This week, Indian.

Stella dreaded the day when, fully recovered, Lucie must inevitably return to London. Stella had no plans to go back, but in the last weeks distantly recognized that she liked life in Tewksbury because Lucie was there too. She had tried encouraging Lucie to stop researching and actually begin writing her true-crime bestseller. But, easily side-tracked by other stories or another avenue of research, Lucie hadn't progressed to page one. If Stella had planned a way of keeping Lucie in Tewkesbury, nothing was more effective than telling her about Roddy March's murder.

Stella placed her empty mug on a Tewkesbury Abbey coaster and going into Google Play Store, she downloaded a podcast app.

Her brain a fug, Stella had forgotten the title of the podcast and was trying to remember when Lucie breezed in on wafts of lavender bath gel and the dry shampoo she used regardless of the all-body power shower. In her combats and a combat jacket not unlike Roddy March's, Lucie operated as if reporting from a war-zone, hence dry shampoo. Garlanded with the Bluetooth earbuds that were a permanent accessory, she clutched a bag of figs in one hand, phone in the other.

'There's a press conference at 11 a.m., gotta be there.'

'No.' Stella hadn't heard Lucie get up. Since Janet had called her observant, Stella was observing how much she failed to observe. 'You can't let Janet see you here.' *Damn, that was the cat out of the bag.*

'Janet? No don't tell me.' The penny had dropped.

'Don't rock the boat,' Stella said. 'I intend to do just that. *Imagine* her face,' Lucie cackled.

Stella felt dread pump through her veins. Janet already had Stella as a suspect; how much worse when she discovered Stella had lied, if by omission, about Lucie? Stella uttered the first thing that entered her head and the last thing she meant to say.

'Janet is trusting me with stuff about the case that she would never tell any other reporter. She's treating me like Terry. If she sees you, she'll cut me out.'

'Wise idea.' Lucie was fiddling with her phone. 'I'll stay undercover for now.'

'I can't remember the name of Roddy's podcast.' Stella diverted Lucie in case she changed her mind.

'*The Distant Dead.*' You can't pull the wool over that kid's eyes. 'I started listening last night, but fell asleep. Draw your own conclusion.'

'Let's listen now.' Stella connected her phone to the Bluetooth speaker Jack had given her after one of their cases.

'He has three subscribers. I'm betting, mum, dad and the cat.' Lucie tapped at her phone screen. 'There, now he has four.' She settled into the creaky old recliner she had called her cockpit and which, feet pointing upwards, she rarely left.

'One of the subscribers could have murdered Roddy's murderer,' Stella said.

'I *like* that notion. Murderers can be arrogant, but pretty stupid to leave a digital trail.' Lucie fussed with her notebook. 'You said March was full of himself; men like that get on people's tits. The few minutes I heard confirmed that. He makes drama out of a non-event.' Chattering happily, Lucie nipped off the end of a fig from her new bag.

'I didn't say he was full of... he was just...' *What had Roddy been?*

'Let us sit comfortably and listen.' Lucie nestled in her cockpit.

'This podcast contains serious and graphically violent scenes. If you are affected by anything you have heard, contact your nearest crisis centre. Be aware I have been prepared to go the distance in my quest for truth...'

Stella was unprepared for the shock of Roddy's voice coming through the speaker almost if he was in the room. Whereas at the Death Café Roddy had rattled on about his podcast, now thanking the design company who had sponsored the series, he was ponderous, each word lined up after the other. Also, he sounded Australian.

'I'm Roddy March and you're listening to *The Distant Dead*. Over the next weeks I will take you through my investigation of a chain of brutal, callous murders that span generations. As the March hare I chase scents until I catch the answer...'

'He mixes metaphors good enough to drink. Oh, and hares don't chase they are chased,' Lucie scoffed. 'You didn't mention he was an Aussie.'

'He didn't talk like that last night.'

'Some of the best true-crime podcasts come from down under. March was after a global audience. Shame he sounds like a satnav.' Lucie twirled a fig on its stem.

'I begin with the brutal slaying of Professor Aleck Xavier Northcote, Home Office pathologist, in the sitting room of his home in Tewkesbury on a cold November night in 1963. But wait on, Northcote's death was the effect, not the cause.' A pause was filled with piano music that must be intended to heighten a sense of suspense. 'Why is this date familiar? Older listeners will recall Friday the twenty-second of November as the day President John F. Kennedy was assassinated in Dallas, Texas. Meanwhile, in the ancient market town of Tewkesbury, the inhabitants woke up on Saturday the twenty-third to the unbelievable news that there was A. Murderer. At Large.'

'Honest to God, March's delivery. Could. Make. *Me*. A. Murderer.' Lucie munched on her fig.

'Widowed, his grown-up son living in London, his housekeeper out at the cinema, Professor Sir Aleck Northcote was alone in his grand house hard by the River Severn. Julia, his wife, unable to handle the cruel privations of the war, blackout, constant air raids, rationing, had hung herself twenty-odd years earlier...'

'*Hanged*, not hung,' Lucie said.

'The Northcotes, prominent auctioneers, had owned the house in Tewkesbury set in the English county of Gloucestershire for centuries. A picturesque market town where people existed happily, going about their business. *Or did they?* Aleck had abandoned business for his own pleasure: pathology. From the mid-thirties, now living in an equally big house in London, Julia and Aleck were strictly weekenders. Some of you will have heard, if not of the murdered pathologist, then of the Quarry Murders case in 1941 and the Bodies in the Basement after the war in 1951.' More piano music. 'Sir Aleck was more used to examining a corpse than to being that corpse himself. I'm Roddy March and you're listening to *The Distant Dead*.'

'*Kinell*,' Lucie scoffed. 'These podcasters haven't an iota of journalistic training. They think all you need is a tape recorder and a bedroom.'

Stella knew podcasts were one of Lucie's hobby-horse gripes. Another horse being that training was pointless: 'the only way to learn is on the job.' Lucie was comfortable with holding two opposing views.

'Northcote's murder was solved and his murderer judiciously hung in April 1964. The Northcote case gathered dust in police archives, solved, signed and sealed. What's the mystery you could ask?' The piano.

'I could ask,' Lucie said. '*Hanged*.'

'Many bad books have been published about Northcote's murder. Lots of sensational inaccuracies, but the biggest is that no one knew the real killer. What was the truth of what went on in that cavernous house on that stormy November night? No one has questioned the judge's verdict. Until. Now.'

'Another pot-boiler rushed out to catch the zeitgeist while it's bubbling on the stove.' Lucie thought nothing of mixing her own metaphors. Happier talking than writing, Stella was increasingly certain Roddy's murder was to be Lucie's latest excuse for abandoning her own true-crime book.

'...prove to you that the man hung on the morning of the eighteenth of May at HMP Pentonville – only weeks before the end of capital punishment in Great Britain – was as innocent as the spring day on which his neck was snapped. I will show that, after the supposed killer left Cloisters House, Professor Northcote got another visitor. His. Murderer.'

'Da da da *dah*. Actually the last hanging in Britain was on the sixteenth of December 1969 so that's tosh for starters. ' Lucie sang as she ripped the top off another fig. 'Sadly, that style works, listeners lap it up. No editor to correct gigantic holes in his grammar.' Lucie often railed against her editor at the *Chronicle*.

'That evening, when Northcote was opening the door to his visitor, most Brits were glued to their TVs reeling from the death of America's president. If Northcote shouted for help, his cry went unheard. There was no witness. Or. Was. There?'

As he had at the Death Café, March promised to reveal the name of the murderer at the end of the series. 'This is a living podcast, I'm unearthing secrets by the minute and as I do, I will share them with you. I don't know how many episodes this will take, but please come with me on what will definitely be a bumpy ride... Giles Northcote was the Northcotes' only child – could the great man have been slain by a boy he'd dandled in his arms over twenty-five years earlier? That the professor's middle name of Xavier, like everything I tell you, is a brick in the wall of this fifty-year-old mystery. Like so many deaths, the accessories are clues. Holmes had his pipe, we have a cigarette lighter, a tailor's ticket and... well, why not wait and see?'

'I love how he compares himself to Sherlock Holmes.' Lucie was busy writing in her notebook as Roddy had the night before. 'No shame.'

'You call me Sherlock,' Stella said.

'A fair comparison.'

Stella was glad that, engrossed in her notes, Lucie didn't see her struggle not to smile. Lucie was a harsh judge, so that was a compliment.

'We know that Giles Northcote called his father earlier that Friday requesting to see him. The renowned professor knew his son's reason for coming was not filial affection. We know Aleck poured Giles at least one whisky; Giles's fingerprints were on a glass and the decanter. In his police statement Giles confirmed this as he admitted tapping Northcote Senior for a loan to pay off a substantial gambling debt. His father refused. Giles claims he "took this on the chin". On his return to London, he got drunk and didn't waken until noon on the Saturday to headlines in the papers that Kennedy was dead. And in smaller print how his own father had been bludgeoned to a pulp with a poker. Giles's girlfriend had dumped him so, alone in his flat, no one supported his alibi. Scotland Yard found Giles's smudged thumbprint on the poker and his fate was sealed by the discovery of a silver cup Giles had pinched from his father and hidden in a cupboard.

'But what if Giles was cool with his father's refusal of money? The silver cup was worth five hundred pounds which easily covered his debt. Giles claimed he'd raked the fire with the poker, and maybe that's all he used it for. Why would he kill the golden goose?'

'To benefit from the will, one would suppose, young March,' Lucie said.

'If Giles did kill him, he did nothing to cover his tracks.' Stella took down notes as Roddy gave more background.

Giles Hugh Northcote, twenty-six, single, no children. Expelled from Eton for going to the races. This surprised Stella, she'd rather expected it to be mandatory curriculum to know about horses. Giles was 'booted out' of the army for being drunk on duty while serving in Aden, now Yemen, then a British Protectorate. His voice deepening, Roddy said, 'Aleck was alive when his son left. Not long after there came another knock on the door and, expecting Giles come back to plead, Northcote answered it. He admitted his visitor. It's by this unknown person's hand that the pathologist sustained the ugly and vicious attack that ended his illustrious life.'

'Save us.' Lucie pressed a button on the recliner and her feet went up several inches.

'Aleck drags himself to the hall telephone but, fixed to the wall, he can't reach it. The housekeeper comes back from the cinema and notices the receiver dangling. Then she sees her master in a pool of blood on the hall floor. Professor Sir Aleck Northcote died the way he'd lived, a mutilated corpse on a mortuary slab.' More piano chords then Roddy said, 'Check out our website for photos and pics of the key players. Join in the conversation: do you know about this case? Have you spotted an anomaly?'

'Mortuary slab. Catchy notion until you pick it apart,' Lucie commented. 'And he can't keep to one tense. What a dog's breakfast.'

'I was reading that some podcasts have got people out of prison.' Stella saw a dog's breakfast as a good thing.

'Now let's turn back the clock to the nineteen thirties when Aleck is plain Dr Northcote but already swarming the pole. His unrivalled knowledge of contusions has just done for the Brandy Snap Strangler.'

Stella wished they could turn the clock back. Clive's insistence that time was a concept should mean Roddy was still alive. Turn it further back and she hadn't gone to the Death Café nor been frightened on a country lane. *She and Jack were still together.*

'Armchair forensic specialists schooled on box sets and podcasts, we're alert to fake news. But imagine a world in which one man can inspire such veneration that a twitch of his finger sways a jury to hang a man they should let walk free. Northcote was that man. As you'd expect, such a man gains enemies. *Who? Were. They?*

'First up, Northcote's colleague and arch-rival Gerald Bradman. Known amongst his colleagues as the Butcher, Bradman blagged his way through autopsies and trials. More than once Northcote was brought in to do a second autopsy. Incidentally, a nasty twist is that the pathologist who cut open

Northcote and his son after their deaths was none other than the Butcher. With Northcote gone, Bradman stepped into his shoes.

'Did Professor Bradman kill his rival? Supposedly in the clear, he had signed into his club on that cold rainy night in November. A taxi driver was driving him home to his house in Harley Street at the same moment as Northcote's housekeeper found Northcote dead. But never make an assumption. In episode two we will examine this alibi with the same level of detail that Northcote himself would apply…'

Was Stella someone's enemy? When she walked out on her own life, she had walked out on other lives too. Jack. Everyone at Clean Slate. Her mother and, although he lived in Sydney, her brother too. The piano music broke into her musing.

'…the flipside of respect and awe is envy and hate…'

'Wrong. It's disrespect and disdain.' Lucie chomped on a fig.

'Police arrested Giles the next afternoon at the Cheltenham races where he won more than enough to pay off his debts without selling that cup. Giles was found guilty. After the frenzied attack, the judge said Giles had coolly replaced the poker with the other fire irons and had the presence of mind to destroy his bloodstained garments. I'll leave you to spot the double irony.'

Stella couldn't spot double anything, nor by the look on her face could Lucie.

'Ponder how, given the alcohol Giles had put away at his father's and later at his flat, he was capable of so comprehensively disposing of bloodied clothes? How did Giles travel unnoticed from Tewkesbury to London, in bloodstained clothes? And winding back, what fit twenty-six-year-old lets his elderly dad hop up to the fire with the poker? Giles took that task for himself, ergo fingerprints on the poker…'

'A twenty-six-year-old bloke happy to nick his dad's silverware and squeeze him for a few quid, that's who,' Lucie said.

'…was hung on circumstantial evidence. Fingerprints, and that the housekeeper opened the door to him as she left for the cinema…'

'Hung? Giles wasn't a ham, for God's sake.' Lucie was getting spiteful.

'…Let's look at this fingerprint. It was the print for a right thumb on the poker. Giles Northcote was left-handed. Motive? Yes, Giles would inherit, but he knew that his father had willed his son got nothing until he reached thirty-five. Nine years away. Aleck Northcote was worth more to his son alive. In summary, milud, the trial was a car-crash…'

'I skimmed the first pot-boiler that was out of the trap, *Hate Father Hate Son*.' Lucie waved her leather-bound Kindle at Stella. 'In it, Giles's barrister, a James Dudeney, tells the author that in his teens, Giles hurt his left arm in a rowing accident on the Thames, so he learnt to compensate with his right. March never checked. Honest to God, the boneless wonders who churn out these podcast-dreadfuls never do the legwork.' Lucie subsided into her cockpit.

'All the same, a poker isn't so heavy. Isn't it likely Giles's instinct would have been to use his left? He may not have touched the fire and if he did kill his father then it was probably in the heat of the moment,' Stella said.

'True, oh queen,' Lucie said. 'March should have got you on board. Pose an argument, counter. Get your listeners sure it's red, then reveal it's yellow.'

'This murder upended every convention about how true-crime stories usually unfold.' Roddy went on, 'Where how a murder investigation is meant to go turns a somersault. Where each break in the investigation appears to raise more questions than it answers. Northcote's murder is the first clue in a story that will not go the way you expect. By the end, you will learn the identity of Sir Aleck's other visitor on that fateful winter's night.

'A visitor no one feared, to whom no one attributed evil. That person went to Cloisters House with only one purpose. Murder.'

More piano, then Roddy again, '*The Distant Dead* is brought to you by March Hare Productions. I'm Roddy March and you're listening to *The Distant Dead.*'

'Tosh and *tosher*. I bet March had no idea who did it.' Lucie gnashed at a fig.

Roddy's podcast did have a third-rate feel, sensational with overblown emphasis to keep the listeners' interest. Recalling his scared expression, his struggle to speak as he died in her arms, Stella realized she'd wanted his podcast to be a legacy, a great thing to remember him by.

Janet had said Stella's experience was traumatic, but Stella diminished it; lots of people went through much worse. Suddenly she felt crushed by a terrible sensation in her abdomen, raw grief for a man she'd hardly known. At the end of the only episode of his podcast that there would ever be, Stella felt as if Roddy March had died all over again. *Now was only silence.*

Chapter Seventeen

December 1940

'A thirty-tonner hit three shops and pulverized the flats above.' The ARP warden let them through the safety barrier. 'No casualties, but then what happens? The all-clear goes and that bloody thing only smashes into the hole.'

'Fatalities?' Cotton gazed down at the mangle of twisted metal scattered with bricks and burnt timber nose first in the crater. Only the swan was visible of a Swan Vesta advert on the side of the 27 bus which had never reached Highgate.

'Female clippie, four passengers at the front downstairs, a babbie and the mother on the top deck...' Whatever the warden said next was lost as a District line train clattered over the viaduct.

Cotton reckoned more died in blackout accidents, fires and structural collapse than by direct hits from the Luftwaffe's Blitzkrieg.

'Hey you.' The warden was distracted by an Express Dairies float negotiating the edge of what must be a twenty-foot drop. Cotton felt triumph as the float made it to the other side and, engine whining, trundled away. ARPs were jumped-up idiots acting like police.

Maple worked for Express Dairies.

Cotton and Shepherd trod across rubble and around the corner to Turnham Green station. They dodged women, some lugging string bags that bulged with tins of ham, vegetables, parcels of meat, others peering into shop windows. Some of the fronts were rimmed with cotton wool snow and adorned with tinsel, baubles and plaster Father Christmases. It could be a usual winter's day before Christmas. Cotton had forgotten what was usual. This year June was having Christmas lunch with her fiancé's family, it would be just him and Agnes. At least they would all have *Aladdin* together.

The J. Sainsbury next door to a boarded-up violin-maker's said *Business as Usual*. Agnes said those three words summed up the British spirit. Cotton didn't fight her, although his notion of the British spirit was that represented by the looters who stripped homes bare like dogs tearing at a carcass.

Beyond, a dolls' hospital was intact as, Cotton was thankful to see, was Bright's Tailoring. In the last months he'd lost count of the times he'd gone to see a suspect or interview a victim, only to be directed to the morgue.

After the glassy stares of the – presumably 'cured' – dolls in the window of the dolls' hospital, came the life-size manikins displayed at the tailor's. All done up in garments dearer than anything Cotton could afford.

Since he was the one who found the ticket, Cotton let Shepherd take the lead.

A black cat with white-booted paws at the foot of a dummy in an evening dress scrutinized them through the glass before curling back into a ball.

A man in a Sunday best suit was switching the sign to 'Closed', but seeing them, pulled open the door.

'How can I help, gentlemen?' His grizzled hair was thinning, deep lines scored sallow cheeks either side of a smiling mouth.

'Mr Bright?' Shepherd reached for his badge, while Cotton guessed from Bright's overeager manner that Bright already knew they were police. He ushered them in and shut the door.

The low-ceilinged room was lit by strong bulbs in a line behind the counter, like an actor's dressing room in the pictures. A ceramic bar fire glowed in one corner. Along one wall bolts of material were slotted into pigeonholes. Cotton decided that the rack of dresses and suits shrouded in tissue paper could be bodies in an abattoir. Agnes would say, you would, wouldn't you.

'Is there a problem?' The tailor, needlepoint-neat, his hair cut short back and sides, regarded them over wire spectacles. Cotton saw a resemblance to Humphrey Bogart and had no doubt that women – Maple? – did too.

'Can I see your papers?' Shepherd's no-messing tone suggested he too was on the case. He shot his cuffs, perhaps to appear less off the peg, and to let Bright know if he'd murdered Maple Greenhill, they were on to him.

'I'm a legal Jewish refugee. I came here in 1933, we saw what was coming with Hitler even before he was made chancellor. I am *British* now.' He spoke with a lilting foreign accent that Cotton found pleasant to the ear.

Cotton caught the name on the ID that Bright produced. Joseph Ivan Bright. Cotton's mother had been Jewish which made Cotton and his brother Joe Jewish too. But she'd drummed into them that they were Londoners, born and bred. Cotton's Uncle John was in the Black Shirts. He'd been decapitated leaning out of a train window shouting obscenities on the day war was declared. God's ways weren't so mysterious after all.

'Who is the owner of the item of clothing referred to on this ticket?' Shepherd asked stiffly. He slid the ticket across the counter.

Bright lifted his glasses and examined it. 'Ah yes. A tear in the sleeve. She caught it on a hook, as I remember. Unfortunately, she blamed it on the material, but it had torn, it was not frayed. As I do, I mended it without fuss. Her husband collected it, as a surprise, so he didn't have the ticket.' Bright added, 'After I mended the rip, you couldn't tell.'

Cotton liked a man who made no bones about his skills.

Northcote was like that. Cotton's mother used to say, if you couldn't stand up for yourself in a high wind you deserved to be knocked over. Bright wasn't exaggerating, the coat had looked good as new.

'Who was her husband?' Was he Maple's fancy man?

Before Bright could answer they were all startled by the bell above the door as a woman, trim in an astrakhan coat like the coat in the window, burst into the shop.

'Mr Bright, I was sure I'd missed you. I've searched high and low for that damned ticket, turned the house…' Seeing Shepherd and Cotton the woman faltered. 'Do excuse me, I didn't see you had customers.'

'How extraordinary, madam, we have it.' Bright held up the ticket. 'It is not lost. The police have this minute returned it.'

'The police?' The woman blanched. Cotton was used to people looking guilty when they discovered he was a police officer, but rarely were they of this woman's class, nudging forty and a couple of rungs below royalty.

No one was too wealthy to murder. Cotton paid the brim of his hat through his fingers as a theory formed.

Wife discovers husband has mistress. Wife arranges to meet Maple in the empty house and, trusting, Maple goes there. Sensing no threat, she turns her back and is strangled from behind. In the struggle the ticket falls out of wife's handbag. That didn't work, Cotton interrupted himself. *Ticket in pocket. Husband has no idea when he picks up the coat and, on a whim, thinking Maple would look fine in it, gives it to her. Maple finds ticket, so knows coat belonged to her lover's wife. He's married. Knowing she will die, Maple tucks ticket in coat cuff to tell police that her killer is the wife. Wife sees Maple is wearing her coat, goes mad, kills her.*

'Who might you be, madam?' Cotton stepped forward.

'Inspector, this is my best customer.' Bright came around the counter, talking as if they were meeting at a tea party. 'This is Mrs Northcote.'

Cotton heard the woman's name and his theory fell apart.

★ ★ ★

'I'm too old for pantomimes.' June was sulking over her mushroom soup. 'Gerry took me to the new Humphrey Bogart at the Warner cinema, a proper grown-up picture .'

'For goodness' sake, June, proper grown-ups can be kiddies sometimes. Try not to be ungrateful, Poppet, these days, we're none of us too old for a good laugh.' Agnes laid her hand over Cotton's on what she'd declared was a lovely white tablecloth. 'I'm in heaven, Georgie.'

George's Christmas treat – *Blitzmas* the papers were calling it – the matinee of *Aladdin and his Wonderful Lamp* at the Coliseum followed by a slap-up meal in Lyons' on Oxford Street – the Mountview Café, no less – hadn't impressed June. His girl was growing up. Did his little girl have secrets like Maple Greenhill? Not likely, and the diamond ring on her finger wasn't a Woolworth's bargain.

All afternoon, diverted by the pantomime, falling about at jokes about air-raid sirens and tripping over the bed in blackout, Cotton had been briefly transported from Maple's murder. It was back with a vengeance and, appetite gone, Cotton forced his soup down.

'Penny for 'em, love?' Agnes was tipping her soup plate away to get the last drop. The soup tasted bland and watery – her calling it heaven put a gloss on it, she could make better at home. 'It's that poor Maple, isn't it?'

'Sorry.' He shouldn't mention work when they were having a night on the town.

They'd been married a month when Agnes had persuaded him to tell her about his day. He'd wanted to keep from her the man's rotting body strung from his bedroom door in an Earl's Court mansion block; the two kiddies gassed by their father because his wife was leaving him. Cotton didn't want Agnes to have in her mind the pictures which haunted his.

'If I'm going to be a proper wife, I must share everything,' she'd insisted.

In twenty-two years of marriage, Agnes had listened to stories of murder, suicide, traffic collisions, violent burglaries. She'd walked with him into his seamy underworld. Agnes truly was his better half.

So, when Cotton told Agnes about Maple Greenhill, he'd left nothing out. How Maple had lain twisted on a rug, her arm flung wide as if, even as her soul left her, she was pointing to her murderer. He had told Agnes about the mending ticket, the coat, the lighter. He stopped as something else occurred

'He had scratches on his arms, from gardening, he said.' Cotton wiped his hands down his face, 'Aleck's never been a gardener, he always says it's Julia with the green fingers.'

'Shocking. Poor lamb, she must have fought for her life. Now it's her mum and dad I feel for. Those pictures in the *Express* showed her as a nice-looking girl. If I lost June that would be me done with. I'd tell the Nazis, do what you like you can't hurt me.' Agnes brushed the back of her hand on June's cheek.

'I can look after myself and it won't be me being strangled, I'm not a prostitute.' June recoiled from Agnes's hand.

It seemed to Cotton the room fell silent at the word. But with the quartet – playing some Fats Waller tune – and the murmur of other diners, no one had heard. He expected, too, that the pillars encircled with lily-shaped lamps and circular lights in the high ceiling acted as baffles.

'Maple wasn't a prostitute.' He was patient. 'She was engaged to her sweetheart like you are.'

'Not like me at all.' June clattered down her spoon. 'If Gerry took me to a dance hall, he'd walk me to my door.'

They looked at their laps while the Nippy took their plates away and brought the main course: Empire beef, potatoes and carrots. Then Christmas pudding with carrots substituting fruit. Agnes said, 'Everything tastes better when someone else has cooked it.'

Cotton could only think that one thing worse than failing to solve a murder was when you had solved it and the solution was worse than not knowing.

'We should go. I don't want to be caught in the St Martin's Lane shelter, it smells.' June broke into his thoughts. Cotton waved for the bill.

'You always say the solution to the murder is there if you do the legwork.' Agnes might have second sight.

'If I forget, you remind me.' Cotton smiled at his wife. Never in his life had it occurred to him to have an affair. Agnes was everything.

'Dad.' Out in the cold street, taking his arm, June gave him a sheepish smile. 'Gerry never takes me to places like this, he says now we're engaged we've got to save.' She kissed him on the cheek. 'Thanks for a lovely evening.'

'Gerry's a sensible chap. 'Sides, if it's not down to your old dad to treat his two best girls once in a while, what's he for?'

'That's better.' Agnes did up her coat. Cotton saw the tear in her sleeve from a nail. Since she'd joined the AFS, Agnes neglected herself. There was that astrakhan coat in Bright's window. Hang the expense. It must be hers.

Waiting on the Underground platform, already packed with shelterers, Cotton kept his family close. Some of the public were no better than the Nazis.

On the occasions when scraps of cloth or a stray button solved a murder, Cotton had raised his pint of London Pride to there being one villain fewer in London. Never more than now did Cotton wish he could be Cameron or Tither working in the coroner's officers' cosy room at Hammersmith's mortuary. Or that Maple's murderer was a vicar in the grip of the devil. Nothing in his career had prepared George Cotton for what he had to do next.

Chapter Eighteen

2019

Stella

At a prearranged meeting, arrive first. At the moment the nominal enters, before they adopt a social mask, watch them. In that flicker of a second, they will inevitably reveal themselves. Stella's dad had taught her to choose a position with a wide-angle view that included entrances and other exits.

Stella arrived at 9.50 a.m. at the Abbey Gardens teashop and bagged a corner seat with a view of the door and the servery. Everything had returned to normal: tables and chairs at which sat customers eating pastries and drinking coffee. Occasional snatches of conversation told Stella that only one topic was being discussed. The murder of Roddy March.

Stella had been surprised to discover that, since the abbey was closed, the teashop had remained open. But Janet said it wasn't a crime scene and besides, her team had taken statements from all the Death Café attendees.

When Janet had suggested meeting at the teashop, Stella had panicked. Was the plan to get her relaxed then pounce with a killer question? Stella had told Lucie she had an extra cleaning shift at the teashop to prevent Lucie tagging along, or lurking on the yew path. Stella hadn't told Lucie the cleaning company had cancelled her shifts. Naturally, the manager had said, Stella would need to recover from finding a body in the abbey. Code for 'not tainting the company name with murder', Stella had been let go.

Recalling last night's Death Café, Stella felt far from relaxed. She was riddled with guilt. She had not told Janet that Lucie was in town and she *had* told Lucie information that, since it hadn't been reported, Janet must be withholding. Roddy March's dying words. Word. Stella had told Lucie it had sounded like 'chamomile'. Lucie said Stella had misheard. Stella felt sick at the memory of Roddy's terrible efforts to make her understand. He had died knowing she had not got it.

Lucie had promised Stella not to be at the 11 a.m. press conference with the police, but Lucie's promises had a short use-by date.

Although the fire was lit, damp from the rain, Stella was trembling and cold.

Janet locked eyes with Stella as soon as she walked in. Terry never said what to do if the nominal you were meeting was a police officer.

Mindful of not engaging with props when she was shaking, Stella refused coffee then changed her mind. A drink would be warming and perhaps it was better to have something to do with her hands.

'After last night we both need blood sugar.' Janet returned with a tray of coffees and a chocolate brownie with two forks. 'I can't tell you how relieved I was when my sergeant gave your name as the witness. I said to myself, there can only be one Stella Darnell, detective extraordinaire.'

'I'm a cleaner.' Stella took a sip of coffee. She wanted nothing to do with murder.

'Don't get me wrong, once the team have got over my not being the bloke who just retired, they'll shape up. But it's all so by-the-book – not like with Terry or his daughter.' She grinned at Stella.

'Terry worked by the book,' Stella said.

'Terry made the rules work for him. Think how he got to grips with PACE. Others moaned it was a show-stopper, but not your dad – he made the pros work for the cons. At least I can discount you as a suspect.' She divided the brownie in half.

'I'm not a suspect?' Stella spluttered coffee.

'*Duh*. No?' Janet attacked her half of the brownie with the side of her fork. A hand over her mouth she went on, 'Sure, you had means, but when and where did you dispose of the weapon? You were soaked in March's blood, but the stains were the result of staunching his stab wound, not spatter from an attack. Motive? Aside from meeting March a couple of times, we can't find evidence you knew the guy. OK, so the timing is right, March was stabbed just before you – *allegedly* – found him, but I know this because you told me yourself. You could have lied and said you got there later.' Janet flipped through her notebook. 'Stella, when you commit a murder it will be perfect.'

'You've ruled me out with an argument that rules me in,' Stella said. 'What if this *is* my perfect murder?'

'Help me out here – rule yourself out. I'm ducking under the thin blue line because I need your eyes, ears and definitely your brain. *Eat*.' Janet pushed across the other half of brownie. 'Were he here running this, Terry would be talking to you.'

Looking around the tearoom, Stella imagined the Death Café group around the table, faces in shadow. Since her dad's death, she had understood he'd respected her. Nowadays this feeling was mutual. She had found a relationship with Terry after his death. On the day before he died, Terry had rung her for help on a case, but she'd changed her number and forgotten to tell him.

Janet had had Terry's back. Stella owed her.

'Honestly, Stella, don't let me down. I need you as my sanity check. I leave London for a slower pace and find myself locked in an Agatha Christie novel.'

'Not sure how I can help.' Reaching into her rucksack, Stella got out her own – *pretend* – police notebook.

'You are my star witness. Tell me anything and everything that comes to mind about this creepy death group you've joined.' Janet rested her elbows on the table.

'OK, so there were seven of us there. Including me.' On a clean page, Stella drew a circle marked with the names of each participant. Roddy on her left, the nice landlady Gladys Wren, Andrea the abbey gardener, then Clive who had actually known the murdered Professor Northcote, then Joy the organist. Felicity had been on Roddy's left. Stella slid the book across the table to Janet.

'You've put March close to you, was that deliberate?' Janet took a picture of the diagram on her phone.

'I didn't mean to, but actually he did sit nearer to me than anyone else did around the table.'

'To hear Mrs Wren, first name Gladys, you'd think the sun shone of out March's everything.' Janet sat back with her coffee. 'He'd take her shopping, do the bins, sit up drinking sherry which, Roderick, as she called him, always brought himself. Such a lovely fella. He told her he wasn't the marrying kind, I said get away with you.'

'They never said they knew each other, although I did notice Gladys liked Roddy.' Janet's bad imitation of Gladys's accent made Stella feel protective of the only member of the group who she had liked. 'Felicity was cross when she thought Roddy came with me – maybe he warned Gladys it was best to pretend they were strangers.'

'Mrs Wren's nest is a tall rickety house opposite the Tudor House Hotel. From the outside it's a dump, but it looked like you had waved a wand in there. The five-star hygiene rating put me to shame,' Janet said. 'Apart from Gladys Wren and Roderick March, did you get the sense any of them already knew each other?'

'I thought I was the only stranger. I'm sure Joy and Clive did, they were quite offhand with each other.' Stella looked at her diagram. 'Joy's patience with him was thin, but it was with

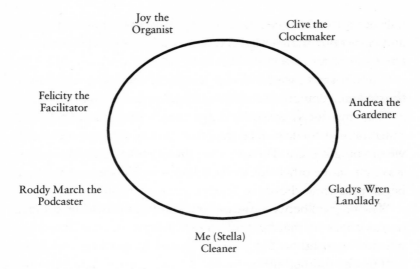

Joy the
Organist

Clive the
Clockmaker

Felicity the
Facilitator

Andrea the
Gardener

Roddy March the
Podcaster

Gladys Wren
Landlady

Me (Stella)
Cleaner

Gladys too. Andrea the gardener didn't know anyone. I got the strong feeling she wished she hadn't come. It was Felicity's first time, and she got annoyed that everyone kept straying off death; Joy was the only one who answered the questions properly.'

'Felicity Branscombe, retired Home Office pathologist, she's lived in Tewkesbury for five years. This will make you laugh, she told me when she was an "eminent pathologist" her nickname was Cat Woman. Tony my sergeant said it's in a true-crime book on that Salt Cellar Murder in the eighties which was solved because of her autopsy.'

'She told us she was known as Cat Woman at the Death Café.' Stella felt less amused than surprised. Felicity had struck her as not the sort to accept a nickname. Stella wouldn't mind being known as Cat Woman.

'In her youth, she was as agile as a cat and wore close-fitting black. She reckoned it was important to stand out from the men.' Janet pulled a face. 'Not a bad idea, I thought. I looked her up. Felicity Branscombe was considered the cream of her generation.' Janet was reading from her notes. 'She didn't seem bothered that Roddy March crashed her Death Café. But if she had been, it hardly merits murder. Unless she planned a Burke and Hare body snatch for old times' sake. She actually offered to come out of retirement and do his PM. She's seventy-odd.'

'I doubt she's lost the skill. I read Felicity does world lecture tours.' Stella couldn't admit it was Lucie who'd googled.

'Slap my ageist wrist. Why not? She's brighter than I feel.' Janet tapped Stella's diagram. 'Joy Turton was on the organ when you got there. That puts her in the abbey with March if it was him on the other side of the pillar. You said she stopped then began practising chords so she had the opportunity.'

'The interval between the music and the chords seemed short, it was silent in that time. Wouldn't Roddy have shouted out when he was stabbed?'

'He was stabbed in the back. The blade went right through. Initially he may not have comprehended he'd been stabbed.' Janet walked her fingers on the chequered tablecloth. 'Then Joy scoots away and lands back at the organ where, flustered, she can only bash out chords.' Like Janet, Terry had brainstormed crime scenarios with Stella as bedtime stories. Stella loved hearing them, but her mum had said it was one good reason for leaving him.

'Or she chose chords because they are louder. The organ was deafening.' Stella couldn't see Joy getting flustered.

'Felicity the Facilitator can obviously wield a knife, but since she left after you, how did she get past you?'

'I would have seen her,' Stella agreed.

'I see what you meant about that Andrea Hammond, the gardener. Boy, was she hard work. However, for all she's a sulky bitch with a pruning knife, CCTV backs up her story that she was cycling off along the high street before you called it in. Oh, and she did know people, she too lodges with the redoubtable Gladys Wren. She had passed March on the landing by the bathroom, but claims not to have said more than hello. I didn't get the sense Mrs W was keen on Andrea, but I also got the sense that she likes blokes better.' Janet moved her finger around

Stella's diagram of the Death Café table. 'That clock man, Clive Burgess, is as thin as a pin, but we've established it doesn't take strength to stick even a strapping man like March in the back. He said he hadn't seen March before that night and I tend to believe him. Gladys Wren had more to lose than gain by March's death, no more gratis sherry, she's lost a lodger and her tears were definitely real. Of all of you, she's the only one who seems genuinely sorry.'

'I don't see her killing anyone.' Stella resented the implication she wasn't sorry.

'That leaves the perfect stranger.' Janet groaned. 'A copper's nightmare.'

It was all a nightmare. For the umpteenth time, Stella wished she'd stayed in the flat. *Takeaway, chat with Lucie, bed, then up early to clean...*

'...according to the tox report, Roderick March's blood alcohol level was normal. He tested positive for coke and we found a small amount in his flat which would definitely grieve Mrs Wren.'

'In his podcast, Roddy claimed to know the identity of the real killer of Professor Northcote who was murdered in that house beyond the wall. If Northcote's killer is still alive then that's a motive to murder him,' Stella said.

'What bilge that was. Produced with Sellotape on a shoestring. A reason to bump him off might be to prevent him making more episodes.' Janet flapped a hand in front of her face. 'The Northcote case was clear-cut, it pointed to the son. I asked Mrs Wren if March talked about his podcast. She said he'd kept it under his hat, he wouldn't say who he thought killed Northcote. My guess is March was stirring dead embers. You can tell from that vacuous first episode the podcast would have been all hope and hype. From the one I've heard and from various descriptions, he appeared grandiose, a fantasist. I'll keep an open mind for now.'

'He said he was receiving death threats.'

'He never mentioned that to Gladys Wren, which since she told me they had gossipy sherry evenings is odd. We're checking every cloud, as surely he's saved his stuff somewhere. Nothing so far.'

'If the son was innocent, someone might want to make sure that never comes out.' Against her judgement, the podcast had piqued Stella's interest. 'Roddy is dead – doesn't that increase the likelihood his theory about Giles not being the killer holds water?'

'Up to a point and I will chase that down. I'll have a hard time pushing for a fifty-year-old solve, which left no room for doubt, to be reopened on a flimsy basis. It's not that we'd have the hurdle of going against the techs of the time – with no more than March's saying Giles Northcote was innocent, my boss wouldn't front up the budget and nor could I blame him.' Janet looked impatient. Stella was reminded that, Terry's daughter or not, Janet would see her as an amateur with no idea of how to operate in the real world of policing.

'I'm more inclined to go down the stranger route. A gold candlestick is missing from that chapel and, sad though it is, robbery is motive enough. It's possible that March went for playing hero and tried to do a citizen's arrest.'

'That means his killer didn't catch him by surprise?' Stella tried to remember if she'd seen the candlestick the last time she cleaned.

'One bloke goes for the candlestick, March grabs him, doesn't see the accomplice and is stabbed. While you're spotting Roderick's beanie, they make a getaway down the Three Kings' aisle and leave without you or the grumpy organist knowing they were there. Terry always said how often the more colourful murders have a banal solution.' Janet did quote marks.

'It's possible.' Stella tried to recall what happened after she had got up and seen the beanie. Unconvinced by the banal explanation, she wondered out loud, 'Did Giles Northcote have children?'

'No, but March wanted to clear his name so why would any offspring want March dead? I've got the techies on his laptop where we may find any research and, if he bothered with one, a projected plan of the series.'

'He told the Death Café group that he knew who the real killer was – that's a finite group of suspects.' Stella knew, as she did a lot these days, that she was arguing for the sake of it.

'He said it on his podcast,' Janet said. Stella didn't repeat Lucie's view that the number of listeners was in the low single figures.

'He left about fifteen minutes before the Death Café ended,' Stella said.

'Joy the organist said she unlocked the doors when she came to practise. March can only have entered the abbey after her.' Putting on her coat, maybe Janet had concluded she'd overestimated Stella's observational powers. Or she'd remembered that, at the end of the day, Stella was a cleaner not a detective.

'Did you find his notebook?' Stella tried to delay Janet leaving. 'It was in his jacket pocket when he left the Death Café.'

'Nope.' Janet frowned.

'What if the candlestick was stolen before Roddy went into the chapel?' Stella tried to conjure up the little altar, the cloth on the table, the shadowy starved monk. Had there been a candlestick then?

'His pockets were empty. If he had a wallet that had gone too.' Doing up her coat, Janet wasn't listening. 'We found photocopies of newspapers from the war, 1940 during the Blitz, in his room.' She brightened. 'Actually, one article featured our old stomping ground, a woman strangled in a house by the Thames in Hammersmith, murderer never caught. He'd scribbled "Retro Murders" on one of the cuttings. We'll check them out, but I'm guessing they were ideas for yet another podcast.' Janet glanced at her watch. 'I should be gone. Media circus is in half an hour, boss'll be antsy if I'm not prepping.' She tossed a couple of pound coins onto the tablecloth.

Outside, Stella pulled up her hood against the relentless rain.

'After that I'm taking March's parents to view his body,' Janet said. 'They've flown in from Australia. Roddy came from a hick town outside Perth, no wonder he was a thrill-seeker.'

'They got here quickly, the flight's about thirty-six hours.'

'That's the sad thing, they were coming over anyway – a family reunion after five years.' Janet gazed up at the abbey, the tower lost in the mizzle. 'They got here yesterday. They missed him by hours. Remind me, Stella, why do I do this job?'

Stella couldn't think of a reason why anyone would.

She pictured the small chapel, the cold stone of the starved monk's tomb seeping through the fabric of her anorak as Roddy March's warm blood soaked her trousers.

'Word to the wise, Stella, keep whatever it was March said as he died to yourself, OK?' Janet checked her hair in the tearoom window. 'I don't want the press getting wind of it.'

'OK.' Stella fixed her own gaze on the abbey tower.

Chapter Nineteen

December 1940

Chief Superintendent Robert Hackett's office was on the top floor of the police station. While a part-glazed partition split CID in two, Hackett's oak-panelled affair sprawled across the entire square footage. A football-field-sized desk, four-seater chesterfield and conference table still left room enough for, as Hackett liked to say, swinging a villain. However, like CID, the metal casements did not deaden the clatter of trams and lorries on Shepherd's Bush Road below.

When Hackett's long-suffering secretary told him to go in, Cotton was unsurprised to find the room empty. The top brass offices included showers and water closets which, a memorandum sent before the move last year had said, 'enabled dignified preparation for functions'. Or, as Shepherd reckoned, they enabled undignified hanky-panky with secretaries. Cotton knew Hackett, deacon at his church and self-styled pillar of the community, was unfaithful. With this, and a martyr to piles, he made full use of the facilities.

Prepared for a wait, Cotton sat on the other side of Hackett's desk. Passing out himself, Hackett had the photograph of them all framed on the wall – Hackett had made Cotton's present rank in his late thirties and chief super at forty. Alone, the men reverted to friends sharing a pint in the pub across the road, their wives swapped recipes and family news, but at work their roles were strictly observed.

Cotton fiddled with the galvanized metal pencil sharpener affixed to Hackett's desk, turning the handle as if every crank would grind down the problem.

An embroidered homily hung above Hackett's chair: *Home Sweet Home.* Perhaps Betty Hackett's swipe at Bob's long hours, which Cotton knew were spent mostly on the Richmond golf course.

Agnes had sent him off that morning with a greaseproof packet of fish-paste sandwiches and a lingering kiss on the cheek.

'Georgie, you've got enough for a jury to find him guilty many times over. Not but what that lazy so and so Bob Hackett will claim the glory. I wouldn't be surprised if it's not Dr Northcote's first time...'

'Anything in that prostitute case?' The door behind Cotton burst open and Bob Hackett strode across the thick carpet, planting himself on his air-cushioned chair with a fleeting grimace.

'Maple Greenhill wasn't a prostitute. She had a sweetheart,' Cotton snapped.

'Decent women don't end up in empty houses with their knickers down.' Pain made Hackett crude.

'Her brother claims she was engaged.' Cotton had brought his notebook but he didn't need it, the facts were at his fingertips.

'Not according to this.' Hackett flourished some papers and Cotton recognized the carbon of Northcote's pathology report which he'd sent by internal mail the previous evening. 'Girl hoodwinks a chap with her sexual advances then extorts more cash.'

'Northcote doesn't say that.' Had Northcote talked to Hackett? *Get your chap off my back, he's questioning my results.*

'No need.' Chin on elbows, Hackett winced. 'George, don't go making her one of your lame ducks. Banks won't thank us for inflating a common or garden murder when there's decent Londoners dying for their country.'

Wolsey Banks, the west London coroner, adjourned and reopened his inquests as often as it took to locate witnesses, suicide notes, wills, shopping lists, everything that might determine cause of death. Frustrating when a guilty man walked away scot-free because a scribbled note cast the slightest doubt on the crime, but today Cotton was counting on Banks's diligence. Tither and Cameron, the coroner's officers, would back him up.

'Actually, sir, I'm about to make an arrest. I know who killed Maple.'

Home Sweet Home. Cotton cranked the sharpener handle.

'I will have to charge Dr Aleck Northcote. With murder.'

A shower of shavings trapped in the housing fluttered to the carpet. Outside on the street, neither man registered the clop of horses' hooves as a coal merchant trundled by.

Shifting on his rubber cushion, Hackett barked, 'For heaven's sake, George, stop doing that.'

'Mrs Northcote said her husband was working the night Maple was murdered.' Cotton had lain awake all night rehearsing the words. 'His secretary confirmed, however, that, at Northcote's request, she had made a retrospective entry in his work diary for when he was called to the hou—'

'*Stop.*' Hackett had gone white. 'George, this bombing is getting to us all. Invasion any minute, we're all under strain. Agnes told the missus you were at your parents' grave the other day.'

'The cemetery is opposite where Maple Greenhill lived. I didn't go in.' Cotton knew Hackett's MO was to pull you down a peg or two if he didn't like what you said.

He listed the evidence starting with the scratches on Northcote's arms. Yes, the lighter on its own could be explained. It was untypical of Northcote to leave a personal item at a murder scene, but we all make mistakes. Trickier was the tailor's ticket in Maple Greenhill's coat. Then the coat collected from the tailor by Northcote himself and which, Bright believed, belonged to Julia Northcote, the pathologist's wife.

'She admitted as much, sir.'

'I'd call you shellshocked if you'd ever fired a gun for your country,' Hackett said.

'...two cigarette butts in the grate, a fingerprint on the radiogram and on a paperweight on the mantelpiece which Northcote had no reason to touch. Cherrill from the Yard had confirmed they belonged to the pathologist. He'd assumed Aleck had picked it up to confirm if it was the murder weapon.'

'How do you know they're his?' Hackett growled.

'They're on the Yard's files.'

'Why the dickens is he on their system?' Hackett was as surprised as Shepherd had been.

'They've got you and me too, sir. That time he gave us a tour? It's useful for elimination when we're at a scene.'

'You can ruddy well eliminate Northcote.' Hackett banged his desk. 'Kindly explain how, if Dr Northcote killed this girl, that his PM report says its murder? Don't you think he'd have called it an accident? No one would have questioned it.'

'Any half-decent pathologist would have seen the broken hyoid bone. If he'd omitted that and there'd been a second autopsy, someone like Bradman would have enjoyed destroying his rival's reputation. This way he puts us off the scent.'

'For God's sake.' Hackett dabbed the back of his neck with a hankie. 'George, do you realize what you're suggesting?'

'I'm not suggesting anything, sir,' Cotton said. 'I am saying I have more than enough evidence to charge Aleck, Dr Northcote, with the murder of Maple Greenhill.'

Bob Hackett made his way around the desk; instinctively Cotton tensed, but Hackett was going to the washroom. He called out over his shoulder, 'Detective Inspector Cotton, you are to take no action until I've informed Wolsey Banks of this very queer turn-up. It will be in his hands.'

'Sir.' The meeting had gone to plan. Cotton knew that lily-livered Bob Hackett hadn't legged the greasy pole only to slide down with his pension in his sights. But Wolsey Banks was made of sterner stuff. He would not let a man, whoever he was, get away with murder.

Chapter Twenty

2019

Stella

When Stella returned to the flat, she was relieved to find Lucie in her cockpit transcribing the episode of Roddy's podcast. Seeing Stella, she adopted a noble expression of self-sacrifice which meant she had kept her promise not to go to the police briefing. In case she let slip she'd been with Janet in the teashop that morning, Stella took Stanley for a walk.

Stella crossed the bridge over the Severn and went along the lane to Lower Lode. When she reached the river, she followed the bank past the boathouse, through churned-up mud at the start of the footpath to the meadow beyond.

Stanley badgered her for a ball but then, diverted by a myriad of smells, he abandoned it. Stella strolled to the lightning-struck tree. Stripped of leaves and smaller branches, the scorched oak emerged through the mizzle, angular branches stark against the white-grey sky.

Out of habit – Jack said never assume you are alone – Stella checked for anyone up ahead or behind her then clambered through a break in the undergrowth to a spot where she had spent many hours since coming to Tewkesbury. Although it faced the river and the opposite bank, the little clearing was screened by bushes from the path. It offered Stella the space she craved. Leaning against the trunk of a horse chestnut, she concentrated on leaves and twigs drifting by on the water and tried to relax. Stanley settled on her lap.

Her fragile calm was shattered as, barking, Stanley launched off her lap and tore back through the gap. Hearing a voice – annoyed tones – Stella scrambled up and returned to the path.

Stanley was dancing around a person standing by the lightning-struck tree. From his exuberance Stella imagined it was Jack, but then saw it was a woman.

'You should watch your dog, cattle graze here.' It was Andrea the abbey gardener.

'There aren't any today.' Stella recalled how rude Andrea was at the Death Café. The solution was to demonstrate being nice. 'How are you, after the…'

'After the murder, is that what you're pussy-footing with?' Andrea said.

'Yes. I mean it was pretty shocking for all of us.'

'Not for me. I didn't know him.' Andrea nudged Stanley away with her foot. This only encouraged him to fuss around her more so Stella grabbed him and clipped on his lead.

'Nor did I, but just the fact of a man dying,' Stella said. 'But don't you live at the same lodging house, the one run by Gladys Wren? You didn't see him there?'

'Who told you that?' Andrea looked distinctly unhappy. Stella couldn't believe she'd asked the question; she'd hate someone asking her about her living arrangements.

'I don't know, maybe Roddy.' Janet had told her, but she could hardly say she was as good as hand in glove with the police. Stella felt bad using Roddy. Lucie would applaud her quick thinking since, being dead, he wouldn't deny it.

'Roddy had no right to go blabbing to you,' Andrea said.

'I wouldn't call it blabbing…' Stella wished she herself had not blabbed.

Andrea appeared to be about to say something else, but abruptly with a noise of exasperation she stalked off toward the boathouse without saying goodbye.

All hope of calm having gone, Stella returned to her secret haven by the horse chestnut tree – not secret now – and collected her seating mat and rucksack. She gave the river one last look.

She hadn't noticed the light begin to fail. The path in both directions was in shadow. She couldn't see Andrea. The grey of the day was merging with approaching dusk.

From across the meadows, the abbey bell struck three thirty. Evensong was in half an hour. With what she'd been through in the last forty-eight hours, Stella absolutely didn't want to miss it.

She reached the abbey at exactly four and hurried up the yew path. As she went through the great north door, Stella wondered if Janet would be there scanning the congregation for anyone suspicious. Janet would be suspicious of Stella, for a start. Stella hadn't told her she'd taken to attending evensong. With Stanley on her shoulder, Stella slipped inside.

Organ notes ricocheted around the walls. The choir was singing the Magnificat. No Janet, no police tape or crime scene markers, the abbey was restored. Stella took a seat beyond the entrance where she could see, but was less likely to be seen. Craning up at the stained-glass window of Christ's Journey she gave herself up to the atmosphere. Stanley was already dozing on her lap.

Perhaps Roddy's murder had put off worshippers: there were only three. One woman with a Labrador at her feet and two elderly men huddled near the choir. Stella recognized the men from other evensongs. She wondered if it was Joy on the organ, or if she, like Stella since Roddy's murder, had been stood down. Absently, Stella took up a prayer book and finding the

Corinthians, followed the reading of the second lesson with a finger.

...He hath put down the mighty from their seats: and hath exalted the humble and meek. He hath filled the hungry with good things...

After a bit, her gaze wandered. Beyond the font, there was a shadow.

Murderers returned to the scene of the crime. As the congregation rose for the Apostle's Creed, Stella, paralysed by damp terror, stared at the shadow.

... he shall come to judge the quick and the dead.

Stanley struggled and she had hold him tight to stop him escaping. Dogs might be welcome in the abbey, but not ones who cantered about. The shadow had gone. Stanley began to mew.

Someone had sat behind her.

With the whole abbey why choose there? Filled with rage, Stella reminded herself she could shout for help. But she was like stone, she could not move.

...the Resurrection of the body, and the Life everlasting.
Amen.

Stella shut the prayer book and turned to confront him.

It was Jack.

'Please come home.' Jack came and sat next to Stella and submitted to Stanley's excited slathering and head-butts.

Evensong was over. The chords of Handel's Voluntary had died away. The straggle of worshippers and the priest had left.

'I *am* home.' Stanley only mewed when he recognized someone he loved. She contemplated the area where workmen were restoring the floor at the base of the pillar – the barriers seemed somehow brighter in the dim light from above.

'You live in Hammersmith, not here. Everyone misses you.' Jack addressed the choir ceiling. 'I miss you.'

'Like I said, I'm no use to anyone right now, not fit for human consumption, as Mum would say. I need space on my own. To sort stuff out.' Stanley was curled up on Jack's lap asleep. *He was home.*

'You are *use* to me,' Jack said. 'And you're not on your own, Lucie's with you. Don't tell me she gives you space.'

'Actually, she does.' Stella felt the truth of this. Lucie chatted on about her terrible editor, her unwritten book as if she'd finished it, she read out gruesome stories from the Gloucestershire *Echo*, stopping to heckle, *'Garbage, this kid can't write. Where was the editor?'*

Within Lucie's noise and caper, as if in the eye of a storm, Stella had found peace. Until Roddy was murdered her chief fear had been that, nearly recovered, Lucie would soon return to London and leave Stella behind.

'Jackie and Bev send their love. Your mum said she'd love to hear from you.'

'I only wrote to her yesterday.' From his face, Stella saw Jack didn't know she was in touch with her mum. *That meant he'd made it up.* Had Jackie and Bev sent love?

'What about Clean Slate? You *need* a job. Jackie said you've stopped drawing salary.'

'I can't take money for doing nothing.' Stella contemplated the sleeping Stanley. 'I have a job. Cleaning.'

'Where?' Jack looked shocked.

'Here.' Her turn to lie. She had found whatever space it was she had wanted by dusting off tombs and the bosses, angels with their instruments, a rebec, tabor, zither, one had a pipe, hurdy-gurdies. That was all over. Misery overwhelmed Stella. 'I'm in a team.'

'You were already in a team. *Us.*' Jack frowned up at the gigantic piers supporting the roof. 'Justin and Milly miss you.' He jolted as if with an electric shock and Stella knew this bit was true.

'They have you and Bella. Anyway, the children email me, didn't Bella say?'

'What? They are too young,' Jack said.

'Well, not literally, Bella scans their pictures and emails them.'

'No, she didn't say.' Jack was fiddling with Stanley's ears as if trying to tie them together.

'She sent a story Justin and Milly made up.' She and Jack had vowed never to have secrets or lie to each other. Even when they'd been an item neither had kept that promise.

'What about? Us?'

'No. Stanley was in it.' Stella would not say that in their story the twins' daddy found a big house for Stella *where Daddy and you have a huge wedding*. If she told Jack he'd be in floods. And so would she.

'Even my children can't put you and me back together again.' Jack looked disappointed and Stella wondered if he'd been hinting about their marrying to his kids. No, they were independent little beings, they'd see for themselves their daddy was sad.

'Lucie said you have a case,' Jack said after a bit. 'She said you found a dead body here. Is that why you came to the service? Are you OK?'

'Lucie shouldn't have told you and Roddy wasn't dead he was dying.' She was horrified – who else had Lucie told? What if Janet found out?

'Roddy.' Jack repeated the name. 'Did you know him?'

'No. Although we had met before…' Despite the likelihood Lucie had told Jack, she didn't want to talk about the Death Café.

'I heard March's podcast. I think the case he was investigating, the murder of that pathologist in the sixties, must be connected to his own murder.'

'Professor Northcote was murdered nearly sixty years ago. More likely it's someone with mental health issues, or Roddy was mugged. He was robbed.' That morning she'd disagreed with Janet saying something like that, but now Jack's certainty about the murder had Stella arguing against herself. Jack had chewed it over with Lucie.

'Lucie says you're helping Janet, your dad's old colleague. Fancy her being here, what a coincidence.'

'You don't believe in coincidences,' Stella reminded him.

'No, well.' He stroked Stanley. 'Lucie says Northcote was a Home Office pathologist who used to live near Ravenscourt Square Park. That's not far from me in Kew. We could check it out.' Jack sounded tentative.

'It's a matter for the police,' Stella said stiffly. Lucie would have declared them a team. *Like the old days, darrrling.* Stella wanted nothing to do with murders from the past or in the very present.

'You know as well as I do the police miss stuff. Look, Stell, I get you want space, that we're on a break or... but let's do this, be a team just once more.'

Someone was coming up the north ambulatory. It wasn't... *it was.*

'Hello, Joy.' Instinctively, Stella shifted up to Jack.

'Good evening.' Joy stopped. 'Stella, was it?'

'Yes, I liked your... organ playing. It was lovely.' Stella cringed at the lame comment.

'Ah, you attended our evensong.' Joy gave a confirmatory nod.

'Jack Harmon.' Jack reached for Joy's hand and shook it. Stella expected this to displease Joy but to her astonishment Joy smiled. Jack said, 'I'm Stella's... friend, I am *so* sorry about the tragic event here. How upsetting for you all.' Lucie used to say Jack could charm birds out of the trees. He was working wonders with Joy.

'Yes, it has shocked us all.' Still smiling, Joy tipped her head up at the stained-glass window that depicted the life of Jesus, the image barely discernible now as it was dark outside. 'Stabbed. Stone dead.'

Taken aback, Stella remembered Joy hated euphemisms for death. She was telling it as it was.

'Not stone *dead*, Stella was with him as he died,' Jack said. 'She heard his last words.'

'I beg your pardon?' The smile had gone. 'It was you who came upon our Mr March?' Joy was glaring at Stella. 'I didn't take to him, no, not one bit. I told that policewoman, March used our Death Café to flog his wares.'

Stella tried to change the subject: 'Joy is the abbey organist.'

'I *adore* the organ.' Jack was gazing at the stained glass. 'Especially ones with four keyboards! How do you guys do it?'

Guys. Joy would hate that. She obviously hadn't heard because she said to Stella, 'March was still alive when you found him?' Joy feigned disinterest, but Stella was sure that, like anyone, she was keen to know.

'Something about chamomile.' Jolting in horror, Stella gave the chair in front a kick. She should not have told Joy. *She should not have told Lucie.* 'He was in a lot of pain before he passed, I mean died.'

Roddy, oh Roddy, talk to me, what happened? Reliving her own words, Stella didn't trust herself to speak.

'Terrible way to go.' Jack had seen this, he was helping.

'From the way March swanned over to you last night I was convinced you two were old friends.' Joy swung a leather dossier case.

'How observant, I bet the police loved you,' Jack crooned with unbridled admiration. 'They'd never met before.'

'Actually, we had—'

'What I didn't tell the police was that, with her fancy airs, Felicity is no better than she ought to be. Just because she conducts the choir, she thinks she can lord it over us. I ask you, where would she be without the organ? March was in league with Gladys Wren, anyone could see that.'

Anyone except Stella who, according to Janet, had the observational skills of a raptor.

'Trust me, I know a few things about our Felicity that don't bear repeating,' Joy said.

'Ooh, secrets. *Exciting.*' Jack clapped his hands. '*Do tell.*'

'I am not one to gossip in a House of God.' Joy was prim.

'However, I am concerned that dear Felicity's conducting skills are not what they were. A soprano told me she was off beat last week, poor thing.'

'Felicity runs the abbey choir,' Stella told Jack.

'On whose soul may God have pity,' Joy said randomly.

'How marvellous. I've always wanted to sing with a group,' Jack rhapsodized.

Someone had dimmed the lights, the subtle illumination playing tricks on perspective so to Stella it seemed that the tall font on its stone plinth was a church spire on a horizon. The triforium walk and the vaulted ceiling were lost in gloom.

'Do you have a theory about who murdered Roderick March?' Jack turned serious.

'Kids. A nasty gang is marauding through Tewkesbury. That female police officer agrees. I told her that we'd over a hundred pounds' worth of goods stolen from the gift shop last month. *Nothing* is sacred.' Joy hugged her music case.

'Murder makes suspects of us all,' Jack chirped. 'That must have taken some lugging out, gifts in these shops are usually inexpensive.'

'We only sell objects of quality.' Joy's smile had long gone.

'I came for evensong.' Stella changed the subject again.

'Me too,' agreed Jack. '*Divine.*'

'There's a recital here on Thursday evening. We contemplated cancelling after the nasty incident, but we've rehearsed so it would be a great shame. Bach – *JS*, not the other one – and some Dupré.' Joy slipped a hand in her dossier.

'Ah, Jacqueline,' Jack brayed. '"The Swan" kills me every time.' Stella silently urged Jack to stop while he was losing ground.

'Marcel Dupre's "*Cortège et Litanie*",' Joy corrected him.

'Sublime.' Jack glided over his misstep and, in that instant, Stella recalled exactly why they'd been a team.

They all walked out of the abbey and Joy locked the door. High up in the tower, the bells rang for six thirty. The chimes were muffled by the steady rain.

'Straight out of Ngaio Marsh,' Jack said as they watched Joy trot away down the yew path, her bag swinging. 'Detective writer from the thirties.'

'I know who Ngaio Marsh is,' Stella said, although she did not.

'Here, take your boy.' Jack passed her Stanley's lead. 'Stella, I am sorry about the ambush, I forgot Lucie works with what *might* not be reality and I was happy to buy in to it. If you won't come back, would you at least let me research the case? Gen up on this Professor Northcote. Don't forget the National Archives is round the corner from my house. I could see if the case has legs.'

They had reached the abbey gates. What Lucie called Jack's chiselled features were like carved stone in the lamplight. Tall, dark and handsome, Lucie and Jackie called him.

'I'm a cleaner, not a detective,' Stella snapped. 'And it's not up to me what you do. Janet is moving towards thinking it's a gang, like Joy said. Roddy's wallet was missing.'

'You said.' Hands plunged in his coat pockets, Jack hunched into his collar. His dripping fringe, in spikes, hung over his forehead. 'Goodbye then, Stella.'

It was good to see you. She formed the words too late. In his long black coat Jack had merged into the darkness. The pavement was empty.

Rooted to the spot, Stella became aware of the distant thunder of the weir, water crashing through the sluices into the Severn. And above the tumult, Roddy's dying whisper, '...*Cah... ca... wo... my...*'

Car Wo My. Car Wo My.

Roddy March's dying words had become a mantra. But no amount of repeating what amounted to a series of sounds, Stella could make no more sense of what Roddy had been trying to tell her.

Chapter Twenty-One

December 1940

'After Ernest, my sister and her husband are chivvying me to put a toe in the water. They took me to the Palais, to get acclimatized, nothing more. Sue went to powder her nose, David was getting drinks, that's when I saw them. Clark Gable doesn't say it. He reminded me of Ernest; the way he danced he must have had proper lessons. She was unremarkable, but love transforms a face. Daft, but watching them I felt the chance of romance hadn't after all died.'

Cotton circled Clark Gable in his notebook. He knew Una Hughes had meant the man with Maple really did look like Gable. Her own features would once have been attractive if not dulled by bags under her eyes. She had told him she was the walking wounded from grief and, with warnings coming thick and fast night and day, got no sleep. Recently he'd noticed Agnes looked worn out. She spent most nights on the substation telephone and, if they asked, making tea for the regulars. The Auxiliaries had to make their own.

'What time did they leave?' he asked.

'Let's see, well, Moaning Minnie went off at ten thirty. We decided to stick it out, it's exhausting reacting to every warning and half the time nothing happens. When I looked again, I couldn't see them. I could have cried. Sue, my sister, said stuff and nonsense, they weren't Romeo and Juliet, makes no difference to you. But you see, it did. It spelled The End.' Una Hughes patted her rolled fringe. Cotton felt saddened; widowed at twenty-five like so many other girls, Una Hughes was too young to be deciding her life was over.

'When Maple – a pretty name – popped up on the screen before the newsreel, I nearly fainted. *Poor girl.* There's people dying every day, but Maple Greenhill and her chap were meant to be spared. A girl like her being dead, it's like Adolf has won.' Cotton, somewhat of a romantic, was inclined to agree.

Mrs Davis had come to the station asking for Divisional Detective Inspector George Cotton. She'd started talking before he'd even got her sitting down with a cuppa. 'Her face popped up on the screen at the Carlton up town. I'd gone with my mother to the new Errol Flynn... really, Inspector Cotton, it can't have been Maple's chap who did it, he looked so respectable. Debonair, actually bit like Errol Flynn now I mention it.'

'Would you recognize this man if you saw him again?' Cotton said.

'Oh yes. I can see him now clear as day.'

Sitting in the library of Northcote's palatial home in Ravenscourt Square that evening so, Cotton observed, could he. *Clear as day.*

'I need this.' Aleck Northcote was pouring himself another whisky from the crystal decanter on a drinks trolley. Snapping his teeth on the stem of his pipe, he relaxed back in his armchair. 'Hell of a day, George. Six warnings, one being the bomb that hit the docks and burst a watermain. It closed off the Whitechapel Road and delayed me on my way to the mortuary. I tell you, the Führer had me in his sights. I'm a liability – where I go the

Hun follow. To top it, Jumble's fractured her damn leg at the Hippodrome, doing high jinks with some fancy man. Thank God today is over.'

'Poor Miss Porter.' Cotton was surprised to hear Northcote's secretary – Jumble was Northcote's pet name for her – got up to 'high jinks'. He'd refused a whisky, although he too could do with it – he was still on duty.

'Poor *me*,' Northcote wailed. 'I can't begin to say, I am at sixes and sevens without her, my fool of a lab assistant is useless.' He tamped down his pipe and lit it. Puffing, he asked, 'Any luck with that prostitute? I gather old Bob wants it bagged. Good as said you were wasting too much time on it.'

'Hackett said that?' Cotton hadn't known the two men were on first-name terms.

'I asked him, mainly to stop him asking me about his damn haemorrhoids. I advised, keep taking the ointment and lay off the sauce – that depressed him.' Northcote held his pipe aloft.

Cotton was startled when the door opened. To his dismay Julia Northcote walked in. Seeing Cotton, she gave a start. When he'd called to arrange to see him, Aleck had said his wife would be at *some dull old lecture on nutrition for the poor*, so Cotton had expected to find the coast clear. He stood up.

'Good evening, Inspector.' Her gaze slid off him.

'You know each other?' Northcote gestured to the drinks trolley. 'One of your gins, dear? You fought free and escaped the spinsters then?'

'I met the inspector at the police shindig you dragged me to.' *Why had she lied?* 'I didn't escape, they're good women, it ended early to beat the Nazis. Nothing for me, I feel thoroughly second-rate. I'm off to bed. I'll leave you to... your business.' This time, Julia Northcote looked at Cotton properly.

'George and I are chewing the cud of crime and punishment.' Northcote was cheery.

'Inspector, I wish you every success with your investigation.' Her hand on the door, Julia Northcote was still looking at Cotton and, although it felt rude, he made himself hold her steady gaze. 'I'm confident you will find the monster who soiled that girl then snuffed her out.'

'I hope to, Mrs Northcote.' *Julia Northcote knew.*

'George puts Sherlock Holmes to shame, dear, but on this I can't share your confidence. George and I know that in sordid cases like this, the only hope is when, or if, the chap kills another girl, he makes a slip.'

Julia Northcote didn't reply. Bidding Cotton goodnight, she left the room. After the faint creaks on the stairs had receded, still standing, Cotton said, 'He *has* slipped up.'

'You didn't say.' Northcote's face stiffened. His eyes were cold, cruel and unstinting.

Cotton felt he could read what was passing across the pathologist's mind as he rapidly assessed the situation. His high-flying career had convinced him he was invincible, he would never be found out. If he had been, he would have been confident that the police, the coroner, his colleagues would protect him. Julia Northcote's parting words might be spelled in the cloud of blue pipe smoke.

'I'm confident you will find the monster who soiled that girl then snuffed her out.'

'I wish this wasn't happening.' Cotton went to the door, although Northcote wouldn't make a run for it and he knew that Mrs Northcote would not return.

Standing sentry, Cotton repeated all that he had told Bob Hackett. The elements of evidence: the scratched arms, the lighter, Northcote's print on a paperweight, the radiogram, *You knew Maple had been strangled, you had no reason to touch it.* Another on the radiogram, *on the other side of the room where you had no reason to go.* That Northcote arrived within minutes of the call had seemed impressive. 'You said you lived around the corner but I've just come from Chiswick and it took me just over a quarter of an hour. The PC who made the call reported that you got there in little more than three minutes. Perfectly possible if you were already in the vicinity, waiting until you could have legitimately got the message.'

'George, I've always respected your common sense and fine judgement, don't fall at the fourth now.' There was no mistaking the warning in Northcote's tone.

Cotton continued, 'Miss Porter put in the diary that you were at the lab until nine, but the man you called your "fool of a lab assistant" told us that you left at five. You said you were taking your wife out to dinner.'

'George, you are on the rack with this murder. As your friend, why don't I have a chat with Hackett, see if he can't give you lighter duties? Or set you loose to dig for England on that allotment of yours. Maybe you could join your wife at the AFS and put out fires, so much wiser than setting them, don't you think?'

'I could twist facts to make sense of the senseless, but then there is the coat.' Cotton related how they'd found the mending ticket from Bright the tailor tucked in the lining of Maple's coat. 'A coat that belonged to Mrs Northcote. Your wife.'

'Don't you dare bring my wife into it.' Northcote remained seated in the other wing-backed chair, but now his face seemed alive as if charged with electricity. He looked like an automaton; in that second Cotton saw nothing human about him. He should have come with Shepherd. He had come alone to spare Northcote. His mistake.

'However, if we must involve her...' Northcote raised a hand and, without looking, took hold of a china handle at the end of a cord beside his chair.

Expecting a servant or a butler, Cotton was astonished when Mrs Northcote reappeared. Wrapped in a silk kimono, Julia Northcote stepped into the room. It was so soon after her husband had pulled on the cord that Cotton suspected her of listening from the hall. So, from his expression, did Northcote.

'Julia, please would you put the inspector's mind at rest? There's been some confusion in CID – comprising two men

– regarding that silly business with your coat that Bright the tailor claims to have given to me. It is pretty ghastly, but the ticket you lost, and indeed the coat, have been found on the corpse of that prostitute strangled in Chiswick. Although there will be other such coats in London, the valiant Cotton here declares them a match.'

The ensuing pause was broken by the siren. Moaning Minnie, as Una Hughes had called it. Una Hughes who, so impressed by Maple's debonair dancing partner, had not forgotten him. Glancing at a folded newspaper photograph which Cotton happened to leave on the table, she had recognized the pathologist with the film-star looks whose forensic work on corpses pointed police to the killer as the man she'd seen with Maple.

The siren stopped. Julia Cotton gave a sigh. 'This again?'

'I'm afraid so, darling.' Aleck sat, legs crossed at the ankles, fingers intertwined, at home in his home.

Cotton hoped to God Agnes, not on shift tonight, had taken June to the shelter. Although she hated him doing it, if she was on her own, she preferred curling up under the kitchen table to their damp dug-out.

'As the inspector knows, I lost the ticket for my coat, I went to Bright's to collect my coat only to find you had already done so,' Julia Northcote said. 'Now you're saying that, all the time, the coat you gave me and the mending ticket for which I turned the house upside down looking for yesterday, were in the possession of a dead tart?'

'You went to the shop?' For the first time Northcote looked disturbed.

'Didn't I say?' Mrs Northcote flapped pipe smoke away with a hand. 'I was expecting to collect my coat, a thoughtful gift from you.'

'Why didn't you tell me?' Northcote's smile filled Cotton with dread.

'I preferred to put it out of my mind, the affair is too sickening. I shan't be using Bright again, he's clearly unfussy about the standard of customer. I want nothing to do with the whole, frankly revolting, business.'

'If you had told me, we could have saved Cotton here a *lot* of trouble.'

'If Inspector Cotton wants an explanation, here it is: Mr Bright accidentally – or on purpose – eyeing a bargain, sold my repaired coat to the first comer. A whore who, with airs and graces, then lured some poor unfortunate man with no more brain than the chair you are sitting in, Aleck.' Julia stifled a yawn. 'Bright will no doubt come up with some story to cover his tracks. Lucky for him, without the ticket I can't prove he ever had the coat. However, I'm sure that the nice inspector knows who to believe.' Again, she looked at Cotton.

'I have a witness,' he said.

Chapter Twenty-Two

2019

Jack

Jack was in the Kew National Archives – as he'd reminded Stella, he lived just around the corner. He had not told Stella that, regardless of what she'd said, he would work on the case. Without Stella, what else was he to do with himself?

Last night, on the drive back to London, his spirits in his boots, it had sunk in that Stella didn't see their relationship as on a break, she considered it broken.

Lucie had texted that if he discovered a link between Northcote's murder in 1963 and March's two nights ago, she was sure Stella would be all over it. *And by extension you too, Jackanory.* Jack knew Lucie's view could be more fanciful than his own, but when she predicted what he yearned for...

Wrangling with his conscience, Jack concluded that, although Stella didn't want them to be a team on Roddy March's murder in Tewkesbury Abbey, she'd said nothing about the case featured in March's putative podcast. How pleased she might be if Jack discovered the real killer of Aleck Northcote in Cloisters, the professor's house adjoining Tewkesbury Abbey, fifty-six years ago in 1963.

He had followed a paper files trail, stared at the computer

screen until he felt seasick. Although he'd scanned material to his phone, gifted with a photographic memory, Jack could summon images and screeds of text at a mental press of a button. When they were a team, Stella handled information capture and populating colour-coded spreadsheets. She'd make them pause and take stock. Jack dealt in impressions and imaginings, ghost voices in subways and at window panes. Now he had to cover both angles.

Jack had come armed with a potted biography of Aleck Northcote. Born 1901, father a Guildford GP who suffered a fatal heart attack when Aleck was ten and at boarding school in Gloucestershire. Scholarship to King's to study medicine. In 1925 Northcote married his secretary, Julia Barnes. Giles was born the following year. A marriage not underpinned by love, Jack pondered, but of convenience? Northcote swooshed up the career ladder to be a pathologist by thirty. Not possible now, Jack knew, forensics was more complicated.

Luck played its part. Northcote was at the right crime scene at the right time. The 1933 Triplets in the Lake Murders came in while Northcote's boss was holidaying in France. His discovery of a thumbprint on one of the bodies led police to the father and Northcote to stardom. He sent Giles to Harrow, bought two palatial homes, the London one and Cloisters House in Tewkesbury, where, on 22 November 1963, Professor Aleck Northcote was beaten to death aged sixty-two.

From newspaper articles Jack traced Northcote's London house to Ravenscourt Square. The seasick feeling had begun as he combed the fine print in volumes of the electoral roll from 1933 onwards until he finally found the Northcotes at the Laburnums – too posh for a house number. After 1941 Julia's name was no longer there. And from 1942, the Laburnums was occupied by the Smith family. On Street View, Jack found the house a disappointment, just visible through a lychgate with a pitched roof that better belonged on a village church. Had the Northcotes divorced? It happened during the Second

World War, Julia could have been killed by a bomb. Although he knew nothing about her, Jack hoped she'd gone on ahead to Tewkesbury. His interest piqued, he dug deeper and in an article printed in the *News of the World*, got a shock.

> Police were called to a respectable London square on New Year's Day Eve after reports of a man causing a disturbance. They arrived to find eminent Home Office pathologist Professor Aleck Northcote distraught, being comforted on the kerb by neighbours. Northcote led them upstairs to where he had found his wife of fifteen years dangling lifeless from a length of rope.

A week later the *Daily Mirror* reported the inquest at which *Professor Northcote was a key witness. He told the court that recently he'd suspected that the balance of his wife's mind was disturbed.* The coroner, the weirdly named Wolsey Banks, ruled suicide although no note had apparently been found.

Jack felt unaccountably flat. His motivation for being at the Archives – that he clung to – was the slimmest chance he might win Stella back. Personally, he doubted Roddy March's theory that Giles was innocent, and he'd been annoyed by Stella referring to the dead podcaster as 'Roddy'. As if they had been friends. If anything, this made Jack more inclined to think Giles Northcote had murdered his father. Having had little love for his own father, Jack could put himself there.

However, Jack did know that where murder was concerned, more than one person often paid. It could be the judge who had dished out the sentence, or the barrister whose defence had fallen short, so why not the pathologist who delivered incriminating evidence in what *The Times* called a mellifluous baritone?

Whether the person in the dock was guilty or innocent, Jack knew only too well that the relatives of victims nursed grudges for decades. Until one day they instituted punishment of their own.

Giles Northcote may have been framed. And what sweet revenge if, before bludgeoning him with his own poker, his killer had paused to tell the pathologist that Giles would hang for Northcote's murder.

The more Jack read, the more he began to suspect the truth about the murders of Northcote and the podcaster lay in the past. Events often came in threes. If this was a chain reaction, then who was murdered first? Or who would be murdered next?

Chapter Twenty-Three

2019

Stella

When Janet suggested they meet at the bookshop on the high street at 4 p.m. precisely, Stella pictured a shop like the various Waterstones she had cleaned over the years, bright, colourful with a coffee shop. The New Leaf, oddly named as it sold second-hand books, occupied a sixteenth-century half-timbered building squeezed between an Indian takeaway and a shop selling bric-a-brac.

Leading Stanley around two women browsing crime paperbacks that were heaped in tottering towers along a stone-flagged passage, Stella ascended a rickety staircase, then another. On the third floor she was again relieved to find she was there before Janet. She needed time to prepare her befuddled mind for Janet's rapier-sharp questions.

Six foot in height, Stella had to stoop beneath exposed ceiling joists. A sloping floor gave her the impression that a stack might topple on to her. The damp air smelled of plaster and old books and old dust. It would be a challenge to clean. Stella sighed as she considered again how she needed another cleaning job. Surely not every company would see her knack of coming across dead bodies – only twice – as an obstacle to employing her.

Stella scanned the subject labels on the shelves: ontology, divinology, graphology… her mind became more befuddled. No café, she noted. After the Death Café, she'd had it with cafés. Although since seeing Jack and existing on scant sleep, she craved caffeine.

'Sorry I'm late, it's crazy at work.' Janet did a circuit of the room establishing that they were alone which, watching her opening a cupboard under the eaves at one end of the room, Stella thought she should have done.

'How is it going?' Glimpsing cleaning equipment in the cupboard, Stella regained solid ground.

'If only Terry could see you now.' Janet flashed her a smile and Stella saw that the older woman looked as tired as Stella felt. 'Bet you wish you hadn't torn up that police application Terry gave you for your eighteenth.'

'The police are not for me.' Ashamed of her teenage moment of temper, Stella knew if her dad had told Janet, it meant Stella ripping up the form had upset him even more than she'd suspected it had. And she had been a detective: Jack and she had worked as a team. *Not any more.* Even at eighteen, Stella had had the mind of a cleaner, not of a detective.

'Yet here you are, ready to help me out.' Janet dropped her voice.

'I'm not sure I can.' Stella did want to keep tabs on Roddy's case. She'd been in at the beginning and she wanted to make up for not understanding his last words. And, she told herself in pompous defence, since Janet wished to use her as a sounding board, it was her civic duty to comply.

'We found a mint imperial behind what you called a cadaver tomb. With traces of March's DNA. Probably got knocked out of his mouth when he was attacked.' Janet ran a forefinger along the book spines as if testing for dust. 'Any more luck on what March said before he died? Car something?'

'Car. Wo my, or mo. Or me.' Stella snatched at the fading memory.

'Car. He did have a jeep. We just found it parked on a yellow near the abbey, with a sheaf of tickets. Any chance he was trying to tell you that?' Janet pulled a face. 'Bit sad if his last words were fear of being nabbed by a traffic warden.'

'What with the bells, I couldn't hear,' Stella said.

'What bells?'

'The abbey's bells, they struck ten.'

'That fits in with when you called the ambulance.' So Janet had checked that Stella was telling the truth. Rummaging in her coat Janet waved a packet of mint imperials. Seeing Stella's expression she clicked her tongue, 'OK, so I'm suggestible. Want one?' Stella shook her head. 'We found Roddy March's phone in a bin near the Rose Theatre. No SIM card. Rather than the magnificent Death Café seven – if we include you – more and more I'm erring on the side that this is robbery-murder.'

'How were Roddy's parents?' Stella didn't agree, but was that just because, as Janet had as good as said the day before in the tearoom, the solution to most murders was banal?

'She was chatty, going on about a memoir she's writing about her time in Africa before her parents moved to Australia. Frankly, that was weird. He was matter-of-fact, wanted to know if there was a will, did we have the key to Roderick's lodgings. How much money was in his account and had it been tampered with.'

'Maybe not having seen Roddy for five years, it felt remote.' Stella imagined that if someone she loved died – her mum, her brother... Jack – she'd be in overdrive asking practical questions. Jack might talk about memoirs if she died.

'I got the sense Roddy was the black sheep of an otherwise fluffy pristine white flock.' Janet tossed another mint imperial in her mouth and, tucking it in her cheek with her tongue, said, 'His bedsit was a mess. Bed unmade, dirty clothes on the floor and he was literally living out of a suitcase.'

'What about his laptop?' Stella asked.

'We didn't find a laptop. No phone, nor the notebook you mentioned. Still can't find anything on any bloody cloud. As I said, those newspaper clippings on retro murders is all we have so far. It's like he intentionally deleted his footprint.'

'Or someone else did,' Stella suggested.

'He'd kept letters from four exes, two offered to kill him for dumping them by text. What an arse, would you believe it?'

'Are they suspects?' Having dumped an ex by text, Stella could believe it.

'No, they all have alibis. As do your Death lot.'

'Three have alibis, Felicity Branscombe was at home arguing with the vicar, or whatever he is, over choir music, Gladys Wren drove to the Morrisons out of town. She's on their CCTV in the veg section. Clive Burgess walked home. He was seen by no one on his journey, but frankly he's not high up there as a brutal killer. Andrea was seen by another lodger. So all in all, your Death Clubbers have no motive.' Janet was swiping through her mobile, 'We've got extra patrols in the town, I'm doing the telly news to warn the public not to approach anyone acting suspiciously... yadda yadda. Personally, I miss *Crimewatch*; decent coverage and we'd round up these shit-arses in no time.' Janet crunched on the mint and, flapping her gloves at Stella, went to the stairs. 'Catch you soon, Stella.'

As Janet's footsteps died away – she'd asked Stella to leave a couple of minutes after her to avoid them being seen together – Stella pondered if, after all, the mystery of Roddy's murder was a nasty mugging gone wrong. Not the kind of death she imagined Roddy would have envisaged for himself. Stupid, because Roddy hadn't expected to be murdered.

Five minutes later Stella made her way down the uneven stairs out to the street.

It was raining heavily, not the light shower forecast on her app, making the abbey a black ink sketch against the sky.

'If it isn't the Cleaning Detective.' In a fur hat with earflaps, his threadbare overcoat buttoned to his chin and ski-boots, it was Clive the clockmaker. At the Death Café Clive had said time wasn't on his side but, to Stella, the ruddy-cheek and glittering eyes promised years yet.

Clive regarded her with a knowing, amused look from beneath the rim of his umbrella. Stella was struck with horror. Had he been in the bookshop? Had he listened to her conversation with Janet?

'You never told us you're a celebrity.' He twirled the umbrella handle which, Stella noticed, was decorated with clock faces.

'I'm not.'

'Modesty is unbecoming. I do hope you're going to solve our little murder.' Clive moved closer as Stella stepped back. He leaned confidentially towards her. 'I've got a clue to get you started.'

'You should tell the police.'

'Think John Lennon.'

'What have the Beatles to do with it?' Stella hated riddles.

'Who mentioned them? Consider when time ran out for John Lennon.'

'If you know something you should go to the police,' Stella repeated.

'Take my advice, never get involved with the police.' He put up his hands, the knuckles swollen, probably rheumatic. Stella wondered if he still mended clocks.

'Come to my house tonight. Around eight. Address: 1 Stag Villas. Cross the weir at Fletcher's bridge and turn right.'

Before Stella could refuse, umbrella held high above evening shoppers, Clive Burgess had lurched away into the rainy darkness.

The rain was pelting now. Her hair plastered to her head, Stella swept Stanley up and hurried along the street to the flat.

In her staff cleaning manual for Clean Slate, Stella had written, *Operatives must never enter premises without informing HQ of their location.* Following her rule, if not her judgement, Stella decided to ask Lucie to go with her to 1 Stag Villas. She didn't fancy being alone with Clive.

Chapter Twenty-Four

2019

Stella

The Victoria Pleasure Gardens gleamed in sporadic moonlight. The river had risen above the banks, it lapped across the paths and lawns. Sharp gusts of wind drove forward the encroaching water, the surface pocked with yet more rain.

In the daytime, the gardens were another of Stella's refuges. She and Stanley wandered the paths soothed by the geometry and neat rows of winter planting. She sat on a bench watching the river, which made up for missing the Thames. Tonight – with no Stanley – each step felt like an advance into oblivion.

'Wait for me.' Never had Stella been so grateful to hear Lucie, tottering and slipping in high-heeled boots several metres behind. She stopped and, catching up, Lucie clawed at Stella's sleeve. 'Christ, will the rain ever stop? This town is underwater.'

Lucie May's dress-code was either war correspondent in cargo pants and combat jacket or an outfit in which she 'dressed to kill, darling'. In tonight's faux-fur jacket over a shimmering black dress that showed off her too-thin figure, she must be freezing.

'This was a dumb shortcut with a murderer about.' Lucie splashed into a deep puddle. She shouted over a distant rushing sound.

It *was* dumb. Glad to have Lucie and striving to keep them both upright, Stella made for the gate by Fletcher's Mill.

'So, this is the drill. You point me at Clive the Clock, stand back and watch me go. In no time at all he'll be spilling his beans.' Lucie stamped a booted foot, soaking them both. 'Whoops, *damn.*'

'Clive asked me to go there, I doubt he'll need encouragement to talk.' Having seen Clive Burgess's chatty efforts with Gladys Wren and the surly Andrea at the Death Café, Stella doubted he'd need luring with Lucie's particular charm. *He could clam up.*

They stepped onto St Mary's Road where, in the shifting shadows of scudding clouds, the row of higgledy-piggledy cottages seemed to jostle for their rightful place. The rushing intensified to a roar as they passed the weir. A thundering torrent, sheened moon-silver, streamed over the sluices into a cauldron mass below.

Lucie's heels caught on the planking as Stella attempted to guide her over the footbridge. Pausing to look over the side, Stella was instantly mesmerized. She imagined casting herself into the spume and being spun away by the relentless force.

'*Stella!*' Above the cacophony, Lucie's cry was faint. Gripping the balustrade, she tugged Stella on across the bridge. On the other bank she grabbed her wrists and coming up close, yelled, '*What in hell happened there?*'

Stella's numbed lips were slick with spray, she could only shake her head.

'You were about to throw yourself over.' Lucie shook Stella. '*Shit*, girl, you gave me a fright. When you saw him last night, exactly what did Jack say? You've been a zombie ever since.'

'It wasn't Jack. *I would never ki—*' Stella could not explain her reflexive urge to leap into the river was not suicide, but a bid for life.

The clock on the abbey tower said two minutes to eight. Clive had said around eight. He'd said punctuality was a concept but it could do no harm to be on time.

'It's like all this water, the wind, all the elements, they defy time. We could be here in the past. Or in the future.' Stella felt as though she was channelling words not her own.

'One two three, back in the room.' Lucie's face loomed close. 'We already have Jack out with the tooth fairies.' She took Stella's arm and, holding her tight, attempted to totter on along the towpath.

The two cut a capering pair as they swayed and plunged along the river bank. The elderly clockmaker's house was, as Clive Burgess had told Stella that afternoon, hard to miss.

The reflection of Fletcher's old mill in the treacle-black river cast an air of menace. A lamp-post outside the middle villa was out. The vanishing moonlight robbed the pale line of the towpath of dimension, sometimes it led forward then it climbed to the teeming heavens. The Avon was now a lake, now a vast crater. The wind and the weir combined in an unmitigated roar.

Battered and disorientated by the remorseless elements, Stella fought off the vision of the high-hedged country lane, the van door slowly opening. She huddled to Lucie, more than grateful for her stolid presence, as they battled against easy drowning.

'One false step and we'll be in the river.' Lucie's shout was one of those rare times when she had read Stella's mind. 'It takes no time to shove someone into turbulent waters and whoosh, they're gone.'

Not mind-reading, Lucie had once nearly drowned in a river. Jack would say she was re-enacting trauma.

'Are you OK?' Stella felt bad to have brought her.

'Fine and dandy, Bubsy Bear.' Head down, Lucie patted Stella's arm as she ploughed forward. Two moments later she brought them up short and her mouth to Stella's ear, '*Wssst*. What was that? Did you see it?'

'No.' Stella raked the rain-soaked darkness. Nothing. On the far bank a moored houseboat crouched in a wash of faint light.

'I get the sense we're being watched,' Lucie said.

'I don't.' Stella had forgotten Lucie's tendency to crank up the suspense in life as well as in print.

'Always assume you have a witness, take nothing for granted.' Now Lucie was quoting Jack. *If only he was here.*

'What if Roddy's murderer knows we're on their trail?' Already on the qui vive, Stella was whisked into Lucie's drama.

'Trail? What trail?' Lucie could also abandon her ship without notice. 'If there was and she's stalking us, we'll get her.'

'You think a woman murdered Roddy?'

'Rodders sounds a bit of a bad boy with the ladies, doubtless there's a queue with knives out.' Suddenly, she shouted into the storm. 'Who's there?'

A shape detached itself from the darkness of the Avon. It resolved into a man, the hood of his fleece up, a scarf covering his mouth.

'Evening, la-ladies. La-ate to be wandering alone.' He swayed towards them. Tall, thin. *Menacing.*

'Buzz off, Mr Man,' Lucie barked.

'Ooff. N-n-not ver-r-y nice.' Stamping in a puddle, hands in his fleece pockets, he drew nearer. The escaping strand of dark hair precluded Clive, Stella decided.

'Turn around, Dick Whittington. There's a good reason why I'm only allowed out in daylight hours.' Lucie braced herself.

'Effing lezzies.' The man stomped away towards the weir.

'If he was spying on us, he'd have seen double,' Lucie said when they were alone. 'Old soak missed his way home from the pub. This is Stag Villas, time to see Old Father Time.'

Ahead a pallid shape proved to be a Georgian terrace of three houses. Standing outside, Stella made out three carved stags, one reclining on each porch, slender legs folded. Every window was dark. Dismissive of time, had Clive Burgess forgotten their appointment? She yelled over the wind, 'He's not there.'

'Only one way to find out.' Splashing through puddles, Lucie pulled an iron lever affixed beside the door. 'It's open.' Before Stella could stop Lucie, she shouldered inside.

Peering back to the river, the man had made her uneasy. Stella saw someone crouched on the towpath. Staring hard, it became a yellow salt bin. She hurried after Lucie into the house.

'What is that noise?' Lucie looked nervous.

From all around came a chattering, insidious as cicadas.

Stella found the light switch. Light flooded a spacious hall.

'Christ on a bike, Clive likes clocks.' Lucie's faux fur was like a damp animal draped over her.

Grandfather clocks lined the walls, pale wood, some oak, mahogany, all somehow forbidding. On a marble table stood an ornate clock of porcelain with silver filigree. Stella wasn't up on antiques but through cleaning for clients, ormolu and Louis XIV came to mind. One she could identify, the brass fittings not hidden, was a skeleton clock. Was it, she wondered, the one Clive had said he mended for Professor Northcote?

'Clive?' Stella's voice was hoarse after shouting. 'It's me. Stella. I hope it's OK, I've brought a friend.'

'Coo-ee,' Lucie called.

They ventured into a room on the right and the chattering grew louder. On an oval dining table were more clocks. Stella froze. Each faced across the table, like dinner guests. More clocks were set on plinths around the room and, in each corner, as if waiting to serve food, stood grandfather clocks.

'Useless, none of them tell the time,' Lucie said. Her horror mounting, Stella saw that every face was blank. There were no numbers. No hands.

'At the Death Café, Clive said some clocks keep the time to themselves.' Stella cleared her throat. 'They don't *tell* the time.'

'I *hate* concept art.' Lucie was snappish, not a good sign. Stella needed her to be fearless.

In the living room more clocks crowded every surface, pendulums swinging. Some ticked rapidly like beaks chipping bark, others with a ponderous clunk. The awful chattering set Stella's heart beating faster, faster, *faster*. She fought the impression that every clock had turned to face them.

'Something is very off,' Lucie said. 'He's not in the kitchen. There are two mugs out for tea so he was expecting you.'

'Yes.' Stella knew from experience that a trouble shared was a trouble doubled.

'Where is Clive the Clock?' Lucie stepped out to the hall. 'Clive? If you're hiding in one of your hideous upright coffins ready to jump out shouting "Cuckoo", do not.'

The chattering was getting louder.

Stella flapped aside the living-room curtains. *Nothing.* Through the window, the flooded Avon reflected the clouds tearing across the sky. From habit, Stella did a finger test on the sill. Clean. Then she recalled Clive saying dust was the enemy of time, it clogged the cogs. Or had Joy said it? If only, like Roddy, she'd taken notes. This reminded her that Roddy's notebook was missing.

'Mr Clo-*ock*,' Lucie wheedled. 'Come out, come out, wherever you are.'

'We ought to leave.' Stella came out to the hall and saw Lucie already halfway up the stairs.

'He could have passed out on his bed.' Lucie reached the landing.

Clive was in none of the four bedrooms. All the beds were neatly made without a crease, each room spotless with, thankfully, only one clock in each.

'Yuk, don't tell me that's his aftershave.' Lucie wrinkled her nose at a smell which pervaded all the rooms.

'It's Horolene, it's for cleaning clocks,' Stella knew about cleaning. 'It means Clive was here recently.'

When they returned downstairs, Lucie headed down the passage to the kitchen.

'You looked there,' Stella said.

'I need a cuppa before I face that friggin' towpath again and who knows, in the time it takes to dunk a teabag, Clive might appear,' Lucie said.

Stella was surprised that the kitchen was modern, with white cupboards, white stone counters, white sink and taps. Silver microwave, toaster, kettle, oven. No clocks.

Lucie filled the kettle and skittered about the room, eventually finding an old-fashioned Lipton's tea-caddy.

'There's something on the lawn.' Stella peered out through raindrops streaming down panes in the back door. 'What's that light?'

'Scarecrow lit by the moon.' Lucie joined her.

'There is no moon.' Frantic now, Stella fiddled with the key, eventually turned it, and plunged out into the freezing garden, Lucie behind her.

A lantern stood beside a plinth in the centre of the lawn. The candle was burned almost to a stub and in the guttering flame they made out a bundle draped over Clive's birdbath.

Flash. Flash. Flash. Lucie was firing off photos with her phone. The on-off light revealed the scene in high relief.

Clive was sprawled on the birdbath, staring upwards, his face fixed in a ghastly grimace. *Not a birdbath.* Clive Burgess was impaled on a sundial. Stella dialled 999.

'I'm calling in a murder.' As Stella gave Clive's address, she saw Lucie writing in her notebook.

For the clockmaker time stopped when...

Chapter Twenty-Five

29 December 1940

That terrible swingeing sound. *Crash.* If the house shook, the bomb was within about three miles. A fraction of silence. *Crash.* It would go on until dawn. Extraordinarily, after weeks of the Blitz, so much of London was still standing. Tonight it seemed more terrible, perhaps because for three nights the weather had been onside and the Nazis had left them in peace.

When Cotton walked across Shepherd's Bush Green in the mornings, shops were still there. *Business as Usual.* Houses undamaged, the trams and trains still ran. His own street was intact so that, on a Sunday sweeping up leaves in their garden, he teased himself life was normal, the country wasn't imprisoned in a set of complex rules and regulations for its own good, and that there was not the chance of dying, if not today, then tomorrow.

Cotton hunched on the bed watching searchlights raking the sky. It rained down with flares, incendiaries. Bombs. Agnes had made him promise to go out to the shelter. But he could not when she was at the substation risking her life to keep people safe. How he wished she'd volunteered for something less dangerous. Her captain had told him she was the glue in the outfit, handling messages for reinforcements, the engines, turntables, pumps, in double quick time. Cotton took it as a hint not to prevent Agnes doing her bit.

Another explosion. It drowned out Billy Cotton downstairs on the radiogram. Cotton tensed when the windows rattled, closer that time.

Agnes was the glue at home too. When he'd returned from arresting Northcote last night, she'd got the fire going, using up the coal ration. They had sat watching the flames, drinking hot chocolate as he related what had happened.

'They should hang him.' She snuggled closer. Like him, Agnes didn't hold with state execution. Solves nothing, she'd say. *There were exceptions.*

He'd told her how he'd escorted Northcote to the station where they were met by Chief Superintendent Robert Hackett and the coroner, Wolsey Banks. His first clue should have been when both men had groused that they'd had to come out in a raid. The second when, going into Hackett's office, Banks had told him to wait outside.

'Ten minutes later, Northcote comes out.

'"Night, George." He tips his hat and strolls off down the corridor as if he didn't have a care in the world.

'Next thing I'm hauled in there to be told by Bob in his best King's English how it "was all an unfortunate misunderstanding". Banks is tearing up Una Hughes's statement there and then; he says everything is explained. Northcote "deeply regretted his slip with the lighter, it proves I'm human like everyone else". Hackett and Banks had a good laugh at that.

'Hackett tells me I had gone against his orders, "countermanded" was his word. I had no busines charging Aleck Northcote with murder. Hackett said he'd "expressly told me the matter was in the hands of the coroner".'

Oblivious to the hiss of incendiaries, the Messerschmitts and Heinkels pummelling the city or deafening bangs of returning gunfire, Cotton hunched on the edge of the bed. He was back in the flickering firelight, Agnes holding his hand, saying nothing, just listening like she did.

'"...disgraceful to lay murder at the door of a respectable man who daily gives his life for King and country. Northcote is worth more to the home front than some grubby shop girl." I couldn't believe it was Banks talking.

'I tried putting the case: "Northcote knew the house was empty, he'd performed the autopsy on the owner... the stubs in the grate were the same brand of cigarette, his fingerprints, those scratches—"'

'"Murder by person or persons unknown." Banks is puffing on his pipe.

'"Bob?" I tried to appeal to the bloke I passed out with, we always had each other's backs. But Bob is at the door.

'"Thank you, Inspector Cotton, that will be all." Agnes, you'd never have recognized him.'

'Betty's been funny with me. I thought it was because I saw her getting extra down the butcher's,' Agnes had said. 'He must have told her to keep her distance. He won't have said why, he never tells her anything except if he's won at golf. So, your hard work with Shepherd is thrown away and a cold-blooded murderer is free to kill again all because he's so ruddy important.' Agnes had held his hand. 'Doesn't that man have enough dead bodies that he needn't be killing more?'

Cotton clutched the quilt, wishing it was Agnes's hand. Before she'd gone out to the substation earlier that evening, she'd said, 'Men like that, Maple Greenhill wasn't his first and won't be his last...' She had kissed him and told him to collect up stuff for the shelter. June was out with her man. 'I've told her not to be late.'

Cotton hadn't told her how Wolsey Banks, the man who had swapped allotment tips with him and once described Cotton as the cream of the force, had walked past him as if he wasn't there.

He hadn't been able to tell Agnes his pension was in doubt if he made trouble. She did know that tomorrow, although suspended, Cotton was expected to inform Keith and Evelyn Greenhill the police had not found their girl's killer. Hackett had suggested Cotton 'call the girl a casualty of the war'.

'Adolf didn't strangle Maple Greenhill.' Agnes had been furious. 'Northcote did that.'

Now Cotton raised his head. Through the smoke he could see the distant glow of fires in the east. He wanted June home. At least her man would bring her to the door.

Despite the raid, he went out and peered up and down the street. The moon was obliterated by smoke. It was dark as pitch. Cotton couldn't see the kerb.

This meant when Shepherd found him still standing by the gate half an hour later, Cotton was taken by surprise.

'You've heard then?' Hackett had wasted no time. He'd have to recruit a new team. The only winner was Shepherd – he was getting his way and being shipped out to fight.

'Heard?' In the hall light Shepherd looked sick as a dog.

'About Dr Northcote. I wanted to tell you myself, but I've been furloughed.'

'It's not that, sir. They sent me to tell you. Shepherd clutched his hat. 'The Paddington substation got a hit and Agnes... I'm sorry, sir.'

'Not your fault, lad,' Cotton said.

PART TWO

Chapter Twenty-Six

5 November 1979

The explosion made the bridge vibrate. A spray of light across the sky made multicoloured molten glass of the water cascading through the sluices into the River Avon. Guy Fawkes was long dead, but every year he had to be burnt again. Cotton was a Catholic, but when he'd married Agnes, strict Church of England, he'd let it lapse. Nothing that had happened since had restored any kind of faith.

'Jesus, Mary and Joseph, another one.' Cotton wiped rain-water from his face.

Since the Blitz, he couldn't stand bangs: a car back-firing; a door slamming; fireworks all became gunfire, bombs. On other years at this time he stayed home, headphones on to block out the sound, listening to records from their collection. Agnes's favourites: Chopin, Beethoven sonatas, Vaughan Williams.

Dr Aleck Northcote had found it amusing that the Cottons liked classical music while he, '*eminent pathologist, adored band music. A chap can't get hold of a girl to Vaughan Williams.*' George hadn't put Northcote right. They'd agreed it took all sorts while each secretly admiring the other man for having something more about him.

Cotton checked his watch. *Nearly ten.*

A flare. The scream of an incendiary. He clutched the guard rail and stared fixedly past the old mill to where the tower of the abbey showed above the rooftops. It had survived centuries, the Dissolution. The Blitz. When Cotton had arrived in Tewkesbury he'd gone straight to the abbey and, regardless of his lost faith in God, had lit a candle for Agnes. Then another for June and her babbies. Grumpy teenagers with better things to do than visit Grandad when June came to check on him. He'd found himself thinking how the abbey belonged to the Catholics first, perhaps because in his old age, Catholicism was once again his harbour.

A high-pitched whistle was a V2, Hitler's last hurrah. *Whistle. Silence. Death.* In the end it had never been his turn.

Cotton sensed he wasn't alone. He turned. Too late. His detective's brain registered that his throat would now be cut from the front instead of the back. *Less clean, but as effective.*

Pain was extinguished by the shock when Cotton's body was tipped over the bridge and hit the water. It was quickly carried away on the current, bobbing briefly before it sank. The post-mortem would find that actual death was by drowning.

A firework ended the night's display. It illuminated the bridge, the weir and a terrace of houses along the bank. Cotton's killer was revealed, steeped in white light, like a sculpture of cold steel.

Unlike when Maple Greenhill had been strangled nearly forty years before, this time there was a witness.

Chapter Twenty-Seven

Jack

7 p.m. The night after Jack's abortive trip to Tewkesbury. He slumped on the sofa in his sitting room staring at the fire. His sofa was long enough for Stella and him to lie end to end, toes touching. Just him now.

Idly sifting through Rightmove, a way of weaning himself off being a guest in a True Host's house, Jack had discovered a listing for the house in Ravenscourt Square where Professor Northcote had lived until 1942. Instantly he considered booking a viewing, but thought better of it. Best not to leave footprints, digital or literal.

Then he felt the nearest to happy that he'd felt for two months. There was a Virtual Tour. A devotee of Street View, Jack used to 'walk' routes around London, a reconnaissance for when he did the real thing. Now virtual reality software allowed him to explore a house in what estate agents called 'immersive 3D'. He could wander around Northcote's old home and not a soul would know.

Clicking his mouse pad, he hopped along the faint circular markers which, like stepping stones, allowed him to move through the property.

The house had been modernized since 1942 when, according to the electoral roll and, Jack now saw, on an English Heritage blue plaque, Northcote had moved permanently to his weekend house in Tewkesbury.

The ground floor was open plan – what he guessed was once an elegant hall with a sweeping staircase had been knocked into one with the downstairs rooms. With no nooks or alcoves, it resembled a sprawling modern office. Ceiling spots killed shadow and slants of light. Jack's heart sank – were there to have been a clue to any mystery round Northcote's murder it was there.

Jack 'climbed' the stairs, hopping along the circular markers into each room. There at last were original panelled doors, ceiling roses, alcove cupboards, fireplaces. Handles that Northcote and his wife had turned, cupboards they had opened. Door jambs they had touched during the thirties.

Jack let out a sigh. The top landing was unchanged. Oak balustrades curved round and down to the soulless office three storeys below. Jack had grown up in such a house, he'd spent hours as a small boy peering through the spindles to the perilous drop. Now he zoomed in on the banister, he saw the grain in the wood smoothed by hands over centuries and, immersed in the experience, caught the scent of beeswax polish.

Using the dollhouse view, Jack could turn and twist the cluster of rooms, suspended like a jewel-bright Christmas tree decoration, and peer inside. Stripped of external walls, each room exposed, he was reminded of the Blitz photos in the Archives. Interiors blown open by a bomb, to reveal to the street how lives were lived.

Jack swooped in on the landing where, on New Year's Day 1941, Julia Northcote, the pathologist's wife, hanged herself. Thirty-six and beautiful, her son staying with a friend from his boarding school. She had at least avoided the possibility Giles would find his mother. Jack felt an affinity with the boy and later the man who had sat hunched in a prison cell that last night awaiting a verdict of judicial murder. Giles had worked at the stock exchange, unsuccessfully, Jack guessed, since he'd been in debt. He must have found life a struggle; you never got over losing your mother.

Circling like an albatross, Jack tried to read Julia Northcote's long-gone mind as she prepared her scaffold and, proficient as a Pierrepoint, dispatched herself. No thought of her boy, who would be motherless. Jack's own mother hadn't killed herself yet he did sometimes blame her for leaving him. Across decades, he asked Julia Northcote, 'Why? Why did you do it?'

He shivered. No amount of clicking and zooming about on the landing would turn back time. He hopped along the white markers to the front attic bedrooms, then the back – what were once the servants' quarters.

Jack was not alone.

A man bent by an alcove cupboard, low-slung jeans giving Jack an unwanted view of cheek butts. Automatically, as if to tackle the intruder, Jack leapt the cursor forward. The man vanished.

Now the cupboard door was closed, the room was empty. He clicked back to the door and came in again. This time there was no man and the cupboard was still shut. He pinched out to the Death Landing and tried again. Nothing.

This time, Jack made sure to click on every marker.

There he was. Purple polo shirt, brown Goodyear rigger boots, he crouched on his haunches, sideways to the camera. The glimpse of his face suggested he was about Jack's age, early forties, hair greying at the temples. Perhaps he was the virtual tour photographer and the image file editor had been careless.

Jack's phone buzzed with a text. A supper invitation at Jackie and Graham's. *Bev and Cheryl are coming.* He loved it there, the Makepeaces were the family he'd never had, Jackie's cooking like a mother's love. Not that he could remember his mother's meals. Yet he was suspicious. Everyone would know he'd seen Stella last night. Maybe they were offering him a cleaning shift;

with Stella gone shifts were thin on the ground. No, Stella's gatekeepers, Bev and Jackie, planned to tick him off for going to Tewkesbury. Tempted to ignore the text, Jack abandoned himself to his fate.

'Jackie wants a summit.' Beverly hauled off his coat and tossed it onto one of a row of hooks in the hall. 'I found a clue.'

'I'll go then.' Jack reached for his coat.

'Don't be a nutter, that's why you're here. Plus Jax is trying out the Persian rice cooker me and Cheryl got for her sixtieth, she's doing a tahdig. Lamb with apricots, *sensational*.' Beverly pinched her fingers and kissed them.

In the kitchen, Jack was mobbed. Jackie hugged him, Cheryl, more circumspect, patted his shoulder and Graham thrust a bottle of London Pride into his hand. *Jack was home from home.*

The tahdig was perfectly formed with a golden-brown crust. Graham carved the lamb – otherwise unconventional, the family held to a couple of traditional cornerstones. Jackie sat Jack next to her.

When everyone's plates were full, Bev raised glasses to absent friends.

'Stella.' Jackie named the unnameable. In an undertone to Jack, 'I am sorry Lucie misjudged Stella's mood.'

'You were right, she's not interested.' He felt mild relief that Jackie didn't consider him Stella's stalker.

'I didn't say that,' Jackie said. 'Give her time as well as space.'

'I was checking the catch-all junk mail and found one addressed to Stella.' Beverly glanced at Jack who was frowning. 'Don't look like that, Stella diverted her work inbox to me, not that I found it there. It was sent two weeks ago – I missed it.'

'You can't cover everything.' Jack's frown wasn't judgement on Stella's right to privacy – he knew about that – he was sad Stella wasn't there to check her own email.

'I can actually,' Beverly said. 'It was from Roderick March. The podcaster who was murdered?'

'If it was in the junk folder, that means Stella never got it,' Jack said.

'I've got it here.' Beverly went to her rucksack – a replica of Stella's – and fished out her pretend police notebook. Inside was a folded paper. 'Listen.'

'"Hi there Stella,

Good to link up. As you know, I'm an investigative podcaster. Like the Innocence Project in the States, but better. I seek justice, not for the living, but for the dead, for those who have been silenced."'

'OMFG,' Graham groaned. Jackie sssh'd him.

'Stella said she didn't know March.' Jack felt himself grow hot.

'Which means she *didn't* know him.' Jackie told him. 'March, on the other hand, assumes Stella has heard of him and will want to "link up". Hubris, pure and simple.'

'It gets creepier,' Beverly rattled the paper. '"You've snared a few solves. So, here's one to assist me with. I belled your office and a starchy lady said you're on sabbatical. Awesome. Madam wouldn't spill details, but we investigators can walk through walls. I found your personal email, no sweat.

'"My podcast airs soon and it would be cool to have you on board. I'm in Tewkesbury, ground zero. Can you be here pronto? Should have nabbed you sooner, my bad. Roddy."'

Reading over Beverly's shoulder, Cheryl scoffed, '"Award-winning journalist and crime consultant. How cold is your murder? Call me."'

'Not to be rude about the dead, but what a clown.' Bev flopped back down at the table.

'March must have gone to that Death Café to meet Stella,' Jack said.

'Has anyone heard his podcast?' Graham began clearing the plates.

'Yes,' Jack and Beverly both said. Between them they outlined the 1963 murder mystery.

'Sounds like the bloke was fanning the embers of a failed career, all smoke no fire.' Graham loaded the dishwasher.

'Lucie thought that,' Jack said.

'If, as March claimed, he found this Professor Northcote's true killer, it's obvious who murdered him.' Beverly was making notes, as Stella would if she were there. *Capture even the most irrelevant, it may be key.*

A police siren blared. Jack took his phone from his back pocket, 'It's Lucie. Please keep quiet, she mustn't know you're here.'

'We live here.' Graham tossed a tablet of dishwasher soap from hand to hand like a juggler.

'*Gray.*' Jackie pulled a face at him.

'No need, it's a voicemail.'

'What did she say?' Beverly looked ready to write down whatever was said. *As Stella would.*

'A couple of things. As you know, Janet is secretly keeping Stella updated on the case. Lucie says Janet's homesick and Stella equals Terry.'

'Stella equals *home.*' Beverly's comment silenced them.

Finally, Jack went on, 'Janet met Stella in a bookshop this afternoon then rang her later to say there's a statue of the Virgin Mary and a candlestick missing from a tomb in Tewkesbury Abbey. Apparently, they were there last Sunday and were probably stolen around when March was killed. Janet is thinking it's aggravated robbery or whatever and not to do with March and his podcast.'

'Is that what Lucie and Stella think?' Jackie asked.

'No idea about Stella, but Lucie said it's Janet Piper seeing no further than her nose. Lucie said one of the Death Café people, a clockmaker, has invited them to his house tonight, she's leaving now.'

'According to my research,' Beverly was consulting her notes, 'Northcote's forensic evidence put away tons of villains over forty years from before the Second World War. If March's murder is connected to the murder of the professor, that's a lot of suspects.'

'I think that's where the answer lies.' Jack told them about his day at the archives, Julia Northcote's suicide, that the house where she hanged herself was up for sale and about the man he'd spotted on the Virtual Tour. 'I'm wondering if the two murders we know about are links in a longer chain of killings. Three at least.'

'What's your evidence?' Cheryl asked.

'I don't need it, I use intuition.' Jack pulled himself together; Stella's leaving was making him a nasty person. 'Suppose Julia's relatives blamed Aleck Northcote for her suicide and wreaked revenge? The inquest said she didn't leave a note, but if she did and it was critical of Northcote, he might have destroyed it.'

'Twenty-three years later?' Impatient with intuition, Beverly would be missing Stella's down-to-earth approach. *Stella would understand Jack.*

'Someone murders Northcote because Northcote made his wife unhappy then someone else murders the podcaster for threatening to reveal Northcote's murderer.' Cheryl was following him.

'Stella told me the attendees of the Death Café have alibis,' Beverly said. 'March left first. One fishy customer is an organist who went to the abbey straight after and was playing music. But Stella was there too so either Stella murdered him or neither of them did.'

Stella had been talking to Beverly. Jack couldn't check a flare of jealousy.

'Look at this.' Beverly laid an A4 photocopy of the front page of a Gloucestershire *Echo* on the table.

Cleaner Finds Man Dying in Tomb

'It says he was dying, not dead. Did he speak to her?' Cheryl said. 'If he did, Stella might be in danger.'

Jack felt shame this hadn't occurred to him. Stella had found the body, she was front page news. Any murderer worth his or her salt would see her as a threat.

'She told me it's a matter for the police,' Jack said. 'She's not investigating it.'

'She was fobbing you off.' Beverly could be blunt.

'I think I got that, Bev.' Nasty person was back. Stella had lied. She and Lucie were deep in the case. Bev, perhaps Jackie and Cheryl too, were a team.

'There you go, mate.' Graham put down a fresh bottle of London Pride in front of him.

Gratefully Jack took a slug and looking at the *Echo*, exclaimed, 'That's Roddy March.'

'We know that,' Bev said.

'I mean that's the man on the virtual tour. Wait.' Jack opened the Rightmove app on his phone and found Northcote's old London home. Agitated, he kept missing the right circular marker. At last he found it, and enlarged the man crouching by the cupboard. 'See?'

'Oh, yes. That is March.' Beverly remained calm.

'I recognise that shirt. It's a company called Geo-Space.' Graham leaned over the table. 'We used them for a Jobcentre Plus building. They scan the interior for an accurate reading of the space and stitch in the redesign. It's a more accurate version than the one they use for home interiors.' A council surveyor, Graham was expert in computer-aided design.

'Sloppy editing,' Graham added, echoing Jack's earlier thought. 'Looks like March worked for Geo-Space. What's he looking for?'

'March must have believed Northcote's real killer was linked to that house,' Beverly said. 'When did Northcote leave Ravenscourt Square?'

'Nineteen forty-one,' Jack said.

'The same year his wife committed suicide,' Beverly said.

'Jack, love, send Bev a screenshot of the man by the cupboard to forward to Stella,' Jackie said.

'OK.' *Why couldn't he send it direct?* They were behaving as if he and Stella had split up.

So, if he was single, he could do what he liked. Jack knew what he'd do next.

Chapter Twenty-Eight

Stella

'What's she doing here?' Janet ducked under the 'Do Not Cross' tape. 'Get the hell out. *Now.*'

'I'm a witness, darling.' Lucie bared her teeth in a wolfish smile. 'Stella and I found the body. To save you time, I can confirm our clockmaker has been murdered.'

'You talked to a reporter,' Janet muttered to Stella as she stalked past her into the house.

'It wasn't like—' Stella trailed in Janet's wake, with Lucie shadowing.

'I will tell you what it's like. For the second time in two days you're first to find a body and this time you've brought the gutter press.'

'Three,' Lucie called.

'What?' Janet halted abruptly.

'Three days,' Lucie said. 'We journos worship the god of accuracy.'

'I'm not sure—' Stella groaned inwardly.

'Shut the *eff* up. You've stomped all over my crime scene, no doubt you've done a deal on a syndicated story, I do *not* want her in my sight. Give my sergeant a statement then do me a favour.'

'Anything,' Stella dived in.

'Go home to London.' Janet looked at Lucie. 'If I find you—'

'Tewkesbury is my home. Me and Sherlock are flatmates.' Lucie held on to Stella's arm. 'Come visit, I'm no-carbs, but we can rise to biscuits.'

'Is this true?' Janet wheeled around to Stella. Her expression wasn't anger; she looked hurt.

'I was going to...'

Janet tramped across the grass to a tent already erected over the sundial. Inside, silhouetted figures were a shadow show. When Janet flapped aside the opening, Stella caught a glimpse of Clive's contorted body. The tip of the sundial, gold in the arc lights, was sticking out of his chest.

'No more titbits from the constabulary.' Draped in her cockpit, Lucie stirred a nippet with her devil's headed swizzle stick.

'Nope.' Not much of a drinker, Stella had accepted one of Lucie's nippets – gin dashed over rocks with a splash of tonic – but it did not take the edge off the nightmare. She'd considered emailing Janet to explain Lucie had already known about Roddy's murder. While true, it didn't cover the bit where Stella had told Lucie about finding Roddy, or his dying words, whatever they were.

On the towpath outside Clive's house after giving their statements, Janet had informed Stella that when she got kicked out of the police, she'd blame Stella. Unfair – Janet had chosen to open up to her. Ultimately though, Janet had trusted Terry's daughter as the next best thing to Terry. Stella had let Janet – and Terry – down. She checked her phone, in case Janet had texted.

'Don't bother, kiddo.' Lucie's corncrake voice, hardened by the years when she'd been a dedicated smoker, broke into Stella's misery. The devil's head bobbed as she chased an ice cube around her empty glass. 'We're on our own. A terrible irony that Roddy March cared about victims getting assigned the right killer and now the venerable constabulary will file him as collateral damage in a robbery with violence.' She rose to replenish her glass.

'It's a police matter, we should leave it to them.' Stella repeated what she'd said to Jack in the abbey the night before.

'Off your high-horsey-horse, Stellagmite.' Lucie hooked up the ice and, tossing it into her mouth, crunched it up. 'I'm an investigating journalist, this is my matter too.'

'How hot was the kettle?' Stella suddenly said.

'I didn't make you tea, you changed your mind and went for a nippy-noo.'

'At Clive's house, when you were going to make tea, you didn't have to fill it, remember?'

'Warmish and no, it was pretty full.' Concocting her third nippet, Lucie said, 'I see where you're going.'

'Clive's killer was there just before we arrived. Clive either filled the kettle to make his visitor a drink or because we were due soon. Either way, he was killed minutes earlier. He probably told whoever was there that we were expected.'

'Why did someone want him dead?' Lucie was asking her swizzle stick.

'They had got wind Clive knew something about Roddy's murder?'

'Or... let's suppose our murderer was only on a fishing trip to hook out what Clive knew and while he was showing them his sundial, he or she realized he knew too much.'

'You think they didn't mean to kill him then?'

'No one wants superfluous blood on their hands, although I doubt it was spur of the moment. Impaling a clockmaker on a sundial is such a glorious idea.' Lucie, back in her chair, conducted her swizzle stick in time as she spoke.

'Clive gives a tour of the clocks. He shows how his sundial gleams in the moonlight, turns his back and, *crunch*. He's kebabbed.' Despite sounding jaunty, Lucie appeared sickened by this description. Stella had learnt that the veteran reporter's tough exterior encapsulated a soft heart.

'Of *course*, the man on the towpath.' Stella jolted, spilling gin on Stanley, asleep on her lap. 'That's why Clive's front door was open.'

'Fraid so.' Lucie frowned. 'It was so damn dark down there.'

'We have to tell Janet.' Stella patted Stanley dry with her sleeve.

'We do not. We shall form our own fight club. Wait for Granite-Janet's face when we drop the real murderer into her in-tray.'

'She'll ask why we didn't mention the man on the towpath.' Stella didn't want to get one over on Janet.

'She has no reason to ask and if she does, we forgot. Which we did.' Lucie was undeterred. 'I'm betting it's one of your Death buddies. Roddy March came there to warn the person who was threatening him that he was on to them. Rash move.'

Stella's phone pinged with a text. 'It's Bev.'

'She'll be telling you Jack can't live without you.'

'She's forwarded an email.' Stella opened her laptop and scrolled to her inbox.

'...you might give the guy a break...' Lucie was saying.

'Roddy came to see *me*,' Stella said. 'He wrote to me after we came to Tewkesbury. Bev said she found the email in junk. She's at Jackie's. They said I should see it. Roddy wanted my assistance with his podcast about Northcote's murder at Cloisters House. No wonder he expected me to know him. He must have assumed I was in Tewkesbury because I was interested in Northcote's murder.'

'Cheek of the chap – you, his assistant? But why not talk to you?'

'He tried, but was called away. Then later, at the Death Café, I supposed he was hitting on me, so I gave him the brush-off.'

'*Atta girl*,' Lucie chirruped. 'So, how does Clive fit in?'

'Clive overhears something at the Death Café, or was he in the abbey too? Maybe he saw something that at the time meant nothing, then the next day he learns Roddy has been murdered and whatever it was makes sense. He did say something. I ignored it.'

'Come on, what was it?' Lucie said.

'I thought he was joking, something about the Beatles.' The gin was, after all, smoothing the edges.

'All of them, one of them?' Lucie glared at her. 'John, Paul, George—'

'Lennon. He said "Think John Lennon."'

'That's as code-worthy as chamomile.' Lucie pulled open a bag of figs with such force the bag split, spraying figs everywhere. Chocolate, carrots, figs, Stella admired Lucie's effort to keep off the cigarettes.

'Car wo my. Or mo.' Stella snatched Stanley mid-flight as he aimed for a fig.

'John Lennon was shot around early December in 1980 by a man who had got Lennon to sign *Double Fantasy*, his last album, I remember it well. I had to spend the next day in bed.' Lucie looked wistful. 'Can't see how that helps us now.'

'Clive had met Northcote – what if he killed him? He never got paid for the clock he mended for Northcote. A silly reason, but Clive seemed pretty upset about it when he told us. What if he mended the clock and killed him, like Lennon's killer?'

'Northcote owed him for the clock, killing him meant Clive would never get his money. Stella, by now our killer will know you've bagged a ringside seat at both Roddy and Clive's murders.' Lucie washed down her fig with nippet. 'Your picture's been in the news, the killer could think you know more than you do. Have you seen anyone out of the ordinary?' She was making another nippet.

'No, but I haven't been looking.' *Jack said, 'Never assume you are unobserved.' Or was that Terry?*

'Our murderer will be well aware you're the Detective's Daughter, Hygiene Queen of Crime with a hundred per cent solve rate.' Lucie handed Stella the gin and tonic. 'Drink this, you'll need it.'

'Why?' Stella was back on the country lane, brake lights red in the pitch dark. *She had noticed someone out of the ordinary.*

'Because if I'm right, you could be the next victim.'

Chapter Twenty-Nine

2019

Jack

Sir Aleck Northcote
1901–1963
Forensic Pathologist
Lived here
1929–1941

Jack peered through the rain-spattered windscreen at the plaque. Then at the top floor from where, nearly eighty years ago, Julia Northcote had strung up her noose. Scant comfort that, had she lived, Julia would now be dead. Jack felt as sad as if she had died yesterday and Julia Northcote had been his own mother.

How had Giles felt when he learned of her death? Did he, like Jack had, still write letters to his mummy after supper at boarding school? In his cell at Pentonville prison waiting for his last dawn, had Giles cried for Julia?

Next door, the Coach House which, Jack had read in the *Tatler*, was where Northcote had garaged his Daimler, was now a bijou bolthole of brushed steel and repointed bricks with a separate gate.

11.11 p.m. Jack lived by signs. The time was good luck. He and Stella had got into a thing of texting each other with a heart if they noticed it was 11.11. She wouldn't welcome him doing that now. When he'd seen SJX on a Toyota Hybrid – *Stella Jack Kiss* – that very day Lucie had texted urging him to see Stella in Tewkesbury. Not every sign was a good sign.

When he left Jackie and Graham's, Jack's low mood was lower still. The others were working with Stella and Lucie. Whatever Beverly said about Jack being on the team, if Stella didn't want him, that was that.

Before Jack met Stella, he'd been on a mission. He would find out who murdered his mother and kill them. He was looking for what he called a True Host, one who has murdered or plans to murder. A True Host because Jack gained entry to their home and, secreted in an attic or spare room, became their guest.

Stella had been investigating one of her father's cold cases. After a shaky start, they agreed they had objectives in common and teamed up. But Stella, the police-officer's daughter, hadn't cared for Jack's MO. Hiding in people's houses was illegal, never mind creepy.

Now Jack would return to his old ways. Without a shred of evidence, as he looked across the dark empty street, Jack was convinced that Julia Northcote's suicide held the key to the Tewkesbury murders.

Parked on the corner of Ravenscourt Square, after the virtual tour and a ramble on Street View, Jack was so familiar with Northcote's old house, he might already live there. He could imagine mounting the steps, scratching the key in the lock and letting himself in.

Behind him, a wire fence gave on to the tennis courts in Ravenscourt Park, the nets slackened and forlorn.

11.20 p.m. The square would be bristling with CCTV, but Jack doubted they were monitored.

Only Northcote's old house showed a light. Open shutters displayed the vast soulless downstairs which Jack had explored in his 3D immersive experience. It would not be there that he'd find ghosts.

The thing about estate agents, Jack imagined telling Stella, is, while they are mad to broker a deal, at the end of the day we all take our eye off the ball. Forget to set alarms, lock doors and so... *let's see...*

Jack clicked shut the car door and sauntered to a gate that had once been the tradesmen's entrance. *Often they leave the side gate unlocked... Voilà.*

No security lights came on as he crept along the side of the house and stepped onto a lawn, the grass grey in the light-polluted dark.

At the end of the garden stood a studio which, from growth on the sedum roof, was several years old. Jack edged up to French doors to the left of a back door and applied himself to the task. A network of drainpipes might serve as a ladder, but the ironwork would be slippery and he wouldn't survive a fall onto the paving. No fire escape. Jack tried the sash of one of the downstairs windows. Locked fast.

Jack was staring in through the French doors when he saw a face.

Stop breathing, don't look at the person, make yourself cease to exist.

Like a child, he shut his eyes. *Idiot.*

'Jack.' Beverly opened one of the French doors. 'Hurry up, before someone sees you.'

'What are you doing?' Jack was dry-mouthed with fright.

'Same as you: finding out what Roddy March was searching for in that top room cupboard.'

'Where's Cheryl?'

'At home in bed.'

'Does she know you're here?' Jack asked.

'No. She'd go nuts. I said I needed to pop into the office. She knows I'm being a desk slave to save Stella's business.'

'You lied to your wife? You and Cheryl have only been married a few months.' Jack was dumbfounded. He needed everyone else to be happy. 'She's a lawyer.'

'Yes, I know that, *Mr Perfect Man*, but if I'd told her the truth she'd have come too. I won't let her risk her career.'

'Have you found anything?'

'I was about to go upstairs when I saw you flitting about. Hardly subtle – aren't you meant to be good at this sort of thing?'

'Not any more.' He was gruff. 'Let's get it done and get the hell out. I can't let you risk your career either.'

'What career?' Bev pulled a face. In the torchlight she looked grotesque. 'I have nothing to lose.'

'A clean record is what you have to lose, *come on.*'

'Don't forget these.' Beverly smacked a pair of latex gloves into his hand.

'You carried a spare pair?' Jack snapped on the gloves. Bev really was a mini Stella.

'I brought them for you.'

On the top landing, Jack rested a hand on the banister from which Julia Northcote had tied the rope. He switched on his torch and shone it on the wood.

'There's the faintest disturbance in the grain. If you weren't looking for it, you'd miss it.' Beverly sounded as sad as Jack felt. 'She didn't tie it in the centre, the weakest place, she secured it above that thicker strut to be sure it held her weight.'

'She couldn't risk surviving,' he murmured.

'She had this lovely house, a successful husband and young son. She had to have been very unhappy.' Beverly spoke as if she'd gone over the facts many times.

'That doesn't spell happiness,' Jack said.

The cupboard in the back bedroom where, on the virtual tour, they'd seen March, was now shut. Beverly turned a small brass key in the lock and swung it open.

A clothes rail and shoe rack. Both empty. The carpet inside was different to the one in the room, but the pattern looked nineteen seventies.

Beverly bent and, grabbing an edge, peeled back the carpet. Beneath was dark brown lino which looked new but, with a thrill, Jack saw was original. Lining the bottom of the cupboard, it got no footfall. His hopes were dashed when Beverly sat back on her haunches, having found nothing.

'Pull up the lino.'

'It goes right under this shoe rack... wait. Oh, *actually*...' Beverly tugged at the wooden rack and suddenly giving, she was sent backwards, still clutching it.

'This has been disturbed.' Jack was attacking the lino in the corner that had been beneath the rack. Beverly crawled over and together they wrenched it free.

'This floorboard's loose.' Beverly shifted the only plank that didn't run beneath the cupboard. 'Get my make-up bag from my rucksack and give me my nail file.'

'This isn't the moment for a manicure.'

'Nor is it the moment for one of your bad jokes.' Beverly glared at him.

Rummaging through lipsticks, tampons, mascara, Jack found a metal file. He passed it to Bev and said, feeling the need to regain ground, 'I left my skeleton keys at home.'

'Here we are.' Beverly prised up the plank and reached into the cavity below, producing a cardboard box.

Jack shone his torch. 'Sea, sand and sun will please everyone. And so'll Lyons' Swiss Roll.' A single line drawing showed a sandcastle in the shape of the Swiss Roll. In smaller letters the address of the factory, *Cadby Hall, Hammersmith Road, London W14*.

'My mum liked Swiss Rolls,' Jack said. Or was that a dream?

'Who wants a Swiss Roll on the beach?' Beverly wrinkled her nose. 'Let's get out of here, there could be a hidden sensor.'

'Now you think of it,' Jack said, 'if there were, the police would be here by now.'

Beverly replaced the plank and stamped down the board. They slotted in the shoe rack. It was impossible to tell there had been any disturbance.

On the landing, Jack made Beverly pause. The house was silent, too silent. He tuned into the quiet. It was the deeper silence of invisibility. *Of another heart beating.*

'Someone is here.' Jack breathed into Beverly's ear. 'We are trapped.'

Beverly shook her head and before Jack could stop her, glided soundlessly down to the next floor. He had no choice but to keep close to her.

A creak. Unmistakable. *Someone was there.*

Beverly was an independent married woman in her thirties yet Jack felt responsible for her. Beverly wasn't just emulating Stella. It was him and his True Hosts which had inspired her tonight. If Bev got hurt Stella would kill him.

Beverly was climbing out of the landing window. Jack stifled a shout as she disappeared. They were two floors up. Then her head appeared above the sill.

There was a fire escape on the side of the house. He should have known. He really had lost his touch.

Jack tried to keep up with Bev on what felt like an endless descent. The wrought-iron steps were slicked with icy rain, his palm even in latex gloves stung with cold. One misstep could be fatal. *The person in the house could be waiting at the bottom.*

His worst fear was, for once, not realized.

'This way.' Bev was a shadow amongst shadows. Racing blindly in her direction, Jack found her behind the studio.

'I'll give you a boost.'

'Can you take my weight?' Jack could make out Beverly's interlaced palms.

'Yes, *hurry.*'

Steading himself against the studio wall, Jack stepped onto Bev's hands and immediately she launched him upwards. He grabbed the top of the wall, his coat twisted around him. At last he was sitting astride the brick. He reached for Beverly. At the same moment they both heard a door open.

'Quick.' He hauled Beverly up.

Moments later Beverly was leading Jack around the back of the teahouse in Ravenscourt Park. They crossed the old stable yard where Beverly unbolted a gate and hustled Jack through onto the pavement outside.

'My car's in Ravenscourt Square.' He heaved a breath.

'You can't go back. Honestly, Jack, you're getting soft. How come you didn't walk? Plus, you entered premises without establishing an exit strategy. It's not me who'll get the criminal record.'

'Seriously, thanks, Bev, you saved us.' Jack was humbled. 'I was an idiot.'

'We're both idiots. We should have stayed to see who was there. It had to be Roddy March's murderer – who else has reason to be there?'

'The owner?' Jack said. 'Whoever it was expects us to keep watch, they will have gone by the side entrance to avoid us.'

Beverly's car, parked twenty minutes away in Chiswick High Road, took three goes to start.

'Mission accomplished,' she said as they drove towards Shepherd's Bush. 'We've got what March was looking for and obviously didn't find.'

'Unless he was hiding it, not searching for it.' A new idea.

'Let's open the box at Clean Slate,' Beverly said. 'It feels ages since supper – if only there were Lyons' Swiss Rolls in the box, I could murder one. Let's get some from the mini-mart.'

Bev had circled Hammersmith Broadway three times – to lose anyone on their tail – when Lucie's siren ringtone sounded on both their phones.

We've got another body.

Chapter Thirty

2019

Stella

Stucco had fallen from the tall thin Georgian house. A woody rosemary bush grew drunkenly in an avocado bath set on bricks by the door. A sign suckered to the downstairs window read, 'Vacancies'.

'Well I never. Clive was a silly sod, but I wouldn't wish that on him.' Gladys Wren started talking as she opened the door and hastily, as if they were expected, she ushered Lucie and Stella inside. 'First Roderick, then Mr Know-It-All Burgess. Fancy you being there so soon afterwards. A nasty surprise. Come into my parlour or you'll be catching your deaths. So kind of you to pop in after your shock yesterday. Dreadful.'

Stella wondered if Gladys's last remark was meant as ironic. From the two Death Cafés, Stella had concluded no one should underestimate Gladys. Indeed, Lucie had planned to break the news about Clive's murder to Gladys and study her reaction, but Stella was unsurprised that Gladys was totally up on last night's murder.

Gladys Wren's 'parlour' was overburdened with a dark sideboard on which was an orange plastic bowl of plastic peaches and nectarines and an Bush radio that dated to before 'retro' – the tuning plate recalled the radio from Stella's visits to her nan in the sixties, offering magical far-off lands, *Moscow*, *Luxembourg*, *Frankfurt*, *the Midlands*. Perched on a huge television was a stuffed cotton hen. Antimacassars, two care-home-like armchairs and a bamboo magazine rack overflowing with copies of the *Radio Times* contributed to the time-warp.

'You've collected some treasures.' Lucie spun about the room.

'Roderick wanted to put that wireless on eBay, I wouldn't hear of it. What a bright lad he was.' Gladys Wren snatched a duster from her apron pocket and whipped it over the radio. She turned to Stella. 'Want a cuppa?'

'Yes please.' Lucie flumped onto a leather pouffe and made parched noises. The pouffe put her at a height disadvantage to the armchairs. Stella knew this would be Lucie's intention. It made her appear harmless. Stella also knew that Lucie wouldn't get the better of Mrs Wren. *Gladys, please, we're old friends.*

'Funny-osity,' Lucie said when Gladys was out of the room. 'That dress, mutton and lamb— Ooh, Mrs Wren,' Lucie shot to attention as Gladys returned, 'fancy you being Roddy's landlady.'

'Why didn't you say at the Death Café?' Stella said.

'Roderick wanted me incognito. I had to ask Andrea to keep mum. Goodness, what a temper she was in, I don't know why she came. Roderick had schooled me with what to say about death, but what with Joy and poor dear Clive taking lumps out of each other and Felicity getting steamed up, it went clean out of my head.' Gladys hovered by the door. 'Don't get me wrong, I'm glad I went. It got me out. Roderick was an eye-opener; my evenings are deathly dull now.'

Promising newly baked Dorset apple cake, Gladys went out.

'We need to see March's room,' Lucie hissed from the pouffe.

It was Lucie's idea to get into Roddy's room. Stella had been against it. What a great way to get properly in trouble with Janet and the police. Then Lucie suggested they pay their respects to Roddy's landlady, she must be grieving. Aware Lucie was only trying another way to see where Roddy had stayed, Stella recalled she'd liked Gladys, she would like to know how she was doing.

'His room will be sealed.' Stella was determined to keep Lucie reined in.

Roddy's address was the last bit of information that Janet had given Stella before she had cut Stella loose.

'Our Mrs Wren knew March and your grumpy gardener.' Lucie was consulting her version of the diagram Stella had done of the seating in the Death Café.

'Here you are, girls.' Mrs Wren was back. 'Stella, with you and Roddy being friends and all, you must be heartbroken, I know I am.'

'We weren't—'

'Dreadful, *awful*,' Lucie dug Stella with an elbow. 'So Roddy told you that he knew Stella.'

'He mentioned they were going to work together on his poddy thingy. What a disappointment for you, dear.'

Stella took refuge in what proved to be delicious cake.

'What paper did you say you wrote for?' Her expression peaceable, Gladys leaned down to Lucie.

'I didn't,' Lucie said. 'The nationals, whichever coughs up the right price.'

'Roderick would want me talking to you. "Knock yourself out", he'd say. That did make me laugh. He promised me helping him with his podcast would make me rich. Sitting right where Stella is now. "You'll be able to get a new boiler and pick and choose your guests." I said, a new hip will do me, Mr Prince.'

'Roddy wanted you to help him...' Stella felt herself flush. She'd assumed Roddy had wanted to pick her brains as a successful detective, but he'd asked his landlady too. Was he even serious?

'Every night, we'd have a sherry – or two – and he'd ask his questions. Even though it was about me, I had to think. My memory's not so good. Roddy said it's not Alzheimer's, it's me being a busy businesswoman. The gorgeous boy, always trying to make me feel on top of the world.' Gladys smiled to herself.

Stella noticed Gladys Wren wasn't as smartly turned out as at the Death Café. Her pink shell-suit had seen better days and while she'd obviously combed her hair it looked unwashed. She wore no make-up.

'What questions did March ask?' Lucie was poised over her notebook.

'What the professor was like, was he kind, nasty, who were his friends, that sort of thing. Right down to what he liked to eat.' Gladys Wren cut up the rest of the cake. 'Help yourselves, don't stand on ceremony.'

'How could you know?' Stella said.

'Didn't I say?' Gladys said. 'I was Sir Aleck's housekeeper.'

Chapter Thirty-One

2019

Jackie

'You look as if you spent the night here.' Jackie hoped Beverly and Jack hadn't done something illegal that both would deeply regret. Without Stella, Jack was a loose cannon and Bev would do anything for Jack and Stella. His hands wrapped around a mug of coffee, Jack's sheepish countenance didn't reassure.

'We didn't sleep.' Yawning, Beverly pulled back her hair and secured it with her diamanté scrunchie.

Please not. Squaring off a bundle of dormant customer files she hoped to bring to life, Jackie let the silence reach a crescendo.

'It was Bev, I'd never have asked her,' Jack eventually said.

'Is it always someone else?' Distantly Jackie noted how once quietly pleasurable office tasks had become purgatory.

'I shouldn't have gone. Jack rescued me.'

'I doubt that,' Jackie muttered. Modelling herself on Stella, Beverly rarely lied. Jackie had hoped with no Stella, Bev would keep out of Jack's slipstream. Bev was sunshine incarnate to his dead of night.

'We've arranged everything next door where there's more space to spread out.' Beverly opened Stella's office door. Reluctantly, Jackie followed her.

'Spread what out and you shouldn't have gone *where?*' Seeing Stella's empty chair, Jackie felt her chest tighten. Then she saw that the carpet tiles were covered with papers.

'We've found the murder that caused Professor Northcote's murder.' Beverly knelt down. 'Roddy March was either hiding this box of papers on the virtual tour or he was about to retrieve them and was interrupted. Either way, we've got them now.'

Dead Prostitute Worked in Dead Man's Home. On a yellowed front page of the *Daily Express. Strangler Kills Girl for Extorting Cash* emblazed across the *Daily Despatch.* The *Daily Mail* said, *Greed Spells Girl's End.* All were dated 12 December 1940.

'As you see, newspapers called Maple a sex-worker. In fact, she was an accounts clerk at the Express Dairies which used to be on King Street. She was found strangled in a house owned by a solicitor who was killed fire-watching. Apparently, lots of people were. Police said that she knew the house was unoccupied and lured clients there to, as the *News of the World* said, "ply her trade".'

'How does this relate to Sir Aleck Northcote?' Jackie mustered herself.

'He did the autopsy on Maple.' Beverly's eyes gleamed. 'Jack found the PM report. Her hyoid bone was crushed with, quote, "terrific force from behind". As Northcote puts it, wait...' Beverly scrabbled among the papers and finding a stapled document, read, 'she "put up a struggle but her assailant was too clever for her".'

'How clever do you have to be to grab a woman from behind and squeeze the life out of her?' Casting back eighty years, Jackie felt inchoate rage for the self-satisfied pathologist, even though his own end had been even more grisly. 'His job was to find cause of death, not judge the intellect of the culprit.'

'There's more.' Pulling out one of Stella's visitor chairs, Bev motioned for Jackie to sit while, with an outstretched arm, she stopped Jack from pacing the room.

'So, who killed this Maple Greenhill?' Jackie asked.

'Here's the thing. The coroner, Wolsey Banks, ruled "murder by person or persons unknown".' Beverly held up a newspaper article. 'The press speculated it was a serviceman. The murder rate went up during the war; men on leave found the home they were fighting for didn't exist. Wives had other men or liked their new freedom. Trained to kill, servicemen defaulted to murder. The blackout and bombed or burnt-out buildings were a perfect screen for killing and disposal. A corpse found under rubble might be an air-raid casualty. Newspapers warned of "night blooms luring men into the gaping maws of destroyed homes". Crap. As if the likes of Maple were monsters and their killers, soldiers, ARP wardens, whoever, the innocent victims.' It was a while since Jackie had seen Beverly so fired up.

'Maple Greenhill wasn't a sex-worker,' Jack said. 'In an interview, I read that her brother Vernon Greenhill insisted she was murdered by a man she expected to marry.'

'Who was that?' Jackie stifled a sneeze. An air of damp from the old papers had pervaded Stella's office.

'Firstly, we have discovered an incredible coincidence.' Beverly looked fit to bust.

'There's no such thing as a coincidence, it's a sign,' Jack said.

'What?' Jackie put aside how they'd got the papers, she didn't want to know.

'Maple Greenhill's family used to live in your street. Corney Road.' Beverly added, 'In *your* house.'

'Goodness, my mother-in-law's ears will be burning in her grave.' Jackie gave a dry laugh. 'When we bought it, Violet said the house reeked of an unhappy spirit. She said misery seeped from the walls. Violet was a spiritualist, she made a fortune out of tarot and whatnot. To my mind, she was a charlatan, but her tea leaves were spot on – we're living in the home of a murdered woman.' Jackie looked at the ceiling. 'Sorry, Vi, I should have listened.'

'From December 1940, your house was witness to wholesale grief.' Jack didn't pull punches. 'Grief can be assuaged, it's a happy home now.'

'Yes, thank you, Jack,' Jackie snapped. 'It's nearly nine, in a minute the phone will ring off the hook with customers. Is there more?'

'This belonged to Aleck Northcote.' Like a magician, Bev revealed a plastic Tesco bag with an object inside. 'This gold cigarette lighter was in the box. It's the first clue found by Divisional Detective Inspector George Cotton, the man running Maple's case. It was found at the scene of the crime. Roddy must have put it in this Tesco bag, obviously it wasn't Julia Northcote. Julia must have hoped it would seal his fate.'

'Wolsey Banks accepted Northcote's apology for accidentally leaving his lighter in the deserted house after his in-situ examination of Maple's body. This is him.' Crouching, Jack shuffled papers and gave Jackie a cutting headed, *Severed Leg Mystery Pathologist Provides Answer*. A photograph of a man in a top hat was captioned *Home Office pathologist Dr Aleck Northcote leaves Old Bailey Criminal Court*.

'You're connecting Roddy March being in the Ravenscourt Square house with this box of cuttings and therefore with Aleck Northcote?' Jackie felt resistant to their palpable excitement.

'Don't forget Clive Burgess the clockmaker.' Bev set down the chain of murders on Stella's whiteboard.

'That's not how we're making the connection.' Jack pulled out a folded sheet from his inside coat pocket. They had choreographed their presentation, annoying but, Jackie admitted, quite impressive. If only Stella was there to see it.

With a flourish Jack said, 'We know, because Julia Northcote, the pathologist's wife, told us herself.'

'The woman who committed suicide?' Jackie remembered Bev's outline of the Tewkesbury murder at their meeting the day before.

'Or did she? This is the heart of the matter.' Beverly wrote out the chain of murders with arrows leading to the next death.

Maple Greenhill (1940) → Julia Northcote (1941) → Aleck Northcote (1963) → Roddy March (2019) → Clive Burgess (2019).

As Beverly wrote, Jack read out the letter.

'*If you are reading this then I shall no longer be on this earth. I must restore justice to a girl whom I should want dead were she not already dead. The Hammersmith coroner has ruled Maple Greenhill's murder as by person or persons unknown, her killer known only to God.*

'*I have no allegiance to a pert little madam who, had he been a different man, would have snared my husband for herself without a qualm. Aleck was not that man. If I am writing this it is because I will have been prevented from revealing the truth of the case to Divisional Detective Inspector George Cotton. A good man.*

'*Aleck will have prevented me.*

'*Aleck bought me the reefer coat for my birthday, plum suits me, he said. On her, the coat would have looked as cheap as she was. After they found the ticket in the coat, the inspector came to arrest Aleck. I felt fear and anger. Fear for my darling Giles, condemned forever to be a murderer's son. Anger with Aleck, who had dragged us into his filth.*

'*Cotton and Aleck left in Aleck's car because Cotton is a decent man. I would have packed him into a Black Maria. An hour later Aleck returned. "I had to examine specimens for George." George, he said, like they were best friends. I didn't say that I knew he had lied, and that through the door I had heard Aleck arrested, like a common bank robber.*

'Today, December 29th, as the Nazis cause a row overhead, I'm making sure I write it all down.

'"Did you kill that tart?" I faced him with it this morning. He admitted it readily, said how lonely he got in town when I'm in Tewkesbury with Giles at school. After seeing bodies all day, he needed relief. Did I understand it meant nothing? But the girl demanded marriage and said if he refused, she'd blow the gaff. His term. In a moment of madness, he gripped her throat. She wasn't meant to die.

'A stupid mistake – Banks and Cotton's superior had dealt with Cotton. They dismissed it as a trivial matter compared to the pummelling the Germans are giving us. Cotton is to be farmed out to his allotment. As a pioneer in his field, Aleck is indispensable to the war effort.

'Whoever reads this, I will secrete it in Giles's favourite hidey-hole where Aleck won't find it. For Giles it was sweets; for me it is the revelation of a woman scorned. Whenever you read this, please take it to George Cotton who I trust will seek justice. Should he no longer be alive it must go to Downing Street and straight into the hands of Mr Attlee, another good man, and despite what Alecks says, far superior to Mr Churchill.

'Julia Northcote. New Year's Day 1940.

'PS: Wolsley Banks will accept that I died by my own hand. But if I am dead it is because my husband wanted me dead. I pray it does not come to that.'

Although she knew the contents, after he had finished reading Beverly looked as stunned as Jackie felt. She said, 'Presumably it was never given to Cotton or to Clement Attlee.'

'It's my guess that Roddy was the first to read it. For some reason he chose to leave it where he found it,' Jack said.

'It was Aleck Northcote who got the rope from the shed and strung his presumably unconscious wife from the top banister.' Beverly had gone pink. 'He knew how to make it look like suicide, but he'd never have been doubted. If it had been ruled murder, Northcote would have been the prime suspect; awkward since they'd already got him off the hook for Maple Greenhill's murder.'

'We found the inquest report on the National Archives database before you arrived. Northcote reported returning from work to find his "beloved wife suspended by a rope from the banister. I began to cut her down but knew I lacked the strength to haul her over the balustrade. I couldn't let her fall to the hall below."' Jack spoke in a monotone.

'He should have known to leave her until the police came.' Jackie had the bug – she too was ready to fight for Julia Northcote.

'Northcote told the inquest that the balance of her mind was disturbed by the Blitz and the blackouts. The press took Northcote's side, his wife had abandoned her family,' Beverly said. 'Her death went badly with a public expected to rally round the flag and be "in it together".'

'Virginia Woolf killed herself a couple of months later and the papers gave her a hard time for jumping ship,' Jack said. 'Yet again, Northcote got away with murder. He was knighted, as was Banks the coroner. Cotton's boss Robert Hackett got a CBE for services to his country.'

'Can we try to trace this Inspector Cotton?' Jackie said. 'Sounds like he was the fall guy.'

'If George Cotton were alive, he'd be a hundred and twenty-six. Unfortunately, he died ages ago in 1979 in his eighties. And here's another sign, he's buried in your cemetery,' Jack said. 'We are meant to solve this case.'

'It might be opposite our house but it's *not* my cemetery.' Jackie was sharp. 'OK, guys, I have to ask, how did you find this?'

Jackie kept her face blank as Jack confessed to finding Beverly in Northcote's old house in Ravenscourt Square where he too had planned to sneak in and find what Roddy March had been looking for.

'How did Roddy March know the box was hidden there?'

'I rang Geo-Space, the company who made the virtual tour, just before you arrived. March wasn't down as the photographer, but there had been a Wolsey Banks who did a brief stint for the company.' Beverly paused for Jack to make the connection.

'If he was considering removing it, then someone interrupted him.'

'Did March's killer think he had Julia's letter and try to get it from him?'

'That presupposes Roddy and his killer knew about her letter,' Jack said.

'If the murderer knew the letter was in the house, why not take it? That they didn't suggests they were unaware it was there.' Jackie knew they were too polite to say they had been over this ground.

'Meanwhile, Lucie has texted saying the police are thinking it a stranger murder. They're looking for the gang members responsible for the spate of muggings and robberies in the areas. Which means,' Beverly clapped her hands, 'we're on our own with this case.'

'Not quite.' Jackie began gathering up the papers. She stowed them in their cardboard box. 'Take that with you.'

'Take it where?' Jack and Beverly asked at once.

'Tewkesbury.' Jackie laid the box on Stella's desk. 'We are in this together and we'll come out of it together. You go and join Stella and Lucie's team and, this time, don't take no for an answer.'

Chapter Thirty-Two

Stella

Roddy's room was, as Stella had expected, sealed with police tape. Relieved, Stella was horrified when Gladys peeled off the tape and unlocked the door. 'That lady detective won't know. Lord knows when I can get on with reletting it. Although the very idea of a stranger in Roderick's bedroom…' She rubbed her hip which if, as Roddy had promised and now Lucie was rashly promising too, would be replaced when Lucie's true-crime book was a bestseller.

'His mum and dad aren't even allowed in,' Gladys announced as they stood in the bedsit breathing stale air. Hearing this, Stella's horror that they were trespassing shot sky high.

The smell of dirty washing, dominated by socks. The shape of Roddy's head was outlined on the pillow. Stella imagined him hunched over his laptop pecking out his podcast script with one finger. Sprawled on the bed recording the podcast which, he'd promised Gladys, would change their lives. Stella pictured Roddy slamming shut the laptop, snatching his combat jacket and hurrying to the Death Café.

With no idea it was the last day of his life.

'We should go,' Stella said.

'Nice room.' With a view of a brick wall, dark and dingy even with lights on, it was not nice. Her gimlet eyes scouring every corner, Lucie would be buttering up the landlady.

'I'd give it a spruce every day, not part of the service, but Roderick was up to his ears. Look at this mess, I can't let his parents see it.'

Black fingerprint powder speckled every surface: the corner sink, the small induction hob, a kettle with the lid off lay on top of a mini-fridge. Drawers had been opened and a shirt was caught between the wardrobe doors. Janet had said they hadn't found Roddy's laptop or his notebook. Stella felt hopeless – what could she and Lucie hope to find? Beyond the ruined dreams of a dead man.

'So, Gladys, fancy you being the one to find Professor Northcote dead all those years ago.' Lucie did her Red Riding Hood smile.

'I'll never forget the sight of him there in the hall.' Gladys clasped her hands in front of her paisley overall. 'A great long streak of blood on the floor where he'd dragged himself to the phone. I found it hanging off the hook. Police said Sir Aleck knocked it off the cradle trying to dial. Like I said to Roderick, that young Giles might have been a trial to his father, but what son isn't? He was a sweet soul at heart.' She lowered herself onto the end of Roddy's bed. 'There's evil in this world.'

'Too sweet a soul to commit murder?' Lucie was disguised as a sweet soul.

'Giles loved his dog. They say it starts with animals and children then works up. He needed money and the police said desperate people will do anything. The professor said his son was a lost cause. "Gladys," he said, "the boy's a bottomless pit, his mother spoiled him. One day it'll end badly."' She smoothed the candlewick bedspread. 'Sir Aleck was out of sorts after Giles left for London. Derek came to take me to the pictures, it was my night off, and I wasn't giving that up to stay behind. In the end Derek got a shout, he was a fireman, so we never did see the film.'

'I understand you didn't live in,' Lucie said.

'Sir Aleck was on at me to stay. Since his wife had done away with herself, he said he hated the empty house. Some nights I did make up a bed in the attic.' Mrs Wren gave a peremptory sniff as if warding off any lewd ideas that Lucie or Stella might harbour.

'Julia Northcote died in the early hours of New Year's Day, 1941.' Stella was confirming the date, but felt her tone implied that by 1963 Professor Northcote should have got over it.

'He was never the same man after that, or so he said.' Mrs Wren got off the bed. 'I wish I'd never agreed to go with Derek, but the film was finishing in Evesham that night. If I'd stayed poor Giles would be alive.'

'And perhaps Professor Northcote?' Lucie said.

'Yes, him too.' She gave another sniff.

'If you'd stayed, you could have been another victim.' Stella was surprised this hadn't occurred to Gladys.

'Who do you think did it?' Lucie rounded on her.

'I'm no detective.' Gladys's expression suggested to Stella that she knew that Lucie was preparing to pounce. 'All I know is, whatever people say, it wasn't me.'

'Who used to come to Cloisters House?' Stella interrupted. To her Gladys seemed genuinely upset by Roddy's death. Personally, Stella was sticking to her first impression of Gladys as a kindly woman, not the sort to kill her ex-employer and then Roddy to prevent him exposing her. An opinion based on intuition, usually Jack's domain, that Stella could not substantiate.

'Northcote was generous to all callers, handing out half-crowns to the butcher's boy, the rag and bone man. When it came to the new window cleaner, I said see how he does first, but would Northcote listen? He bought me all sorts too.'

'Apart from Giles, did any of these tradespeople visit that day?' Stella said.

'Harry with the meat, cheeky so-and-so, wanted to marry me. Derek saw him off. Harry's got his own shop now, his grandson manages it. Giles in the evening, of course, poor lamb. No one else while I was there.'

'You must have been young at the time. What are you now, sixties?' Lucie's crooning tone might work on her budgie, but Gladys Wren wasn't fooled.

'Come on, love, you're as bad as Roderick dripping flattery. As you well know, you and me are in our seventies. I was eighteen then, Cloisters House was my first job and last job, because Derek and me got wed.'

'Goodness, not a bad position for someone so young. I suppose Aleck planned to train you up.' Lucie swam over the reference to their ages.

'Sir Aleck was keen to give me a leg-up.' Gladys's eyes glazed – grief was tiring, Stella knew. Gladys was downbeat compared with the chirpy personality she'd displayed at the Death Café.

'Could Northcote's murder have been a random attack?' Stella asked gently.

'Not a bit of it. He knew whoever it was or he'd never have let them in. He never let just anyone over the threshold.' Her agitation now apparent, Gladys worked her lips. 'Ladies, if there's nothing else…'

'So, you telling the police this led them to charge the one visitor Sir Aleck Northcote would have unhesitatingly allowed in. His son. That's why they charged Giles with his murder.' *Pounce.* Lucie might have bided her time, but Gladys putting her at over seventy was tantamount to a declaration of war. 'What about Roderick March, did he have visitors?'

'Only Clive the Clock, as Roderick called him.'

'Wait, he knew Clive?' Lucie said.

'Clive Burgess cleaned a watch for him.'

'They never said they knew each other.' Stella reflected that nor had they said they didn't. 'Did Roddy interview Clive for *The Distant Dead*?'

'Yes, Clive came here after the first Death Café, thick as thieves, they were.' Gladys looked annoyed.

'What did Clive tell March?' Lucie said.

Gladys's eyes glittered. 'I've no idea, dear. Ask me, Clive talking to Roderick is why they're both gone.'

Chapter Thirty-Three

2019

Jackie

'Phyllis, I've never asked if you knew the family who used to live in our house before us?' Jackie sipped deathly strong tea from a mug extolling Lytham St Annes.

Jackie dropped in on her elderly neighbour every week, usually after work, but today it was for elevenses and Jackie was fact-finding. 'Name of Greenhill. They were here during the war, so before your time.' Although Phyllis had grown up in Lytham, she and her husband had lived in the house next to Jackie for over sixty years. Phyllis was the Corney Road Oracle.

'I should say, I'm not that old.' Phyllis stuck out her tongue as, needles clacking, she knitted a garment for another generation of her family. 'I do remember them. Vernon Greenhill had a lovely wife, I did feel for her when he died, ooh, years ago now. Mary, that was her name, she'd been on the buses during the war. They moved out to Windsor, but we exchanged Christmas cards. She died in a home in 1999. Her son Cliff wrote to tell me. The man they sold to was a grumpy old so-and-so, never gave you the time of day, your family was a tonic, I can tell you.'

'I had heard their relative was murdered. Sounds silly, but somehow I feel involved.' Since Jack and Beverly had told her about Maple Greenhill, she felt haunted by the notion of the young woman walking out of their house for a night at the Hammersmith Palais, where Jackie herself had danced with Graham in her teens. Jackie wondered which of the bedrooms had been Maple's. She had grown up in the same house as Jackie's two boys. Maple felt like family.

'Maple was Vernon Greenhill's older sister. Mary said how she could never measure up to Maple, no one could. Vernon opened a car showroom for William to run along with his garage.'

'Was William Vernon's son?' Jackie asked.

'Ah, well. According to Mary, when William was born, just before the war, it was given out he was Maple and Vernon's little brother. I met William when we moved in – he was about twenty. After Vernon died, Mary told me William was Maple's boy. The parents had lied to save scandal.' Phyllis stopped knitting. 'After all that, and Maple never lived to see her little mite grow up.'

'Do you know where William lives now?' Jackie quelled her excitement.

'William went off after Mr and Mrs Greenhill died, Mary said he wanted a new life.' Phyllis swapped wool to a different colour. 'Vernon was keeping the business for him but when he didn't want it Cliff had to step in.'

'Is Cliff still running the garage?'

'Oh yes, our John got a car from them last year.' Phyllis tugged the stitches on her needle. 'King Street, near where the Commodore used to be.'

'Maple's Motors.' Jackie went cold. 'Vernon named it after his sister.'

'So, Maple lived on, it was her legacy.'

Back in her own kitchen, Jackie called Beverly. She and Jack would be leaving for Tewkesbury in the afternoon.

'Bev? I've got a job for you.'

Chapter Thirty-Four

2019

Stella

'I'm guessing if he had to die, Roddy would like the whole starved monk thing.' Lucie was dancing around the chapel. Roddy's murder had invigorated her. She resumed reading from a printout on cadaver tombs.

'"... the monument is a canopied altar tomb topped with an effigy of a skeletal cadaver being crawled over by vermin..."'

It was three o'clock in the afternoon, but the day had been grey and now the tower was lost in heavy mist.

Stella had collapsed into bed at ten the night before, leaving Lucie busy in her cockpit. She was still there, fresh as a daisy, when Stella set about her morning clean. As Stella removed empty fig packets – too many, she should warn Lucie of likely consequences – Lucie remained absorbed in what she was reading. She hadn't looked up when Stella had given her coffee in Lucie's pint-sized mug. She was reading up on the abbey. Lucie's attention to detail was after Stella's own heart and she had felt bad for assuming Lucie's hectic manner mirrored her work process.

'The carver's included every rib.' Lucie bent over the monk. '*Tsssk*. Some ancient squirrel on a stick has carved his initials on the poor bloke.'

'Roddy said those marks are considered of historic value,' Stella remembered.

'*Pish posh.* I call it graffiti.' Lucie traced the myriad marks scored over the carved figure as if with a healing hand.

'It's a legacy.' Stella thought of Joy's comment at the Death Café. 'Roddy was interested in cadaver tombs. I wonder, was his killer's intention to highlight a link between Roddy and the cadaver monk, as with Clive and his clocks?'

'"Time Keeper Slain by Sundial", I get that, but "True Crime Podcaster Dies by Starved Monk" is a bit deep. Who knew March was obsessed with old tombs?'

'Jack told me there was a theory in the nineteenth century that the last image a person saw was imprinted on their eye and could be restored. If that was true, we'd see Roddy's murderer.'

'Optography. Stella, if you don't want Jack, please don't channel him. We need your cool rational mind. If it held water, it's you who would be imprinted on his eyes. Questions: why, instead of going to the police in Cheltenham, did March come to the abbey? He wanted you on board for his podcast so why not talk to you after the Death Cafe?' Lucie went out to the north ambulatory.

'Something changed his mind.' Stella trawled her memory of both Death Café evenings. There had been a mood of frustration, as if the group, although there from their own free will, had been kept back on detention.

'March's phone would tell us who rang him on the morning you met him. The police are treating his missing laptop and phone as evidence of mugging. Assailants take his wallet which tells them where he lived. They get in and strip his room of valuables. Who else had access to March's bedsit?' Lucie stopped by a shelf of second-hand books on sale for two pounds each. 'Here's an idea. Gladys is to meet March in the abbey after the Death Café. She scampers across, stabs March and dumps his beanie on a chair to make it look like he'd been listening to Joy's sublime music. When you steam in searching for God, it was her shadow you saw on the wall.'

'I wasn't—' Stella spotted a novel by Ngaio Marsh, the writer Jack mentioned when he'd found Stella in the abbey. On impulse, she dropped a few pound coins into a box on the wall and took it.

Above the hum of heating and the echo of echoes which filled the abbey with an eerie non-specific sound, she heard a familiar voice. She peeped into the gift shop. A woman was wrapping up a set of abbey mugs and chatting with an elderly couple in matching Burberry macs.

Stella shrank back and whispered to Lucie, 'That's Joy, the organist.'

'We're in business.' Lucie turned on her phone's recording app and, whisking around the Burberry couple, she flapped into the shop. Stella trailed after. This was not going to go well.

'Lucie May. I'm Stella's *best* friend. Joy, I think?' Lucie floated about in front of the counter, tipping her head like a bird as she appeared to admire the gifts for sale.

'Hi, Joy.' Stella executed a wave behind her.

'Stella. You are becoming quite a regular. Have you bought tickets for our recital yet?'

'No. I've been busy.'

'Goodness, haven't you. Finding bodies all over the place. And poor dear Clive to boot. Are any of us safe?' Joy clasped a large green pendant to her embroidered chest.

'Isn't that jade darling.' Lucie loomed at the pendant.

'Malachite.' Joy straightened a pile of abbey teacloths. 'There's a nasty gang going about. I've asked for extra security.'

'We must band together to bring this killer to book before there is a third death.' Lucie sailed about the gift shop nudging display carousels into a gentle spin, sniffing scented candles. 'I only had the pleasure of meeting Clive post-mortem.'

This was the wrong tone to take with no-nonsense Joy. Wildly, Stella snatched up a group of plaster models labelled Nativity Figures and presented them to Joy. 'I'll have these, please.'

'Would you like them wrapped as a Christmas gift?'

'They're for me, it's fine.'

'They'll be half price after the festive season. You didn't hear that from me.' Joy slipped the figures, Mary with Jesus in her arms and Joseph draped in sickly orange robes, into a paper bag and slid it over the counter to Stella.

'Joy, would you be willing to chat with Lucie and me? Lucie's a reporter, she's concerned to find Roddy's killer.' Stella pre-empted Lucie.

'Concerned to get a story, methinks.' Joy tweaked the battalion of Mary and Josephs to close the resulting gap. Unattractive though the Nativity pieces were, Stella was pleased with her purchase. Their heads bowed, Mary and Joseph exuded calm.

'We have to earn a crust,' Lucie cackled.

'You'll earn a loaf of bread and a good few fish too with any story about this.' Joy moved one of the Marys along the line as if in checkmate.

'If you'd rather not get involved...' Lucie beamed.

'Come to my cottage later. I promise not to be dead when you arrive.' Stella was instantly calm, watching Joy scribble her address on an abbey opening times leaflet. Joy would be a match for Lucie.

'Bagged.' Popping a fig into her mouth, Lucie swam out of the north ambulatory and out of the abbey. Stella caught up with her on the yew path. 'Don't be fooled by that air of sanctity, those types are first in line to kill. One down, two to go. Grumpy Andrea and Morticia, Queen of the Death Café.'

'Felicity.' Stella felt bound to tone Lucie down.

The rain had eased, but tumbling dark clouds rolling above the Avon threatened a storm.

'What's he doing?' Lucie pointed at a figure, sketchy in the rain, bending by the wall adjoining Cloisters House.

'It's a woman. That's Andrea,' Stella realized.

'Our eggs are gathering in their basket.' Giving a sniff like the bloodhound Jack said Lucie was in another life, she beetled across the abbey lawn. Sensing action, Stanley dragged Stella after her.

'Coo-ee, Andrea?' Lucie pronounced it 'And-*raya*.'

At the Death Café, Stella hadn't needed an eagle eye to know Andrea preferred plants to people. Where they could, people chose work to suit their nature.

'It's you that is the artist behind these beautiful gardens.' She swept out an arm, taking in the grass and grey tombs wet with rain.

There was no answer to this and Andrea gave none.

'Stella told me *all* about you.'

'Only that I'd met you,' Stella quickly said. 'Lucie's keen to find who killed Roddy. Maybe you haven't heard, but Clive the clockmaker was murdered last night.'

Andrea leaned on the handle of her spade and stared off towards Cloisters House, as if by fixing on the middle distance, she could make Stella and Lucie disappear.

'Are you OK? You know, with... murders happening?' Lucie looked at Stella with a 'we've got a right one here' expression.

'Why wouldn't I be?'

'What a shock, Roddy and Clive both dead. It quite rattled me.'

'You didn't know him.'

Lucie got out her phone. 'Can I record this? Hearing and memory are jiggered. Do *not* get old.' Lucie rarely referred to her age. Stella knew, as did Gladys, that she was over seventy, but Lucie usually portrayed herself as reluctantly staring forty in the face.

'I'm working.' Andrea put a booted foot on her fork. 'Careful, don't squash those crocuses.' She pointed to a clump of purple flowers that Lucie, stepping backwards, nearly squashed.

'We won't stop you. Evenings are more civilized. We're seeing Joy at seven, we can be with you by end of play. I'm presuming you stop digging when it's dark.' Lucie essayed a wave at a dug-over flower bed at their feet.

'I don't talk to journalists.' Andrea threw her fork into a nearby wheelbarrow and trundled it away.

'She's not a gardener,' Lucie said when Andrea was out of earshot.

'Why do you say that?' Stella felt obscurely irritable at Lucie dissing Andrea's skills.

'The blisters on her hands. She's not used to wielding a fork. And she doesn't know her crocuses from her cyclamen.' Lucie was leading them to a shed at the border of the grounds. 'We shall beard her in her grotto later. *Geronimo.*'

'We don't know where Andrea— What are you doing?' Stella watched Lucie drag a heavy man's bike out from behind the shed.

'As you know, my Stellagmite, life is cause and effect.' Lucie propped the bicycle against one of the stone coffins. She dived into her capacious leather bag, pulled out her plastic make-up bag with leopard markings and, gripping a pair of nail scissors, jabbed the front tyre.

'*Lucie.*' Stella felt sick as Lucie twisted the blade into the rubber. In the muffled silence, she heard a hiss as the inner tube deflated.

'It's frog-freezing, let us take a pot of lapsang in the tearooms.' Putting away the scissors, Lucie smacked her hands on her cargo pants.

'We could go to the flat.' Hugging Stanley to keep him dry and her warm, Stella had had enough of the tearooms.

'We shall grab a window table and wait for Lady Manure to clock off. We shall tail her home then pay her a *leetle* visit.'

'She's on a bike, we'll never...' Stella tailed off as she got it.

'Cause and effect, *mon cheri.*' Lucie's soprano tones sang out. 'Cause equals puncture. Effect equals Andrea the pretend gardener has to walk home.'

Chapter Thirty-Five

2019

Jack

Maple's Motors (Est. 1944) was squeezed between the arched entrance to flats above and what in Jack's boyhood had been a sweetshop but was now a flooring company.

'Rare to find a showroom on a high street, the lease costs must be huge,' Jack said to Beverly as they pushed on a glass door and went inside.

'We've owned the building for nearly a century. Low overheads mean we can offer genuine bargains.'

Maple Greenhill. Although Jack believed in ghosts, he didn't expect to see one under strip lighting amongst polished Minis and BMWs.

'Cleo Greenhill, can I help you guys?' The likeness was so strong the woman could only be Maple's descendent.

'We've come to buy a car.' Beverly was keeping to Jackie's instructions.

'I like customers who know what they want, it saves everyone time.' Cleo shook Bev's hand. 'Do you fancy a wander or would you like me to point you in the right direction?'

'Yes.' Face to face with Cleo, brimming with life, Jack felt the measure of Maple's loss more profoundly than from reading newspaper articles.

'Which?' Cleo raised one eyebrow.

'That one.' Bev pointed at a racing green Mini.

As Bev got behind the wheel and purred over the leather seats, Jack quelled impatience – they were meant to cut to the chase and head for Tewkesbury. Bev was taking the role-playing too seriously.

At the rear of the showroom he found a drinks machine and the toilet. As Jack usually did, he took the 'Private' sign on a door as invitation and stepped inside.

At the top of a staircase, he entered the door with 'Office' on the opaque glass in gold letters.

Boxes towered on top of filing cabinets. On top of the cabinet nearest to him was a huge Remington typewriter that was once the latest in office equipment. As had been the cumbersome computers, one with a floating Windows 98 logo on the screen. Jack tracked fumes to an opened bottle of whisky on the furthest of two desks.

A whiteboard on the wall behind it suggested that, despite the bargain prices, sales were little better than at Clean Slate. Cliff had had no sales for the whole of November and nothing in December so far. Cleo had sold two BMWs in the first week of November, but the rest of the month was blank.

Jack guessed that, as he saw at Clean Slate, the pile of stamped envelopes on the nearest desk contained last notice invoices. His eye travelled to pictures on the dirty white pebbledash walls. Car adverts dating back to the seventies – *You don't need a big one to be happy* – for a tiny Mini, unlike the sleek model over which he'd left Bev pretending to salivate. *One Triumph leads to another* showed four bikini-clad women draped on a TR6. Jack switched his gaze to five photographs, portraits of stiff-looking men, the last in colour. John Hamblin, Billy Turton Hamblin, Vernon Greenhill. The last one showed Cliff Greenhill's ruddy cheeks. In one picture, Jack recognized Cleo, but it was oddly in sepia, like the early pictures. Jack's heart crashed against his chest: the photograph wasn't of Cleo. It was Maple.

'Who the devil are you?' An elderly man, grizzled grey hair darkened with grease, his chin unshaven, staggered through a door which, hung with coats, Jack hadn't noticed.

'I was waiting for Cleo.' Often caught somewhere uninvited, Jack was smooth.

'Cars… downstairs.' The man grabbed the whisky, took a swig and wiped his mouth.

'You must be Cliff.' Jack nodded at the picture beside Maple's.

'*Must I?*' Cliff's cheeks were ruddier still in real life.

'You took over from Vernon.' To gain trust Jack often pretended acquaintance with absent people. Vernon having died before Jack was born, he was skating on thin ice.

'What's that to you?'

'It's lovely when a business is passed down through the family.'

'Is it.' Cliff Greenhill opened a drawer in his desk meant for hanging files and took out another bottle of whisky. Seeming not to notice it was empty he raised it to Maple's photograph. 'Thanks to her.'

'How is that?' Jack was briefed, he knew exactly why it was thanks to Maple.

'She gets murdered. We're still paying for it.' He swallowed a belch. 'RIP and all that.'

'You shouldn't be up here.' Cleo Greenhill stood in the doorway.

'No, sorry, I was looking for…' Jack saw from Cleo's face no lame excuse would do. 'Cliff was telling me about Maple. Your great-aunt.'

'Never met her.' Cliff tossed the empty bottle in the bin.

'I wondered if I could drive it away today.' Bev appeared behind Cleo.

'I'd love you to, but it must go through our workshop before we roll it out. Come back in two days, make it three.' Cleo gave a tight smile.

'We can have it ready for you tonight.' Cliff Greenhill found his inner salesman.

'Dad.' Cleo eyed her father.

'Get the lad on it, he's only twiddling his thumbs.' Cliff waved a hand.

'We'll see what we can do.' Cleo's pantomime that Maple Motors had much more business than they could process was painful to watch.

Back in the showroom, Beverly ignored Jack's prods and hisses that her charade should stop. He couldn't bear Cleo to believe she'd got a win.

'I'll have the Countryman ready tonight,' Cleo told Bev.

'We haven't quite made up our mi—' Jack started.

'That's the best news, thank you.' Beverly looked so pleased she almost convinced Jack.

'If you're sure.' Cleo handed Beverly a pack and it dawned on Jack that Cleo had made her first December sale.

'Why wouldn't I be?' Beverly asked.

'That's not why you're here.' Hands on her hips, Cleo confronted Jack. 'Mr Man here was asking about Maple, my great-aunt. What are you, journalists?'

'We're trying to find out who killed Maple.' Jack sat down at Cleo's sales desk. It was do or die. He launched into the whole story. How they had come to connect Maple's murder with the murder of Sir Aleck Northcote in 1963 and with two murders in the last week in Tewkesbury.

'The podcast man.' Cleo got them drinks. 'That's why he looked familiar. He was here pretending to buy a car a few weeks back. He asked for Dad, which was a mistake because Dad sent him packing as soon as he mentioned Maple. I only saw him as he was leaving.'

'March believed he knew the real killer of Aleck Northcote. He probably wanted to know if Cliff's father and grandparents had ever harboured suspicions about who killed her,' Beverly said.

'As you saw, Dad won't talk about Maple, he blames her for him being a car salesman and he hasn't forgiven Maple's son William, my dad's cousin, for escaping. My grandfather Vernon put pressure on Dad to keep the showroom going.' Cleo let out a sigh. 'Like Maple would care.'

'You seem to care,' Jack said.

'I do. Selling cars is the dream job. If only my dad would let me run the show, I'd turn it right around. But he promised his father to stick it and, even though it's killing him, he will. Thanks, mate.' Crossing the showroom Cleo took a bundle of junk mail and brown envelopes from the postman.

'Do you know where Maple's son is now?'

'No. Someone told me he's a doctor. I should be more interested, but if William doesn't want to know us, fine.' Cleo buffed the bonnet of a bright red BMW on her way back to the desk. 'Apparently Grandad never got over Maple's murder. When Vernon's boss left him this place, instead of thinking it amazing, Vernon felt guilty because Maple never got a life. Everything he did was to make it up to her. It drove his wife and my dad crazy.'

'Why did William disown you all?' Beverly looked outraged.

'Vernon only told him he was Maple's son after Maple's parents died. William was angry that they'd all lied to him. He wouldn't touch a penny of his inheritance.'

'It's nice of you to be so frank with us,' Beverly said. 'I promise you won't regret it. We want justice for Maple.'

'What I will regret is you buying a car to get a foot in the door.' Cleo looked stern. 'There's a cooling-off period, as long as you don't drive it to Scotland and back.'

'I won't cool off,' Beverly said. 'What did Cliff want to do, you know, instead of selling cars?'

'Be an archaeologist. Too late now, he can't even manage a gardening trowel.' Cleo suddenly looked sad. 'Listen, guys, Dad won't care if you discover who murdered Maple, but I will. Her murder destroyed our family.'

'Murder does that,' Jack said.

'Next time you and me go undercover, maybe don't follow through?' Jack said as they drove off in his own crock of a car.

'I wanted to spend the money Nan left me on something special,' Beverly said. 'You can't say it wasn't worth it. Now you have a fancy motor in which to go and see Stella. Besides, as soon as I mentioned Maple, it was like a starting gun, Cleo was off.'

'We're not going to Tewkesbury to see Stella,' Jack lied.

Chapter Thirty-Six

2019

Stella

At around the time Jack and Beverly were in Maple's Motors in London, Stella and Lucie, unaware Jackie was sending reinforcements, were tucking into cream teas in the Abbey Gardens tearoom. Stella had taken one bite of a scone piled with cream and jam, when she spotted Andrea the gardener wheeling her bike down the yew path.

In a madcap dash, Stella and Lucie caught up with Andrea and, keeping a discreet distance, trailed her as she cut down the alleyways that criss-crossed Tewkesbury.

The route was circuitous and Stella began to suspect Andrea was onto them and was taking them on a wild goose chase. But finally, they emerged onto the high street near the New Leaf, the bookshop where Stella had met Janet and she'd been accosted by Clive.

Andrea had stopped and was chaining her bike to a lamp-post. With no shops on this stretch there were few pedestrians so Stella and Lucie feigned interest in the menu outside the Tudor House Hotel. Risking a peep, Stella saw Andrea letting herself into Gladys Wren's boarding house.

'We didn't need to follow her, we knew she was Gladys's lodger,' Stella said.

'Never mind. If we'd come straight here, it wouldn't have been half as much fun,' Lucie said.

Stella had never doorstepped anyone. Squeamish, she hung back as Lucie knocked and stood ready to jam her tactical-strength boots into the gap when Andrea tried to slam the door. This wasn't what happened.

'Nice of you to see us, Andrea.' Lucie barged into the hall and, ignoring Andrea's threat to call the police, pounded along the passage. Stella shut the door in case Andrea flew out into the street yelling for help.

'I'd kill for a cuppa.' Seating herself at Gladys Wren's Formica table, Lucie showed her teeth.

'I said I won't talk to you. Leave *now*.' Andrea's whooshing motion was wasted on Lucie who was ferreting in her bag. In the harsh strip-light, her complexion was sallower than outside in the abbey gardens.

'I abandoned a jolly nice pot of lapsang for you.' Lucie took out a package wrapped in tissue. To Stella's amazement, at the sight of what was Lucie's scone, complete with jam and cream, Andrea switched on the kettle and assembled mugs. Wishing she'd had the presence of mind to bring her own cream tea, Stella sat at the table.

'How long were you and Roddy together?' Lucie darted dainty licks at her scone.

'How do you know that?' Andrea flopped down at the table.

'Ooh, where to start? With tea, I think?' Lucie pointed at the kettle as it boiled.

'I don't have to talk to reporters.' A superfluous protest since, clearly, Andrea did have to talk to Lucie. She resumed tea-making – Lady Grey, Stella noticed.

'OK, babes, if you're a gardener, I'm a blue-headed unicorn,' Lucie said. 'Can you even call a spade a spade? You lived cheek by jowl to Roderick March yet, at the Death Café, you were strangers. Not even the nod of recognition we'd expect, given you lived under the same roof. We know March was operating incognito, he'd instructed dear Mrs Wren – she *is* a poppet, isn't she – to act dumb around him. But what were your instructions?'

'Roderick didn't expect me to be there. I wanted to mess up his plan.' Andrea plonked a chipped mug in front of Stella. 'Show him I can't be walked over.'

'Why?' Stella said.

'He'd gone there to ask you out. He'd missed his chance at the Abbey the day before because I phoned him.'

'He couldn't have known I'd be there, I never told him.'

'He saw your name on the abbey's cleaning rota.' Andrea spat out the words.

'How come anyone could see that?' Lucie asked Stella's question.

'It's in the abbey's admin office. Rod sneaked in there.'

'Is that what Roddy told you, that he planned to ask me out?'

'His name was Rod. Rod March, and it's disgusting you can even ask.' Andrea's eyes, like small round pebbles underwater, were hard and unremitting.

'Sorry?' Stella wilted. The trouble with doorstepping was you could end up in a kitchen packed with murder weapons.

'Take it from the top, Andrea, skip nothing.' Lucie accepted her tea from Andrea with a scary smile. 'We're all friends here.'

'We met on Tinder,' Andrea said.

'That's great.' Stella tried to be encouraging. Lucie shot her a look. *Be invisible.*

'Rod was gorgeous, with nice eyes – why was a hunk like him on a dating site? And when he walked into the restaurant – he suggested Nando's – he was as good as his photo. I was smitten.' Her smile faded. 'When I waved him over, he couldn't hide his disappointment. I waited for his phone to ring – my friend Sally was calling me after half an hour so I could high-tail it if he was a dud; he had to have lined up the same thing.'

'Did it ring?' Lucie swiped to a fresh page.

'No. Of course later I knew he'd have upped and gone regardless of my feelings. But I didn't know, so I went into overdrive to keep him scoffing his peri-peri wings. I told him about my private project. About an unsolved murder of a woman in 1940, Maple Greenhill. I told Rod that I knew who killed her and that I planned to expose him.'

'Did you intend it as a podcast, with you as star detective?' Lucie clacked her teeth. A new and unsettling habit.

'All my life I've slaved at a job, nine to five, five to midnight, weekends, no holidays,' Andrea said. 'It was not a bloody podcast... it was for... for me. My private quest, and he stole it.'

'Roddy stole the idea from you?' Stella said.

'Did Rod tell you he was too tired for sex, but not so tired to be up all night on his laptop listening to true-crime podcasts?' Andrea snarled.

'*Ouch*. Let's play nice,' Lucie crooned. 'I'm guessing you're a teensy bit annoyed with the late Mr March. No matter, trot on.'

'Rod stayed, he bought more drinks, ordered a plate piled with those Portuguese tarts and had me tell him everything. We went back to my flat and, after sex, like a love-sick idiot, I showed him my notes. Next thing, he's dumped the cadaver grave thingy for his podcast for *my* murder. It's only cos I threatened to cut off his balls with my Victorinox knife that I got to be assistant researcher.'

'Yet you're a gardener.' Stella felt outrage on Andrea's behalf.

'I actually *knew* they were cyclamens,' Andrea told Lucie.

'I meant, did he pay you for the research?' Getting the picture, Stella doubted it.

'I gave up work and used my savings.'

'That was some step.' Stella didn't know why, but felt Andrea was now lying.

'Whenever he stayed, before going to sleep – after spending every evening under the duvet recording his podcast, Rod was too tired to have sex. He'd put himself to sleep to a true-crime podcast. We had an ear bud each for better sound. He didn't care that they were about real dead people, he skipped the bits where their families cried or said they would never get over the loss. Our first row was when I called him morbid and he said did I need a mirror? I said it wasn't the same...' Andrea drew breath. 'His podcast would be the best since *Serial*. It would add to the greater good, bring closure and restore truth for the victim. I had to make notes on what worked, and what was too sentimental or sensational. I had my uses.'

'A thorough approach.' Lucie would approve of delegating donkey work.

'He was thorough.' Andrea took their half-drunk cups, tossed the remainder down the sink and washed them up. 'Turned out he was doing digging of his own. He found her. *Stellah Dar-nell*. He was so excited he got an erec—'

'*Stop*.' Lucie raised her palm.

'He didn't *find* me.' That was exactly what Roddy had done.

'Then he learnt that in 1963, some doctor called Sir Aleck Northcote was murdered here in Tewkesbury. His son hanged for it. Roddy got a bee in his bonnet that the son was innocent.'

'How come he was so sure?' This earned Stella a venomous look from Andrea and she decided it was wise to leave it all to Lucie.

'He was sure that someone killed Northcote in revenge for his strangling Maple Greenhill. The podcast was, as he said, now on skis. *He stole my project*.' Andrea looked fit to kill. Stella caught her breath. *Perhaps she had*.

'Tough titty indeed.' Lucie turned her mouth down at the corners.

'He said what the podcast needed for ratings status was this cleaning woman, Darnell.' She fixed Stella with a cold gleam. 'He stalked you online. He knew you'd snap him up, said he was younger, brighter and more now and happening than some old hack you worked with. You'd pull in the thinking listeners who hid their true-crime addiction by framing it as a social and cultural experience. When all's said and done, they're just like other armchair rubber-neckers, thirsty for a nasty murder as a bedtime story. It was my idea to contextualise the crimes. I was still trying to impress Rod. "Focus on the victim," I said, "make them live, give them back their dignity." He loved that, he said, "Victims have traction these days, they're all the rage."' Andrea jabbed the washing up brush at Stella. 'You and him planned to elope into murder sunset.'

'That's silly.' Stella laughed accidentally. 'Of course we didn't.'

'I am *not* old, I am more now and happening than March.' Balling up her tissue, Lucie had been simmering. 'And, more to the point, unlike him I have a pulse.'

'Roddy never asked me.' Stella had noticed before how the less guilty she was, the more guilty she felt.

'He rang your cleaners. A woman claiming to be your PA – lah-de-dah – wouldn't divulge where you were hiding,' Andrea said. 'I hoped he'd given up and returned to me.' She slumped in her chair. 'Until he found the cleaning rota.'

'I would never have agreed; I work with the best journalist. We're a team.' Stella looked at Lucie. 'Although I'm a cleaner and him calling me wouldn't have changed my mind.' *Who had wanted Roddy dead? If Giles Northcote wasn't his father's killer, who was? Who impaled Clive on his sundial?* Stella needed answers. Roddy's asking her wouldn't have changed her mind, but his murder had.

'I read he died in your arms.'

'I found him.' Stella's nod was non-committal.

'Andrea, did you kill Roddy March? Hell hath no fury, et cetera.' Lucie liked to provoke. Tensing, Stella did not.

'I warned him against using the name Roddy on our podcast.' Staring off in the distance, Andrea appeared in a fugue state. 'Listeners will take Roderick more seriously.'

'I'm thinking Mr March went for cutesy,' Lucie said. 'I'll ask again. Did you murder March?'

'Since you're so good at this stuff, you work it out.'

Chapter Thirty-Seven

2019

Jackie

> IRENE AND HENRY COTTON
> BELOVED PARENTS OF GEORGE AND JOSEPH
> 15 JUNE 1935
> JOSEPH COTTON 1909–1940

'I knew this story, one of the boys did it for a school project – Mark, I think. The shared death date had fascinated him. The Cottons died in a rail-crash near Welwyn Garden City, it's on the internet now but Mark had to write to British Rail and look up newspapers in Chiswick Library. For years after he'd pick flowers and make us troop over here on the anniversary. Have to admit, Jack, I do see this as a sign.' Jackie shone her torch on the adjacent grave.

> GEORGE COTTON
> 1894–1979

'I saw this the other day.' Unhappiness had made Jack easily annoyed.

'Shame you didn't tell me – I've spent the afternoon trawling the internet,' Jackie said.

'I didn't know George Cotton was significant. I was just...' Jack fell silent. They knew he'd have been up to his old habit of stalking graveyards.

Jackie couldn't argue, it was due to Jack's habit they were there now. The cemetery was locked after dark but he knew a secret way in behind a beech tree and a break in the railings. Instead of showing them Cotton's grave on her phone, they stood before the real thing. Jackie continued, 'George Cotton, as you know, investigated Maple Greenhill's murder. I've been hitting the online sites and on Ancestry found that in 1941 Cotton was an ARP warden which means he must have left the police. Because of the war, there was no census in 1941, and the previous one was destroyed by fire in the forties. I followed a breadcrumb trail of birth and marriage certificates, the Cottons' daughter's birth certificate in 1922. I found that Agnes died in 1940, which may have been why he stopped being a police officer. The 1971 census had George Cotton still living in Queen Adelaide Road where his daughter was born.'

'Why isn't Agnes here too?' Jack raked the area with his own torch.

'For that I went to Find a Grave. Agnes is buried in Liverpool where she was born. She was forty when a bomb hit the fire station where she worked on the phones. Twenty-ninth of December 1940. There'd been a hiatus of raids due to crap weather, it started up again that night. One fatality, many injured. She apparently chatted away to the men digging her out for over an hour. She said, "I'm not hurt much," and died the moment they got her out.'

'I can't bear that.' Beverly groaned. 'What a brave woman.'

'I wonder if maybe Agnes's parents wanted her near them. Poor George, forced to cover up a murder case, then his wife dies.' Jackie shone the torch on George's grave. 'We're lucky we haven't had to live through a war on the home front. Life stopped, the blackout, rationing, a swathe of new confusing laws. And the noise, smoke, the destruction of your home, whole streets went. I couldn't live thinking my children, my family and friends could die at any time.' Jackie stopped. 'Sorry, folks, digging up the past has got to me.'

'My nan's mum got told off for not having her gas mask on a bus. Nan was there, she got scared her mum would go to prison,' Beverly said.

'And they were never needed, thank goodness,' Jackie said. 'June, their daughter, died of cancer the same year as George, in 1979 aged fifty-seven.'

'George had a tragic life,' Jack said.

'I'm sure not. A life distilled to paperwork leaves out lots of good bits. Those days when a beam of sunlight lifts your mood.' Jackie led them back through the secret hole in the railings and switched off her torch. 'According to one of those newspaper cuttings in Julia Northcote's Lyons' Swiss Roll box, Cotton's right-hand man at the time of Maple's murder was PC John Peter Shepherd. He also left the police in 1940. He joined the Royal Engineers in January 1941, survived the war and died three years ago in a nursing home, unmarried and childless. Agnes dying in 1940 might explain Cotton leaving the force, Shepherd could have wanted to fight for his country, but something doesn't feel right. They needed police officers on the home front, so why let Cotton and Shepherd go? From Julia Northcote's letter, I suspect both men were removed from the scene because they solved Maple's murder and got the wrong result. Ah, here's your posh new jalopy, Bev.'

They were drenched in car headlights as a racing green Mini stopped in the circle of lamplight and, climbing out, Cleo Greenhill tossed Beverly the keys.

'She's fuelled up and ready to go. Handles like a dream.' Cleo patted the bonnet.

Jackie detected more sincerity in the woman's tones than she'd expected when Jack told her Beverly had bought a car in fifteen minutes flat. Still, although impulsive, Bev rarely made mistakes.

'Can we drop you back at the garage?' Beverly asked when she and Jack had stowed their bags in the boot and were ready to leave.

'You're fine, my wife's waiting.' Cleo jerked a thumb at a white BMW sports parked further down Corney Road. Jackie knew Cleo had come out for Bev, letting her know she wasn't the only lesbian in town.

Jack and Bev climbed into the Mini.

'I'm guessing it's under guarantee,' Jackie couldn't help saying to Cleo as they watched the Mini's rear lights recede.

'Three years, plus I've extended cooling-off to a month. All I care is they prove that Creep-Bag pathologist Northcote murdered my dad's Aunty Maple. And, if they do find who killed Northcote in the sixties, if he's still on this earth, I'll shake his hand.' Cleo punched a fist into her palm.

'I'm sorry they weren't straight with you. Blame me,' Jackie said.

'I knew they weren't the happy couple they said they were. I could spot Bev a mile off, takes one to know one, and Jack looks like he's lost a tenner and found a fifty pence piece. Beverly was initially less bothered by the Mini's TwinPower Turbo or multi-function instrument display than talking about Maple. Although she must have been listening to my list of deluxe features because she bought the car.' Cleo gave a husky laugh. 'Jackie, please would you do me a favour?'

'If I can.' Jackie liked Cleo Greenhill.

'If my grandad Vernon killed this Northcote, please tell me first so I can prepare Dad?'

Chapter Thirty-Eight

2019

Stella

'I was born in this room,' Joy Turton said.

'Gosh.' Stella had no need for her finger test – an aluminium lamp illuminated a veil of dust on the dining table, window sill, along the top of a large television. She hoped it had been cleaner when Joy's mother was giving birth.

The electronic keyboard, a skirt around the stand that made it look like an altar, and the G-plan sofa were counter to what Stella had expected from Joy's embroidered jacket with animals and arrows. But Terry had taught her not to expect or assume so maybe the stylish décor, tumbleweed fluff and home-spun garments were reflections of Joy's complexity. A tussle with the old and the new. Were it not the best route to the organist's wrong side and would look like touting for work, Stella would offer to clean.

'You didn't know Roddy March before the Death Café.'

'I did know him,' Joy replied.

'I got no sense of that at the Death Café.'

'Why should you have "got the sense"?' Joy hadn't offered a drink. Not that Stella fancied risking her crockery. 'Personally, I was there to discuss death, not to get a sense of anyone.'

'How did you know him?' Stella doubted that any suspect her dad had interviewed had scared him like Joy was scaring her.

'He interviewed me for his podcast.'

'Why?' Stella said. 'You never said you knew Northcote.'

'Do I have to reiterate my motive for going to the Death Café? I was a child when Sir Aleck met his death. I knew him only as an adult one saw about the town. I met Mr March fussing about the abbey. Now I know he was there for his podcast. I do hate liars.' She stared at first Stella, then Lucie.

'Did you hate March?' Lucie's fearlessness had, in the past, twice nearly got her killed.

'You don't fool me,' Joy said. Stella wished she'd properly debriefed Lucie on the characteristics of the group – such as she'd observed – before they'd started interviews. 'I hated Mr March for lying about why he was in the abbey – it was not where his mother worshipped in her youth – but if you're suggesting I left the Death Café, ambushed him by the monk's tomb and stuck him with a knife, you're as much of a fool as March was.' Joy played silent chords on her keyboard. 'Incidentally, will I be remunerated for this chat?'

'March was in Tewkesbury to find out the truth of the Cloisters House murder.' Stella jumped in before Lucie spouted any nonsense about making Joy rich. 'So, you didn't know Sir Aleck?'

'I was ten when he was murdered.' Joy was suddenly defensive.

'Ten-year-olds are the best observers. I bet you were one of them,' Lucie beguiled.

'Your methods are tired, missy,' Joy said. 'Flattery leaves me cold.'

'Lucie wasn't flattering you,' Stella said. 'You've lived here all your life, the cottage is a stone's throw from Cloisters House and the abbey. Can you recall seeing any strangers about that day?'

'I'll tell you what I did see.' Joy's cheeks puffed like a hamster as if her words had been stowed there for this moment. 'Sir Aleck had her against the wall, legs open. Shocking sight for any child, especially a gifted musician. She lied to the police. She never saw that film, she was busy taking liberties and *what's more,*' crouched over her keyboard, Joy looked like the ten-year-old girl she had been, 'I asked her, in the film, who did the murder. She told me I was far too young to know. Yes, ten-year-olds are observant, and I was far too young to observe what I saw.'

'Who was this woman?' Lucie and Stella asked at the same time.

'The housekeeper, Miss Fleming, as was. Aleck Northcote, Roddy March, Clive Burgess. Don't be fooled by Mrs Wren's ditsy manner, she has sharp elbows and sharp teeth.' Joy's cheeks retracted. 'You don't have to look far for your killer.'

Chapter Thirty-Nine

2019

Stella

Girl in the Headlines. Stella read the Wikipedia page on her phone.

It was seven o'clock and the abbey was closing soon. They had timed how long it took to walk from the tearoom to Roddy's death-site. Walking fast, two and half minutes – two if his killer ran.

'The film Gladys Wren told police she saw at the Sabrina cinema in Tewkesbury the week Northcote was murdered. A British noir thriller set in London about a model who gets shot dead. Mrs Wren told us her fiancé Derek didn't want her to change her night off because the programme changed the following day. Then he got called away and she said she watched the rest on her own.'

'Good alibi, you're seen going in and, in the dark, who notices you slip out unless you block the screen?' Lucie said.

'Except Joy swears she saw her in Cloisters House having sex with Sir Aleck.'

'Did Gladys kill him because he wouldn't marry her?' Lucie walked her fingers up the monk's protruding ribs.

'Or Aleck Northcote was jealous of Gladys being with Derek, tried to kill her so she killed him. Then she pretended to find him.' Stella was struggling with bias; she didn't want Gladys Wren to be a murderer.

'Or she killed him in cold blood,' Lucie said.

'Or Joy made it up to divert us from suspecting her.' Stanley made a ruff-ruff sound as Stella raised her voice, 'I *forgot*, Joy did leave the table. She went off to the servery and made chamomile tea for herself and Roddy March. What if she was in league with someone else and took that chance to speak to them.'

'I can't see Joy in league with anyone. Was there a signal between her and Roddy?' Lucie said.

'Only that he must have asked for chamomile because Joy had made him some. When he collected his mug from the servery counter, they could have arranged to meet at the starved monk. Except it happened so quickly, I doubt it.' Stella's dad advised keeping it simple, start with evidence and likely suspects. That was the crime scene. Widen the net only after ground zero has been swept. Working that way Janet had found enough to convince her Roddy and Clive's deaths were muggings.

'He was stabbed moments before you found him. You left last,' Lucie reminded her. 'If Roddy was expecting to meet one of them here, that half an hour start he had on you all is irrelevant. No one else left when he did. Whoever did that needed the two and a half minutes plus the seconds it takes to run a blade into a man's back. Three minutes max.'

'I left about five minutes after the rest. Felicity was still there. I didn't go straight to the monk, I listened to Joy on the organ, then I saw the beanie. By the time I found him it was more like seven or eight minutes after I left the Death Café.'

'Joy is looking good for this.' Lucie crooned to the starved monk. 'If she's not the killer, she's missed her vocation – she's got the hallmarks of a murderer.'

'Janet said that Felicity is Joy's alibi for both Roddy and Clive's deaths, they're planning the Christmas recital. So, if we think Roddy and Clive were killed by the same person, it rules them both out.'

'Or they both did it. Hey, maybe the whole group did it.'

'Joy did say she had expected there'd be no men there. It's the men that were there who are now dead.' Stella was looking at a photograph of the Sabrina cinema on her phone. The flat-fronted thirties building where Gladys Wren, then Miss Fleming, had seen *Girl in the Headlines*. Going by cars parked outside – a VW Beetle and a Ford, the picture dated from the sixties. 'Hang on, the Sabrina closed in 1963. The last showing was Terence Stamp in *Billy Budd* in September that year. Mrs Wren can't have seen *Girl in the Headlines* there in November.'

'Nice work, Sherlock.' Lucie patted the monk's forehead.

'I suppose she might have got the venue wrong.' Stella was startled by her phone buzzing and flashing in her hand. 'It's Felicity.'

'Bet Joy by Nature got on the blower as soon as we left. Felicity will be wanting a starring role in my article.'

It turned out Felicity did not want to feature in Lucie's story. She wanted Stella to clean for her. Semaphoring wildly, her ear to Stella's phone, Lucie made Stella agree to see Felicity immediately.

They parted at the end of the yew path, Lucie to the shop for nippet supplies, Stella for Cloisters House.

'Thank you for coming so soon, you must be very busy.' Felicity flung wide the great front door.

'No problem.' Stella didn't say that since finding the bodies of Roddy and Clive she had no work at all or Felicity might sniff desperation in her speediness.

'Would you like a drink? I'm having one.' Felicity led her into a large sitting room, a parquet floor gleaming in the light of a roaring fire. The floor didn't need polishing.

Stella wanted to scope the job, but Lucie had instructed she milk Felicity for clues. *'A pathologist living in a murdered pathologist's house who hosts a death café. The profile of a serial killer.'* So, she said, 'I'll have what you're having.'

This turned out to be whisky, which Stella disliked, but was too polite to admit. Sitting where Felicity indicated, on a leather chesterfield, she furtively took in the room. Walnut radiogram, open bureau on which were papers and a laptop. A bookcase of leather-bound books, more books in glass-covered cases along one wall. Stella stared at an oil painting above the fireplace – the man's face was familiar, but she couldn't place him.

'Aleck Northcote.' Felicity handed her the whisky. 'The pathologist.'

'The man who lived here?' *And was murdered in this very room.* Stella gulped the whisky, grateful for the burning sensation that travelled down her gut. 'Did you know him?'

'As I said at the Death Café, sadly no.' Felicity looked mournful. 'Every pathologist worth his salt dreams of knowing Sir Aleck. Thanks to him forensic detection is now a credible weapon against evil. He is our father.'

'Did you buy the picture?'

'I *stole* it.' Felicity was stony-faced. Then she threw her head back and uttered a braying laugh. 'Of course I bought it. I bought all this, lock, stock and test tube. I live in his world – my ex-colleagues can laugh all they like. Jealousy, what would they give to live here? There's pressure on me to open it as a museum for the discerning; only over my dead body, I say.'

'Northcote died in 1963, surely you weren't a pathologist then?'

'I was in my first year at King's. A mere kitten on the slopes of the dead.' Felicity poured herself another drink with, Stella noticed, a shaky hand. 'Every day I walk in Sir Aleck's shoes imbibing the atmosphere in which the great man lived.'

'And where he died.' The whisky had loosened Stella's tongue.

'Sir Aleck didn't die, he was murdered,' Felicity snapped. 'There on the hearth. *Not* with that poker, the police took the original. It's in their Black Museum. A shame – removing an object from a context is like robbing Samson of his hair. It loses its power.'

'I see.' Stella believed that the less power a poker had to bludgeon someone over the head the better. 'Do you believe that Northcote's son killed him?'

'Don't be taken in by that silly podcast man,' Felicity admonished. 'I've had the police grilling me to a turn. Of *course* Giles did it, the little blighter.' Felicity's speech was slurred, but her eyes were sharp.

'I wondered if you'd considered that Roddy might have a point.' Stella attempted a couldn't-care-less expression.

'I am interested in his life, not his death. March was out to be famous, sometimes there is smoke without fire. I offered to do March's autopsy – it's rare we get to look inside those we've met in life.'

'Had I better see the house?' Stella nearly said before the light fails, but at nearly eight on a rainy December night that was plainly absurd.

Upstairs, Stella leaned on the window sill of the professor's bedroom, unused, because Felicity said it would be like having sex with him to sleep in his bed. Stella thought this was going a bit far. For herself, Stella didn't think that, in the heavily draped four-poster, surrounded by dark oak furniture, she'd get a good night's sleep.

'This was Aleck's home and now it's mine. You know his wife killed herself?' Gone was the dreamy voice of the Death Café, Felicity sounded furious as if Julia Northcote had let the side down. 'He was the one to find her, naturally she knew that. So cruel.' She stood in the passage that ran the length of the house. 'I'm sorry but there's three lavatories to clean.'

Three toilets, two bathrooms, one an en suite, all this cheered Stella. She knew the answer to her next question, but wanted Felicity's version. 'Did Northcote live here alone?'

'Yes.' Felicity opened another door. 'Guest bedroom and another one over here.' She opened two more doors. Considering how to handle an answer which flew in the face of truth, Stella noted single beds, each with silk eiderdowns. Oil paintings of rural scenes hung on the walls.

'This was the housekeeper's room and one day will be for the carer.' Felicity opened a door at the end of the passage. 'I plan to die in this house.'

'He didn't live alone.' Surprised that Felicity could be so open about her last years, Stella hadn't meant to point out Felicity had contradicted herself about Northcote living alone. Or maybe she didn't think servants counted.

'I heard Northcote's housekeeper was involved with him. Did you hear that?' Stella felt a heel.

'She was *not*.' Felicity's shout made Stella's eardrums pop. 'A disgusting rumour, and out-and-out libel were Aleck alive. Who told you that?'

'I may have got it wrong.' Stella leaned on the slab.

'Was it that man, Roddy March?'

'It may have been.' Stella felt bad for dobbing in the deceased. Even if she had been willing to reveal her source, Joy the organist was a child at the time and more than likely she'd misconstrued whatever she saw.

'I'll send you a quote.' With a shock Stella saw the Bakelite phone on the wall in the hall. Below was a table with a compartment filled with faded telephone directories, most for London. Stella supposed Northcote had phoned through more to the capital than locally in Gloucestershire. She was looking at the very receiver that Northcote pulled off the cradle when, bleeding to death, he had tried to call for help.

'Good.' Felicity had been formal since Stella had asked about the housekeeper. Perhaps Joy was right after all. 'If you hear any more revolting rumours, please scotch them. Indeed, when you work for me, what you see or hear must be scotched at once. I don't like gossips.'

'Always.' Stella felt a burst of the rage which recently had dogged her. She doused it with politeness, 'It's a lovely house.'

'It sat empty for years until the seventies when I got it for tuppence with a legacy from a ghastly aunt. Goddamn scandal. Stamped with Aleck's spirit, it was worth a million.'

'Lovely.' Stella charged for the front door.

After waving at Felicity, shaken by the pathologist living in a ghost house, Stella accidentally cut down Mill Street and was brought up short by a roaring sound, finding herself on the bridge over the weir. Below, foaming water torrented through the filters. In the thin lamplight a stick was being tossed on the spume. Stella watched it spin. It sank then briefly resurfaced before being whirled away into inky blackness.

On the other bank of the Avon she could just see Stag Villas. Again, no lights. Had Clive had neighbours? Stella shut her eyes to the vision of the elderly clockmaker splayed over his sundial, his terrible grimace describing the violence of his end.

The relentless pounding beneath the wooden slats mesmerized her and gazing down at the churning water, Stella swayed as if drunk. She gripped the cold, slick ironwork of the guard rail.

The weir obliterated other sounds so it was only when Stella felt the slats vibrate that she realized she was no longer alone. She had time to see an arm raised and to compute, not feel, terror. Then the arm came down.

Chapter Forty

2019

Jack

Bev wanted to keep costs down and find a bed and breakfast, but Jack said they'd have more anonymity in a hotel. He was on a decent whack with London Underground, so it was his treat. They booked rooms on the third floor of a hotel on Tewkesbury's high street. Peering out of the tiny casement window, Beverly had been delighted to see her Mini in the car park below.

After they'd unpacked, Beverly joined Jack in his room and now they lay on his bed sipping tea and sharing one of the little packets of shortcake biscuits that came with the UHT milk capsules and tubes of instant coffee.

'Shall we have a nose around the town?' Jack jumped up.

'Only if you promise not to call on Stella.'

'Promise.' Jack was desperate to call on Stella, but it was nearly ten and Stella liked an early night. It was wiser to wait until morning.

With only a couple of burger bars and an Italian restaurant still open, the town was quiet. Jack led them down Red Lane, a narrow passage that at one time, he supposed, was one of the alleys which had once been slum dwellings. This alley emerged opposite what Bev said was a derelict flour factory. On this dimly lit winter's night it was every bit dark and satanic.

'This is creepy.' Beverly sounded ecstatic rather than afraid.

They stood on a wrought-iron bridge over what Jack's app said was the Avon, but might as easily be a canal in Venice. Looking into the fast-running water, Jack made a silent wish that Stella would welcome him with open arms.

Returning to the path, they passed a barge moored, the creaking of timber as it eased away from the bank and back again could be groaning. Jack's chest contracted when he saw Tewkesbury Abbey, peeping above rooftops. Since his fleeting visit to the town, in his mind the abbey encompassed Stella. *Was she there now?*

'The abbey is closed. We'll go tomorrow and see where Mr Roddy Podcast was murdered.' Beverly had taken to reading Jack's mind. 'The other dead man, the one who made clocks, lived across the river over there.'

A hum became a roar and suddenly they were by the weir. Water streamed through the sluices and in that moment was smooth as steel before it hit the river and tumulted to a seething mass.

The bridge was more workaday than a Venice version. Jack guessed a clapboard structure housed the sluice controls. The son of a civil engineer, bridges and tunnels were in his DNA; it was no accident he drove an underground train.

'George Cotton died here.' Beverly's torch lit their way between Fletcher's Mill and a low brick wall onto a gantry which angled out to the bridge. 'We've come straight from his grave to the last place on this earth he saw before he fell in,' she said. 'Actually, how was that possible? This railing's pretty high and he was in his eighties, he'd have had to climb it.'

'His daughter had just died of cancer, maybe he came here to die.' Jack could think of worse places.

'Why come all the way here?'

'Tewkesbury was where Northcote had lived. Maybe he too

was interested to know who administered the death penalty twenty odd years after Northcote should have got it.'

'Even if Cotton was obsessed with his unsolved case, why not come before?'

'Like you said, June had died, his police career had ended badly, what had he to live for?' Jack watched water pushing through the sluice and felt his veins fill with terrific velocity as it slammed into the river. 'Come on, the sooner we're in bed the sooner we're up.'

'*Eeugh.*' Beverly held her hand in front of the torch on her phone.

'You're *bleeding*, how did that happen?' Jack gave her a tissue.

'It's not me.' Dabbing her fingers, Bev shone her torch. 'It's here.'

Jack sniffed the smear on the railing. 'Definitely blood.'

'It's down there too.' In the torchlight, drops of blood were dotted at their feet. There was the fraction of a shoeprint, not either of theirs as it was further to the left.

'Probably a fight.' Jack's gaze drifted back to the deluge below.

'Another mugging,' Bev breathed. 'We should tell the police.'

'Tell them what?' Jack got out his phone and aimed the torch towards the gantry. 'It's not like we saw anything.'

'Look, there's more.' Bev's torch pinpointed a trail, the drops of blood closer together.

The drops led over the gantry and stopped on the bank. The injured man could have staggered off in any of three directions. They were about to give up when Jack found another drop by an arch on which the words 'Victoria Gardens' were fashioned in iron. He'd read about the Victoria Pleasure Gardens in the hotel information folder. Built in 1897 for the Queen's Diamond Jubilee, the arch was made when it was Elizabeth's turn in 2012. It was no pleasure tracking bloodstains.

'He went in there.' Bev dropped her voice.

LED lamps lit a path beside the Avon, washing trees, shrubs

and the ghost shapes of dug-over flower beds in pools of icy white light. In some places, the river had swelled over the bank. A mirror to the sky.

'Is the river always that high?' Beverly whispered.

'Tewkesbury often floods.' Another snippet from the hotel folder. Jack's heel skidded and, envisaging blood, he saw the path had become mud stuck with twigs and leaves.

'There's someone on that bench.' Beverly grabbed his arm.

Shadows of branches played tricks with what was tangible and what was in his head. Jack had a bad feeling.

They trod across the once ornamental lawns, now a quagmire. The bench where Beverly had seen someone was empty.

'Damn, he must have seen us.' A first aider at Clean Slate, Beverly would have been set to flex her skills. 'Or I imagined it.'

'You didn't. *Look.*' Outlined under the other Jubilee arch, a figure moved, swaying with the shadows of branches blown in the wind.

'It's not a man.' Bev was already running towards the arch. '*It's Stella.*'

Stella wheeled around as they crossed the car park beyond the gardens. She tried to run.

'Stella. *No.*' Beverly and Jack were brought up short.

In the thin LED light, Stella's face was streaked with blood, her hair matted. Her face, where it wasn't bloodied, was a dreadful pale.

'My poor *darling.*' Forgetting about giving Stella space or any of the rehearsed speeches he'd composed, Jack caught her in his arms.

'Sit on this.' Beverly pulled out a triangular canvas bag from her shoulder bag and passed it to Jack. He recognized it – Lucie had one. A shooting stick.

Standing back, he released the catch and the folded metal sticks snapped to attention. Taking Stella's hand, he guided her onto the saddle-shaped seat.

'Where does it hurt, Stell?' Bev was unzipping her first-aid bag.

'Everywhere,' Stella groaned.

'We're taking you to hospital,' Jack said.

'I'm all right.' Stella waved a feeble hand. 'No need.'

'Christ, Stell, this is a deep gash, did this happen on the weir?' Beverly began dabbing at Stella's face with cotton wool soaked in antiseptic.

'I just need sleep.' Stella's words were slurred.

'You've banged your head. We must get it checked out.' Jack didn't need to know first aid to realize a head injury could be serious.

'I didn't bang my head.'

'What did you do?' Jack felt a chill dread envelope him.

'Someone tried to kill me.'

Chapter Forty-One

Stella

'You're not allowed to work.' Batting at Stella's open laptop, Lucie placed a mug of slippery elm beside Stella. 'Your gru-el, Olee-*var*.'

'The doctor said my skull isn't fractured, no haemorrhaging. Now the painkillers are working, I'm fine.' An overstatement, Stella had the ghost of a headache.

She had woken at six and, fortified by ibuprofen, dragged on a jumper and joggers. Wandering into the front room with the vague notion of doing her usual clearing up, she had found Lucie ensconced in Stella's usual place on the sofa. Lucie directed her to the cockpit where she draped a blanket over Stella's legs and micro-adjusted the recliner until Stella said she was comfortable.

A martyr – as Lucie put it – to heartburn, Lucie went off to make the slippery elm drink that Lucie used as a fast-food supplement and antidote to nippets. Stella fancied a bowl of cornflakes but now accepted it graciously.

Now Lucie was back and had caught Stella setting up a spreadsheet of facts gleaned about what had become a chain of murders. *Date, names, location of crime, narrative of crime, links between players. Suspects.* It wasn't work, she told Lucie;

colour-coded conditional formulas were next best to slippery elm.

'While you were being scanned and mummified in that fetching bandage, Jack and Bev told me they've found Roddy March's unrequited victim.' Legs bunched under her, Lucie consulted her notebook. 'December 1940, a prostitute is murdered in the London Blitz, name like a tree... Here we are, Maple Greenhill. Twenty-three-year-old living at home with parents, younger brother Vernon and her baby boy. The Greenhill mum and dad had passed him off as their afterthought. The senior investigating officer – Divisional Detective Inspector in those days – was George Cotton aged... they didn't say, but here's the thing...' Lucie glugged her slippery elm as if it was vile medicine. Stella was rather enjoying hers. 'In 1979 Cotton died in Tewkesbury on the very bridge where some git lamped you last night. Fishy-wishy, *yes?*'

'Janet reckons the attack was a random robbery – they nicked my rucksack, there was about a hundred quid in my purse.' This loss hurt more than the pain in her head. Stella returned to populating rows with the Greenhills and Cotton the detective, coding 1940 green to differentiate from the grey of the present day.

'Janet being wrong is not a first.' Lucie slammed her emptied mug on the coffee table. 'Thank God your notebook was in your jacket, or the murderer would now know how close we are to fingering their collar.'

'Or, how far away.' Stella saved the spreadsheet just as the doorbell rang. 'It's half six in the morning, who can that be?'

'Who indeed.' From Lucie's wide-eyed look, Stella guessed Lucie knew exactly who it would be.

'Ta-*dah*.' Lucie flung wide the lounge door and with a swooping action presented Beverly. And Jack.

'I hope it was all right to come.' Jack hung back.

'*Naturellement*, Jacaranda,' Lucie crowed. 'Bev, help me get breakfast, you must have left before the hotel was serving.'

'I can leave.' Jack moved to let them pass.

'Maybe you could sit here.' Stella nodded at the leather pouffe in front of the armchair. 'It's not that comfortable, but...' *I need you next to me* popped into her head. 'Could you help with this?'

'A hundred per cent, I can.' Jack was on the pouffe, leaning over the arm of the cockpit in seconds. He looked at the spreadsheet. 'Lordy, how many suspects? If I was murdered, I'd hope the number of those wanting me dead was smaller.'

'You're much nicer than Roddy March.' Stella realized that dying in her arms didn't make March a good guy. He had used Andrea, probably Gladys Wren too, although at least she'd got something back. He'd gatecrashed Felicity's Death Café where he'd mocked Clive and derided Andrea in his notes. She told Jack, 'They could all have killed March, and Clive being the next victim doesn't rule him out as Roddy's killer.'

Beverly and Lucie returned with bacon sandwiches oozing with butter and ketchup. Bev distributed coffee, which was a great improvement on slippery elm.

'Jackie said we're to be one team. Jack and me won't take no for an answer,' Bev announced. 'But we're not asking so you can't say no.'

'Please stay.' Stella touched Jack's arm and, exhausted, she left it there.

'Deal.' Lucie patted the sofa for Bev to join her there.

'What have you both got?' Stella took a large bite of the bacon sandwich and instantly felt better.

'Seventy-nine years ago, on the twelfth of December 1940, Maple Greenhill was found strangled in an empty house near the river in Hammersmith during the Blitz.' Beverly might have been telling one of her dad's bedtime stories: Stella relaxed. Looking at Jack, Bev swiped at her chin. Taking the hint Jack cleaned the wrong side. Stella leaned across and wiped off the ketchup with her bit of kitchen towel. *Ketchup, not blood.*

'Northcote was first on the scene. He'd been called by an ARP officer who heard a woman shouting,' Jack jumped in, his face suddenly red.

'Or that's what Northcote told the police when they were surprised that he'd got there so quickly.' Bev arched her eyebrows. 'What if Northcote wasn't first on the scene but was there all along?'

Stella filled her spreadsheet as Jack and Beverly talked. Maple had lived in the same house on Corney Road as Jackie and Graham did now. From her elderly neighbour, Jackie discovered that George Cotton, the detective, was buried in the cemetery opposite her house. Maple's little boy had been three when his mother was strangled. Stella squeezed Jack's arm. That would have struck a chord; Jack was three when his mother was murdered.

'The case was ruled "murder by person or persons unknown",' Jack concluded. 'Except one thing. Jackie's neighbour, Phyllis Jenkins, was adamant Maple wasn't a sex-worker, and so was Cleo Greenhill at the garage. Vernon, who was Cleo's grandfather and Maple's brother, said that Maple claimed to be engaged. He said the police had found a cheap ring. Maple worked as a clerk for the Express Dairies, but the Greenhills believed it was because Maple was boxed off as a prostitute that the press lost interest. We saw the fuss when the Yorkshire Ripper murdered a student – sex-workers are disposable, even these days.'

'Cleo told me that the family always thought there was a cover-up.' Beverly said. The police knew who had killed Maple, but it didn't suit for the truth to come out. Thanks to a software program from Geo-Space that estate agents use for virtual tours of properties, we can confirm this.' Stella could hardly keep up as she added in dates of Julia Northcote's supposed suicide and the facts gleaned from cuttings that Julia had hastily torn from the press and stuffed in a cardboard box.

'March somehow gained access to the Northcotes' London house and he must have known where Julia had hidden the box on – we think – the day her husband, Aleck Northcote, confessed. He faked her suicide a week later on New Year's Eve. Perhaps she told him she was going to the papers, she would have known not to go to the police.' Beverly balled up her kitchen towel.

'How did March know about the box?

'Perhaps he wasn't there looking for the box, but to hide it again. It had been a safe place since 1940.' Stella switched out of Excel and brought up the Ravenscourt Square house on Rightmove. Jack showed her the white circular marker which revealed March crouching in the top room.

'But why hide it at all?' Jack said.

'If someone was on to him, perhaps he thought it was the last place anyone would look,' Lucie said. 'We haven't talked about the charming Andrea. It's a tedious stereotype, but March has a freshly jilted girlfriend who he effed over; Andrea had the means and the motive to send him to hell.'

'We only have Andrea's word for it she was his girlfriend,' Stella said. 'She obviously loved him.'

'*Did* she love him?' Lucie bit into a fig. 'What if the tedious stereotype was cooked up for our benefit?'

'She made no bones about being angry. If she had killed March, surely she'd have tried to put us off the scent?' Stella looked up from the screen.

'How did Roddy March know Julia Northcote had left a letter pointing the finger at her husband?' Beverly asked. 'Cleo said he'd been to Maple Motors – he was way ahead of us. I don't buy the mugger angle, his podcast might be a heap of poo, but he appears to have been an effective investigator.'

'Someone else thought so too.' Lucie did a doom-laden voice.

'We need to decipher March's notebook,' Lucie said. 'It's our bible.'

'You've got his notebook?' Jack and Beverly shouted at once.

'No, it wasn't on Roddy when I found him.' Stella sent the spreadsheet to print and emailed it to Jackie, attaching photos of those suspects they'd managed to grab from the internet.

'The killer knew March's notes would incriminate them. With it in their possession, they believe themselves safe.' Lucie caught the collated copies churning from the printer. No one spoke as, in gloomy silence, they digested the contents.

Murders			
Date	Victim	Location	Means
1 12 December 1940	Maple Greenhill 23	House by River in Hammersmith London	Strangulation
2 22 November 1963	Aleck Northcote 62	Cloisters House Tewkesbury	Bludgeoned with poker

Narrative	Suspect(s)	Role	Motive
Maple's body found in empty house, not robbery. Wearing coat belonging to pathologist's wife Julia. Mending ticket in lining. Dunhill cigarette lighter at scene. Case unsolved.	Aleck Northcote	Pathologist	Stop Maple telling his wife of their affair.
Found by housekeeper. Northcote refused son money. Son found guilty and hanged. March questions his guilt.	George Cotton	Detective	Revenge for Maple's murder.
	Vernon Greenhill	Brother	Revenge for Maple.
	Maple's Son	Son	Revenge for Maple.

Murders			
Date	Victim	Location	Means
3 18 December 2019	Roddy March	Tomb of the starved monk Tewkesbury Abbey	Stabbed in the back
4 19 December 2019	Clive Burgess, Clock maker	1 Stag Villas	Impaled on sundial

Narrative	Suspect(s)	Role	Motive
Stella met March in Abbey and then in Death Café. He told group someone wanted to kill him. Stella found him dying. Last words Car wo my. March claimed he knew Northcote's murderer.	Felicity Branscombe	Runs Death Café, retired pathologist, lives in Cloisters House where Aleck Northcote murdered.	March claimed he knew Northcote's killer and would reveal on podcast.
	Clive Burgess	Clockmaker	As well as above. Pathologist never paid him for clock.
	Joy by Nature (Turton)	Abbey Organist	As well as above. Northcote chased her off his land when she was a child. Circumstantial, in abbey during murder.
	Mrs Gladys Wren (Miss Fleming)	March's Landlady	As well as above. Did Northcote threaten to tell Derek the fireman he and Gladys were having affair??
	Andrea Rogers	Abbey Gardener	Revenge for being dumped and he stole her idea.
Told Stella he knew something, then found dead when Stella and Lucie visit. Someone knew Stella was coming?	Suspects as for Murder 3. Less Clive.	As above	To stop Clive telling Stella whatever he knew.

'Four murders.' Jack moved to the armchair and, elbows on knees, said, 'It's time to face the elephant in this room. Last night it could have been five murders. Whoever did for Roddy and the Clockmaker tried to kill Stella. They could try a second time.'

'Last night was the second time.' To a thunderstruck room, Stella described the evening on her way to the Death Café when a van had slowed on the lane. 'If another car hadn't appeared, I think that the van driver would have murdered me. At the time, I assumed they had engine trouble, but that's a classic ploy to get an unwitting driver to stop. Now, I think they wanted to stop me linking up with March.'

'So far we know one person who knew you and March might meet.' Lucie flapped her copy of the grid. 'The Grumpy Gardener.'

'Andrea rides a bike,' Stella said. 'We need to find out if she owns a white van like the van in the lane.'

They were all startled by the doorbell. Refusing to be cossetted, Stella went to answer.

'My *God*, Stella.' Janet pointed at the steri stitches on Stella's temple. 'I came to see how you are and you're worse than my worst fears. Are you OK?'

'Fine now.' Stella actually felt dizzy from getting up too fast.

'I need a statement about last night.'

'There's people here, we're...' Stella's dizziness increased.

She didn't want Janet to see that Jack and Beverly were there as well as Lucie. Too late. Striding past Stella into the lounge, Janet said, 'Fancy that, the gang's all here.'

'We're doing your job.' Lucie would never make a diplomat.

'Give me the room, please.' Hands on hips, her anorak collar up, Janet jerked a thumb.

'I insist I'm present while you interview Ste—' Lucie started.

'Before you *leave*,' Janet raised her voice, 'Lucie, here's a head start on my briefing. This morning, we raided a block of flats in Evesham and rounded up the gang who mugged and murdered

March and Clive Burgess. They had the gear, an icon thingy from the abbey, religious stuff from the gift shop, enough purses and wallets to open a leather goods' store. Small-time violent thugs. And, Stella, we linked them to you.'

'Linked them how?' Lucie looked less than grateful for the heads-up.

'The youngest – a fifteen-year-old – had Stella's rucksack. Denied the lot, bare-faced they were.' Janet took in Stella. 'You'll get it back when Forensics are done.'

'You know this is crap, don't you?' Lucie thundered. 'A bunch of kids murder two men for pin money?'

'Let's go for a walk,' Beverly said as she and Jack hustled Lucie out.

It wouldn't be the first time Lucie was charged with assaulting an officer of the law. However, now Stella agreed with Lucie about the muggings and the murders. As their voices merged with the street sounds below, her headache worsened.

Chapter Forty-Two

2019

Jackie

Geo-Space's reception fitted Jackie's vision of a state-of-the-art software company. A theme of orange followed through in rubber flooring, lampshades and the uncomfortable bucket chair in which she sat waiting – *too long* – for Zack Hunt, acting CEO. At least the coffee was good.

'You plan to offer home scans for cleaning customers, way to go,' a voice bellowed.

'We thought...' *Good grief.* Balding pate, excess bulk, pushing sixty. This confounded Jackie's expectation of svelte, too-young-to-shave in Kenzo and Alexander McQueen. Jackie guessed his pinstripe siren suit, à la Winston Churchill, was the cool bit. At least Churchill had the advantage of being a war-time prime minister busy saving the nation from the Nazis. On Zack Hunt, the suit spelled sartorial disaster.

Hunt showed her into his 'pod' and instantly embarked on a presentation projected onto a wall behind her. 'Geo-Space creates a digital doppelganger, for every kind of space...' Jackie was swooped around buildings, homes, offices, gyms, art galleries, then Hunt introduced the team: a gallery of young men dressed to type in sneakers, jeans and T-shirts.

'Who's *that*?' The woman was in her forties, with wavy blonde hair and what looked like the old National Health glasses but probably cost as much as a cheap car. Team mug-shots were meant to reassure customers that they'd get on with people, but Andrea Rogers' filthy expression turned Jackie cold.

'Her? She's the boss-lady. Andrea Rogers started this business.' Hunt's neutral tone betrayed definite dislike.

'I should meet Ms Rogers.' Jackie got out her phone and scrolled to Stella's email. She clicked on one of the attachments.

'I'm as good as it gets, I'm afraid.' Hunt rested his hands on the shelf of his stomach. 'Andrea's away on a long-term project.'

'That is a shame.' But for the siren suit, Jackie would have spared Hunt's feelings. 'I was told Andrea was top of her game.'

'Your informer is misinformed.' Hunt gave a hearty laugh. 'Anyone can scan properties, the true skill is in the editing.'

'Is that what you do?'

'It was, but now we're one man short – one *lady* – I've had to get down and dirty.'

'Did you scan that gorgeous house in Ravenscourt Square? I loved it. The lighting, the dimensions, the... um... the general feel.' Jackie essayed a vague gesture of rapture.

'No. That house belongs to Andrea. She scanned it herself, didn't trust any of us.' Hunt gave a hollow laugh.

'Is Andrea likely to pop into the office today?' Jackie asked. 'I do want to meet the Queen of Virtual Tours.'

'She's away, no idea where.' Hunt was one disgruntled employee.

'Zack, this has been helpful, your tours could augment our service to our upmarket clients, before and after shots, order restored.' At last, the photographs Stella had sent through downloaded.

Dark hair instead of blonde, straight hair for curly. Same colour eyes. But for hair straighteners and a bottle of black dye, the grumpy woman seated at the desk which Zack had made his own was unmistakable.

Zack Hunt might not know where his boss was but, thanks to Stella's photograph, Jackie did.

Chapter Forty-Three

2019

Jack

'Perfect, you can keep watch on March's girlfriend, she's renting a room at Mrs Wren's boarding house right opposite,' Lucie said when Jack and Beverly explained where they were staying.

'We're facing the back,' Beverly said.

'It's a short journey when you pay her a visit.' Lucie was unfazed.

'On what pretext? From what you say, Mrs Wren is a good gatekeeper,' Jack said.

'Pretext schmeetext, Mr Fox. For the man who hangs out with True Hosts, crashing Gladys's hen-house will be a doddle.' Lucie plunged her fork into a fearsome wedge of strawberry cheesecake. She'd requested three forks, but keeping the plate close, neither of them could reach.

'It's bedsits – every room will be occupied at night.' Jack still felt a pressing sensation through his coat where Stella had rested her hand.

'Not every room.' Lucie held up a hand in front of her mouth as she chewed. 'Mr March has vacated. Anyway, go in the day, when Andrea's being a gardener.'

'I'll divert Gladys while you go up the stairs.' Beverly would be itching for adventure.

'You'll be selling holy trinkets in the abbey's gift shop.' Lucie was wrapping up the remainder of the cheesecake in a napkin.

'How is that possible?'

'You'll be answering that ad which is in the entrance to the abbey. Joy by Nature will snap you up as a blessed change from the gnarled grotesques who otherwise will be her option. Once you're behind Joy's counter, don't let her out of your sight.'

Jack nearly asked who put Lucie in charge, but transported by the memory of Stella's hand, knew that if Lucie commanded, he'd dance on a bed of nails.

'What are you going to do?' Bev's intonation suggested she resented being bossed by Lucie. 'I mean, shouldn't we wait for Stella?'

'Stella is cleaning at Cloisters House in half an hour,' Lucie said.

'She should *not* be working.' Jack spilled his coffee.

'Would you like to tell her that?' Lucie beamed her sweetest smile. 'Just when the turtle dove is letting you land in her nest...'

'She's not— Oh, hang on.' Jack got a text. 'Wow. Jackie went to Geo-Space. The people who made the virtual tour with Roddy March in the top room that we showed you?'

'You only showed me this morning.' Lucie had an air of infinite patience.

'The CEO of Geo-Space is Andrea the gardener.' Jack pushed his phone across for Lucie and Beverly to see.

'Wrong hair,' Lucie huffed.

'No, it is.' Beverly enlarged the picture. 'See that mole there, on the line of her chin? Andrea has a mole in the same place.'

'People can get moles removed,' Lucie said.

'Yes, but she hasn't, that's the point.' Beverly was exasperated.

Lucie was a poor loser, so Jack trod carefully. 'Jackie says this Andrea owns Northcote's London house, the one in Ravenscourt Square where we caught March in the virtual tour. Jackie suggests that Andrea found Julia Northcote's Swiss Roll box with her letter and the newspaper cuttings when she was living there.' Jack was on the edge of his chair.

'This is a game-changer,' Beverly said. 'Andrea finds the box, Roddy steals her idea for his podcast. Did he even know she was filming him?'

'I'm sure he never noticed the camera in the middle of the room on a tripod.' Lucie dabbed up crumbs on her plate. 'In answer to your question about what I shall be doing, *Bev-er-lee*, I shall be taking cupcakes with dear Gladys.'

'Where?' Considering the cheesecake, Jack nearly asked how.

'*Lo*, the wren has landed. *Coo-ee, Gladys.*' Lucie waved one of her forks at a small woman, startling in a silver jacket and a pink and yellow scarf heading their way. Lucie hissed, 'The boarding house is vacant, Jack. Embark on tasks now. *Shoo.*'

It was too easy to enter Mrs Wren's house. Jack wondered if her tenants knew she kept a key under the back door mat.

Lucie had said no one would be there, but Jack was wary. Andrea Rogers might have called in sick. The size of the house suggested at least four rooms to rent: Andrea's, March's bedsit was sealed, and a 'Vacancies' sign in the front window implied one at least was empty, but the other? Jack disliked unknowns.

No sound. A stale smell of meals past, all fat-based.

Gladys Wren had entertained Stella and Lucie in her front parlour, a gloomy room at the front of the house. Through nylon curtains, Jack could see his hotel opposite. He sniffed mothballs and polish. The smell of Isabel Ramsay's house, his neighbour when he was boy. Formidable to many, Isabel had been infinitely better company than the hyper-critical pillar of disdain who would bid Jack call her Grandmama and mind his manners.

Jack was about to mount the stairs when a clanging jolted him out of his skin. A telephone in the hall was amplified by a speaker on the landing above. Jack shrank back down the hall passage as he heard thumping on the stairs. The receiver was picked up.

'Wren House. Who is this?' A whiny-sounding man answered. *A lodger.* Jack had been right to assume nothing.

'Who? No one called Harmon lives here... I'm not divulging my name. Are you trying to sell me something?... You tell me your name... Thought not, slime-ball.' The sound of the receiver being replaced on the cradle.

Jack dared not move. He knew from Stella and Lucie that the lodgers had the right to use Gladys Wren's kitchen. What if he decided to make himself a cup of tea now that he was down there?

A draught cooled the passage. Peeping round the turn in the stairs, Jack saw a sliver of light. The front door opened then shut. Jack pattered up the corridor into the front parlour in time to see a man, suit jacket flapping, crossing the road. A letter in his hand suggested he wouldn't be gone long, then, the man turning, Jack saw a shoulder bag strapped over his chest and gave himself up to half an hour.

When he crept back to the hall, Jack caught sight of the telephone and replayed the lodger's side of the conversation. The caller asked for someone called Harmon. That was Jack's surname. *There was no such thing as coincidence.*

Whoever had rung was sending him the message that they knew he was there. They knew his name. Stella had said the killer was at least one step ahead of them. She was right.

Nerves jangling, Jack knew he should leave, but couldn't with his allotted task incomplete, and now he was alone. Or was he? *Had the caller rung from a mobile phone in a room here in the house?* Jack dialled 1471. 'The caller has withheld their number.' Typical for a salesperson, but Jack's unease increased.

Outside March's room, the police tape looked undisturbed. Jack couldn't tell that Mrs Wren had peeled it off to gain entry, as Lucie and Stella had told him. The woman was a pro. Jack knew Andrea lodged on the floor above.

He knocked on both doors, ready with how he'd found the front door ajar and was checking for intruders. No reply. Unlike when he'd gone to Northcote's London home, this time Jack had his trusty set of lock picks.

As a surgeon practises needlework on pigs' skin, Jack had spent many a dull evening – without Stella – picking his collection of locks. He too was a pro and now he had the tumblers in the lock of the door released in moments.

Jack snapped on latex gloves and did a fast but efficient sweep. No business card, nothing to connect Andrea to Geo-Space. In the wardrobe, a couple of dresses and smart women's shoes and two pairs of pristine denim overalls. Andrea's disguise.

A crumpled leaflet for the Death Café lay on the nightstand. Next to this, Jack was startled to see a copy of *Cranford* by Elizabeth Gaskell. The novel was a blip in either the profile of the sullen gardener or high-flying tech executive. It warmed Jack to Andrea and he began to hope she wasn't a budding serial killer.

He homed in on a laptop which shared the veneered dressing table with a mascara stick and a black eye liner, both Jo Malone, likely vestiges of Andrea's true identity. She hadn't got to grips with the rigours of being undercover.

Jack wasn't as deft with computers as he was with locks. With her logical brain, cracking passwords was more Stella's territory. For the sake of doing something, he tapped in 'March'. Not having met Andrea he had no idea what else mattered to her. He guessed that, an IT geek, Andrea hadn't gone for a pet's name or her street name. Idly he typed in 'Geo-Space' and was amazed to see he'd cracked it. Andrea was into double bluff. Was that a clue? Or perhaps she had nothing to hide.

Jack soon found out that this wasn't true. In a folder marked 'Homes' were several files of virtual tours. Each file contained a different property, a couple of flats in West London, an architect plan. *Boring*, Andrea was more of a workaholic than Zack Hunt had suggested to Jackie. Then Jack froze.

In the file called 'Cleaning' was a property he recognized. Not at first, he'd only been there once. But as the image spiralled out of dollhouse mode then zoomed into the sitting room, Jack felt icy sweat trickle down his forehead. It was Stella and Lucie's flat. With a trembling finger, he clicked along the circular markers, moving around the room where he'd sat hours earlier. He avoided the bedrooms, even entering virtually felt wrong. Not as wrong as Andrea scanning Stella and Lucie's private space.

Jack fumbled in his wallet and fished out his USB stick. He fitted it into the side of Andrea's machine and swiped a copy of the folder onto it. As he did so, he heard the front door open. He clicked the laptop to off. More perspiration as it took ages to close. He fought the urge to shut the lid; it would only fire up when Andrea lifted it and she'd know someone had been there. Footsteps on the stairs, the step too light for the lodger with the letter.

Jack had forgotten about the mystery caller who had asked for him by name.

The only hiding place was the wardrobe. Opening the door, Jack eased himself inside and pulled it to. As if it made him invisible, he screwed his eyes shut and held his breath. *If you can feel someone watching you, you are unaware of them when they're not.* Jack had to look.

The handle turned slowly, hesitantly. Jack pictured someone outside on the landing. Playing with him. Had he left a drawer open? Had he accidentally pressed restart on the laptop? None of that mattered if they knew he was there.

Footsteps in the room. Jack imagined breathing although there was silence. He hadn't had time to crouch or hide himself behind Andrea's overalls. If the wardrobe was opened, that would be it. Would he be number five in the chain? As if to calm himself he recited the names Maple, Northcote, March, Clive the Clockmaker. *Jack Harmon.* He would never see Stella again. *Never hold her…*

Jack was about to burst out of the wardrobe, surprise his only weapon, when he heard the door shut and the key turn in the lock. His hearing tuned for a pin dropping, he caught the slightest tread on the stairs. The click of the front door. Could be a trick, but he could not stay where he was.

With feathery fingers, it took him longer to pick the lock. Jack was ready to faint when he finally emerged onto the landing and risked a look over the banisters. No one. He would not be trapped a second time. He rightly guessed that a third door on the landing was a lavatory. Inside, he stood on the pan and succeeded in thrusting up the window sash. He came face to face with a rusting pipe and a twenty-foot drop onto slimy concrete below. Was whoever might be waiting for him more dangerous than the pipe and the concrete? He had only to think of Roddy March and Clive the Clockmaker to know the answer.

Jack got stuck halfway out of the window. It took all his gymnastic initiative to wriggle through the aperture. He gripped the pipe for stability, not cheered by noticing it shifted slightly. It was raining heavily and although he was cold, he welcomed the stream of water soaking his face and neck.

Jack nerved himself to let go of the window sill and relinquish himself to the soil pipe. He whispered a prayer to any god out there who might listen as he made sense of something fixed to the wall of the house. *A ladder.*

When he reached the ground, he raced down a paved garden to the back gate. It was locked and, fresh out of patience with picking locks, Jack took a run at the wall. On his second attempt, he got a grip and hauled himself over. He landed badly on the other side. He was in an alleyway. It took him to a road which in turn led to the high street. Blinking back rainwater, Jack looked into the window of Phonz Cheep, the accessory shop beneath Stella and Lucie's flat.

'Is it OK for me to come up?' Jack spoke into the intercom. 'No worries if not.' *Lie, damn lie.*

'I've missed you,' Stella answered.

I've missed you. Splashing about on the pavement in the neon light of Phonz Cheep, Jack was Gene Kelly.

Chapter Forty-Four

2019

Stella

I've missed you. The words had tumbled out. Now Stella said, 'Let me get a towel for your hair.'

'Have you?' Jack had heard it then.

'Yes.' Unable to think what else to say, Stella busied herself making tea.

'Jackie said to ignore you if you refused to let us help. But seriously, I will head off if that feels more comfortable. I mean, Bev could stay perhaps?' Jack had his brave face.

'Don't.' In the lounge, Stella resumed her corner on the sofa; Lucie's cockpit was too Lucie for comfort. Seeing Jack going to the armchair, Stella heard herself implore, 'Please sit next to me.'

'Stella, I've found something.' Jack took the other corner, Stanley leapt onto his lap. He held a USB stick. 'It comes with a "creep you out" warning.'

'OK.' Unsure she was ready to be creeped out, Stella put her laptop in the space between them on the sofa and inserted the stick.

'Lucie gave me and Bev tasks.' Scrubbing his head with the towel, Jack's voice was muffled.

'She shouldn't have.' Once Stella would have resented Lucie taking over a case but since living with her, she didn't mind. However, she didn't like Lucie bossing Beverly. Jack could handle himself. She listened, incredulous, as Jack outlined what Lucie had asked them to do.

'I had no trouble checking out Andrea's bedsit, as you'd guess.' Jack peered out from under the towel. 'Bev can't come to harm in the abbey gift shop and she's a sensible woman.'

'Roddy was murdered in the abbey, possibly by Joy. We should stick together. And if she was that sensible, Bev wouldn't have broken into Northcote's London house.' Without thinking Stella batted Jack's leg. 'Nor would you.'

'We didn't break in, we found the key.' Jack finger-combed his hair. 'But you are right. Stella, can you forgive me?'

'No need.' Stella clicked on the USB stick, labelled 'Jack's Contraband' – Jack liked to walk on the wild side. A geometrical shape appeared on the screen, spun around, then resolved into their lounge. There was Lucie's cockpit, the pouffe. Stanley's bed was empty. 'I don't get it, is this some kind of graphic software?'

'I wish.' Jack folded the towel. 'It's a CAD scan of this flat. Like that virtual tour with Roddy March in the film.'

'No, that's not now.' She realized the papers on Lucie's cockpit were pages from her putative true-crime book on The Playground Murders in Hammersmith and not the biography of Northcote which Stella had been reading when Jack called.

'Did you get this off the letting agents? Is the flat on the market?' Stella had been putting off whether to extend the lease after Lucie left. Had the decision been taken out of her hands?

'I found it on Andrea's computer.' Jack's face was serious.

'Andrea was living here before us?' Stella fought off panic.

'It wasn't scanned for an estate agent.' Jack directed the cursor to the left of the room. See, there's your rucksack by the coffee table. And isn't that Stanley's Mr Ratty?'

'You're saying Andrea broke in here?'

'It would seem so,' Jack said.

'Is this some kind of warning?'

'If she planned to send it you, yes. But more likely she was doing a recce. This gives her offline access to every inch of the flat.'

Jack got Stella to open the other files in the folder. It took them round the abbey. Stella clicked along the ambulatory to the chapel with the tomb of the starved monk where her heart rate doubled. She could almost see Roddy's body slumped against the plinth. Jack asked Stella to check the other two files, but the interiors meant nothing. If the people who lived there were in any danger, they had no way to warn them.

'Whoever killed Roddy and Clive was calculating, even if they committed the murders on impulse. They left no clues and, since the police are charging those boys in Evesham, the real murderer has got away with it,' Stella said.

'I agree, and right now Andrea is my prime suspect,' Jack said. 'She had reason to murder Roddy, he was cutting her out of the podcast in favour of you. You are obviously in her sights. Like me with True Hosts, Andrea preps before taking action. Unlike me, she's designed her own software so she can prowl around a home without leaving her chair.'

'Is she a True Host?' Stella was determined to sound OK about Jack stalking killers and living in their closets. No one was perfect. Least of all her.

'She could be.' Jack steepled his fingers. 'We might no longer believe that when someone takes our photograph they steal our soul, but with this scan Andrea has stolen your privacy. How did she know where you live?'

'She would have seen my name on the cleaning rota; she could have followed me home. Then all she had to do was call when Lucie and I were out. But how did she get in?' Unconsciously Stella shifted closer to Jack on the sofa until their thighs were touching.

'I'm afraid a Yale lock is no challenge.' Jack closed the file and removed his USB stick from Stella's laptop. 'Stella, you're not safe here. I'd like to swap – you take my room at the hotel, then if Andrea dares break in again, I'll be waiting.'

The abbey clock struck midday. The mugs of tea had gone cold. Outside there was a lull in the rain. Neither Stella nor Jack could have said when they began clasping hands.

Chapter Forty-Five

Jack

Rain fell in a slant across the abbey close; a gargoyle above the north buttress spewed water which, whipped by the wind, splashed against the stone wall. The bells in the tower tolled four o'clock. Two figures and a small dog huddled beneath an umbrella hurried up the path between two lines of yews into a pool of yellow light spilling on to the flagstones and entered through the north door.

Retracting the umbrella, Jack dried his face on his coat sleeve. Stella was already halfway up the right-hand side. He found her with three life-size alabaster models of the kings, a motley crew lurking in the gloom of the south ambulatory.

Jack felt in the grip of an awakening that was less to do with God than that he and Stella had spent the previous few hours making love. Afterwards, they had lain in each other's arms as if resting on a fluffy white cloud. Then they'd made a plan.

'That's the Grove organ Joy plays,' Stella whispered, as with Stanley the poodle swaddled in a towel on her lap she settled on a chair. Seemingly now expert on the abbey, Stella told him that the north transept was fifty-eight feet high.

'It's horrible to think of the men who died building this.' Jack admired fine geometrical tracery around small pointed windows. 'Beneath beauty lies ugliness.'

'Beneath ugliness there's more beauty.' Stella's optimism made Jack want to kiss her right there.

They crossed the nave to the western end where, putting Stanley down, Stella showed Jack the font, a giant octagonal receptacle carved, she informed him, in Purbeck stone. Abruptly she said, 'Jackie said Zack Hunt at Geo-Space had taken over Andrea's office and behaved like he was in charge.' Stella pushed the towel into the rucksack she'd bought from a luggage shop in the high street. Even when the police relinquished the bag that was stolen by the mugger on the bridge, Stella didn't want it back. 'Andrea said Roddy stole her project – the murder of Maple Greenhill then later the consequent killing of Aleck Northcote at Cloisters House – for his podcast and ousted her. Zack Hunt is ousting her from Geo-Space. It's a bit like me.'

'No one's ousting you from Clean Slate.' Jack sought to reassure her.

'No, I know. But what if Andrea needed to take a break, find what mattered to her? Like I did.' Stella brushed his fingers. 'She realized she loved Roddy.'

'Meantime lovely *Roddy* was after you. *Whoa.*' Jack spread his arms before a gigantic stove caged in mesh. This was more an object of worship than the glittering altar or the mysteries depicted in the stained-glass windows. 'A *Gurney*, what a Victorian invention! And here's one in operation. Isn't the "London Warming and Heating Company" a magical name?'

'Rather long, but yes, nice.' Stella's willing interest made Jack want to whirl her around and shout how much he loved her. Except that wouldn't go down well.

'If who Andrea discovered was Roddy, I feel sorry for her. She didn't matter to him.' Stella peered through an iron grating into what was called the Clarence Vault.

Somewhere, Stella remembered reading that the vault contained the remains of George, Duke of Clarence, and his wife, Isabel, who had died of poisoning.

Murder was never far away.

'You mattered to March. If Andrea killed Roddy and then Clive and, mad with jealousy, attacked you, she doesn't get my sympathy vote.' Wracked with his own jealousy, Jack felt no regret that Roddy March was out of the picture. *What if Stella and March had worked together...*

'Time to go undercover,' Stella announced.

Stella had suggested Jack visit Joy in the gift shop. Since Beverly had texted that Joy had hired her, Stella wanted to check up on her to know she was safe. Jack had warned Beverly he'd be *incognito, treat me as a stranger.* Bev texted back, *Who are you?* Jack would try to gauge if Joy was the harmless organist she portrayed herself as.

Stella sat where she had seen the shadow on the wall the night March was murdered. Nervous for her safety too, Jack wanted Stella to come with him, but Stella was adamant, he'd learn more alone. She and Joy hadn't hit it off.

Confirming there were a good few people around, Jack left Stella perusing 'O Come, O Come, Emmanuel' in a copy of *Hymns Ancient and Modern* with Stanley. Still with misgivings, he slipped around the pillar to St James's chapel.

Jack had read that, compared with the chapel housing the starved monk, St James had got a raw deal. The chapel had gone to wrack and ruin, lying open to the elements for centuries until it was walled off and used as a schoolroom. Jack felt uncomfortable treading on the tombs of the men beheaded at the battle of Tewkesbury – the Dukes of Somerset and Devon and more – interred beneath what was now the abbey's gift shop.

For all that St James's Chapel was dedicated to Mammon, Jack felt his spirits lifted by the bright objects and myriad scents of candles, potpourri oil and branded soap. Spotlight tracks across the vaulted ceiling shone on abbey mugs, boxes of abbey chocolate and fudge. A table was piled with rose and lavender hand cream, framed pictures of Christ in the stable and saints hung from wire strung from one cladded pillar to another.

No sign of Joy or Beverly. Their absence surely an invitation to any muggers Janet hadn't nabbed. A sign warned CCTV was in operation. Jack located the camera and gave it a long stare. That should smoke Joy out from her sarcophagus. When he'd met her after evensong in what was now a different 'without Stella' life, Jack had felt something was off about her. Or was it that Joy had got to spend two evenings at a Death Café with Stella? *Jealousy kills.*

Jack gravitated to a carousel dominated by fabric hen doorstops. Easter leftovers, they were reduced to £5.50. He toyed with getting one for Stella before coming to his senses.

'Are you looking for a specific item, sir?' In abbey gift shop uniform of cream shirt, navy cardigan and tabard, Joy looked sterner than in the multicoloured knitted jacket of last time. Of a similar age to Stella, they were chalk and cheese. Stella dressed forever young while Joy's cream tea and Christian outfit suggested timeless middle-age. If Joy was their murderer, she was in perfect disguise.

'It's a stocking filler, for my partner.' While not foolproof, Jack's principle of opening his mouth in the hope the right words came out generally served. On the pretext of admiring the shop, Jack scanned for Beverly. '*Gosh*, do you manage this lovely emporium alone?'

'I have a girl.' Joy didn't expand.

Damn. Stella had warned him not to sweet-talk Joy but, intent on nuzzling her neck, he hadn't paid heed. Joy was no-nonsense.

As were Roddy and Clive's murders.

'Thank heavens, it's a lot to manage.' Jack swept an arm around the empty shop.

'Does he or she like jewellery? Some nice earrings and necklaces have come in.' Joy was all business.

'No.' Stella would hate 'nice earrings'. Catching sight of a miniature Joseph carrying a lantern with a lamb snuffling in his robes and a Mary with baby Jesus, Jack crowed, 'Perfect. It must be a gift that brings peace. She recently had a shock.'

'Five pounds for the pair.' Ignoring the reference to shock, Joy was supremely professional. Or she was a psychopath.

'She was attacked on that bridge by the weir.'

If Joy had attacked Stella, she might now recall that she'd met Jack before. Yet her expression remained inscrutable. Jack prattled on, 'What with that terrible murder here, well, not *literally* here, at the Wakeman Cenotaph. Terrible to die violently in a sanctified space. Or perhaps a comfort.'

'I doubt Mr March was bothered by the scene of his death or that he was stabbed with a sharp knife. He'll be where he belongs now.' Joy slid Mary and Joseph across the counter towards Jack.

'So right. Do you think it was this gang of boys the police have arrested?' Jack imagined Mary and Joseph were himself and Stella. *Concentrate.*

'These days it's as likely to be a female. One knows where one is with boys.' Joy was animated. *Did she know March was killed by a woman?*

'Do you feel safe here?' Not a kind question, but proof boys weren't so reliable.

'Why wouldn't I?' Joy shook her head and said, 'We have hens going cheap.' Her face betrayed no sense this might be humour so Jack didn't laugh.

'Don't they look fun? After her *shock*.' He did want a hen. *True Hosts could read your mind.* 'What with these murders, she's set to hightail it out of Tewkesbury. Boo-hoo, I say.'

'We don't get murders every week and Clive probably slipped and fell on his sundial. That was him all over.'

'Oh, crikey.' Jack clasped his hands. 'You knew the poor gentleman? I am so very, very sorry. I gather he was a clockmaker.'

'Clive had more enemies than clocks – he overcharged.' Joy was emptying Mary and Josephs from their boxes onto the counter. 'Not to mention wandering hands. Some deluded souls, naming no names, put his disinhibition down to dementia. Clive Burgess was as sharp as a pendulum, he was born an octopus.'

'Did, um, did Clive wander in your dir...?' The Marys were lined up in the front of the Josephs.

'Do you want a set?' Joy waved a hand at one of the carousels. 'Or a hen?'

'Yes and *yes.*' Jack snatched a hen from the stand and speaking confidentially to it, 'My partner read somewhere that the murdered podcaster, Ron Marsh was it, received death threats.'

'*March.* Roderick. She may also have "read somewhere" that a little knowledge is a dangerous thing.' Joy shoved two Marys into a box and, snatching the hen from Jack, snipped off the price label. 'Due to saving the planet, we don't gift wrap, do you want a bag?'

'I'll give them to her now, dwelling on Christ's birth and his um...' Jack clasped the Easter hen, '...resurrection will be calming.' He caught a movement out of the corner of his eye.

Beverly was crouched in a corner unpacking gigantic candles, shaking her head. *Yes, OK, wrong tack.*

'A couple of plastic Nativity icons won't satisfy a lust for gossip. Try the internet. Or perhaps you have.' Game set and match to Joy.

Chapter Forty-Six

Stella

'I keep inviting you at short notice. My father called me impulsive, I wanted to clarify that you're not just my cleaner, not *my* cleaner at all, you clean *for* me.' Felicity was wheezing slightly as she led Stella into her – *once Northcote's* – drawing room. 'I felt we had a rapport at that frightful hash of a Death Café, at which the only good thing was meeting you. I hope you like scones, I cooked them especially.'

Stella had told Jack that she'd see him at the flat later.

'Did you miss evensong?' Felicity's eyes glittered in the firelight.

'Yes.'

'I apologize for dragging you away. Do you want to shoot back for the Voluntary?'

'It's nice to see you.' Stella's head wound ached and she'd rather return to the flat and rest. She touched it gingerly.

'Would your doggie like water?' Felicity laid a plate of scones beside Stella.

'He's just had some, thanks.' Stella knew Stanley would prefer scones.

'Was dear Joy about to bash out ditties on her organ?' Felicity winked as if this was a shared joke.

'I think today is one of her days in the gift shop.'

'You are well up on abbey life.' Felicity was cutting her scone with a knife surely meant for tougher material.

'I used to clean there.' If only cleaning in the abbey was all she still did.

'Used to?'

'The cleaning agency heard that I found Roddy Marsh dying and were worried employing me would attract the wrong kind of publicity. They cancelled my shifts.' No point pretending that she was rushed off her feet.

'I thought Roddy was dead when you found him.' Felicity paused mid-bite.

'He died soon after.' *The police had kept that back.* Spreading too much cream on her scone, Stella hoped that now there'd been arrests that slip didn't matter.

'Did you capture any last words?' Felicity flourished her napkin. 'For his loved ones?'

'No,' Stella said.

'That's wrongful dismissal, you should take the cleaning company to court.' Felicity looked suddenly indignant.

'They said I needed a rest and would be in touch when I felt better.' A burning log tumbled to the edge of the grate.

'Charlatans. Start your own company, that would be my response.' Grabbing the poker, Felicity whacked the log to the top of the pile where it was engulfed by blue-yellow flames.

'I don't want the responsibility.' Stella was startled by a swishing sound in the hall. From her tour the day before she guessed it was the green baize door to the kitchen. She had assumed they were alone.

'Come,' Felicity commanded, her head cocked.

Luckily Stella had swallowed the rest of the scone because when the door opened and in stockinged feet, tatty gardening jacket glistening with raindrops, Andrea skated in and stood by the fire.

'Didn't realize you had company. I've been calling out.' She was gruffer than ever. 'I've come for my money.'

'I left it outside, on the kitchen window sill. There was no need to come in here.' In an aside to Stella, 'Andrea is my gardener – you met.'

'Hi. Small world.' Stella's rictus smile wasn't reciprocated. *Andrea is my gardener.* Andrea, it seemed, was not invited to tea.

'You left it outside?' Andrea scowled. 'It will be soaked.'

'Call it laundered and don't spend it until it's dry.' Patting her chest Felicity seemed to enjoy her own joke.

'I didn't realize you knew each other,' Stella said.

'She made me act like a stranger. She wanted me there to bulk up the numbers. Strangely, the advert to do to a Death Café got few takers.' Andrea's wet clothes gave off steam from the hot fire. 'I'll go and find my money, then, shall I?'

Perhaps as a Home Office employee with a good pension, Felicity didn't understand the anxiety of getting paid on time and with respect. A respect all the more important when paying a woman who may have murdered the last two people who upset her. Stella made up her mind to warn Felicity. Yet what if Andrea was innocent? If Felicity sacked Andrea, it would be down to Stella.

'A difficult madam, I told her not to come the second night after her rudeness. Extraordinary behaviour,' Felicity said to the closing door. 'Heigh-ho, it's what comes of employing staff without a reference.'

'You didn't ask me for a reference,' Stella said.

'You came with a track record. I did my research.' Felicity began gathering up the tea things. *If Felicity had done her research, she'd know Stella owned a cleaning company.*

'Let me help.' Stella wanted to check Andrea wasn't in the

kitchen waiting for Stella to leave before she attacked Felicity with a gardening implement.

'You are *not* here to clean.' Felicity's warmth contrasted with her treatment of Andrea. Stunned by Felicity having researched her, Stella was astonished when she said, 'I invited you to see my morgue.'

'Can I just grab a drink of water?' Stella had to assure herself that Andrea had gone. Little comfort, Andrea could have opened and shut the dividing door to fool them, then sneaked upstairs. Stella gulped the water, then, her hearing tuned for the slightest sound, went with Felicity down to the basement.

'Shall we take the key?' Stella said when Felicity left the key on the outside of the basement door. Andrea could take them prisoner.

'Are you worried we'll be locked in?' Felicity began descending a long flight of stone steps.

'It's happened before,' Stella said. 'I tell my staff—'

'What staff?' Felicity was waiting at the bottom of what must be a very deep basement.

'I used to run a cleaning company.' Stella couldn't see in the dark.

'I didn't know.' Felicity flicked on the light. 'Aren't you a detective?'

'Not now. I only clean.' The top of the stone staircase was lost in gloom. Stella became aware of being cold. *Jack had said Andrea was his prime suspect, but what about Felicity?*

'Are you worried someone's there?' Felicity's voice was like melted chocolate.

'There's something I should tell you.' Feeling dreadful, Stella told Felicity about Andrea's software. She kept back that Andrea and March were lovers. 'She's not really a gardener.'

'I dislike being taken for a fool.' Felicity's features darkened.

'I could be wrong,' Stella said. 'Perhaps she just wanted a career change.'

'As I understand it, you are never wrong, Stella Darnell.' Felicity opened a door and the temperature plummeted. A hand on Stella's back, she said, 'After you.'

The first thing Stella saw was a mortuary slab.

Chapter Forty-Seven

2019

Jack

Gone to see Felicity.

When he read Stella's text Jack was plunged into doom. He'd hoped their time in bed meant Stella and he were a team but now she'd gone to tea with Felicity by herself, he could have gone too. Did Stella regret the sex, and saying she loved him? Was she scared she'd lost the space she'd found in Tewkesbury? If he rang, Stella might feel pestered. She'd think he was desperate. *Which he was.*

In anguish, keeping out of the lamplight, Jack wandered the abbey close. The rain had stopped, the grass was soggy and soon his shoes were wet through. He told himself he was looking for Andrea the gardener, although she wouldn't work in the dark. *One, two three.* He reached the wall of Cloisters House. *Two more steps.* Through the gate into the garden.

Jack reasoned that if he watched Stella through a window, it could help the case. *She need never know.*

The house was a hundred or so feet away, the top windows were unlit, but a lamp glowed on the ground floor. His heart skipped. Stella was in there.

Jack shut the gate and, aiming the beam of his Maglite down, trod carefully over a carpet of dead plants and leaves. Stakes stuck into the soil every which way seemed to tilt in the torchlight. The garden was a wasteland. Felicity, retired pathologist and Death Café host, didn't have green fingers.

He tripped against something hard. It was a raised bed supported by sleepers. Jack saw he'd done Felicity a disservice – he was in her veg patch. His torch picked out a compost bin and a water butt beside a couple of cold frames. It recalled the garden at his boarding school, a refuge from the bully who'd nearly broken his spirit. Skirting a lavender bush, Jack found a grave.

Not a grave. Since his mother was murdered, death was Jack's default. He gave himself a break, it was just that the plot looked the right length and breadth. Weeds and clods of grass lay piled to one side, the soil was freshly dug. Adjusting his beam, Jack saw a spade under the lavender bush. He pulled it out and dropped it.

It was streaked with blood.

Chapter Forty-Eight

2019

Stella

It didn't get much more suspicious than having your own morgue, a rack of cutting and sawing implements, specimen jars and a body freezer. Stella paused to wave to Felicity still in the hall; the tall willowy figure elegant in the lamplight didn't wave.

Her wound properly throbbing now, Stella hastened up the high street and turned into the abbey close. She picked her way through the puddles on the grass to the back gate of Cloisters House. She needed to be sure Andrea was not in Felicity's garden waiting to pounce. Now she was equally, if not more, worried for Andrea. With pathologist's skills – and a slab – Felicity could slice, dice and dispose of Andrea in an hour. Stella heard voices.

'*What did you do?*' The distress was animal.

'Chopped off the head, if you must know.'

Stella crept into the garden and stopped short.

'I'll swing for you, I swear.' *Jack.*

'Why don't you?' *It was Andrea.*

Stella saw torchlight, broken by foliage, dart this way and that. Desperate to get to Jack, she tore forward and stumbled on a twist of vegetation. Momentum carried her on, then her legs gave way. She landed on her knees in a pool of light.

'Oh, look who's risen from the dead,' Andrea said.

'Stella, oh my God, Stella.' Jack knelt down and clasped her. So tight it rather hurt.

'*Ow*,' Stella managed at last.

'I thought she'd killed you too,' Jack choked.

'What do you mean "too"?' Andrea barked.

'You have blood on your spade.' Jack helped Stella to her feet.

'I told you, it was a pigeon. Felicity's horrible cat mauled it then left it dying. I had to finish it off. Please could you stop shining that in my face?'

Andrea did look distressed about the pigeon, but she might be a good actor. Lucie said her readers complained about graphic descriptions of animals' deaths in her articles, but couldn't get enough human murder.

'We shouldn't be here,' Stella muttered to Jack.

'I'm the gardener, I'm allowed,' Andrea said.

'Not at seven at night,' Stella said. 'Besides, we need to talk.'

'I told you and your reporter sidekick I'm not playing your detective games.' Andrea stomped out of the garden.

Jack and Stella chased after to where Stella knew Andrea kept her bike. In time to see Andrea opening the door of a white van.

'When you tell us the truth, we'll leave you alone, Andrea.' Stella stood by the bonnet. 'You might start with why you stopped on a lane the night before Roddy was murdered?'

'You were lucky I didn't tear you limb from limb.' Andrea slumped onto a stone coffin by the abbey's south wall. She didn't look capable of being rude, let alone bashing a pigeon with a spade.

'I think we have exposed a charade. Andrea Rogers, chief exec of an IT company, is undone.' Jack was being unnecessarily dramatic.

'Are you OK?' Stella asked Andrea.

'The bastard *robbed* me,' Andrea groaned.

'Felicity?' Stella recalled the wages, paid reluctantly, in soaked notes.

'Her? She always robs me, tight bitch,' Andrea said. 'No, Roddy. The rest is true, I did meet him online. I wanted a mature man who didn't show off and demand endless sex. A life companion, someone to love me.'

'Instead you got March. And for this bloke you found on an app, you gave up Geo-Space, a software company making CAD 3D films for estate agents, developers and architects.' Jack sounded superior. OK, Stella hadn't got him off an app, but as Lucie said, she'd got him by lurking on a dark night near where his mother was murdered.

'We know you're selling a house you only bought six months ago which was the home of pathologist Sir Aleck Northcote. It was where his wife hanged herself.' Jack was setting a trap since they knew Julia Northcote was murdered.

'She didn't commit suicide, Northcote murdered her, as he murdered Maple.' Andrea clamped her hand over her mouth but, too late, the words had flown.

'How do you know that?' Jack crooned. 'Shall I nudge you? Lyons' Swiss Roll and a letter from a hanged woman.'

'How did you find it?' Andrea looked all-in.

Jack handed his phone to Andrea. Stella saw he'd brought up Andrea's virtual tour of Northcote's Ravenscourt Square house. *Andrea's house.*

'Your point is?' Andrea was moving, virtually, through the rooms.

Jack leaned over and clicked the marker that, like the wardrobe door into Narnia, revealed Roddy March on the top floor.

'The. Total. Fuckwit.' Andrea's voice carried across the Avon. 'Zack *effing* Hunt's useless editing. I knew I shouldn't have asked him. *He's fired.*'

'Is this the same Zack as the one occupying your office and passing himself off as CEO?' Jack said airily.

Andrea looked so dreadful that, in rescue mode, Stella joined her on the coffin.

'Not so fast, Poirot.' Andrea was busy on Jack's phone. She thrust it at Stella.

Blurred lamplight. Pavements, railings, kerbs, three cars and, beyond, a scribble of houses. A counter at 6.34 a.m. rolled in real time. Not Street View then. CCTV.

Leaning across Stella, Andrea tapped the image. It speeded up. The lamp-post went out, the scene was washed in grey light incrementally brightening. 10.13 a.m. The street was sketched with diagonal lines. Rain. Puddles appeared. Cars and front doors became tinged with colour as time passed. Occasionally umbrellaed pedestrians shot across the frame. Hours rolled. Light diminished. Dusk. 4.54 p.m. The lamp-post lit up. On time went. The rain eased. A woman opened a gate of the nearest house and drifted up the path. She looked up. Andrea froze the image.

'That's you,' Stella said.

'Date and time?' Andrea indicated the bottom of the screen.

Stella read out the numbers on the frozen screen. 'Oh, *that's*—'

'—when Clive Burgess was murdered. Oh, and by the way, the pathologist is in with the lab people here. *Boy*, does she like a gossip. She told me how both men died.' She glared at Stella. 'No doubt you've updated Felicity on my true status?'

'Where is this street?' Unrepentant, Stella had clients who, while demanding confidentiality, would, as Lucie put it, spill everyone else's beans.

'It's my dad's place in Chertsey. Two hours away by road. Proof that I wasn't here in Tewkesbury nailing dirty old Clive to his sundial.'

'Clive could have been killed in a botched robbery. His death might be unconnected to Roddy's murder,' Stella said.

'It proves you didn't kill Clive,' Jack said. 'March stole your project and dumped you. Revenge is a motive served at any temperature.'

'I'm a woman scorned. Hell hath no fury?' Andrea shook her head. 'I thought you prize detectives had Roderick and Clive Burgess murdered by the same killer. Ergo, to be innocent of one murder makes me innocent of both.'

'Good point,' Stella admitted.

'If it's a consolation, I'm sure March would have used Stella then spat her out too,' Jack said.

'Let's be clear.' Stella got off the coffin. '*One*, had March asked me, I'd have refused to work on his podcast. *Two*, I didn't fancy him, and three, I love Jack.'

'How touching.' Andrea did a slow hand-clap.

Jack and Stella's phones went off. The ringtone, Gloria Gaynor's 'I Will Survive', fractionally out of synch. Stella read her text.

'Jackie's found William Greenhill.'

Jack was reading his text. 'Seems we don't know everything, do we, Andrea Greenhill?'

Chapter Forty-Nine

2019

Jack

'*I love Jack.*'

Basking in Stella's words in the abbey close an hour ago, Jack struggled to concentrate. Over pizza and beer in the flat, the team was debriefing. Jack and Stella skipped how they'd spent part of the day. Stella, beside him on the sofa, was updating her spreadsheet. Stanley snoozed on his bed, his chin on Mr Ratty. Lucie was in her cockpit, Bev was curled in the armchair and Jackie was perched on top of a pile of empty pizza boxes via Zoom. Jackie was walking them through her sensational discovery.

'It's in plain sight on Ancestry. I put in William Greenhill and there it was. Andrea's pretend identity was thin. Although I only found it because I went looking.'

'So, Andrea is Maple Greenhill's granddaughter,' Beverly said. 'Let me get this straight. William is her father. He was three when his mother, Maple, was murdered nearly eighty years ago.'

'William Greenhill is now eighty-two.' Lucie had done the maths.

'Andrea's mother was fifteen years younger, but died of cancer last year,' Jackie said.

'Andrea told us that the rumour the Greenhills heard that William was a doctor was correct. Guess what sort?' Jack said.

'No games.' Lucie was still sulking that Stella and Jack had got Andrea talking when she'd failed.

'A pathologist?' Jackie's ceiling shot into view when she jogged her laptop. She righted it and reappeared.

'*Bingo.*' Jack pointed at Jackie, on Lucie's laptop. 'Not a coincidence, but I'll come to that. After his wife died, Greenhill, or, calling him by his new name, Rogers, told Andrea about Maple and that the killer was never caught. Until then he'd said his parents died when he was young. He confessed that, when he was twenty, Vernon, the man he'd known as his older brother, told him his parents were his grandparents. This was 1958, eighteen years after Maple was murdered and—'

'We *know* this.' Lucie was ripping into a fig.

'Cleo Greenhill had told Bev that, learning this, William took off. Vernon never saw him again. It broke his heart. He'd lost his sister and her child. He named his garage after Maple and made his son Cliff keep it going for when William returned. Bev and me saw what being second fiddle to a missing cousin has done to Cliff. He sits at his desk drinking. Meanwhile, William Greenhill never came back and is a successful pathologist in the mould of Northcote. As for mending cars, Andrea said he can't change a tyre.

'Privately, he must have wanted to know about his mother because he went on Ancestry, obtained Maple's death certificate. He collected newspaper cuttings about her murder, tracked down the man in charge of the investigation, Inspector George Cotton, on his allotment living out what we suspect was an unhappy retirement. Cotton told William everything he knew.' Jack paused for Stella to catch up on her spreadsheet. 'Cotton told William who had murdered his mother.'

'Flipping creepy he's a doctor. Why not help poor dear Vernon with his garage?' Lucie flicked a fig stem into the waste-paper basket.

'Vernon told William he'd remembered Maple saying she was going to marry a doctor and that, one day, William would follow in his new father's footsteps. William snatched at his mother's dream and made it true.'

'Andrea said her dad wanted to fulfil Maple's dream. He went for pathology because he wanted to ensure dead women received respect. Cotton had told him Northcote called his female corpses Annie: "my Annies", he'd say.'

'Revolting.' Beverly scowled.

'Sounds like Andrea was a proper motormouth,' Lucie huffed. 'Didn't Vernon tell the police Maple's fiancé was a doctor?'

'He only remembered she'd said it when he read in the paper that Julia Northcote had taken her own life. He did go to the police. By then Cotton and Shepherd had been moved off the force. The case was unofficially closed. Cotton told William that his boss had plenty of evidence pointing to Northcote, but the powers that be, specifically the coroner, buried it. This was 1940, the Blitz was in full swing and the government needed the public onside. The last thing they needed was for them to discover that a toff thought the rules didn't apply to him and had strangled a decent girl from a respectable home. They hushed it up.'

'So, this is the project that March nicked from Andrea.' Lucie broke the ensuing silence.

'As she told us, Andrea confided in March to keep him, but he stole the idea and cut her out in favour of me,' Stella said to Lucie. 'He never got the chance to ask me because he was murdered.'

'Horses for courses,' Lucie said obscurely. 'If Andrea didn't want March rootling in her past, why come to Tewkesbury with him?'

'Have you ever been in love?' Jack said, then regretted it. Lucie had been in love with Stella's dad and neither woman needed to be reminded. 'Any hope of keeping March was dashed when he discovered Stella's name on the abbey cleaning rota.'

'So, it was Andrea who tried to kill you on the country lane, on your way to the Death Café?' Lucie said.

'She says it was meant to be a warning to stay away from Roddy. Had she got to speak to me I'd have been able to say I'd only met Roddy once. On that morning in the abbey by the cadaver tomb.'

'She'd never have believed you,' Lucie said.

Jack saw Stella and Lucie exchange a look. Since sharing the flat, they'd formed a bond. It should please Jack, but he felt a twinge of jealousy that Stella had always made space for Lucie. He kept to himself that he too had believed Stella and March were an item.

'Andrea followed you to the Death Café?' Beverly asked.

'No. Felicity was worried about having so few people for her session so she paid Andrea to go. When she arrived on the second night, Andrea found Roddy there. That convinced her I was in cahoots with March. But it was Andrea herself who told him I'd been there the first night which I'm guessing is why he came.' Stella saved her spreadsheet. 'Before you ask, Andrea didn't attack me at the weir last night.'

'Pigeon blood on her spade? A grave in the garden? She played you both.' Lucie still had Andrea as top of the suspect chart.

'The grave was a potato bed,' Jack said. 'She showed us the dead pigeon.'

'You plant potatoes in March or April. Just saying,' Lucie said. 'My turn.'

Lucie put her phone next to her laptop so Jackie could hear it and played her illicitly recorded chat with Gladys Wren in the tearoom that morning.

'*...he'd said he would marry me. I'd have left but I needed the job and he'd have made my name mud in the town. That night, before Derek and me went to the pictures in Evesham, Derek proposed. He'd blown his wages on a gorgeous ring. Look.*'

'She's showing me her diamond,' Lucie said.

'*...I'd just said yes when Derek gets a shout to attend a barn fire. He wanted me to hand in my notice that night. He knew I hated it there, not that I'd said why or Derek would have*' *swung for Sir Aleck. I went back all cock-a-hoop and told Sir Aleck I was leaving to get wed. He made me submit, one last time. I said no, but that didn't bother him. I was up against the wall in that sitting room. It hurt worse than ever, while he was... while... he kept saying I'd led him on. That I was a common tart, did Mr Wren know that? That sort of language always got him in the mood. That time he had me by the throat.'* There was silence during which Jack could hear the clatter and chatter of the tearoom. *'...I was scared stiff he was going to murder me.'*

'So, you killed him,' Lucie's voice said softly. *'I know I would have.'*

Jack knew Lucie would have fought and doubtless Northcote would have strangled her as he had Maple. Gladys Wren had gone for survival. Of a sort.

'No,' Gladys Wren hissed. Another silence in which Jack thought Gladys had left. Then, *'...I was halfway home, we lived in Bredon's Hardwick, outside of Tewkesbury, when I saw my brooch was gone. I'd sneaked it from my mother's drawer to wear for Derek, I had a notion he'd pop the question. It must have come off when... I had to get it back.'*

'You weren't worried Northcote would rape you again?'

Jack shut his eyes, Lucie had no soft pedal.

'If Mother found her brooch missing, she'd go to the police. She'd never think it was me, I was a goody-two-shoes. I planned to creep in through the kitchen. By then he should have gone up to bed. But when I opened the baize door, there he was. Dead in the hall. I called 999. When they came to interview me, Derek told me to say I'd been at the film in Evesham until it finished. He said, if they didn't find someone for the murder, they'd blame me.'

'And you never told Derek what Northcote had done to you?'

'He believed he was my first. Soon after, I discovered I was carrying. For the next months I was sure I was bearing the Devil's child. But God forgave me. John had Derek's chin and that winning smile of his. There was nothing in him of Northcote.'

'Do you know a woman called Joy Turton?'

'Joy, the blacksmith's daughter, runt of the litter. The kids called her Spotted Dick after she got the measles. Joy told Roderick she'd seen me that night. She was on at me about who murdered the girl in the film. Well, I didn't know, did I. The minx said the murderer was a girl who'd seen her husband kissing another girl in the lounge at the back of the house. From jealousy, she bashed her on the head with a poker. I couldn't tell on her to her father because I had lied and she knew it. Roddy looked up the film on the internet, although Mary my friend who worked at Moore's auctioneers had gone over what really happened, so I knew. Joy had lied to let me know there was no escape.'

They heard a loud rat-a-tat-tat, like gunfire. Stanley jumped up and woofed his head off.

'She's banging her teaspoon on her cup,' Lucie explained.

'Good guard dog.' Stella calmed Stanley.

'I'm waiting for her to go the police. She is biding her time, giving me her Cheshire cat smile when we pass in the shops.'

'That's it.' Lucie had her own Cheshire cat smile.

'Joy was keen that Lucie and I suspected Gladys.' Stella said.

'We can rule out Gladys.' Beverly was hugging a cushion. 'I wish I could murder Northcote all over again.'

'I agree with Bev, Gladys is too obvious a suspect,' Jack said.

'Often the simplest solution is the one. She had a strong motive for wanting Northcote dead.' Stella sounded reluctant to point a finger at the former housekeeper for whom Jack knew she had a soft spot. 'But if Northcote had carried through his threat to tell Derek Wren he'd been with Gladys, she'd have lost everything.'

'She'd have lost everything if she'd killed him with Joy watching.' Beverly would be upset that Stella wasn't simply 'onside'.

'She would have.' Stella's fingers flew about the keys as she added in the latest information. 'Gladys's story rings true to me.'

'I agree,' Jackie said from the pizza boxes. 'You said Gladys Wren is the size of a wren, we know from photos that Sir Aleck Northcote was a big bloke. How did she overpower him?'

'The same way Roddy's killer got to him – by catching him unawares,' Lucie said. 'Gladys Wren finds Northcote zizzing in his chair. Grabs the poker and with one whack fells him. Another and he's unconscious. Presuming he's dead, she finds her brooch and scarpers.'

'If Joy was watching at the window, she'd have seen everything.' Jackie's picture momentarily pixelated. 'You said she's a Christian steeped in morality, would she witness a murder and say nothing? And why protect a woman she doesn't like?'

'Joy had a better idea,' Lucie said. 'After I accidentally stopped recording, Gladys told me that, for fifty-seven years, Joy by Nature has been blackmailing her.'

Jack had to hand it to Lucie, she was consummate at the grand finale.

'Why hasn't Gladys gone to the police?' Stella sounded outraged.

'Why indeed? Suspect round-up.' Lucie's good mood was restored. 'Gladys Wren is paying out on a murder she claims she didn't commit. Madam Joy wins the jackpot every month for being a peeping Tom. Felicity Branscombe knows how to use a knife and has a morgue in her basement *and* a creepy crush on Northcote. Andrea the Fake Gardener is granddaughter to the first victim in our grisly daisy chain and jilted girlfriend of the third. All four are steeped in motive and opportunity.' Lucie was riding high. '...*kinell*, let's do eeny-meeny-miny-moe.'

'If Gladys killed Northcote, and then Roddy to stop him naming her in his podcast, why not murder Joy too?' Stella coded the *suspect* cells on her spreadsheet a light blue.

'What if Joy murdered Northcote for Gladys and that's why she's paying her?' Beverly said. 'And she told you Joy was blackmailing her because she's strapped for cash.'

'Felicity and Andrea could have teamed up.' Lucie waved a fig.

'Felicity said pathologists revere Northcote – she'd surely want the true killer revealed.' Jackie raised her voice over the hubbub of theories.

'And see Roddy March get the credit?' Lucie said. 'Ooh, Andry-Pandy just texted.'

I love Jack. Stella's words echoed as if she'd whispered in his ear. *I love Jack.*

'...you go, Jack?' Stella was looking at him.

'Sorry?' Jack blinked.

'Andrea's texted Lucie: William Greenhill wants to see her. She's insisting you go with her.'

'Me?' Jack ran a hand through his hair.

'She might want to make a pass at you to get back at Stella. But it's a chance to see Maple's son, another piece of the jigsaw,' Lucie cackled.

'Do you mind?' Jack asked Stella.

'Why would I?' Stella took his hand. 'I love you and I know you love me back.'

Chapter Fifty

2019

Stella

The next morning Jack went to meet Andrea in Stella's van to drive her to Chertsey to find out why William Rogers (Greenhill) had summoned his daughter. There had been a contretemps before they left when Jack and Stella found Lucie hidden in the back of the van under a heap of groundsheets.

'She could lead you off the beaten track and bash your brains out with her spade,' Lucie had protested as they bundled her out. 'Jack, you'd never let Stella go off with a woman who is likely a murderer.'

'She's right,' Stella had said.

'I don't think Andrea is a murderer.' Promising to keep them posted, Jack had sped off down the high street.

This had delayed Stella getting to Cloisters House to clean for Felicity. The front door was open. Stella knocked and waited. The door was probably open for her. With the tip of her finger she pushed on it.

'Felicity?' After finding Clive dead in a house with the door ajar, Stella feared the worse.

She told herself Felicity was making a point about punctuality. She had disapproved of Andrea being late for the Death Café.

Or Felicity had forgotten Stella was coming and had gone out without locking up. Stella stamped on the tiles to announce her presence.

'Hi, Felicity, I've come to clean.' She pushed on the green baize door and ventured down the passage. Light from the kitchen cast a sheen on the brick floor. Distantly, Stella noted it was clean. The door to the utility room where Felicity stored mops, vacuum and other cleaning equipment was shut. Stella felt unwilling to open it although it was precisely where she could legitimately go. Heart in her mouth, she turned the handle.

A body was spread-eagled on the stone flags, the head jammed against the washing machine.

For a split second, Stella supposed it should be in Felicity's morgue, then she realized. *The body was Felicity.*

'Felicity.' Stella flung herself down beside the motionless figure. She put a finger to her neck but she couldn't feel a pulse.

'What's happened?'

The voice came from behind Stella. Whipping around she saw Joy framed in the doorway. 'Call an ambulance, now.'

'Is that necessary?' Clutching some papers, Joy remained motionless. 'Of course, I will, but even paramedics can't wake the dead, as Felicity would be the first to tell you.'

'Not another murder,' Stella gasped.

'No wild theories please. Felicity is an old woman. It'll be a stroke or she missed her step and hit her head.' Joy put her papers on the washing machine. 'Let me.'

She squatted beside Stella and leant down, putting her ear to Felicity's chest. Then she sat up. 'Oh dear.'

There was a noise. Gurgling. A groan. Felicity opened her eyes.

'She's *alive*,' Stella shouted.

'I told you it wasn't murder.' Joy hauled herself to her feet and took up her papers. She reached into a small fabric bag strapped across her chest, with, Stella noticed without noticing, Tewkesbury Abbey on the side, and fiddled with it. Seeing Stella's glance, Joy said, 'I've got brandy in here somewhere.'

'I hate the stuff.' Felicity began to turn over.

'Stay still. You might have broken something. Joy, could you get a cushion from the lounge?' Stella wished Bev was there, Stella's first-aid training wasn't current.

'I am a doctor, my knowledge of anatomy is second to none. *Physician heal thyself.*' Felicity pushed herself to sitting and rubbed her temple. 'I have merely suffered a blow to the head.'

'*Merely?*' Stella spotted something on the floor. An iron, the plastic casing cracked. She picked it up, gathering shards of the casing from the floor. Looking at a shelf above the washing machine she asked, 'Did this fall on you?'

'I wish.' Felicity got to her feet. 'Someone sneaked in when my back was turned and,' she looked at Joy, 'I assume the iron was the only weapon to hand.'

'I hope you're not accusing me.' Joy was hugging the cushion she had brought.

'What are you doing here?' Felicity began to get up.

'I came to give you the revised service sheets, to save you a trip to the abbey. Goodness knows I wish I hadn't if I'm to be held responsible—'

'Calm yourself, Joy,' Felicity rapped. 'Who's doing the solo for "Once in Royal David's City"?'

'You know we choose on the night, like at King's.' Joy tssked. 'Perhaps now you won't be up to coming, though?'

'The swine only gave me a tap, my skull is as strong as an ox. I *shall* be there.' Moving carefully, Felicity pottered up the passage. 'Although, with this rain and so many yellow flood warnings, it will doubtless be cancelled.'

'I for one shall play to an empty abbey,' Joy said as she and Stella followed Felicity to the front room. 'We're doing the King's 1940 service – I think we could show some wartime spirit, don't you?'

'We might be better doing Noah's Flood.' Felicity was examining her forehead in the mirror above the fireplace. 'See? I've not lost my sense of humour.'

'Did you see who hit you?' Stella asked.

'They would have been dead next to me if I had,' Felicity snapped.

'*Coo-ee?*' The call echoed in the tiled hall. 'Anyone home?'

'In here.' Stella was relieved to hear Lucie then sick with worry. *Had something happened to Jack and Beverly?*

'Fancy.' Lucie saw Joy. 'Three's a crowd, four is a *party*.'

'This is not a party. Joy says she was dropping something off and Stella is here to clean.' Felicity was frosty. 'Have we met?'

'I'm Stella's minder.' Lucie did her trademark cackle. 'After she was attacked on the weir the other night, I'm keeping a weather eye. She hates me fussing, but fussing saves lives.'

'What attack?' Felicity looked shocked. 'Stella, you never said.'

'I'm fine, they only took my bag.' Stella was annoyed. 'Is it Jack? Or Bev?'

'Who? Never heard of them. *No.*' Lucie flapped a hand.

'Felicity was just attacked too.' Wilting with real relief, Stella sat on the sofa beside Felicity then promptly got up. She was there to clean.

'Failed robbery, not like poor Stella's beating. Did they find anything valuable?'

'No.'

'If Stella and, of course, Joy hadn't come when they did, the thugs would have— The little *shits*.' Felicity was staring at the mantelpiece. 'They've taken my cartilage knife.'

'What did it look like?' Joy asked.

'A knife is what it looked like – with a sharp blade.' Felicity eyed Joy.

'The police will insist you provide a detailed description and estimate of value.' Joy seemed unfazed by Felicity's impatience with her.

'It belonged to Sir Aleck Northcote, it was in that case.' To Stella's surprise, Felicity was fighting tears as she pointed at a leather case open on the mantelpiece.

'That's quite dreadful,' Lucie said. 'We must call the police.'

'I'm not wasting their time over a knife.' Felicity blew her nose on a tissue. 'I'd rather put this whole thing behind me. I need a lie down.'

'What concerns me is, taking two murders out of the equation, this is the second attack in Tewkesbury within a week.' Lucie settled on the sofa beside Felicity. 'There are many expensive objects in this lovely room which the robbers passed over. That Alexa is surely a gold watch to a magpie, yet they stole a knife.'

'I said, they were interrupted when Stella arrived.'

'The door was open,' Stella said.

'They could still be here.' Lucie shot out into the hall and, sighing, Felicity got to her feet. They trailed after Lucie.

Darting into corners, slamming doors flat against walls, peering under beds, after checking each room Lucie yelled, '*Clear.*' Finally, returning to the hall, 'OK, Prof, you may rest easy in your bed.'

'I always do.' Felicity wandered back to her sofa. For all she sounded annoyed, Stella guessed that Felicity was grateful for Lucie's trouble.

'However, and she's going to kick off, I'm taking Stella home.' Lucie put out an arm. 'It's too soon after Stella's own bang on the head to be wearing Marigolds.'

For the first time in as long as Stella could recall, she felt relieved not to clean. Confirming Felicity was all right to be left, they all trooped out.

'Why are you doing the King's 1940 service?' Stella had read up on the year which was Maple Greenhill's last. She felt a connection to the dead woman and the time she had lived in.

'Christmas in the Blitz, barbed wire mingled with mistletoe, guns with tinsel, when Christians demonstrated fortitude amidst suffering. Great Britain refused to deprive the nation's children of the one day in the year which brought them joy. Nothing could cancel Christmas. It's a message to those who bring evil to this town that we shall overcome. '

'I thought Christmas was in God's hands.' Lucie did a pious face. 'Are you OK, Joy? Rather a shock for you, too, finding Felicity apparently dead like that,' she said.

'Perfectly, thank you. It wasn't me she attacked.' Joy flapped the service sheets, 'Botheration, I forgot to leave these. I should go back.'

'*Who* didn't attack you?' Lucie loomed in front of Joy.

'Whoever hit the doctor with her iron. *Obviously.*' Joy scowled as droplets of rain began to fall. 'I'm not going back now. Felicity will have to fumble her way through like she always does.'

'What makes you think Felicity was hit by a woman?' Lucie was a dog with a bone.

'*He* then.' Joy was properly cross. 'I've said before, girls are worse than boys.'

'Do you think it could have been Mrs Wren? What with her history of violence?' Lucie said.

'I don't think anything.' Joy looked annoyed.

'I was thinking, if it *was* Mrs Wren, she is now armed with a knife,' Lucie continued in a merry voice.

'I can't stand here gossiping, I'll be soaked.' Seemingly heedless of the water forming a shallow lake, Joy plashed up the yew path to the north door of the abbey.

'There's a liar if ever I heard one,' Lucie said when, the rain now heavy, they had fled to the tearoom and ordered coffee and doughnuts.

'Joy?' Stella bit into her doughnut then baulked at the red jam. *Everything was blood.*

'Felicitations the knife,' Lucie said. 'She was lying her head off saying that, after nearly being dashed away with a smoothing iron, muggers purloined her cartilage knife.'

'It does sound far-fetched.' Picturing Felicity crumpled on the floor, Stella believed she had been attacked. 'When I found her, she was barely conscious.'

'She was bashed, she has a bruise smack bang on her temple to prove it. Something doesn't fit, what is it?' Not a question, Lucie knew the answer and suddenly so did Stella.

'She was facing her attacker.' Stella scalded her mouth on hot coffee. 'She knew who hit her.'

'Because her attacker was *there*, listening to her every word.' Lucie was triumphant.

'That's why Joy said the attacker was "she". It was her. Could Joy be blackmailing Felicity too?'

'What about you and I trotting along to their rehearsal tonight?' Lucie had jam on her cheek.

'There will be floods, no one will go and really, nor should we.' Stella leaned over and wiped the jam off with a corner of her napkin.

'A little water won't put off us, we're Angels of the Thames.' Lucie hugged herself.

'You can't swim.'

'Wartime spirit, Stella. It's all arranged.' Lucie beamed. 'Beverly will finish in the gift shop and save us seats. We must support your Death Café chums.'

'How come you knew Joy attacked Felicity?'

'I didn't.'

'Why did you go to Felicity's?' Stella knew Lucie's concern for her had been a ploy to get into Cloisters House; any concern was ever for the story.

'Like I said, to check on you, Ducky-Doo. If you won't take care of yourself, I have to do it for you.'

Chapter Fifty-One

2019

Jack

'By the way, when we get there, you're my partner, we met on Tinder.'

'Andrea, I get you're angry that March wanted Stella, but it wasn't Stella's doing.' Jack slapped the steering wheel. 'Stella doesn't do petty so she doesn't get it when people try it on her. And, she's too certain of me to be jealous. You and I could go to the moon, she'd just wish us a good journey.' Jack felt brilliant. *I love you.*

'You think that's what this is about?' Andrea was slumped against the van door. 'Typical bloke, it's not all about you. You and your merry band have missed the point. If you want to get past first base, you need to do what I say. If my dad thinks you are anything like Roddy you will be out on your ear. If Dad thinks you're there for me and not to solve a murder, he'll be halfway polite.'

'I am not pretending to be your partner.' Even pretending was betraying Stella.

'Your choice to be an idiot. You and Roddy are peas in a pod.' Although already stifling, Andrea turned up the heater. 'You want to abort this mission, then tell Dad you and your cleaner girlfriend are poking into his mum's murder. If you've got any sense at all, you will trust me.'

'It's wrong to lie.'

'Says the liar,' Andrea said. 'Roderick March was one dipshit, but my fate is to fancy dipshits. Nice blokes like you don't do it. Dad'll probably see through it, but at least give it a try?'

'No.'

After that they drove in silence.

'Dad, this is Jack.'

'You're my daughter's latest man off the internet.' Greenhill was so bowed by osteoporosis that to scrutinize Jack he had to twist his head to the side.

'I met Andrea in the abbey grounds.' Jack tried to placate Andrea. 'She's jolly nice, Dr Greenhill.' *He wasn't supposed to know this was William Greenhill.*

'Westminster Abbey?' Greenhill loomed into Jack's chest. It felt sobering; he'd once have been as tall as Jack.

'Tewkesbury.' Jack felt Andrea's eyes lasering into his back. Turning he mouthed *Sorry*, but Andrea was as grim as the reaper.

'What the hell were you doing there?' Greenhill looked past Jack to his daughter. Jack had just aborted the mission.

To the man whom Divisional Detective Cotton had divulged that his mother had been murdered by Sir Aleck Northcote, Tewkesbury would clang a loud bell. 'That was in confidence. This man isn't in love with you. Even I, a dull-witted doctor, can see that. He's a reporter.'

'He's not, Dad. However, he does care about Maple. He's working for your family, the Greenhills.' Andrea was talking fast to keep her father there.

Seeing Greenhill's face Jack knew it wouldn't work so, risking his lovely leather lace-ups, he inserted his foot in the doorway.

'Your cousin Cliff, he's Vernon's son, and Cliff's daughter Cleo want to know who murdered Maple. They need closure.' Jack wasn't sure that, through a fug of alcohol, Cliff Greenhill cared, but to Cleo who, Bev had told him had given her a silly deal on the Mini, it mattered very much.

'Closure? That's crap.' Greenhill tried to shut the door.

'Ouch,' Jack said.

'Cliff wasn't alive when my mother was strangled. It was me wearing a jumper that she'd taken so long to knit for me, it was tight.'

'Dad. Please. Let us in.' Gone was the Heathcliff demeanour, Andrea was pleading.

'Just you. He can sling his hook.'

'Know what, Dad? This is also about me.' Andrea's moment of pleading switched off like a light bulb. 'I traipsed after Roddy to Tewkesbury because I want the truth. You lied to me the way they lied to you. Although not for a good reason. You throwing him out sent Roddy March after a woman he thought would win you round. A poxy Mrs Mop. He dumped me.'

'He would have dumped Ste—'

'Enough. Roddy fancied Stella, she wouldn't have refused him.' Andrea was fizzing. 'Dad, Maple might have been your mum, but she was my grandmother. I never met her, she never got to know me, but she's family and I will avenge her.'

'Don't do anything rash…' Jack mimed *sorry* again.

'We all owe it to Maple to know about her last moments. To live those last moments with her. Then Maple can be at peace.'

'Jolly good.' Jack was impressed.

'Please be quiet,' Andrea fumed. 'And before you say it, the victim thing was my idea, not Roddy's.'

'Northcote was never charged with murder. Cotton was a bitter man spreading false rumours.' Greenhill shambled into the house.

Andrea followed him in. When Jack hesitated, she hissed, 'Are you coming or not?'

'George Cotton told you it was Northcote, but the man couldn't be charged, he was needed for the war effort,' Andrea said to her father.

'Ex-coppers get obsessed with failed cases. I saw that. The war stopped Cotton retiring, then it killed his wife. He was a broken man. All he had left was that case. He actually told me that. Northcote's career soared while Cotton's had gone south.' Stiffly putting out a steadying hand on a stack of *Lancet* journals, Greenhill lowered himself into a more recent vintage of Lucie's cockpit. At his feet lay scattered pages of the *Telegraph* as if, after reading, Greenhill dropped each one.

'You told me Cotton said Julia Northcote had promised him she would tell the world. Northcote murdered her before she could put anything down.'

'If there was anything to tell, she took her secret to her grave,' Greenhill said.

'Why are you doing this, Dad? Don't you want to help your mother?' Andrea paced the room. Jack felt for her: for whatever reason, Greenhill had changed his original account.

'I bought Northcote's house.' Andrea was speaking quietly, Greenhill's state-of-the-art hearing aids must have ensured he heard every word because he was as white as a sheet. 'I was scanning the house when Roddy found the box under a floorboard. Julia Northcote had kept her promise to George Cotton after all.'

'So that's how it happened,' Jack said.

'I was a fool,' Andrea flashed at him. 'On his first date, Roddy turned up. I had to pay for the meal in the expensive restaurant he'd said was dreamy. Take note of how a relationship starts, Jack, it's a good hint for how it will go on.'

'Men are liars and toads,' Greenhill spluttered. Jack caught the west London accent beneath his finely tuned doctor's voice.

'We know Northcote murdered his wife,' Jack said.

'She killed herself, I've seen the path report.' Greenhill shook his head vigorously. 'His wife was ill.'

'Old boys' network – the pathologist had his own career to think about. He flipped forced hanging to suicide. Julia Northcote left a letter and newspaper cuttings in a Lyons' Swiss Roll box in the dressing room. It states categorically that Northcote confessed to strangling Maple and that, if anything happened to her, whoever read the letter was to tell Clement Attlee who Julia Northcote seems to have admired. Roddy said the letter would make our fortune.' Andrea gulped for air. 'Julia probably planned her letter as insurance against her husband hurting her. But Northcote was a risk-taker and he killed her anyway. His risk paid off, he got away with it. Until the night of Friday the twenty-second of November 1963.'

'I've seen the letter, sir.' Jack was scrupulously polite. 'I'm sure it's genuine.'

'You stole it.' Andrea couldn't possibly get any angrier with him. Yes, she could.

'That's not quite right,' Jack said. 'Julia wanted it to be read.'

'Julia, is it?' Andrea spat. 'Found an affinity with *the distant dead*, have we?'

Jack judged it best not to admit that he had. Julia and Maple were almost friends.

'It is likely a soldier or a corrupt ARP warden murdered your grandmother. There was a lot of that.' Greenhill looked defeated.

'Is this the medical profession looking after its own?' Andrea said. 'Since Shipman we all know doctors can kill.'

'I don't like rushing to judgement.'

'Maple Greenhill was murdered in 1940 – hardly rushing.'

'Someone wanted Northcote dead,' Jack said.

'You're like her other man, making mystery where there is none. Haven't you got a better way to spend your time than leading on my daughter?' Greenhill looked at Jack with pure distaste.

'Dad. He's not leading me on. This is about me.' Andrea got up. 'I believe George Cotton and so do you. Why are you doing this?'

'As you said, my mother has been dead a long time. It won't help her to destroy people's families. And their reputations.' Greenhill looked uncomfortable. Had someone got to him?

'Northcote killed her, we have the proof. I want her story to be told.'

'Why did you change your name?' Following a thought train, Jack was surprised when Greenhill answered him.

'I grew up in the shadow of my sister's murder. Maple was a millstone around all our necks. My parents – grandparents – were destroyed. Dad said Mum couldn't bear him to peck her on the cheek after Maple died. They couldn't be pleased for Vernon when his boss left him the garage or the birth of Cliff, their first grandson, second if you include me. Dad died the day he retired. Mum soon after. They'd died in spirit in December 1940.' Greenhill spoke in a monotone. 'Then big brother Vernon dropped the bombshell. I was Maple's illegitimate kid and he was my uncle. They had fooled me. I changed my name to be rid of the dead.'

'Jack's mother was murdered when he was a boy,' Andrea said. They had agreed she'd use it as a lever, but still Jack felt as if he'd been punched in the face.

'Don't fib, dear.' Greenhill was the severe dad.

'She was strangled next to the River Thames in 1981.'

'Did they catch the killer?' The doctor's tone softened.

'Not at the time.' Jack's tongue stuck to the roof of his mouth.

'Jack and his partner identified her killer in 2012.' Andrea was on a roll.

'Did that bring you closure?' Greenhill was faintly acid.

'I wanted her killer dead, but when that happened, nothing changed. Revenge would have satisfied me briefly before it wore off. Only my mother returning would do.' Jack hadn't fully thought this before.

'I'll make tea.' Andrea left the room.

'If you could find your mother's killer, would you want revenge?' Jack asked William.

'I don't like to call him her killer, it creates a link that was never there in life.'

'Maple told her brother Vernon she had a secret fiancé who was a doctor. Northcote was seen with her at the Hammersmith Palais – isn't it likely he murdered Maple?' Jack went for it. 'Dr Greenhill, did you kill Roderick March because he was going to reveal you are the actual murderer of Sir Aleck Northcote?'

Chapter Fifty-Two

2019

Stella

Stella had asked Lucie to go to the Christmas rehearsal at the abbey. Amidst the turmoil of murder and Stella's growing fear that, rather than make a pass at Jack, Andrea would try to kill him, Stella needed peace. Lucie hadn't needed persuading, she'd zipped and buttoned herself into her Driza-Bone against the rain and was out the door. Perhaps she too needed peace. Stella's phone buzzed.

Stock-taking for Joy. Will quiz her.

'We should pull Bev out of there.' Stella paused for Stanley to lift a leg against a tree trunk on the yew path.

'Give Beverly a chance to shine, Stella. Ah, looks like Felicity was right and Joy was wrong.' Lucie was reading a notice on the abbey door.

Due to severe weather, rehearsal postponed.

'We have to at least check on Bev.' Stella tried the door. It opened. 'Besides, Joy said she'd play whatever the weather.'

They gravitated to chairs near the choir where Stella had seen March's beanie.

'Northcote murders Maple Greenhill to save his rep then murders Julia, because she's going to dob him in for Maple. Sickening.' A puddle of water from her coat had collected around Lucie's feet. 'Northcote in turn is bumped off, supposedly for refusing son Giles a handout. If we are to believe Rodders and Virtual Andrea, Giles went to the gallows an innocent man. Who wanted Northcote dead?'

'It had to be out of revenge,' Stella said. 'That narrows it down to anyone who cared about Maple.'

'Or held a grudge against him. And since he seems to have been an evil genius, our net widens again.' Lucie was flipping through the hymn book.

'Gladys Wren had a lucky escape,' Stella said.

'Not if, according to Joy by Cheque, lovely Gladys murdered Northcote.' Lucie began to hum the carol she had open in the book. Stella could see it was 'O Come, All Ye Faithful', but didn't recognize Lucie's version.

'I think Gladys's story of faking her alibi rings true. We know that murder ensnares those with secrets of their own.'

'Ooh, I like that.' Fumbling in her bag Lucie scribbled the phrase in her notebook. 'But Joy said she saw Gladys.'

'I think she saw Northcote raping Gladys and conflated the scene with hearing he'd been murdered. She was a child, she probably only made sense of it as an adult and seems to have seen mileage in her knowledge,' Stella said.

'At ten she was a peeping Tom; what she saw made her older than her years.' Lucie was swooshing water off her sleeves.

'Dad always said start from the simple solution and work up. We're into the very complicated.'

'If only that was how he had conducted his personal life.' Lucie flicked to 'Once in Royal David's City'; Stella hoped to goodness she wouldn't attempt to sing it.

'Sorry to rain on your parade, Stells, but Mrs W is steeped in motive. Northcote left her a small legacy, doubtless he told her that to get his wicked way with her. He threatened to tell her fiancé. Gladys told me Derek would have forsaken her if he'd known she wasn't a virgin. The bounder. Northcote only had to touch his flies and she'd have to be there. During their sherry evenings Gladys understands this podcast thing Roderick's doing will point the finger at her. Easier if you stick a knife in the back and don't see their eyes.'

'And Clive?' Stella realized the abbey was silent. Joy wasn't playing after all.

'I'm guessing he saw her do it or Joy told him Gladys killed Northcote. Clive sounds like a weaselly old squirrel, probably saw a chance to move in on Mrs W himself. Face it, Stell, why hand over cash to Joy if she's innocent? I'm there with Gladys. Mind, she's the victim here. She's also top of my suspect tree. She lied about her alibi, said she was at the Sabrina Cinema when she can't have been since it was closed.'

'I think that was a mistake. The police would have known the Sabrina had closed down. In her chat with you, Gladys said they were going to Evesham to see the film. I think she felt guilty, soiled. Somehow to blame. Few people would have believed her about Northcote. The only one who had seen it was Joy and she blackmailed her.' Stella was passionate. 'If Gladys killed Northcote she'd have been splattered with blood. Her family would have seen.' Sticking to a hunch felt alien, but Stella felt Mrs Wren's account of that November night fifty-six years ago was the truth. 'Had there been no barn fire, Gladys and Derek would have watched *Girl in the Headlines*. No, I'm certain that after Giles and Gladys left, Northcote had another visitor.'

'Out goes Andrea as a suspect: Roddy March stealing her story is a weak motive and, like she told you, his podcast planned to expose her grandmother's killer. It pains me, she's a grumpy sod, but...' Lucie deleted Andrea from a list in her notebook. 'And you can have Gladys Wren. We're left with Felicity, Joy and you.'

Baring her teeth, Lucie warbled the first line of 'Once in Royal David's City'.

'There were barriers.' Stella leapt up and went over to the column near the choir. 'Workmen had been repairing this area, and until after the night Roddy was murdered, it was closed off to the public. The barriers started from that pillar. On the south ambulatory. Although it was blocked off, I went that way to avoid Joy.'

'Ambulatory, is that rude?'

'Roddy March must have approached the starved monk from the north side because it was where he left his beanie.' Stella rocked Stanley in her arms.

'Meaning?' Leaving a trail of drips, Lucie wandered over and joined her.

'That Roddy would have passed the Grove organ to get to the tomb and, as she was playing at the time, Joy must have seen him. She told Janet, and us, she saw no one. Maybe she expected him after the business with the chamomile tea. Maybe they had conferred.'

'Suppose his killer met him there and, like you, moved the barrier. You said March was chucked out fifteen minutes before everyone. He had time to be installed with the hungry monk before Joyful got going on her organ.'

'Roddy might not have come straight to the abbey.' Stella buried her face in Stanley's damp fur. 'Roddy is following a lead of his own. Something at the Death Café gave him a hint. He's heading to their house because he knows that at that moment it's empty. He gets a text from his killer asking to meet at the abbey. He sits for a bit, that's when I saw his shadow on the wall, then he goes to the starved monk, via the other way. Follow me.'

Stella crept down the north ambulatory and, keeping close to the cases of second-hand books, edged past the panelling that housed the organ. There was no one there.

'Looks like Joy bailed out after all that talk of braving the floods to play.' Lucie snorted.

'Stanley's coat is wet.' Stella was clutching Stanley.

'Funny that.'

'Roddy's hair was wet, I assumed it was blood, but he was stabbed in the back. It must have been water, Roddy was caught in the rain.'

'Does it ever stop raining here?'

'It wasn't raining when Roddy left the Death Café,' Stella said. 'Andrea muttered that it was a shame, he wouldn't get soaked. Joy said it would be his fault if he was. Felicity said she felt bad ejecting him, but must abide by Death Café rules. Since everyone except Felicity and me appears to have disliked Roddy, him going can't have mattered. To have got wet, Roddy must have gone somewhere before the abbey.'

'Have you heard from Jackanory?' Lucie suddenly said.

'No.' Jack was on a motorway at night. He'd be all right, he was a confident driver. He'd been sure Andrea was innocent and, with his thing about spotting True Hosts, Jack would know. Stella told herself.

'Hang on, look.' Lucie was pointing at a spotlight on a gantry high up above the nave. 'The shadow of that pillar is slanting across the wall as it would have that night. If March was in that chair in front, his shadow would be there too. Stay where you are.' Lucie went and sat in the chair. 'Can you see my shadow from there?'

'Yes.'

'When Joy was cantering on her Wurlitzer, she would have seen the shadow.'

'That means...'

'It means we have our murderer.'

'Beverly is stock-taking.' Stella pulled Lucie behind the pillar.

I'll quiz her.

The same thought occurred to Stella and Lucie. Beverly had a tendency to jump more than one gun. Jack had found her in Andrea's house in London and since Gladys had said Joy was blackmailing her, Beverly's money was on Joy.

Seeing light spilling out of the gift shop, Stella felt dread. If Jackie were on the spot she'd have watched out for Beverly. Stella had taken her eye off the ball.

The shop was shut. Stella let herself breathe. Then she got a text. Disappointment that it wasn't Jack was mitigated by *Bev Mob*.

At Mrs Wrens. Joy on way, will trap her. I'm on it! B.

'We have to stop her.' Stella spun around. 'Is this the chance to shine you meant?'

'Bev on her own with two likely killers? No, *hot damn*.' Grim-faced, Lucie voiced what Stella couldn't bear to think.

Another text.

'Felicity knows who attacked her,' Stella said. 'She's asked to meet me at our flat and go with her to the police.'

'Tell her to come here. Find out who it is then text me. We're not handing this to Janet on a plate. I'll go and rescue Bev.'

'Take Stanley, his bark is scary.'

Flinging up the hood of her Driza-Bone Lucie zipped it up to her neck and, like a giant bat, flew along the north ambulatory. Stella heard the door slam.

She was alone.

She stared through the grille into the gift shop. Through the bars, a carousel of fabric hens might be in prison. Bev had warned her that Jack had bought her one, so she could arrange her face when he gave it to her. No need, she'd happily accept the lot. Bev said Joy got easily upset.

Bev might be the youngest in the team, the least experienced and terrible at filing, but she was sharp and brave. Too brave. Stella WhatsApped her.

Don't do ANYTHING. Lucie coming, me too soon. Be NICE to Joy, DO NOT make her upset.

Listening out for Felicity, Stella pressed send.

Through the grille, Stella saw a light on the counter. She heard a buzz. Glimpsing two Yuletide candles Stella supposed they were electric. She looked at her phone. One grey tick against her message to Beverly. Two grey ticks signalled that the other device had got the text. Two blue ticks told you the recipient had read it. Beverly had not read it. Thinking to attract her attention, Stella resent the text. Another buzz. Another light on the counter, not the Yuletide candles. Propelled by the buzzing, a pink object juddered past one of the candles and stopped by a cluster of Mary and Josephs, like the couple Stella had bought. Her mind raced.

Beverly had texted from Gladys Wren's lodging house on the High Street. Yet her phone was here.

'There you are, Stella.' Felicity's cheeks were reddened from the cold. She swung a black umbrella that explained why she was perfectly dry.

'We have to go.' Stella turned to go up the north aisle. 'Bev texted that Joy is going to Gladys's lodging house, Beverly believes Joy killed Roddy March the podcaster and... she's right.' Why hadn't she listened to Beverly?

'Go where?' Felicity was peering through the gift shop grille.

'To the lodging house.' Felicity wasn't getting it. Stella felt screaming frustration.

'We'd be better calling the police.' Felicity sounded reasonable. 'Better yet, let's tell them when we go to the station.'

'There's no time.' Stella knew fear for herself, but fear for someone else was another thing. Her teeth started to chatter.

'Stella, it looks like Joy tricked you like she tried to trick me.' Felicity gave a grim smile.

'Tricked, how?' Stella couldn't speak properly, her mouth was dry, her breathing fast. 'I'm being dense. Beverly couldn't have texted from Mrs Wren's, her phone is in there.' Beverly had never left the gift shop.

'Beverly,' Stella shouted. She wrenched on the grille as if she could yank it from the thick wooden door into which it was fixed. 'Bev is in there, injured or...'

'Stop. Joy is here in the abbey. She told me she was going ahead with the rehearsal with or without the choir. You were there, you remember. I wanted to see you at your flat to avoid her, but when you said you were at the abbey, I had to come. We have to get out now.' Felicity tottered, as if telling Stella had brought it home. She clutched the umbrella like a spear. 'Joy wanted me to come, not to sing or to hear her play, but to kill me.'

'Why you?' Stella was picking up on Felicity's nerves.

'Not just me. She will murder you too. She knows March told you his killer's name. Clive knew, that's why he's dead. Joy thinks you told me too.' Felicity was scouring the abbey. 'She's here. Listening to every word.'

They heard a click then a grinding sound. The sound of stone rolling on stone. In the cavernous abbey they couldn't tell where it came from.

'It was Joy who attacked me. I saw her. She attacked you at the weir and left you for dead.'

'What's that noise?' Stella whispered to Felicity. There were too many chapels, too many pillars and dark corners.

'That way, from the Wakeman Cenotaph, the bitch, she's teasing us.' Fear had made Felicity look somehow younger. Pale and waxen.

'Roddy March didn't tell me his killer's name.' Stella raised her voice for Joy to hear.

'Joy won't believe you.' Felicity got the ruse. 'She has outplayed me.'

'She's got Beverly.' Joy had outplayed them all.

'Sshhh.' Felicity gripped her shoulder, 'It's a double bluff. Beverly will be at Mrs Wren's. Joy's not interested in her, it's me and you she wants.'

'I'll call Janet... I mean the police.' Stella's limbs were jelly. Bravery is a quality attributed by others in retrospect, terror consumes in real time. Why hadn't she made Janet listen, sent her the spreadsheet? Because, as Andrea had said, Stella wanted to play detectives.

'It's too late for the police.' Felicity put a finger to her lips. 'Come with me. Stay close. Joy is dangerous.'

They had moved only a few feet when Stella spotted the source of the noise. A large glass marble lay in the middle of the ambulatory.

'She threw it to distract us,' Felicity breathed. 'Make us think she is nearer than she is. Mind games.'

At that moment the lights went out.

'Don't move,' Felicity breathed in her ear.

It wasn't properly dark. The sconces had dimmed. Stella made out the myriad arches, chapels shrouded in gloom. Shafts of moonlight drifted through the stained-glass windows.

'This is hopeless, Joy could be anywhere.' Stella tried to work out where the door was. The marble said Joy knew exactly where they were.

'I know where she'll be,' Felicity said. Stella felt a flood of gratitude. Felicity had come to the abbey when it would have been safer for her to call the police from a public place. Stella didn't need to ask Felicity where Joy was. She knew.

Joy had returned to the scene of her crimes. The tomb of the starved monk.

Chapter Fifty-Three

2019

Jack

'What do you mean, you know who killed Roderick March?' Janet burst into the interview room with notebook and takeaway coffee. They hadn't even been offered water.

Jack felt as exhausted as Janet looked. A crash on the M4 had put four hours on the two-hour journey. He'd been sitting with Andrea and William Greenhill at a sticky plastic-coated table for a long half hour. Janet intended them to suffer. Their news, highlighting a series of police mistakes, would not improve her mood.

The electric wall clock said two minutes past seven o'clock. The room's high ceiling did nothing to dispel stifling heat pumping from a tubular radiator or the odour of overused furniture and compounded fear.

'We know who murdered Maple Greenhill and Julia Northcote in 1940 and 1941, and then Aleck Northcote in 1963.' Jack wanted Stella there, but when he'd tried calling from the gents' toilet in the police station and several times in the interview room, she hadn't picked up.

To her credit, Janet said nothing while Jack – his account spliced with Andrea's snappish interjections – *bitch, shitbag,* and one worthy of Lucie, *fountain of crap* – outlined each discovery. March's crouching image on the virtual tour of Northcote's London home, the Lyons' Swiss Roll box with Julia's account of her husband's confession which she'd secreted in the house before Northcote murdered her too. How Divisional Detective Inspector George Cotton told William he had evidence – a coat, a mending ticket, a cigarette lighter – leading to Northcote as Maple's murderer. At this William Greenhill had shouted, 'This is *hearsay*.'

'Dad, we've been through this, you heard it from George Cotton, that's the horse's mouth.' Andrea had found patience for her father.

'You don't agree, sir?' Janet didn't look up from her notes, taken despite her request to record the interview, informal as it was.

'It's not a question of agreeing,' Greenhill said. 'Northcote can't defend himself.'

'Why are you defending him?' Andrea went pale. 'Did you do it? Is that why? Revenge for Maple, your mother?'

'Is your daughter correct, Mr Greenhill?' Now Janet did look up.

'No, she's not.' Jack saw it all. 'Or not *exactly*. William, let me tell them what you have believed for, what, fifty-six years?'

'Don't meddle, son.' William shrank into the collar of his raincoat. Not, Jack knew, a sign of guilt.

'Get on with it, Jack,' Janet said.

'William believes that the visitor Aleck Northcote received after his son Giles had gone was Vernon Greenhill. I'm guessing Vernon told William he wanted Northcote to hang. When the pathologist's housekeeper found Northcote dead on the hall floor in 1963, William believed Vernon had carried out his threat. Vernon's granddaughter Cleo also fears this. I thought so too for a while. Seeing the state of Vernon's son Cliff, so does he. Cotton told William the truth about Maple's murder, did he also tell Vernon? Did Maple's brother decide to take an eye for an eye?'

'Vernon is dead,' William said. 'It does no good to rake up the past.'

'I'll be the judge of that, sir.' Janet perhaps agreed, thought Jack.

'Northcote was murdered out of revenge,' Jack said. 'That's pretty much a no-brainer. But the person who smashed his skull with a poker was not Vernon.'

'Who then?' Andrea didn't look happy.

'The same woman who would later murder Roddy and Clive because they discovered the truth. Through a jungle of blackmail, ill-temper and deceit we should've seen it.' Jack saw dismay as Janet comprehended the extent of her mistake. 'Two people were not killed by a gang and nor, half a century ago, did a young man murder his father in a fit of filial fury.'

Stella, the daughter of Janet's detective hero, should be here.

'Do you have evidence?' Janet's face said she was on board. 'This man was a pillar of the community with no previous convictions and a lot of gongs. We can't just go accusing a murdered man of rape and murder.'

Jack was trying to think of how to fudge that they had no evidence but then Andrea leapt up.

'*Yes*,' she cried. 'Come with me.'

Chapter Fifty-Four

2019

Stella

'Stay close, Stella. Do *not* underestimate Joy. She is dangerous.' Grasping Stella's elbow, Felicity crept along the darkened ambulatory.

At first Stella thought the Wakeman Cenotaph was empty. Two candles cast a glow over the starved monk and made fabric draped across the front of the small altar appear woven with threads of gold.

Joy had lit the candles. The right-hand side of the chapel was screened by the carved fretwork beneath which was the monk's tomb. Felicity paused. Stella realized she must be scared. Strangely, this gave Stella courage. She edged to the left and peered around the tomb.

Joy was on the floor, her head forward, hands cupped on her lap. Her palms were filled with blood like an offering. It had drenched her chest. Blood welled from a slit in her neck. Joy slowly lifted her head. She gazed past Stella as if to something beyond. Stella got the scene immediately – Joy had tried to kill herself. She was dying.

'Joy, can you hear me?' Fear evaporating, Stella knelt before the recumbent body. Desperately she looked about for something with which to staunch the blood. Her scarf. She unwound it from her neck and bundled it, pressing it against Joy's neck.

'Felicity, 999, *call an ambulance*,' Stella shouted.

Silence.

Stella leaned into the wound, trying at the same time to maintain Joy's airways.

'Help is coming.' Fleetingly Stella noted she was trying to save the life of a multiple murderer. Joy's eyes looked less vague, they were focused beyond Stella. Stella looked round.

Felicity was illuminated by the candles on the altar table. In her outstretched hand, held perfectly steady, was a knife. Stella knew instantly that it was Sir Aleck Northcote's cartilage knife, the one stolen from Felicity. *By Joy.*

'Don't hurt her,' Stella implored Felicity. 'You of all people know that Joy must face a fair trial. Don't implicate yourself for Northcote, he's long dead and he wasn't worth it.'

'If that wasn't pathetic, it would be funny.' Felicity gave a peculiar high-pitched laugh. 'Leave her, Stella.'

'Please don't do this.' Stella held her scarf against Joy's neck. Joy appeared to be using every ounce of strength to implore Stella not to let Felicity hurt her. 'Felicity, you're a doctor, think of the Hippocratic Oath.'

'I don't save people's lives. My bible is the corpse.' Felicity pointed the knife at Stella. 'Leave her.'

'I can't,' Stella said as Joy's head dropped forward again.

'This way, Stella.' Felicity sounded almost kind.

Chapter Fifty-Five

2019

Jack

'We can't search Ms Branscombe's home without a warrant. Please come out of there, Ms Rogers.'

'My name is Greenhill.' Andrea thrust her spade into the bed of soil which, the night before, Jack had supposed was Stella's grave. 'I can be here, I'm her gardener. Jack, for God's sake, hold the torch steady.'

'Without a warrant, anything you find will be ruled inadmissible by her lawyers.'

'I'm planting the rosemary and lavender bushes as Felicity asked me. I would have put them in earlier, but I had to visit my elderly father, *milud*. Madam Felicity would be cross to find the bushes still in their pots.' Andrea was heaping soil beside a deepening hole. 'Anyway, she'll be at her rehearsal.'

Jack looked beyond the veg patch to the house. Every window was dark. Lucie, Stella and Beverly would be at the rehearsal too.

'Is this enough evidence?' Andrea waved a Tesco Bag for Life at them, then kneeling on rotting foliage emptied out the contents. Two sealed plastic bags. 'That poker matches the description of the one given by Northcote's housekeeper which in her autopsy of him, Felicity said matched the wound in Northcote's skull.' Andrea waved the other, larger bag at them. 'This is Felicity's disguise, the fruits of various charity shops, she easily fooled them both. Stella Darnell and Lucie May no doubt gave signed statements they'd seen a drunken old man swaying along the footpath?'

Janet didn't respond.

Jack's phone rang.

'Stella, are you OK?' White sound, rushing so loud Jack had to hold the phone from his ear. 'Can you hear me, Stella? What's going on?'

The line went dead.

'Something's wrong.' Jack never had trouble following a hunch. The phone rang again, it was Lucie.

'Darling! Don't worry. Stay calm. Bev and me have narrowed the suspects to two. Joy and Felicity. Or both. Whatever, I was lured away and left Stella in the abbey. We're on our way there now, when will you get back from Chertsey?'

'*I'm here.*' Dashing rain from his eyes, Jack leapt over the makeshift grave and tore across the abbey green. He pushed on the great heavy door and raced up the nave. He didn't need to be told where Stella would be.

Chapter Fifty-Six

2019

Stella

Spumes of water thundered through the weir. Soaked by rain Stella was at the mercy of the elemental. A primal roar that stirred the depths of every fear she had ever felt. The black floodwaters were not her only enemy.

'You should have stuck to cleaning.' Felicity was seemingly oblivious of the water welling up through the footboards on the bridge and the deafening crash of the swollen river pushing through the sluices. 'You had to meddle.' Again, that strange fluted laugh. 'With that podcaster and my idiot gardener trailing in your wake.'

'Andrea is not a gardener; if you were genuinely interested in your garden, you'd have seen that. She is a brilliant 3D software engineer. Her scan of our flat initially put us off your scent. It was intended as a warning to me to leave Tewkesbury, so she could have Roddy March to herself. Not even your morgue got me worried.'

'Stella, you are not such a bright girl.' Her back to the sluice-housing, Felicity appeared monstrous. 'You and your gaggle of playmates. They'll be scuttling around the abbey now. They've found Joy the Poison Pen bled out and lifeless. Like headless chickens they'll be tearing into every nook and cranny, every tomb and chapel looking for you. As a cleaner in a little flat in Tewkesbury we could have been friends. You were my ally at the Death Café, I was so disappointed that didn't come off. Then you spoilt things. Like the fools who ended up on my slab.' Felicity tapped the cartilage blade on the gantry railing. It made a sound like a Tibetan bell. Clarity within the tumult.

'Why did you murder Roddy March and Clive Burgess?' Stella clung to the age-old tactic of keeping Felicity talking.

'Clive overheard me outside the tearoom telling March to meet me in the abbey after the Death Café. Gentleman Clive had spent his life opening doors for silly women he despised, it never entered his mind that one of those women would kill him.'

'You must have been there when we...?' Stella was soaked through. Everywhere was water. '*You were the old man.*'

'See what I mean? Not so bright, are you? If only you'd left well alone. I did try another way. Andrea was rabidly jealous of you and March,' Felicity shouted above the cacophony. 'Isn't it frustrating how dense fools like March, with puny egos, capture the hearts of clever women? Though with those manners, Andrea was lucky to have him. I encouraged her jealousy. Let her be the one to drive you out of Tewkesbury.'

'She didn't *have* March, he used her.' Stella could not bear that the last moments of her life might be talking about March. A stupid thought in itself.

'We used each other. I killed March to stop him using me. He would have destroyed my reputation with his trashy podcast. His life was nothing and Clive was a vile woman-hater. As for you, I resent that you have put me in this position.'

'*You murdered Aleck Northcote.*' If this had dawned sooner, Stella wouldn't be hanging over a raging weir with a murderer deciding when she would die.

'Stella the Slow Detective.' Felicity's breath smelled of peppermint. Her clothes of formalin. Smiling like a best friend, Felicity laid the flat of the cartilage blade against

Stella's neck. 'Don't worry, Stella, this is not how you will die.'

'Why did you murder Northcote?' Stella forced herself to sound calm. 'At the Death Café, you said he was your hero.'

'I wanted to a be a pathologist ever since I was twelve when I discovered one could cut up human bodies and see their insides for a living.'

'You must only have been about twenty.' Lucie had warned that no age was too young to murder. Joy, the blackmailer, liar and a snoop, was ten and, until half an hour ago, the prime suspect.

'Too young to die, too young to murder.' Felicity ran the side of the blade down Stella's neck. If she slit her skin, Stella was too numb with cold and fear to feel it. 'Too young to be raped.'

'Aleck Northcote raped you?' Stella blinked away water that ran down her face like borrowed tears. If she wet herself the rain would disguise it. *Death would disguise it.*

'A fellow student boasted how he'd taken his copy of Northcote's autobiography, *Mind over Murder* to Tewkesbury and called on Northcote. He was invited in for tea. Northcote signed the book, "To my successor". Sebastian, that was his name, got low marks, I corrected his mistakes and helped him revise. He was a less than mediocre pathologist.'

'Northcote probably wrote that in every book.' Stella was reassuring Felicity. *Anything to be allowed to live.*

'Only for men.' Felicity pressed the blade against Stella's skin. 'Women have to work twice as hard to astound and astonish so that we cannot be ignored. When I visited Northcote, it would be a meeting of supreme minds across the generations.'

A siren. The town was flooding, Lucie and Beverly would be trapped in the abbey. Jack wouldn't reach Tewkesbury. 'Felicity, please let me go, people need help.'

'Don't plead, it's pathetic,' Felicity grated. 'I intended to find Northcote alone, Sebastian said the housekeeper left at six. At Paddington, newspaper hoardings said that JFK had been assassinated. Perhaps this was why one selfish individual chose to jump in front of a train so I didn't get to Tewkesbury until that evening. No matter, I too was welcomed in. Aleck and I were locked in a discussion about facial reconstruction. He was genuinely fascinated by my theories. He was charm itself, I was transported. My career was made. Here was the greatest living pathologist caught in my spell.

'It started with a hand on my leg. He oozed compliments. *You are quite something, aren't you, dear.* Then he grabbed me. He was savage, clumsy. Revolting. A rabid dog. *A dog that had to be put down.*

'Later, on the train back to London, I read the inscription: "For my Girl in the Headlines". The film Northcote said Gladys, his housekeeper, was seeing that night. Joy told me Gladys lied.'

'That's what Clive meant about John Lennon,' Stella exclaimed. 'You got Northcote to sign a copy of his book and then you killed him.'

Felicity waved the knife impatiently, 'One night Joy told me that Gladys Fleming, as was, had been with Aleck that evening. Joy believed Gladys had killed him.'

'How come Joy told you?' Stella's jaw ached from her effort to stop her teeth chattering. The river crashing through the sluices expressed the roar of terror Stella felt. In the sky, ragged skeins of white cloud became sooty black as they passed across the moon.

'When I bought Cloisters House, I joined the choir. I've always loved choral music. Joy came to Cloisters with one of her fussy musical arrangements. After several glasses of brandy – "medicinal, the organ plays havoc with my lower back" – her tongue loosened and out it poured. No friends as a child. She spied on others and bartered secrets to get friends. But she had kept one secret. That Aleck had an affair with his pretty young housekeeper, the gorgeous Gladys. She'd seen them "in this very room". Giles Northcote hadn't murdered his father, she said. It was Gladys Wren who'd bludgeoned Aleck with the poker. This was the real music to my ears: *I was safe.* If there was doubt about Giles Northcote's guilt, Gladys was next up as culprit. That was until that scoundrel March arrived in Tewkesbury with other ideas.'

'You let an innocent man hang?' Stella should not be shocked; were Roddy March's suspicions true, someone had let Giles Northcote die to save their own skin.

'Holier than thou doesn't suit you, Stella. I killed Northcote because he raped me. I wasn't his *successor*, I was his sex doll. Should I have given myself up to the police for his son, a gambler and a drunk?'

'How did Joy find out you killed March?' Stella's measurement of time was in inches as the water rose. If she leapt in, what chance would she have? At least she'd control her own death. *I love you, Jack.* Stupidly it occurred to her that it was two days until Christmas and she wouldn't see him.

'March called me that night at the first Death Café. It was him threatening me, I never as much as sent him a poison pen letter. I dismissed all of you and told him to meet me by the cadaver tomb after the rescheduled session the following night. I already had it in my mind to frame Joy – here was the perfect chance. I stabbed him and was out of there before Joy had finished playing.'

'But he was listening to the music.' Stella struggled to recall that evening.

'That was me. For such a ghastly woman, Joy's music was angelic, couldn't resist it. And you had arrived so I couldn't leave.'

'But his hat was on the chair.' Stella had an idea. 'Did you move the plastic barriers?'

'March left his hat and I had asked him to move the barriers. It would lead the police into thinking that the murderer would have passed Joy.' Felicity didn't appear to mind that she was soaked through. 'All in all, I had March set up his own murder.

'Clive saw me visit Northcote that night. I gave him some guff about being the pathologist on the scene. He seemed to swallow that, but over the years he began coming out with remarks apropos of nothing. *Time* was his to bide, he'd say. *Truth will stop the pendulum.* I tried to stop him coming to the Death Café, but could think of no good reason. When I saw Clive talking to you in the high street, I had to do something and fast. Joy told me Clive had instructed her to go to the police if anything happened to him, but the fool didn't believe him so came to me instead.' Felicity shouted over the raging turbulence. 'You are not distracting me, Stella, I, too, can bide my time. You are a deserving listener for a story which, sadly, isn't in my autobiography.' Felicity yelled, 'March was not supposed to come to the Death Café. That threw me.'

'Northcote raped you. You know better than me that you'd get manslaughter,' Stella yelled back.

'It was my first time, I bled on his carpet. If they'd kept the carpet, they could now test it for DNA. That would be that. But since they had their man, they burnt it. I threatened to tell the police and Aleck laughed. I was dressed in black, my alter ego was Cat Woman. One must stand out from the herd. *They'll think you a common tart.* Stella, when the other side doesn't play fair, it's idiotic to stick to the rules.'

'That will be taken into account.' Stella was clutching at straws, but the rage fuelling her terror was for Felicity. Something pinged in her brain. She jerked her head. *Car wo my.*

'Keep still,' Felicity yelled.

'*Cat woman.*' Stella gripped the railing. In the moonlight, the water might be liquid steel. 'Roddy tried to tell me. It *was you.*'

'Oh dear, Stella. Several steps behind. Always the bridesmaid, never the bride,' Felicity taunted her.

Stella didn't believe in ghosts. That was Jack. But staring down at the spume, Stella felt the presence of George Cotton. She held his last moments as another piece of the jigsaw fell into place. As Felicity had said, too late.

'George Cotton worked out that you killed Northcote. He came to see you.'

'One step at a time, don't tax your brain.'

'Why did you kill him? He didn't like Northcote any more than you did.'

'Cotton was a police officer at heart. No murderer should get away with it even if the victim was a killer. He and his wife Agnes had never held with capital punishment. He wanted me to give myself up.'

'You murdered three people to avoid being caught for murdering Northcote.' *Soon it would be four.*

'There you are again, like Joy, moralizing. Northcote knew he could thrust himself into me, button himself up and pour himself a Scotch. I put a stop to him – after me there were no more rapes. I killed the fatted calf. The golden goose. The man whose work had inspired me. I was his successor. Cotton, March, Clive were collateral.'

'Did he mention Maple?'

'Here we go. What about me? Maple was a silly cheap missy with aspirations way above her station. She did not come up.' Felicity's words were caught up and whipped around like hornets. 'Maple Greenhill left her son at home during an air raid to cavort with Aleck Northcote. It's the Maple Greenhills who paved the way for me. How could Northcote respect my sex with girls like her out to bleed him?'

'He never promised to marry you. He didn't pretend he liked you. He bought Maple gifts, he dated her.' Stella was fighting for her own life. 'If you don't intend to stab me, stop doing that with knife.' *Never antagonize the enemy if you can't escape.* Stella ignored her father's advice.

'Stella Darnell, what a trouper. Perhaps we could have been friends.' Felicity lowered the knife and rested her palms on the railing. 'I remember being confounded by the splinters of bone, grey brain matter, blood. I expected Northcote to be greater than human. A god made of gold. Even after he'd raped me, laughed at me, discounted me, Northcote the pathologist was the point of my life. I didn't understand how he could look like any other corpse.'

Water slapped over the boards. Foam spewing through the teeth of the weir appeared phosphorescent. Stella pictured Jack. *Don't think about Jack.* It had been Felicity who mentioned legacy at the Death Café. Stella's legacy would be the manner of her death. This felt more terrible than death itself.

'... saw Northcote speak at UCL in my first year, his rich brown voice, his sheer brilliance, my heart soared, as if he spoke only to me.' Felicity was back with her story with Stella nothing but her captive listener. 'After he... after... I went upstairs and drew a bath. After that, I made sure to clean where I touched – this was 1963, like I said, no DNA, but there was fingerprinting, blood types, hair samples. I was a brilliant young pathologist, I made no mistakes. Not like Northcote. I agreed with Cotton, leaving his lighter at Maple Greenhill's murder scene was basic.'

'Your clothes must have been bloodstained.'

'I burnt them in his stove. I took a shirt from his wardrobe, laundered and starched, it smelled of him. When I left, I took the poker – never leave the police a weapon.'

'What if you had been searched?'

'As Northcote told me, the police ignore the least likely suspect. They still do. That woman they had on the murders of March and Clive never as much as considered me.' Felicity spoke as if the murders were nothing to do with her. 'I booked into the Tudor House Hotel, it's not far—'

'I know where it is.' Stella had cleaned there.

'After breakfast I went across to Cloisters House to get my autograph. Only to display profound shock when the police officer outside informed me Northcote had been murdered. I sobbed, real tears, I cried for the professional who was my personal deity. Just then Professor Max Watkins, Home Office pathologist, came out of the house. He remembered my intelligent questions at his lectures and autopsies.

'"Young lady, career-defining cases come rarely, come with me and keep your wits about you."'

'I watched him cut and bottle Northcote. I agreed Northcote was bludgeoned with a blunt instrument – not quite blunt, I tentatively proffered – could those indentations on his skull indicate some kind of pattern, could Northcote have been attacked with a fire-iron? "Clever child," Watkins said. He invited me to motor back to town in a Daimler that "Poor old Northcote himself flogged to me when he got his Rolls." When Giles Northcote was charged, Watkins was cheerful. "Zeus kills Cronos, the old make way for the young." As I held the jar containing Northcote's liver to the light, I blew him a kiss.'

'Giles Northcote was innocent.' Stella's throat was on fire from shouting above the deafening sound. They were ankle-deep in water. *Did Felicity plan to die with her?*

'Don't spoil it, Stella.' Distracted by water swirling at their feet, Felicity snapped into the present. 'I'm seventy-four with an international reputation, I speak at international conferences, as Northcote once inspired me, so I guide the young. I won't be felled by armchair detectives like you and Andrea who have something to prove to their fathers.'

'My father is dead.' Stella was telling herself as much as Felicity.

'Police will be swarming around the abbey, Forensics will be all over Joy. I watched your man friend sneaking about in dear Andrea's room from across the street. I called the house and left a message with one of Gladys's greasy lodgers. Soon smoked Mr Harmon out, I can tell you. What a shame he can't come to your rescue, Stella, but all the roads into Tewkesbury are cut off by floodwater. As pathologist on call, they'll be ringing me.'

'You have retired. They won't be calling you. *Ever*.' Stella lost it. She had in fact nothing to lose.

'...how sorry I will be when I'm told the river has claimed you. I shall treat you with care. My report will state water in your lungs indicates you were alive when you went in. Northcote taught me the corpse is a narrative, my bible. Your bloated cadaver will tell your story. The police will assemble facts and make five. Joy attacked you, and in self-defence you killed her. At Fletcher's old mill, with only the moonlight to show you the way, you slipped and tumbled into the rushing waters.'

'You won't get away with it.' Not every ending was happy. Felicity was plausible. Respected. Jack and the others thought Joy was their killer. She would get away with it.

'Stella.' *Jack's voice.* Wishful thinking was skewing reality. Jack was stuck on a road outside Tewkesbury with Andrea – harmless grumpy Andrea. *Jack would be annoying her with how he loved Stella...*

Rain etched silver lines across the lamplight on St Mary's Lane. The moon was out. Something floated downstream. A dead sheep, sodden and bloated, was pale in the thin light. *Stella saw herself.*

'Stella.'

Felicity turned.

Torchlight, the strobing lamps of squad cars and ambulances. Armed police were on the gantry below the old mill. Stella made out Janet at the other end of the bridge. *And Jack.*

'Keep back.' Felicity again pressed the cartilage knife to her neck. This time not the flat of the blade.

'I can say it was Joy who killed Northcote,' Stella shouted at Felicity. 'That you saved me.'

'How will you lie to your chap? Isn't honesty important to you?' Felicity appeared interested. Stella felt a flicker of hope.

'I lie to Jack all the time.' *Don't plead.* 'I'll say Joy was blackmailing you.'

'Clever, it could work.' Felicity spoke into her ear. Stella felt more scared of her now that she was being pliant.

'I'll say you found me on the bridge and stopped me from falling in.'

'Perfect.' Felicity's laugh was high, strange. 'Ah, Stella, I almost feel sorry for you. You underestimate me and, as Aleck found out, people do that at their peril.'

A scream, louder than the water pounding below, rent the air.

'Jack.' Stella felt thuds, heard shouts. She was inches from the black river.

'I've got you, darling.' Stella felt Jack around her. Then she was on a stretcher. Jack held her hand. *Voices, faces.* Stella touched her neck, it was wet. *She was dying.*

'Not a mark on you, popsicle.' Lucie's face swam into focus. 'Before she jumped, she let you go.'

'She jumped?'

'The rescue launch is out. A budget-breaking wild goose chase. Ask me, Felicitatus does not intend to be rescued.'

Cat woman.

Stella imagined Felicity slinking out of the water and running nimbly up the bank. Then she passed out.

Epilogue

Jackie

'Shall I be mother?' Bev waved at the array of teapots on the table and at a murmur of assent, poured Earl Grey, bog-standard and gunpowder tea (Lucie) into a cluster of Tewkesbury Abbey mugs.

Eight minutes past ten. Christmas Eve morning. The Clean Slate Detectives, as Bev named them, had been first into the Abbey Gardens tearoom where, as Jack had noted, everything began. A large stuffed hen was wedged between Stanley's jaws as he lay on Stella's lap. He had claimed Jack's present to Stella for his own.

Passing round cakes, doughnut for Lucie, chocolate brownies for Bev and Jack, Jackie opted for a Portuguese tart, but couldn't persuade Stella to share. Jackie's second family was reunited, for the first time in months she could relax. When she'd come to Tewkesbury the night before, Stella had told her she was coming home and would start work after Christmas. Clean Slate would rise from the ashes.

'It began in December 1940 in the middle of the Blitz,' Stella said. 'Aleck Northcote strangled Maple Greenhill.' She raised her mug. 'To Maple, dead long ago, never forgotten.'

'Cleo says William is changing his name back to Greenhill. Andrea's sacked Zack for embezzlement.' Bev had been on the phone to Cleo Greenhill as they all walked to the tearoom. 'Andrea's scanning a virtual tour for Maple's Motors. Cliff is going into rehab. When he's out, Cleo is encouraging him to start an archaeology course and leave the showroom. Cleo has asked Andrea to be co-director. Maple's granddaughter kind of fits with Vernon's dream of Maple's son joining. Cleo and Andrea are the dream team.'

'At least that's one good outcome from this sorry tale.' Lucie sighed. 'This chain of murders could not have a happy ending. Maple Greenhill's own dream proved to be a nightmare, Julia Northcote failed to send her husband to the gallows, Roddy March's parents lost their only child. Clive at least had a fitting end.'

'Is there such a thing as a fitting end?' Jack wondered.

'I want to die in my sleep and know nothing about it,' Beverly declared.

'OK for you, but a tragedy for the rest of us,' Lucie said. 'Me, I expect there's a few who want me to shuffle off the mortal coil. My winged idiot of an editor for one. What a hash he made of saying how pleased he was that I'm coming back to work.'

'Joy will never play the Grove organ again,' Stella said.

'My heart breaks,' Beverly snapped. 'Joy-*less* was a first-class nasty person.'

'She loved playing in the abbey.' Stella did feel sorry for Joy. Unhappiness had made her nasty. It hadn't made Stella all that nice.

'The first organist in the country to be blackballed for blackmail. There's her legacy right there.' Lucie scribbled the phrase in her notebook.

'Gladys Wren is exonerated,' Jack said.

'I'm pleased for her.' Beverly sounded heartfelt. 'She never did anyone any harm. She didn't even murder the man who had

abused her for years. I wouldn't have blamed her if she had. I
don't blame Felicity that she did.'

'Can I join you?' Janet was detective-smart in a black suit,
white shirt and mac with the collar up.

'Please do.' Jackie pulled out a chair when no one spoke and
made everyone shuffle round.

'I went to Gladys Wren's boarding house; she said you were
here. I want to apologize, Stella, I should have listened. Lucie,
you too,' Janet added with, Jackie guessed, monumental effort.
Lucie had been the bane of what was now the Met Police's
Central West division for too many decades. 'I got it wrong.'

'Not the first— *ouch*.' Lucie winced when Jackie kicked her
ankle.

'There'll be an enquiry, from which I'll emerge stinking of
horse-shit.' Janet sat forward, her hands between her knees.

'You followed the evidence,' Stella said. 'Like you – and me –
were taught. If I'd been the SIO I'd have got it wrong too. I only
realized Felicity was the murderer when she had a knife at my
throat.'

'I'd have solved it.' Lucie was not gracious in victory. 'All I
lacked were the resources of a county constabulary.'

'We have retrieved Felicity's body from the Avon. It was
caught in reeds miles downstream.'

Lucie was cutting her doughnut in half. Jam dripping, she
passed one piece to Stella. Jackie knew it was Lucie acknowledging
that, cold-blooded killer though Felicity had been, Stella would
mourn her. Felicity's life had been ruined by Northcote. A kind
of murder.

'The irony is,' Janet accepted a mug of tea from Jackie, 'Roddy
March's laptop and notebook along with his wallet were in a safe
in Felicity's basement mortuary. Not that the notebook would
have led us to the killer. The only person he had a good word to
say about was you, Stella. He thought you, observant with the
makings of a forensic cleaner as well as "not a bad looker".'

'I don't know how he could think any of that,' Stella snapped.

'The only time the guy had it right, I'd say, except he missed out first-rate detective.' Janet shot her a smile. 'We finally found his podcast files in a cloud under the pseudonym, Charles Foster Kane, as in *Citizen Kane*. March outlined the rest of the series and revealed the name of Northcote's killer. It wouldn't have helped any of us, the dill-brain pointed the finger at Joy Turton. He reckoned Joy was jealous of Gladys having, as she supposed, an affair with Northcote and to deprive Gladys of him, killed him. He was both right and wrong. Joy didn't take her jealousy out on Northcote, but on blackmailing poor Gladys, who became a handy source of income.'

'Joy made sublime music.' Stella made no sense of that. All that made sense to her now was that she loved all the people sitting around the 'séance' table in the teashop.

'Just think,' Janet sipped her tea, 'Dame Professor Felicity Branscombe could have gone to her grave with her reputation as a top pathologist whose evidence put violent murderers where they belonged intact. We might never have known she'd murdered Northcote and Cotton. Because *yes*, Cotton had worked out Felicity killed Northcote. A detective, haunted by the man who had got away with murder, he'd gone to an exhibition of pathologist artefacts. It included the copy of Northcote's autobiography signed for Felicity which her ego had propelled her to contribute. Cotton must have made sense of "To the Girl in the Headlines", the housekeeper's alibi for Northcote's murder. It's on record that Felicity had been in Tewkesbury that night. The book was evidence she'd met Northcote.'

'March got the wrong woman.' Lucie tapped Stella's plate, urging her to eat the doughnut. Jackie was euphoric when Stella took a bite. They had their Stella back.

'Gladys Wren refuses to charge Joy Turton with blackmail,' Janet said. 'Claims she's destroyed Joy's letters. Joy is selling her cottage so that she can pay back every penny she extorted from Gladys.'

'Good.' Beverly was hot on justice.

'That's the beauty beneath the ugliness.' Stella wiped her mouth with a napkin.

'Gladys won't let her. That Joy can't play the organ is punishment enough. I doubt I'd be so forgiving.' Janet got up, 'Stella, I do hope our paths cross again. Not my place to say, but... well, Terry would have been effing proud of you.' She tucked her chair under the table. 'He said pay attention to the irrelevant, the peripheral and the outlandish, it can lead to the truth. I didn't do that. His daughter did.'

'I didn't.' Stella got up and, edging past Lucie, touched Janet's shoulder. 'Dad also said the police welcome information from the public. I should have told you my suspicions.'

'Enough with the *mea culpa*, girls,' Lucie cried. 'Blame Aleck Northcote. He wrought trauma on women for decades and got every gong in the book for slicing up more. I'll be there when they rip his plaque off the wall of Cloisters House.'

After Janet had left, everyone ate and drank in what Jackie felt was companionable silence.

'Do you plan to write a true-crime book?' Jackie asked Lucie.

Stella shot her a reproving glance, she was protective of Lucie and the true-crime books that never reached fruition. But Jackie wasn't teasing Lucie, she thought that, unless another murder came along in the meantime, this chain of murders spanning 1940 to the present day might be the one to take Lucie over the finish line.

'Books *schmooks*.' Lucie sat back as a second doughnut with a fresh pot of tea was put in front of her. Again, she shared her doughnut with Stella and again Stella polished off her half.

'The future is in podcasts,' Lucie said. 'I'm doing one.'

This time the silence was of astonishment.

'Andrea's got the material, I'll script it, and me and Andrea will co-present.'

'You'll be better than March, better than any podcasters I've heard.' Stella licked sugar off her upper lip. 'You'll tell it fairly and without sensation.'

Jackie wasn't sure she shared Stella's confidence.

'You listen to true-crime podcasts?' Jack stared at Stella. Jackie wondered how Jack would be with the new Tewkesbury-improved Stella who liked true-crime podcasts and attended evensong.

'We will bring Maple back from the dead. Listeners will meet a vivacious clever young woman who was cut down before she could begin her life and be a mother to her son.' Lucie slurped tea. 'We'll give William Greenhill his mum.'

Jack jolted as if he'd received an electric shock. Jackie saw Stella see it too. Stella moved closer to Jack, their shoulders touching. Lucie meant well, but nothing and no one could give back William Greenhill or Jack their murdered mothers. Perhaps, though, their sons might learn to feel the love of those who loved them. Perhaps William could find peace with his estranged family; and his daughter, now she knew the truth about his past, could forge a new relationship with him.

Jackie only had to look at them to see Jack and Stella had found each other again. Stella had told Jackie she could accept Terry's death, she carried him in her heart.

'Andrea needs me for journo credibility; as a designer she deals in pictures and code. I had thought the podcast would be just you and me, babe.' Lucie was rummaging in her Driza-Bone. 'Hope you don't mind, Stellagmite, we'll have you as consultant.'

'This is Andrea's story.' With Stanley snoozing on her lap and Jack holding her hand, Jackie could see Stella was in seventh heaven. 'From now on, I'm sticking to cleaning. No more solving murders.'

'And my mother was a bright red rooster.' Lucie raised the hip flask she'd recovered from the depths of her coat and took a generous swig of nippet.

'Here's to our next case, Sherlock.'

Acknowledgements

During the night of 10 December 1940, my grandad, an officer at London's Pentonville Prison, sat with Jose Wahlberg, a young convicted spy. The note of gratitude that Wahlberg wrote to Albert Nelson, on a cigarette packet perhaps minutes before he was hanged for treason, is still in our family's archive box. I haven't dramatized this in *The Distant Dead*, which is a murder mystery, but it did inspire me to set the novel in the 1940 London Blitz.

The Distant Dead was written in 2020's first lockdown. I planned it before Covid-19 overtook the world, but it didn't take a genius to find parallels between the privations and strictures of the Blitz and those set out by Boris Johnson's government to protect the National Health Service. The pandemic slogan, *'We're in it together'* was a wartime rallying cry too.

In 1940 rules made criminals of the law-abiding, for leaving a chink in a blackout curtain or a gas mask at home. In the pandemic too, well-intentioned people ignored, bent or broke rules around 'Bubbles' and high days and holidays. Living with limitations on movement, seeing businesses vanish and reading of the daily death toll, I felt an affinity for the civilians on Britain's home front in 1940. History was just a breath away.

Lockdown meant cancelling appointments with e.g., the National Archives, the Metropolitan Police Archives and the University of Sussex archives at the Keep. These collections have material online, but nothing beats handling actual documents.

I did make extensive use of UKPressOnline, the BBC's British Genome Project and of the British Newspaper Archive. I read many texts, watched government propaganda films. A core book was *Murder Capital: Suspicious Deaths in London 1933-53* by Amy Helen Bell (Manchester University Press, 1988). Myth speaks louder than reality and from this book I read that while shelterers in the tube did huddle over board games and sing Vera Lynn songs, in dark stations and stairways, women were raped and murdered. Crime was rife. The Nazis weren't the only enemies.

In 1940, nineteen-year-old Maple Church, a 'respectable' clerk with Hackney Borough Council was murdered in a bomb-damaged building after a night out in London. My character Maple bears no resemblance to Maple Church, however her name is by way of tribute. I hope Maple is resting in peace.

As a novelist, I am proud to be part of a wonderful team. Against the thorny backdrop of furloughs, staff shortages and home-schooling, Head of Zeus worked hard to bring *The Distant Dead* into being. Thank you *so much* to:

Christian Duck – Production, Liz Hatherell – Copyeditor, Vicky Joss – Marketing, Anna Nightingale – Editorial Assistant, Lauren Tavella – PR, Mark Swan and Matt Bray – Cover design, Jon Appleton – Proofreader. I am lucky to have the fabulous Richard Attlee reading the audiobook.

Laura Palmer who, has for nearly a decade, helped make my novels the best they can be.

Always thanks to Georgina Capel and all at Georgina Capel Literary Agency, including Irene Baldoni, Philippa Brewster and Rachel Conway.

Thanks as ever, to retired Chief Superintendent Stephen Cassidy and to 'The Detective's Mother' – Shirley Cassidy.

Friends and family have been vital in this tough time, I've valued your support and encouragement.

Heartfelt thanks to my fab cousins, Tasmin Barnett (adopted 'younger sister'), Roger Goodwin, Ronnie Rees. William Nelson and Katherine Nelson. To my Uncle and Aunty, Peter and Lynn Nelson. To my dearly loved Aunty Agnes who, being looked after in her care-home, has been painfully out of reach and died of Covid four days after receiving the vaccine.

Thank you, Elizabeth Anscombe, Teresa Andow, Sarah Barclay, Laura Barnett, Melissa Benn, Philippa Brewster, Jenny Bourne Taylor, Kathryn Burton, Jonny Burton, Elaine Butlin, Stuart Carruthers, Marianne Dixon (aka Vikasini), Helen Eve, Susan Eve, Hilary Fairclough, Katrina Heather, Nigel Heather, Flis Henwood, Lisa Holloway, Christine Muscato, Emma O'Grady, Steve O'Neill, Shirley (Sam) Margerison, John Pumphrey, Tina Ross, Rick Ross, Ruth Ussher, Paul Ussher, Guy Warner, Joann Weedon and Harriet Wood. My particular thanks to Juliet Eve for her gimlet eye.

Libby's Patisserie became a take-away during Lockdown. Our lattes and brioche, brought to a bench across the street on a tray by Libby's partner Matt, became more special than ever.

The highest of fives to the fellow members of the 'Crime Trio', Elly Griffiths and William Shaw, who, as fellow writers and good mates, keep me up and running. Here's to more rainy-day meetings on a grey windswept beach, hopefully only for old times' sake.

A special mention goes to Domenica de Rosa (11.11).

Where is a writer without readers? Thank you all for your wonderful messages. Those requests to write faster spur me on!

My gratitude is due to all bookshops which during the pandemic yet managed to get fiction to readers. To the bloggers whose 'Tours' were spiced with particular value in this Virtual Time. A big shout out to David Gilchrist and all who run the treasure that is the UK Crime Book Club. If you're not a member, don't miss out!

It's rare my novels include an autobiographical element. However, like Stella with Stanley, I've spent hours in Tewkesbury Abbey listening to Evensong with our dog Alfred napping on my lap. On our last visit, in front of two security guards, he disgraced himself and me, by lifting a leg against a pillar in the north ambulatory. Despite this, I'm grateful to Alfred for his company and for those lockdown walks he made legitimate.

I wouldn't have put fingers to keys without my beloved wife, Melanie.

Lesley Thomson
Lewes, 2021